THE WINTER WARRIORS

Also by Olivier Norek in English translation

The Lost and the Damned
Turf Wars
Breaking Point
Between Two Worlds

Olivier Norek

THE WINTER WARRIORS

Translated from the French by
Nick Caistor

OPEN BORDERS PRESS
LONDON

First published in Great Britain in 2025 by
Open Borders Press
an imprint of
Orenda Books
London

www.openborderspress.co.uk

9 8 7 6 5 4 3 2 1

First published as *Les Guerriers de L'Hiver*
© Éditions Michel Lafon, 2024

English translation © Nick Caistor, 2025

A CIP catalogue record for this book is available from the British Library

ISBN (HB) 978-1-916788-76-3

Map © Emily Faccini

Designed and typeset in Minion by Libanus Press, Marlborough
Printed and bound in Great Britain by CPI Group (UK) Ltd, Croydon, CR0 4YY

IN MEMORY OF ALL THE LIVES LOST

———

This is a novel.

However, the passages of dialogue often come from archives or have been provided by enthusiasts, military sources and historians. None of the battle scenes has been invented. No act of bravery has been exaggerated. Although these events will soon have taken place a century ago, they point us to contemporary history and serve as a warning. War often takes us by surprise, and there has to be a first death on our land for us to truly believe in it.

O.N., February 2025

For a just cause with a pure sword.

Carl Gustaf Mannerheim,
Chairman of the Finnish National Defence Council, 1931–9

———

When the non-stop deadly Russian artillery fire started up, thousands of white-hot hammers echoed in the heads of the Finnish soldiers. One man giggled inanely, another wept hysterically.

Erkki Palolampi,
Finnish Army Information Officer on the Kollaa front line

———

You've no doubt heard of Hell. It is the same here. But not even the Devil would understand what is happening here.

Soldier Tšurkin,
150th Infantry Division, Soviet Army

Contents

First Prologue

Light streams over his closed eyes, over his prostrate body and its stilled heart.

All around him, the last day of war has littered the ground with bodies in their thousands, staining the snow red. Amongst the other corpses, he is no-one. No more precious, no more important. Elsewhere, he could be a father, a brother, a friend, a husband. Elsewhere, he is everything.

In death, only their uniforms set them apart. They were enemies, now they lie side by side. Here, hands touch; elsewhere, lifeless faces confront each other. They have spent the whole winter killing one another.

The dead from earlier weeks are half-hidden in the earth. Only vestiges remain: still visible helmets, occasionally parts of their backs. Their arms are like aerial roots, as if growing out of the ground itself, ready to rise, get to their feet, and haunt all those who decided on this war.

Their blood saturates the ground, their flesh nourishes the trees, mingles with the sap. They will be in every new leaf, every new bud.

There were more than a million of them, and when, tomorrow and beyond tomorrow, the wind blows through the branches of the forests of Finland, it will also carry their voices.

There had been happy days, a cherished peace.

There had been a before, in the days leading up to the Hell.

Second Prologue

For many years Finland belonged to someone else.

For centuries, it formed part of the kingdom of Sweden. For a further century, it came under Russia's sovereignty. It was not until 1917 that it gained independence.

In 1939, therefore, Finland was 22 years old. Twenty-two years are hardly sufficient to make a man, let alone a country.

In a storm of lead and fire, Stalin's Red Army, the largest in the world, swept through this neutral, poorly armed nation, launching a bloody conflict known by history as the Winter War.

The hellish events that are the subject of this novel took place in that year of 1939 at Kollaa in Finland. But also on its isthmus, in Karelia. On the ice fields at Petsamo. From the shores of its gulf to the distant reaches of Lapland.

Imagine a tiny country. Imagine a huge one. Now imagine them clashing.

Twenty million shells. The Earth almost cracked in two when Russia pounded its crust in the same place day after day for more than a hundred days.

Tank columns against old-fashioned rifles. A million Red Army soldiers against workers and peasants. But past conflicts tell us it takes five soldiers to face a single man fighting for his land, his home country and his own people, hands clutching his carbine, a sentinel behind the door of his barricaded farm.

And a single man can change the course of history.

*

At the heart of the harshest of its winters,
at the heart of the bloodiest war in its history,
Finland saw the birth of a legend.
The legend of Simo Häyhä, the White Death.
And yet there had once been happy days, a cherished peace.
There had been a before, in the days leading up to the Hell.

map

1

The days before the Hell,
a forest near Rautjärvi, a village in Finland

Crushed grass, snapped branches, tufts of fur caught on juniper bushes, prints in the soil whose pattern signposted the way taken by whatever had left them: without a sound, Simo was reading the forest.

He could hear the trees soughing in the wind, the pulse of their sap, the rustle of animals; hooves on dry leaves, their hides rubbing against bark, their hearts beating. For those who can read it, there is no noisier silence than that of the forest. Simo never forced his way in, he was always invited. Simply invited. And so as not to offend the forest, he took from it only what he needed. Sometimes an elk, at others a wolf, partridge, crow, or one of the ermine whose coveted furs had adorned all the capes of the kings of France.

To take proper aim on the Finnish Civic Guard shooting range Simo had to delve inside himself, blot out everything around him. But here in the forest he was alert to every murmur, every silence, every sound of running or flight.

Twenty metres ahead of him, a fox's fiery coat stood out against the green needles of an ancient spruce's drooping branches. The animal's body pulsed slightly as it drew breath. Simo controlled his own breathing and aligned it with that of his quarry. For an instant they breathed in harmony as the young man became the animal he had in his sights, until he could sense what movements it would make. The fox sniffed the ground and the air, trying to discover why its instinct was warning him of danger although he could not detect the reason. He approached his earth and dropped the lifeless body of a blackbird from his muzzle. Exactly 23 metres away.

No-one is more adept than a person who has learned the skills from his father, and Simo's father had taught him the art of judging distances, following his own peculiar teaching method.

"How far?" he would ask his young son, pointing to the burnt-out trunk of a tree struck by lightning the previous summer.

Simo told him his estimate, walked over to the trunk, counting his paces, and stood behind it.

"The bullet traces an arc. If your estimate is too short by a metre, the missile will bury itself in the ground. But if your estimate is a metre or two long, it's going to lodge itself in your belly," his father threatened.

Of course, the threat was never carried out. And yet, when Simo got it wrong, his father's words were as wounding as a bullet:

"Son, you're dead. Let's go and eat."

*

And so, while others were enjoying a rest after their meals, letting their bodies recover from the hard work in fields and farms, Simo donned his boots or took down his pair of skis and headed for the forest, disappearing into a primordial green that must have given birth to every other shade of green. He would roam through the trees until he chose a landmark, calculate its distance and verify this by counting the number of steps to it. He had followed the same routine every day, every week, every year from the very first time he had picked up a rifle.

"That fox. How far?" he heard his father's voice say inside his head.

Simo gently rested his first finger on the trigger, then squeezed harder and harder ... But an instant before the shot rang out and roused the forest, a black muzzle appeared from the earth. A female came lumbering wearily out, belly heavy with a pregnancy that curved her spine towards the ground.

Simo eased his finger on the trigger and silently backed away until he was out of sight. It would be wrong to see this as compassion. He had not spared the animals, simply postponed their meeting for a while. Being able to do something and having to do it are not the same.

To be able to shoot or to have to shoot. To be able to kill or to have to kill.

*

Back at the farm, a fat grey partridge in his bag, Simo propped his unloaded gun against the stone wall, hung his heavy cotton jacket on the rack, and sat down to a plateful of buttered sugary biscuits placed in front of him. Before eating, he let the flames from the hearth warm his back and ease the knots in his muscles. Stretched out on the flagstones, the family dog thrust its front paws forward in his dream's imaginary chase.

"Toivo and Onni came by to see you," his mother announced without looking up from her knitting, two long needles in her hands and her body sunk in the cushions of an armchair as old as her.

Simo shrugged. Toivo and Onni were neighbours and friends from childhood. They would see each other at some point. No hurry.

"Onni showed us his wedding ring," his mother went on, all innocence. "He even said he'd gone down on one knee."

In front of the kindly fire, Simo's nieces – one knee-height and the other not much taller – were plaiting each other's hair, pushing flowers into their blonde locks. Since the conversation was taking a turn they all knew very well, the two girls mimicked an adult voice to recite reproaches they had heard so often.

"Simo Matinpoika Häyhä, it's not by spending all your days in the forest that you'll find someone who loves you," the first one said.

"Unless of course you want to marry a doe," the second one said.

"Do you want to marry a doe?" they chimed in unison.

In another second the young man would have chased them round the room and made them suffer for their cheek. However much they giggled and pleaded with him, he would have untied their plaits and afterwards the day would follow its course. But at that second the father came into the kitchen and sat at the table, restoring calm simply by his presence. The girls were still laughing, and Simo gave them a warning look: he wasn't finished with them.

The father weighed the still warm partridge in his hand. The blood around the bullet hole in the neck was already dry. Pleased with Simo's efforts, he blew gently on the few light feathers stuck to the palm of his hand, then turned to Simo.

"Are you ready for tomorrow?"

Simo looked first at his gun and then at his father, who sought at once to erase his son's over-confident smile.

"You must show yourself worthy of Rautjärvi, because there'll be 1,700 against you …"

Simo's smile only widened.

2

The following day,
Finnish Civic Guard Rifle Championship, Helsinki

The strained expression on the faces of the other teams was a tribute to the squad of marksmen from Rautjärvi. Although everyone respected them, many would have preferred their truck to have had an engine problem, or for its wheels to have skidded off the road, leaving them in a ditch: any unforeseen accident that meant they did not arrive at the shooting range in time. But the engine did not fail, the wheels stayed on the road, and no obstacles got in their way.

"*Perkele!*[1] The lads from Rautjärvi have arrived," groaned one young man.

"Is Simo with them?" another youngster said, because the marksman's name was what was making everybody else so anxious. Every one of the 1,700 other competitors in the national championship had uttered it at least once on the roads converging on Helsinki from all over Finland.

"I don't know. I haven't seen him yet."

"The wolves and foxes never see him either. And yet his coats are made of their fur."

"I reckon people overestimate that kid," another team captain said, determined not to leave without a trophy.

*

Nobody had ever really doubted that Simo would win the competition. A farmer and reserve soldier like most Finnish young men, he was discreet and modest and scarcely taller than his rifle, but rarely gave the other competitors a chance. It was in his blood, the blood that pulsed at the end of his trigger finger, blood the same colour as the centre of the target he never missed. Never ever.

So the group around Simo had already finished their congratulations. Even the officers who had organised the event had come over, as it was one of their number who had challenged Simo:

"How often can you hit the bull's eye in one minute?"

Simo's look was enough to show he accepted the challenge.

Led by Onni and Toivo, the Rautjärvi team began to take bets.

Onni, the one soon to be married, whose hair was so blond the sun sometimes lent it silvery glints, held out his upturned helmet to receive the money.

Toivo, the best friend, whose perfect beauty made young girls and their mothers blush at dances, wrote the bets down with a coloured pencil on the first page of a novel he had not yet begun.

Simo was nothing more than a trainee soldier in the Civic Guard. His rival was a career officer, and so the odds naturally fell in the officer's favour.

"Five marks on the officer. He's an instructor. How could he be beaten?"

"I'll add ten marks on the officer!"

"There's no hurry, gentlemen, you will all have the chance to lose your precious money," Toivo taunted them.

"Come on, don't be mean, empty your pockets, I've got a wedding to pay for!" Onni said.

The officer to the stand. Simo to the stand.

Two hundred metres away, the new target.

The officer lay down, and the stopwatch began. The exploding gunpowder made the rifle's muzzle rear, so that after each shot he had to realign his sights, control his breathing, then shoot again. By the sixtieth and final second, the officer had hit the bull's eye fourteen times, although there was some doubt over the twelfth bullet, which some argued wasn't altogether in the centre. The officer had found the target fourteen times with an automatic weapon that did not require reloading after every shot.

It was Simo's turn to lie flat on the ground. The officer glanced at him, confident and condescending. What did he have to fear from this Sunday soldier, barely one metre fifty tall, who looked so babyish it seemed incongruous for him even to be holding a gun.

The murmurs among the spectators grew when they realised that, as promised, Simo would indeed be using his M28/30 manual-loading rifle, which meant he had to load a fresh round after each shot. So he had to aim, fire and deal with the recoil, just as the officer had done, but also eject the bullet case by clearing the breech, pick up another round from the ground, load it, aim, fire, control the recoil and start all over again. Simo lined up his rounds in front of him; on the signal, his dancing hands stupefied everybody fortunate enough to be present that day. The speed of his gestures, the machine-like precision, a manoeuvre he had repeated millions of times: in the permitted minute, Simo hit the bull's eye sixteen times without a single impact being in doubt.

For a man to fire more accurately and more rapidly with a manual-loading rifle than someone with an automatic one was quite simply impossible.

At least, that was what everyone had believed until that day. The defeated officer left the stand without congratulating his adversary.

*

In the truck taking the victorious squad back to Rautjärvi, everyone was singing raucously, passing the trophy from hand to hand.

"I hope there was a *Ryssä* spy there today,"[2] Toivo said.

"They're everywhere, even under our beds," Onni said.

"Then he'll have seen you, Simo, and he'll tell his friends how good we are with a weapon in our hands."

There were shouts of "*Huraa*", and Toivo shook Simo by the shoulders, even though his friend was abashed at being the centre of attention. To embarrass him further, the others began to cry "Simo! Simo!" as the trophy was returned to its place between his legs. It swayed to and fro as they drove along the bumpy roads back to their village on the Russian border. Despite the discomfort, many of them fell asleep, heads resting on their neighbour's shoulder.

Toivo, who was still wide awake, whispered: "My cousin in the army came to visit. He said their headquarters had forbidden all officers to take leave until further notice. He also said we're going back to the defensive lines on the border, to strengthen them."

"Again? We did that only last summer!" Onni protested. "Haven't the Russians asked us to abandon them?"

"And if they ask you to abandon your wife, will you do it?"

"I hope they at least give me time to marry her! But ask me again in a few years, and perhaps I'll go myself and dump her in Moscow!"

*

At nightfall, the Rautjärvi team jumped down from the truck in the middle of their village, saying goodbye to one another as they reached their homes. Eventually only Simo and Toivo were left.

From first light the next morning, at an hour when only peasants are out of bed, the Finns would return to their fields and farms. Men and women, foreheads bathed in sweat, were building a country that was prospering. Even though there were still some well-off families and rich individuals, there were few who allowed themselves the kind of bourgeois lifestyle found in wealthier

18

countries. Finland had only been independent a little more than 20 years, and everything was still to be done.

This meant the only leisure activity for young peasants and workers was the Civic Guard. In town and country, they were taught the history of Finland, and how to defend it. They were taught the ideal of the patriotic Finnish male, with a virile body and educated mind. But perhaps above all, enrolling in the Civic Guard gave these youngsters the chance to broaden their minds and travel round the country on military exercises or for rifle competitions.

In a country desiring only peace, they were also taught the art of war, and both in the village and their Civic Guard regiment, Toivo and Simo were united by an unbreakable bond.

"See you when I see you, and the sooner the better," Toivo said, taking Simo's hand.

Simo repeated the same, and the friends parted.

3

Before it was plunged into terror, nature had chosen to pamper Finland with the most beautiful summer. The hay had grown in leaps and bounds; harvests had been abundant. The sun shone by day and the rain fell at night, without ever getting in each other's way.

Toivo was with his cousin, a career military man. They were sitting in the shade of a big rock, gorging on the red and black bilberries and whortleberries. Lips still stained, his cousin lit a cigarette and they shared it, gazing out over the fields of barley awaiting the autumn harvest. There were rumours circulating in the countryside, at the mill where wheat was taken to be ground, at the market stalls and in factories. Rumours of a possible war. Some believed them. Others thought war was unthinkable. Toivo could not make up his mind, and was hoping his cousin could clarify matters.

"Finland has never been a threat to Russia. So why would Stalin be so scared he would threaten to invade us?"

"He couldn't care less about our pitchforks," his cousin assured him, in a cloud of cigarette smoke. "It's the Third Reich that keeps him awake at night. If Hitler wants to attack Leningrad, he'll only have to march from Berlin through the neutral countries – Denmark, Norway, Sweden and Finland – sweep down our coast, cross the isthmus of Karelia, and Nazi Germany will be in Russian territory without having fired a shot. Stalin isn't afraid of Finland; he's afraid that Finland will do nothing if Hitler invades us."

He spat out a strand of tobacco sticking to his lip before passing the cigarette to Toivo. He went on:

"Why do you reckon Stalin is asking us to hand over entire regions and allow him to station his troops on our territory? Making war outside his own country is far easier, if you ask me. Our government is about to mobilise all professional soldiers, the reservists and the civic guardsmen, in order to reinforce our defences on the Russian border. We'll be told it's a special military operation, nothing more than an exercise to test our readiness. It reminds me of those animals that farmers fatten up. They must think we're very kind to feed them so well, until their throats are cut."

"Do you really think they'd prepare us for war without telling us?"

"What I really think is that if Finland and Russia come to blows, it won't have much to do with our side. Everything will come from Moscow. I also think you and your friends should make the most of the end of summer, Toivo."

4

Woken in the middle of the night, the colonel was now in the Kremlin's Great Palace, sitting stiffly in his dress uniform on a carved gilded chair in a corridor as long and wide as a street, lined with white columns beneath a painted ceiling with a row of chandeliers that could hold as many as a thousand candles.

Sitting there, his face crumpled, and with maps rolled up on his thigh, the colonel had been roused from sleep by fists thumping on his door.

"I have no idea," he told his worried wife.

For two years, Stalin had embarked on a massacre in his own country. His insistence on Western conspiracies and internal betrayals, fed by his acute paranoia, had led him to despatch more than ten million of his fellow countrymen to the gulags, and to kill a million more with a bullet to the back of the head. It was a period of history that would forever be known as the Great Purge.

Consequently, however many awards or medals one had, there was always great trepidation when you were summoned in the early hours to the Kremlin.

"Go to your sister's," he told his wife, kissing her hands. "I'll find you there."

An hour later and the colonel was none the wiser. As he felt for his fob watch in his inside pocket, a poorly fixed medal came loose from his chest and clattered to the floor. The metallic echo reverberated down the immense corridor, making him feel yet more alone and tiny, despite his rank.

A door opened in the distance. The guard took a whole minute to reach him, approaching steadily, heels clacking on the polished wooden parquet.

Invited to follow the man, the colonel hastily gathered his things under his arm and strode after him. He noticed a clock above the huge double doors that closed behind the guard, leaving him once more on his own in a meeting room into which a school or a theatre could have fitted, and across it a table where two weddings could have been celebrated.

The colonel heard the voice of Vyacheslav Molotov, the People's Commissar for Foreign Affairs, long before he saw him enter the room.

"Colonel Tikhomirov, thank you for coming."

Wearing a pair of small oval spectacles, with a round, amiable-looking face and well-trimmed moustache, Molotov sat down at one end of the table. Tikhomirov still had no idea why he had been summoned. Congratulations for his unswerving loyalty? Not at this time of night. A bullet to the head? In those years, a rumour could condemn you as surely as a cancer, but why call him to the Kremlin when the deed could be done in a discreet alleyway or out in the countryside?

"Are we expecting more people?" the colonel asked, uneasy at being all alone.

"No. And this meeting must never be referred to. I need six men for a mission of the utmost importance. A driver, a gunner and four soldiers. Only nine of us will know about this operation. You, me, the six men you choose, and Comrade Stalin, of course."

No congratulations then. No execution either. Tikhomirov felt jubilantly alive, and promised himself to find the time to watch the sunrise.

Still standing to attention, the colonel assured Molotov: "I'll find you the very best among our elite men."

"No, that will not be necessary. Have you ever visited the gulag at Belomorkanal?"

Before the colonel could envisage this question as a threat, Molotov said:

"Don't worry. I'm sending you there because that's where your mission begins. If Finland continues to refuse our demands to annex territory, they will have to declare war on us."

"War? Against us?" Tikhomirov was astonished. "I don't think they have the means. Or any wish to do so. It would be suicidal, to say the least. Why would they contemplate so rash an act?"

"Because we're going to force them to," Molotov said with a smile.

5

Finnish National Defence Council,
21 Korkeavuorenkatu, Helsinki

As chairman of the Finnish National Defence Council, Carl Gustaf Mannerheim cut an improbable figure. In his seventies, tall and rangy with a prominent moustache and a lively, penetrating gaze, he looked more like a dandy or a Conan Doyle private detective.

Having married the daughter of a general to advance his career, he had been a wretched husband until their divorce, but his two daughters made a good father out of him. A loving, protective father. Escaping a Finland that had the same opinion of homosexual women as much of the rest of Europe, Anastasia had settled in Paris, her sister Sophie in London. In these capital cities that they hoped were more enlightened, they could live and love freely. And it was to the Parisian Anastasia, living far from the threats looming over her native country, and to her alone, that Mannerheim could confess his despondency.

> *I am going to tender my resignation to the President once more, as nobody seems willing to listen to me. And if they won't listen, they should at least understand Stalin's demands. If he wants part of our country, a port or a military base, if he wants to station soldiers on our territory to guard against the rise of the Third Reich and his fears over an Adolfus who is marching across Europe, let him have his way! I was a soldier of the Tsar when Finland still belonged to Russia, and know how determined they are. I know them better than they do*

themselves. We ought to give way a little so as not to lose
everything. Because here we are in the middle: innocent, vul-
nerable, busily preparing for the Olympic Games – the place
for noble competition, as our President constantly reminds us.
But competition is not war, and I've never seen any nobility in
war. Not to heed Stalin's demands is unwise. Not to foresee
his anger is a huge blunder. Yes, we're stuck in the middle
between Eagle and Bear, protected by our neutrality, but that's
a very weak shield. We seem to think the storm will pass with-
out us getting wet. Ragnarök *is on its way, I can feel it. And if*
our future means war, we're not ready for it, of that I'm sure.

Mannerheim read this through, massaging the hand crushed
many years earlier by an old nag weighing half a ton, an accident
that meant he was forced to write in a curious manner, his fingers
holding the pen like a pair of sugar tongs.

Surrounding this perplexed head of the Finnish armed forces,
scarcely leaving room for the few paintings hanging from the
walls, 7,000 volumes of books on history and geography were
stacked in a library too heavy ever to be moved. Carl Gustaf
Mannerheim knew that the decisions his government was about
to take would write the history of his country in the pages of
the national novel that would one day find its way into this very
library. His name would appear there. It remained to be seen what
would be said of him, and what Finland would be remembered
for – if it still existed, that is.

He signed the letter "Gustaf", as he did all his personal correspondence. He was laying down his pen when the office door
opened: it was Aksel Airo, a former cadet at Saint-Cyr military
academy in France. His most trusted assistant.

"Is the Ghost ready?" the field marshal said, picking up his
baton.

6

Aksel Airo made Mannerheim wait by the side of the 1915 Rolls Royce Silver Ghost convertible, the field marshal's official car. A shiny black and powerful panther, with leather seats and walnut trim, two gigantic headlights and a streamlined body, the car would make even the most timid of drivers look impressive.

In front of them, an officer was checking that the sub-machine guns in the boot were loaded, while another was peering underneath the chassis to make sure there was no bomb.

"Is this really necessary?" Mannerheim said impatiently.

"Cars have been blown up."

"You listen to the radio too much, my friend."

"You're protecting Finland. Let me protect you."

"I'm protecting Finland," the field marshal repeated to himself. "That's amusing. Don't tell anyone, but I have absolutely no idea how to get us out of this mess."

"I find that hard to believe."

"If we give way to Stalin by offering him territory, I'm afraid he'll only want more. And then make the whole of Finland as Russian as it was hitherto."

"That's why you are also preparing the country for war."

"A war we will be certain to lose. So if we give way we will lose; if we fight, we will perish."

For weeks now Mannerheim had been living with two radically opposed states of mind: a diplomat searching for peace; a military leader preparing for a deadly conflict. He was both at the same time. Airo took a seat next to him in the now inspected Rolls Royce.

"While we're still negotiating, I don't think there'll be any war-like move," Airo said. "Stalin would never dare to fire the first shot, especially on an independent country."

"Ukraine, too, wanted its independence. And he starved it. Four million dead can testify to that. Are you sure your reading of the situation is correct? I don't know how he'll do it, but if Stalin wants to move against Finland, he'll find an excuse."

On its way to the Esplanadi quays where they had a meeting with the president in his palace, the Rolls Royce did not go unnoticed: Mannerheim and Airo in the rear, and in front of them, next to the driver, their escort, who kept a tight hold of the loaded gun on his lap. Mannerheim searched in his jacket pocket.

"Here are two letters and some money. One for Paris, the other for London."

"Money? But you sent your daughters some only last week," said an astonished Aksel.

"The future looks grim. I prefer to be prepared."

"So you really believe there will be a war?"

Mannerheim believed it so strongly it kept him awake at night. And whether you worried about the ambitions of a greater Russia or feared an attack by the Nazis, Finland was caught in the middle.

"That would be a catastrophe," Mannerheim admitted. "If the negotiations fail, we'll exhaust all our wealth on the battlefield. The day will come when we'll be forced to ask married couples to melt down their wedding rings to recover the gold and silver."

Hearing this, Aksel Airo instinctively twisted the gold ring on his finger. He thought of his wife Wilhelmina and his two daughters, Aila and Anja. Debate with words, beat with fists. Once the very last words had been uttered, the last hopes for peace exhausted, that would leave only weapons. Both at the front and in the rearguard, nobody in Finland would be safe any more.

"I am sure we can still avoid it," Airo said, to reassure himself.

"What do you think I spend my days and nights trying to do?"

"I know, Field Marshal. I do the same."

The Silver Ghost came to a halt, but nobody got out.

"Are you ready?"

The future of Finland was at stake in this meeting.

"I'm too old to shilly-shally. Either the president allows me to mobilise my soldiers, or I resign."

7

The president had listened, and Mannerheim had not resigned. And so as the field marshal had envisaged, a general mobilisation for defensive purposes had been ordered. And yet not even Mannerheim liked the idea. It left a bitter taste, and was a cruel, underhand strategy. But he accepted he would not be able to hold his head up high if it came to war.

"Make a company of soldiers out of the sons of the same village, then on the battlefield there will be brothers, friends, neighbours, so that they will have what they must defend before their eyes. It will not be people they do not know dying next to them, it will not be strangers whose lives they will want to save. They will have no choice but to fight, because who would dare to desert when his brother is calling for help?"

*

Like blood coursing through the veins, emissaries travelled along every road in Finland. On horseback, in cars, on bikes, on foot and by boat. No farm was ignored, even if it was surrounded by lakes or marshes. No reservist or able-bodied member of the Civic Guard was spared.

Pietari, with the jet-black hair that was almost unknown in Finland, heard the spluttering old car even before he saw it. He closed the door to his little red-painted farmhouse with its white-framed windows, rolled the grass stalk he was chewing to the corner of his mouth, and folded his arms determinedly.

"Pietari Koskinen?" the visitor said, rummaging in his bulging satchel as he jumped out of his vehicle.

"You know who I am. We've met in the Civic Guard," Pietari said as gruffly as if he was telling a stranger to get off his land.

The messenger did not come any closer, warned not only by Pietari's coal-black hair but also by his face as angular as a badly knapped flint and thin, razor-sharp lips that looked as if they never broadened into a smile.

"I'm sorry, I've been told to check everybody's identity. I have your call-up papers here. For your younger brother Viktor as well."

Pietari looked back at his house, checking it was still silent.

"Viktor is dead," he flung back at the man. "Of sunstroke. During the harvest."

The emissary looked at him disbelievingly and took out two letters.

"You mean Viktor Koskinen? The one I saw at the village celebrations a few days ago? I didn't know the dead danced so well."

Fists clenched, Pietari swallowed his lie. Inside the farmhouse, hidden by the lace curtains, Viktor was listening intently through the half-open window.

"I'm sorry, Pietari. All able-bodied men who have undergone military training must take part in these special manoeuvres."

"You know very well what these manoeuvres are. You know why we're being sent down there."

From first light, the emissary had personally handed this same bad news to heads of families, young married men, and others barely adult. Like Viktor.

Finland was divided in two. One half still refused to believe in Russian aggression and saw this mobilisation as no more than a military exercise of the kind organised once or twice a year. They received the messenger impatiently, keen to be of service to their country. The other half showed more reluctance, not to say frank suspicion, and hands had often trembled as they took the letter. Two of those called up had even run off into the woods, but to no avail. They could not stay hiding forever, and even before they joined their regiment they would face disciplinary sanctions.

"Orders are orders. So unless someone is an invalid, gravely ill, or too old, there is no excuse."

Pietari repeated the words in his head. Viktor was not old or sick. Unfortunately.

"Give me a minute."

Pietari soon came out of the small tool shed grasping the long wooden handle of a sledgehammer. Without a word, he walked past the messenger. Tapping his clogs against the house wall to remove the mud, he disappeared inside.

To refuse to run the risk of getting a bullet in your hide shows not so much a lack of courage as plain common sense, so Pietari did not feel ashamed when he laid eyes on his younger brother crouching terrified in a corner of the room. Sweeping aside the plates and cutlery already laid for lunch on the big kitchen table, he took down a still damp washing-up cloth and held it out to his brother.

"Bite on this. And put your hand on the table."

The hammer rose above Pietari's head and, with all the love he had for his younger brother, he crushed three fingers with one blow.

The scream penetrated the house's thick walls. The messenger wrote in pencil on his list: Viktor Koskinen. Invalid.

*

His automobile took him to the next farm. He knocked on the door. For the first time that day, he was certain the young man who lived here would not run away or receive him with a heavy heart.

Adjusting the satchel on his shoulder, he greeted the woman who came to the door: "Good day, madam."

"*Hei*," she answered briefly, kitchen knife in hand, its broad blade stained with a rabbit's warm blood.

"I've come to see your son. I have his call-up papers."

She had had five sons, and four of them had already made her weep. Antti had disappeared in a war more than 20 years earlier; Juhana was injured in that same war. Tuomas had been felled by sunstroke on a building site, and Matti had left one day, never to be heard of again. The call-up must be for her youngest, the only one left. The peasant woman became a wolf.

"*On koira haudettuna* with your story of a military exercise,"[3] she said suspiciously.

"I'm only obeying orders."

"If my son doesn't return, remember that I know where you live."

"I've been threatened like that all day," the messenger said with an unconcerned smile. "The Javanainen family promised to drown me if the six brothers did not all come back, and the Lankinens will take me behind the sauna if their three brothers are not there for Christmas.[4] But if there is to be a war, and if a man like your son doesn't come back from it, there's not much hope for the rest of us."

With a quick flick of her wrist, the woman cleaned the blood from her knife, sending a scarlet jet that streaked the threshold and ended up on the tip of the messenger's boots. He concluded that if her son had half the spirit his mother had …

"You'll find Simo in the barn. He's already preparing his things."

*

Late on the same day, the car pulled up on the drive to a house encircled by a river. Leena was washing mud and sweat from her laundry in its clear water. When she raised her head to ease her neck muscles, she saw her father deep in conversation with a young man carrying a satchel.

Loosening her hair, Leena wiped her hands on her long dress and left her washing on the riverbank to go and join them. It was only when she drew closer that she saw the bundle of banknotes in her father's hand, the letter in the visitor's, and heard snatches of their conversation.

"This is not about money," said the stranger, raising his hand in front of his face to show his refusal.

"It's always about money! How much more do you want?"

As if caught out, when her protective father saw Leena he stuffed the small bundle into his pocket, and the messenger could finally address the person he had come to see.

"Leena Aalto?"

"Who is asking?" she challenged him.

"I have your call-up papers."

The father lowered his eyes, acknowledging his defeat; when she read her name, the young woman's face lit up.

8

Onni found Simo by the fence next to the Häyhä family's stables. He had hay on the end of his pitchfork, clogs on his feet, and sweat on his brow.

Having also received his call-up papers, Onni was one of those not in the least concerned about it. He and Simo talked about the weather, the harvests and the latest comedy featuring the national clown Lapatossu,[5] advertised at the local cinema. The comic actor was even more popular now that sound had been added to the images in a film. The two of them talked about Onni's wedding, which should have taken place at the end of August, but which had been postponed on several people's advice until a time when relations with Russia were less tense. September had given way to October; August was a long way behind them, and if the event was delayed much longer, Onni feared he would have to go to church on skis, he in his brand-new suit, and his bride-to-be in her beautiful white dress. That would be a great shame, because in fine weather Finland was a magical country, the perfect setting for a wedding.

Those summers when daylight lasts for eighteen hours and the sun constantly skims the horizon, as if too heavy to climb to its zenith, when bodies cast giant shadows, and you can read in the middle of the night or, with a bit of effort, sunbathe at four in the morning. On one of these never-ending days, the couple would have said their vows, got drunk, eaten more than they should have, bathed in one of the 180,000 lakes in Finland, and danced in the light at midnight, casting their elongated shadows on the surrounding houses like a dance of merry spectres come to celebrate their happiness.

The chaotic international situation had dealt a blow to this joyful wedding. But while Onni was complaining about it, something else was on his friend Simo's mind.

He disappeared into his house, painted the colour of wheat as though to harmonise with nature. When he reappeared he was carrying two glasses of fresh milk, and had a long case under his arm.

"For me?" Onni said, astonished.

Simo had been counting on giving it to him on his wedding day, but was afraid that what their government had termed a "mobilisation for special manoeuvres" was in fact a call-up for war, which was something not everyone returned from. Onni opened the case and whistled through his teeth.

"Your very first rifle? The Westinghouse? Are you sure?"

Simo patted him on the shoulder to confirm it was something he had thought through. The defence budget never having been a national priority, not all the reservists and Civic Guards had their own weapon. Even army uniforms were not complete: casual trousers were worn with military jackets, uniforms with everyday shoes, and the blue-and-white Finnish insignia was worn on woollen caps, a motley mixture of war and peace.

As the best marksman in the Rautjärvi Civic Guard, Simo had his own M28/30. Toivo, who was no slouch himself, had his own M/91 Mosin Nagant. Onni, though, was empty-handed. Now Simo was arming his comrade for whatever the future might hold. And Onni had seen it as nothing more than a wedding gift, whenever that was finally celebrated.

9

Leena Aalto presented a problem for her parents. In fact, they did not really have much to complain about, except that she was a Lotta.

"Lotta". As a child, Leena had heard this name in passing, and her mother had satisfied her curiosity.

"Her name was Svärd, Lotta Svärd. A long time ago, Finland belonged to Sweden, and when more than a century ago Sweden fought against Russia, we were dragged into the war alongside the Swedes."

"Did Lotta fight as well, then?" Leena wanted to know.

"No, my dear. Women don't go to war, not a hundred years ago, and not today. But History tells us she followed her husband right to the front."

"She must have loved him very much then."

"Unfortunately for her, she did … The soldier Svärd was killed. As you can imagine, after that any young woman would have returned home, but Lotta wasn't any young woman. So instead she stayed to take care of the wounded, to save lives at the risk of her own."

Without suspecting that years later she would come to regret it, Leena's mother had planted the seeds of the anxiety that she felt now, because ever since adolescence Leena had only been waiting until she was eighteen to finally become another Lotta.

"You can never join up!" her father had thundered with the authority of a patriarch at the head of the table. "I won't allow it!"

"It's not for you to say," Leena had defied him, newly impervious to his authority. "Today I am an adult. And young men have the right to join the Civic Guard, don't they?"

"Ah! So that's it … Young men! So all this fuss is about them, is it?"

"I couldn't care less about those idiots. I simply want to be useful."

"But you are that in Finland," her father exploded. "Here you can do everything! In Europe you wouldn't have the right to answer back your husband or your father. Even working is frowned on for women, whereas here you can do what you like. If you have strong arms, you can roll your sleeves up and work on a farm or in the fields, carry bricks and sacks of cement on building sites, work in the sugar factory or sawmill. If you have a lively mind you can become a journalist or a politician, or occupy any position in the civil service. Luckily you have both strong arms and a keen mind, but nothing satisfies you."

"Don't worry, I'm sure I am going to be one of those. Being Lotta is only for my free time."

"What if one day our country is at war again, what do you think will happen? You'll leave with the men. To the frontline!"

"Women don't go to war, Papa. Not a century ago, and not now."

"*Perkele!*" Her father knew when he was beaten. Nothing was more stubborn than a daughter!

*

Now, four years later in October 1939, Leena was 22, the same age as Finland. And following the messenger's visit to their farm, her parents' worst fears had become reality.

They would have preferred Leena to be frivolous, uncaring, or even utterly selfish. But they had brought her up so well they had only themselves to blame. Hearts gripped by anguish, they watched as she struggled to close her small suitcase.

When Leena arrived on the station platform as her call-up

papers required, her grey uniform perfectly ironed, the woman responsible for the Lottas examined her from head to toe.

"Cook? Canteen assistant?"

"Nurse, madam. And I'm also a trained telephone operator."

"Then you're in the wrong place."

She pointed her vaguely towards the far end of the platform. As Leena made her way there, a tall blond beanpole of a man bumped into her and she almost dropped her suitcase.

"So sorry, sweetheart," the young man apologised, winking broadly at her.

*

The men of Rautjärvi had been taken away. Levied for the nation, like a tax in flesh and blood. The same in every town and village. Next it was the turn of their horses. Sixty-four thousand of them. And the women left behind were already grumbling. The villages had lost their manpower, and since there were now no animals, they knew that for the length of those special manoeuvres they would be the ones pulling the plough, with only the strength of their legs and shoulders to rely on.

A third of all the horses in Finland were requisitioned, led by the halter to cattle wagons of trains whose smoke sometimes covered the entire platform so densely you could not see your closest neighbour.

Gradually, the confident smiles of some of the conscripts helped to ease the general apprehension. An exercise. Nothing more than an exercise, kneeling fathers told their worried children, while the air was filled with the national anthem "Our Country", whose words everyone had learned since almost before they could speak.

In stations, on roads, throughout Finland, 300,000 men and 100,000 women left their homes that day. In the village of Rautjärvi, they woke up to find there were 372 men and 182 women fewer.

Toivo pushed his way through the crowd on the platform, and

jumped over the suitcases in his way, forcing apart the kissing couples. Onni struggled to keep up with him.

"Look, over there, I can see Simo!"

He went faster still, almost knocking over a young girl.

"So sorry, sweetheart," he apologised, winking broadly at her.

*

Half of the cattle trucks had been fitted out. Ranged around a wood stove that needed constant replenishing, long benches were almost comfortable. Everybody found room, the late arrivals pushing their way in. Soon, friendship and the pleasure of being reunited dispelled the uncertainties of their journey.

"You're wearing your wedding ring?" Toivo said, glancing at Onni's ring finger.

"Yeah, we didn't want to wait for the priest. We'll do it according to the rules when I get back. But at least we're hitched!"

Pietari soon came to join them, but could find no place to sit. He made do with throwing his kit bag on top of the others, and using them as a mattress.

"Did you hear that, Pietari? Onni gave his future wife a ring just before he left … Doesn't that remind you of a song?"

An easy question, as the tune was played on the radio almost 20 times a day. And the response came immediately, because you didn't have to insist much to get a Finnish man to sing. Onni found himself the butt of a musical joke as a wagonload of soldiers burst into song after Pietari had hummed the opening words: "Oh Emma".[6]

> *Oh Emma! Do you remember that night*
> *when the moon was full and we left the ball?*
> *You gave me your heart, vowed to love me*
> *and promised to be mine.*

Believing you, I promised in turn
and offered you a ring.
I vowed to be yours
but you broke your promise,
And used my ring
to make a pair of earrings.

Taking it in good heart, Onni himself sang the last couplet; and yet his heart clenched a little when the train began to move.

"We'll only be gone a week or two," Pietari reassured him. "She'd have to be really fickle to forget you so quickly."

10

The railway tracks went no further. The train stopped in open country.

After two days' travel, the men from Rautjärvi were formed up on the platform amidst a cacophony of contradictory orders. They were 20 kilometres from their camp, and the officers shouted that the distance was to be covered *on* foot. To make things worse, the sky had become heavy with the threat of imminent rain. All along the border with Russia, trains were discharging more regiments.

Toivo, Onni, Pietari and Simo had all received the same posting: the 6th Company of the 2nd Battalion of the 34th Regiment of the 12th Division of the IV Army Corps, stationed at Kollaa.

"Kollaa," Onni grumbled, adjusting his rucksack on his shoulder. "I couldn't even place it on a map. Does anyone know the region? What's it like?"

Only a few kilometres from the Russian frontier, the region of Kollaa looked uninviting. Thick forests of silver birch and firs bordered by marshes and lakes surrounded by granite plains that left people exposed to the elements, with only one road wide enough for soldiers or Russian tanks to travel along. More than enough reasons for thinking you would have to be a poor strategist to mount an attack on Finland through here.

*

Lieutenant Colonel Wilhelm Teittinen, commander of the 34th Regiment, had his field tent erected and then summoned his twelve officers. By the dim light of an oil lamp, and with the buzzing sound of radio tests in the background, Teittinen smoothed a map over a trestle table with the back of his hand.

"Officially," he announced, "the exercise is a preparation for a possible conflict. Establishing a rear camp around Lake Loimola, creation of a frontline along 30 kilometres of the Kollaa River, digging trenches and anti-artillery shelters, installation of a perimeter of artificial bramble,[7] weapons practice, forced marches, and taking up attack and defence positions."

The officers round the table, all of them career soldiers, had been told weeks earlier that all leave was cancelled: an order which, in military parlance, revealed more than any other an outcome they all feared.

"As long as the negotiations between the Kremlin and Helsinki continue, headquarters is instructing us not to stir up any trouble on the border. Not to show any warlike intent, not to give them the least excuse to feel threatened."

"Threatened? By us? You could fit 50 Finlands into the Soviet Union."

Teittinen searched in his uniform jacket, took out a blue Saima packet, and lit a cigarette.

"All the more reason not to antagonise them," he said. "Let's stay as unobtrusive as possible. For now, let our soldiers take up their positions, form their companies, put up their tents, stable the horses, collect their things and munitions, and meet their officers."

"Speaking of officers," one of the others said in a worried voice, "the quartermaster has found one of them dead drunk, rummaging in the alcohol supplies."

"You mean Aarne Juutilainen? The legionnaire? He's wasted no time disgracing himself. What company does he command?"

"The 6th."

"Poor them," was the thought shared by all those round the table, as the pounding from thousands of soldiers marching along the muddy ground grew louder and louder.

11

In the general mêlée, the 6th Company's four platoon commanders, Suuronen, Lehelä, Karlsson and Liimatainen, were searching in vain for their lieutenant, the infamous Aarne Juutilainen. The other units, meanwhile, were regrouping, and the most prepared were pitching their tents in an area where they had felled enough trees to leave them invisible in the midst of one of the region's thousands of forests.

Three of the four officers were already complaining about being wet nurses.

"Are these exercises any use? It's not by making them dig foxholes and put up tents that we'll make combatants of them."

"Besides, no-one ever won a medal teaching reservists and Civic Guardsmen to become real soldiers."

"Will we have to change their nappies as well?"

Up to this point, Karlsson had remained silent, but he had a very different opinion and had no intention of keeping it to himself.

"If war breaks out, they will die the same as anyone else, medals or no, soldiers or not. And I advise you to teach them everything you know. One of them could save your life."

The three rebuked officers looked down at the tips of their boots.

"Anyway," Karlsson said, "a bit of sympathy from you won't do them any harm. They don't know yet that they're answerable to the redoubtable Aarne Juutilainen."

"Why redoubtable?" Suuronen said. "What's so special about him?"

"Apart from having a face only a mother could love?"

"Yes, apart from that."

Karlsson had often heard talk of Juutilainen, so thought it worthwhile to fill the others in with a few more details about the person who would be shouting at them over the coming days.

"Aarne Juutilainen, lieutenant and commander of our 6th Company. At the age of fourteen he had already forged parental agreement to join the army. He was a cadet at military college before he was thrown out, only to return a year later and be thrown out again due to his 'inappropriate lifestyle.'"

"Meaning what?"

"Fighting and drinking, if you prefer. All he could do was enrol in the French Foreign Legion, where apparently they aren't as fastidious. So he signs on, spends five years in North Africa, and gains French nationality and his nickname, 'the Terror of Morocco' – or simply 'the Terror', if you get to know him."

"For the legionnaires to call one of their own 'the Terror,'" Suuronen said under his breath, "he must have really put himself about."

"When he returned to Finland," Karlsson went on, "he became a staff officer but was sacked for excessive consumption of alcohol. The following year he was head of a Civic Guard unit deep in Lapland, but was again dismissed for excessive consumption of alcohol. As the saying goes, a leopard cannot change his spots, because the next year—"

This description was suddenly interrupted by the very person they were talking about, who, living up to his legend, was already barking orders at the 300 men of the 6th Company, as they rushed to form close order ranks in front of their officer.

"And the next year, gentlemen," Karlsson concluded, "is this year, and it's on us that this little ray of sunshine has come to shine."

12

A belt with a buckle in the shape of the lion of Finland, a blue badge to pin to their caps, a tin cup, metal canteen, a fork-spoon, a mess tin and a small spade: this was the basic equipment issued to every Finnish soldier. In addition, each company had an axe, a saw, a crowbar and one big shovel.

Once his troops had received their gear, Juutilainen reviewed them, his ice-blue eyes shooting daggers at them all. A criticism of their uniform, a punch to the stomach to get them to stand straighter, now and then an insult to offer them a show of his authority. In front of him stood factory workers, farmers, secretaries, university lecturers, masons, men with an average age of thirty – none of them accustomed to such treatment, or to being shouted at or pummelled.

Among them were the six Javanainen brothers, the three Lankinens and the Rautjärvi schoolmaster, whose pupils had watched him rush out of the classroom and jump on his motorbike the moment he received his papers. Not even the village chaplain had escaped. He must have spent hours struggling with his conscience and with the Almighty whose teachings he preached, for him to accept to pick up a rifle, now that force of circumstance had made a soldier of him. Just like the other 290 men of the 6th Company.

Juutilainen did not know any of them. It was time to find out what they were made of: their courage and their willingness to sacrifice themselves were the legionnaire's only yardstick. He turned to his four platoon commanders.

"Get them loaded up, we're going on a march," he barked.

A loud muttering rose from the assembled ranks.

"Excuse me, Lieutenant, sir," Karlsson said bravely, "but the men's backs are stiff from a two-day train journey, and their legs are aching from a 20-kilometre march. They're tired and covered in mud, night is about to fall, and they haven't put up their tents or even had time to eat."

Juutilainen screwed up his eyes as if trying to focus on the face talking to him.

"And you are?"

"Karlsson, Lieutenant, sir, commander of *Sissi* 1.[8] I introduced myself to you yesterday."

"There's nothing so distant to me as 'yesterdays'. I seldom remember 'yesterdays'. And what was it you told me yesterday?"

Karlsson gestured behind his back for the other three platoon commanders to step up.

"Sergeant Karlsson, of *Sissi* 1. And this is Liimatainen, *Sissi* 2. Suuronen, *Sissi* 3. And Lehelä, leader of *Sissi* 4."

By the time Karlsson finished, Juutilainen had obviously forgotten how he began, so opted to simplify things.

"I'll remember your numbers; that'll do. Numbers are good. Numbers survive. Those who have them, a lot less often. And I only remember the names of brave men, of women I've had, and soldiers who annoy me. So, Karlsson, what was it you wanted to tell me?"

Since the lightning was not going to strike them, Liimatainen, Suuronen et Lehelä, now to be known as *Sissi* 2, 3 and 4, took a step back and left Karlsson to face the lieutenant's wrath.

"I was saying that the men have been travelling for two days, that they've already marched 20 kilometres, and that they haven't yet been able to eat … Lieutenant, sir."

"Are they wounded or dying?" the Terror of Morocco snapped.

Karlsson gave in and lowered his eyes.

Already on this first day, the 6th Company was writing its legend, and its men were commanded to begin their first march.

*

Leena had not had much time to get installed either. Even before she could open her suitcase, she found herself swept up in the general commotion. Obeying orders, she piled clean, warm blankets on one side, lined up camp beds on the other, and at the end of the day, still cheerful, she helped with an exact count of the stock of bandages, dressings and small medical items.

When she finally emerged from the first-aid post, day was taking its bow, and she stumbled on the pegs of a tent that had not been there a few hours earlier. Whereas all the other tents were white, this one's canvas was as black as night. Curious, she stuck her head inside, but could see nothing. Absolutely nothing.

"You have no reason to be here, little one," an officer warned her as she emerged.

On her first day, Leena should have gone on her way, and, as her father had so often told her, minded her own business. But if her father had failed, what chance was there an army officer would do any better?

"Why is this tent empty when we need room in the others?" she said stubbornly.

"So you're a nurse, are you?" the soldier asked, inspecting the young woman's epaulettes and the insignia sewn on them.

Leena nodded.

"Well then, I promise you that you will not want to see it full," he told her.

*

By the twelfth kilometre, in a night as black as ink, one man from Juutilainen's 6th Company collapsed to the ground. His ankle was hurting, and his everyday shoes were torn by the uneven terrain of the forests and slippery granite boulders.

"Get up, Onni," Toivo urged him. "Don't draw attention to yourself."

"But I don't have boots," Onni complained. "And my feet are bleeding."

Simo and Pietari stood either side of him and tried to pull him to his feet, but they too slipped on the muddy earth. All of a sudden, a powerful hand took hold of Onni's coat collar and tugged him upright as if he weighed no more than an eight-year-old.

The four friends turned to the newcomer, who was smiling at them from on high and said in answer to their unasked question:

"I'm Hugo."

"I don't recognise you," Pietari said. "You're not from Rautjärvi, are you?"

"I don't even know where that is," Hugo said. "I'm from Rinkilä."

Twenty-seven years earlier in Rinkilä, Hugo had been pronounced dead the moment he was born. According to legend, his body went to Tuonela, the country of death surrounded by black waters on which floats a swan. But it was said in Rinkilä that the swan was so moved by the pure heart of this newborn that it carried him back to the shores of life, and just as the doctor was preparing a white cloth to wrap him in and take him away, Hugo began to breathe again, and then to cry until he was put on his mother's breast. He had been without oxygen for a little too long, but everything seemed to be functioning. Well enough for him now to be marching on the border with Russia, at night, far from home, under the command of an alcoholic, without really comprehending why.

Mannerheim had wanted men from the same village to be in the same company, but as many villages were too small, it had been necessary to amalgamate several of them to make a complete unit. And hamlets such as Rinkilä had served to make up the numbers.

"Well then, Hugo from Rinkilä, thank you," Onni said.

"Are you the only one from your village?" Toivo said.

"No, there's Janne, so that makes two of us."

During this brief nocturnal exchange, the beam from their torches gave away this little group of soldiers as clearly as a false note in a quartet. With a look like thunder, Juutilainen pounced on them like a predator on its wounded prey, one hand on the pistol at his hip, a grin of pleasure on his face.

"In Morocco," he shouted, "the soldiers marched even if their bones were sticking out of their boots, and they didn't complain! They didn't stop, because they knew that if they did, I would have put them out of their misery!"

As he turned, he bumped into Simo, who lost his balance and fell on his back. The Terror bent over him menacingly.

"You look to me very small to hold a weapon. Very small for anything, in fact."

Then he turned to the rest of the 6th Company.

"You are being paid five marks a day, so at least try to earn them!"

Without asking, Hugo seized Onni's rucksack and slung it on top of his own. Back in their ranks, Pietari laid his hand on the shoulder of his friend, who was now suffering in silence, teeth clenched.

"One week, Onni. Two at the most, then we'll be going home."

13

Forty-five days later

It seemed that the order to demobilise would never come, and that the negotiations between Russia and Finland would never end. Everywhere in Finland people were beginning to doubt whether their Soviet neighbour really did have warlike intentions, and to think those called up had been away far too long.

In the Kollaa camp as in all the others, the news each week was starting to resemble the news of the previous one. The soldiers searched for any anecdote they could write about to enliven their letters and conceal their tedious, exhausting daily routine.

In letter after letter, Onni promised he would soon be home. His bride-to-be sent him news of the farm, adding salacious postscripts that made him blush in secret.

Pietari did not receive any reply to his letters to his brother Viktor, and was starting to worry. What had happened to his crushed fingers? Did Viktor bear him a grudge? Was what he had done even necessary?

Toivo wrote for two people. Once he had finished his lines, he sat beside Hugo who, even if he wasn't illiterate, had the strange problem of mixing up the letters in words, making what he wrote incomprehensible.

As for Simo, he loved his family without having to say so and had not yet sent any news. And even if he had been forced to, what could he have shared that would interest them?

The soldiers had spent the whole time digging. Shelters here, kilometres-long trenches there, here pits for machine-gun emplacements, there others for mortars; and all this without ever firing a single bullet or shell. They were playing at war with real weapons and real men; their only horizon was the black tip of the fir trees and a rare reflection of the November sun on the metal of the "artificial bramble" rolled out all round their camp.

Morale sank to its lowest as one storm followed another and showers came and went. They shivered side by side, hands in their sleeves and heads sunk in their coats. At the slightest pause they fell asleep from exhaustion, their fatigue constantly stoked like a fire at risk of going out.

Every time it rained, the earth turned to mud, smearing everything from boots to uniform collars, as well as the fabric of the tents. When violent winds dried out the ground, it crackled like desert sand and turned to dust that infiltrated everywhere. The first raindrops turned it once again into this heavy, sticky mud that seemed to want to cover them and engulf them. Wet, heavy uniforms that were impossible to dry properly despite the stoves in the middle of their tents; exercises and marches through forests and marshes; guard duty from dusk to dawn: all this to prepare a defence against a hypothetical enemy.

Every company suffered the same fate, but not one of them, despite what was apparently equitable treatment, had any wish to be moved to the 6th Company. And at every bellow from "the Terror", the men not under his command appreciated how fortunate they were and congratulated themselves with a rueful nod of the head.

*

In spite of the lack of any sign of aggression from Russia, one of the regiment's missions was to patrol the neighbouring villages to try to convince the farmers and peasants to leave their land in case of an attack that by now nobody believed in. The situation was hardly likely to persuade a family who owned land to leave behind a lifetime's work; since the arrival of the troops, only ten or so had considered it wise to leave the region. Worse still, weary of there being no sign of any invasion, some had already drifted back.

Time and again, the soldiers marched the kilometres separating their camp from the Russian border, previously settled by myriad tiny Finnish villages that made up the municipality of Suojärvi.

"Sixth Company! Form up! We're returning to preach the good news," Juutilainen roared at his three hundred exasperated men.

Toivo met this news with a smile the others found hard to comprehend.

"Are you out of your mind?" Pietari said with astonishment. "There's really no reason to celebrate."

Toivo put his arm round Simo's shoulders, and the others gathered closer to listen.

"We'll be at Suojärvi this evening," Toivo said in a low voice, "then in the village of Hyrsylä the next day. And I've heard that in exactly three days they're organising a celebration. Soldiers, Lottas and little peasant girls, all together at last. A bit of alcohol, a bit of music, and pretty women: do I still need to explain why I'm smiling?"

This pleasing thought changed everyone's mood. When all was said and done, a two-day march was not so much.

14

Sixteen hours' forced labour a day, just enough food to prevent them dying of starvation, and regular beatings. The Belomorkanal gulag was there to build the White Sea canal over their dead bodies. And yet the prisoners had once been soldiers and officers of Mother Russia, some of them traitors, others communists, many of them innocent of any crime. No matter, their punishment had been decreed by a Supreme Leader who aroused such fear that people understood very clearly why he was known as Him with a capital letter.

Escorted by an armed guard, Colonel Tikhomirov strode down the gulag's underground corridors, with beaten earth floors and bare stone walls lit just sufficiently to allow him to distinguish those who were still breathing in the cramped cells from those already dead. Putrefaction, sweat and excrement: the smell was so overpowering that a handkerchief over the nose offered no protection, and the colonel prayed that his eyes would get used to the darkness as rapidly as possible to help him find the last man in the squad he had come there to assemble, for the mission Molotov had entrusted him with.

"Azarov," the guard shouted. "Are you still alive?"

Two filthy hands with broken or torn-out nails gripped the cell bars, then a face appeared, obscured by long white greasy hair.

"Azarov. That's me."

Tikhomirov studied him, wondering how many days this emaciated prisoner would have lasted without his visit.

"You're a gunner, is that right?"

"I once was."

"Perfect. Then I'll get you out of here if you accept—"

"*Khorosho*,"[10] Azarov cut him short. "Even if you want me to kill Hitler, Stalin or my own mother. I accept whatever you want, comrade."

15

No-one paid any attention to the van followed by three pairs of horses pulling a heavy covered cart. At night, this strange convoy had travelled the few kilometres between the Belomorkanal gulag and its destination, drawn in a red circle on the map Azarov had been given. There they waited patiently until the appointed time.

"And we're going to be free?" one of the men said.

"As much as one can be in Russia," Azarov said.

Only the wheels of the cart stuck out below the stretched tarpaulins, and it was not until the agreed moment that the load was revealed: three 76 mm. guns, almost two metres long. Three artillery pieces on the edge of a dark wood, as Russian as the soft earth they sank into, as Russian as the targets they were going to aim at, as Russian as the men about to fire them.

Azarov checked the coordinates one last time.

The first shells were loaded into the breeches of the three guns. Six identical shells with five-kilo explosive charges were awaiting their turn.

The first salvo was ready.

"Fire!"

*

Mainila, Russia, 15.45 hours

It was not the roar of guns that alerted the two soldiers on guard duty. They knew a lot of exercises took place in the region, and that countless shells of all sizes were fired as soon as they came off the production lines in factories that had been working day and night for months.

Despite their lack of combat experience, the two guards also knew that the likelihood of being the target of artillery fire grew the longer you could hear a shell whistling through the air. And those whistling sounds seemed never to end.

From their guard post they first saw the cabin of a transport lorry explode in the centre of the garrison courtyard. No soldiers were on board, but the petrol tank burst into flames in a blinding flash that turned the mechanic filling it into a human torch. The two other shells ploughed into the garrison approaches, sending a ton of earth into the air, earth now falling back to the ground in a shower of dust and gravel.

Only one shell exploded from the second salvo. The first one overshot noiselessly; the second one tore through the fabric of a tent and landed between two beds, where two miraculously spared men believed in God from that moment on. But one lethal shell, the third one fired, scored a direct hit on the command post, where it blew apart two soldiers and an officer. Their bodies acted as shields and saved the others, who ran out screaming, covered in blood, eardrums shattered.

There was only one shell in the third salvo, and you would need to have been alongside Azarov's guns to know why. The shell hit a log pile; thousands of wooden splinters wounded another eight soldiers.

In the midst of general pandemonium, with confused orders from terrified officers and cries of pain everywhere, silence returned.

*

Three hours later, the van transporting Azarov and his five men entered the empty hangar of a disused aerodrome that was now an aeroplane cemetery, also marked in red on his map. Azarov cut the engine when they pulled up beneath the missing wing of a giant Tupolev bomber whose fuselage still bore the marks of the anti-aircraft fire that had brought it down fifteen years earlier. As agreed with Colonel Tikhomirov, he ordered his five soldiers to stay in the van, walked away a few steps, pulled the pins from two grenades, and rolled them under the vehicle, then took cover behind a wall. The van was lifted two metres into the air, split in the middle from the heat and the impact, and fell back in almost exactly the same spot. His conscience pricking him, Azarov fired a bullet into each of the charred bodies.

He waited several minutes for Tikhomirov's car to come and collect him. He swung his rucksack onto his back when he saw it approaching along the main runway. As it drew alongside, the first thing Azarov realised was that the colonel was not on board. Then, as the barrel of a gun pointed at him through the lowered rear window, he smiled at having been so naive.

Secret missions do not like witnesses.

*

Tikhomirov made his detailed report for Comrade Molotov's eyes only. Then the story was embellished, with words authorised not only by the Kremlin but by Stalin himself. An objective inquiry was set up, headed by a colonel above all suspicion.

Russian press release no. 291
Unprovoked provocation by the Finnish military clique

At 15.45 hours on November 26, 1939, our troops stationed one kilometre to the north-west of Mainila were treacherously bombarded by artillery fire from Finnish territory. The Finns fired a total of seven cannon shells.

Three Red Army soldiers and one non-commissioned officer were killed. Seven Red Army soldiers, one non-commissioned officer and a sub-lieutenant were wounded.

This provocative act created boundless indignation among our troops. Despatched to the scene, the commander of the 1st Division of the regional headquarters, Colonel Tikhomirov, has been appointed to lead an inquiry.

16

Sometimes, all that a peasant in Finland could see from the threshold of his house was land that he owned.

It took only a few farms to make a village. Beyond it would be a lake, a thick silver birch forest, then four or five other dwellings that formed another village. Seventy-six of them altogether, some of which, built round a pulp factory or a sawmill, had increased in size over time, because here work was either the land or timber.

Suojärvi was so close to the Russian border that its inhabitants spoke not only their mother tongue but also an abstruse mixture of Russian and Finnish that had emerged thanks to trading back and forth. The men from Rautjärvi could follow this strange language even if it wasn't completely transparent to them. Further south, the Finns were also within touching distance of the frontier; they too worked the land and timber; they too had always traded with their neighbour, now potentially an enemy.

The 6th Company had been divided into platoons that went from village to village, everywhere greeted by the echoes of a widespread scepticism: "A war? Really? Where would that be?" So, as in the fable, the little shepherd boy had cried wolf too often, and no-one was frightened of the animal's teeth or claws any more. All day long, the platoons were met with repeated refusals to move.

On this particular day, however, nothing seemed able to quench the unusual good humour of the 6th Company, because when that day was done it would be evening, and finally that evening they would be able to forget their misfortune for a while.

*

All the village doors were open to the soldiers. They had been able to take advantage of the saunas to have a wash at last. Naked, sweating in the steamy cloud from cold water poured onto burning stones, they felt as if their fatigue was dissolving with the dirt, and so were Russia and the crazy Juutilainen. Above all, they no longer stank. The dance could begin.

Pietari raised his voice to drown out the local orchestra and introduce himself to the young woman sitting on a bale of hay, heavy coat round her shoulders, bare legs only partly concealed by a thin dress. Her pleasant face was lit by the coloured lanterns running all round the square; her head was crowned with white flowers.

"Are you dancing?"

"If I'm invited," the young woman said with a smile.

Jumping down clumsily from her perch, she almost lost her balance, and laughed out loud. Just in time Pietari caught her by the waist and held on to her as he led them to the middle of the square. First one tune, then another; by the third she had rested her head on his shoulder without worrying about following the beat or the steps. They would have carried on dancing gently, holding each other, even without the music.

At first Onni, Simo and Toivo had made fun of the dancers, but soon found the joke was on them as they sat in a corner, clutching a bottle of *viina*,[11] watching the others and cursing their own timidity.

"Are you dancing?"

Simo dug Toivo in the ribs when it seemed he had not grasped he was the one the Lotta was talking to. She stood in front of him, a beguiling smile on her face, wearing her nurse's uniform: grey dress, skirt exactly 20 centimetres above the ground, white collar and cuffs, scarf on her head, and flat shoes. Round her neck she was wearing a shiny swastika made of metal coloured the blue of Finland – the symbol of the rising sun and good fortune, even if elsewhere it was the symbol of something very different. Toivo gazed speechless at the myriad freckles on her face.

"*Kirottu!* I've chosen a deaf and dumb partner," she mocked him. "My name is Leena. Don't you remember me?"

"Er …" Toivo stammered.

"You almost knocked me over on the platform at Rautjärvi station."

When the orchestra struck up the tune "Emma", Toivo's comrades pushed him forward, and the soldier and the Lotta disappeared hand in hand among the small throng of couples dancing the waltz.

For his part, Onni refused first one and then another invitation to dance. His steadfast refusal at least allowed him to notice not only Toivo and Leena kissing beneath the lanterns, but also an old man seated on a log pile, rifle on his lap, staring angrily at Pietari and the pretty countrywoman he was holding. Onni pointed him out to Simo, who pushed his way towards the couple and whispered something in the ear of his friend, who did not seem to be aware of the danger. The young woman turned around and, seeing her father's grim expression, reckoned that it was time for them to part.

"You should change partners. My father has a good aim, he's not an easy man, and I'm engaged to a man who is even worse."

With regret on both sides, Pietari freed her from his hold.

"Will we see each other again?" he said.

"No," she said with a smile, "but I won't forget you, because even if there is no war, I'll have saved a soldier from being shot."

*

The next morning, the plain where they had bivouacked appeared calm beneath a sprinkling of hoar frost, like hair turned silver with age.

Aarne Juutilainen had also enjoyed the celebrations after his own fashion. He had not danced or chatted, but he had drunk a lethal amount, so that even after 08.00 the next day he was flat out on his camp bed and had not yet bawled at anyone. It was this lie-in that allowed Toivo to reappear without getting caught, smiling beatifically.

Pietari was furious that, thanks to a protective father with a rifle, his own flirtation had come to nothing, and there was a hint of envy in his voice as he greeted Toivo.

"So, what about your Lotta?"

"Her name is Leena. And if you're expecting me to tell you about my night in detail, think again. I've been well brought up."

"Of course you're going to tell us."

"Yes, of course I'm going to tell you. Any coffee?"

Simo handed him his scalding tin cup. Toivo almost spilled it when Karlsson, the commander of *Sissi* 1, stormed in, attracting the attention of most of the company, as well as a group of Lottas who were tipping the steaming breakfast oats into the kitchen vat.

"The Russian garrison at Mainila has been bombarded!" Karlsson said falteringly, as if he himself had just heard the news on the radio connecting them to headquarters.

It was news that made no sense. A fox would never attack a bear. And since no-one seemed able to credit that Mannerheim would decide to point his guns at this small, isolated Russian garrison, Karlsson repeated:

"We've just declared war on the Soviet Union!"

17

Some men are like certain tools you use only occasionally, if at all, and then no longer remember where you put them. So Field Marshal Carl Gustav Mannerheim had to be reminded where to find Vilho Nenonen, because after the Mainila incident this discarded old implement had at all costs to be located.

"Your head of armament planning?" Aksel Airo asked in astonishment.

On a lacquered wood desk brought back from his travels in Asia, Mannerheim twisted his maimed fingers to write a single word on a piece of paper. He folded it in two and placed it in an envelope he handed to his faithful adjutant.

"We're on the verge of plunging our country into a conflict we cannot afford. Believe me, I'd never have imagined that crazy genius Nenonen might be the only one who could help us avoid it. He's also the only one who has the answers to our questions. By firing deliberately or accidentally on Russia, we've just given Stalin the excuse he was looking for. Take the Silver Ghost, there's no time to lose."

Finnish Ministry of Defence, 8 Eteläinen Makasiinikatu, Helsinki

Although it was fifteen years since he had been minister of defence, Vilho Nenonen had never left the ministry building. An expert in a government that had little interest in war and defence, he had been made to change offices, had seen his team progressively reduced, and had even been obliged to descend first one floor and then another, only just avoiding being sent to the basement. He was sidelined, all but forgotten.

When Aksel Airo was escorted to Nenonen's department, he scarcely gave the guard time to announce him before bursting into the room. Surrounded by walls plastered with drawings of weapons, cross-sections of cannon, rifles and munitions, and facing a kind of complex clock face scrawled over with distances, coordinates and a host of mysterious figures, the man with his back to Airo seemed immersed in his calculations.

"Do you know what I'm looking at, Aksel?" Nenonen said.

Airo did not have much time, but knew it was prudent not to risk irritating the man he needed so much.

"It's a firing trajectory circle," he said, like an obedient schoolboy.

"And what is a circle like this for?"

Since there was no way of hurrying Nenonen, Airo took off his coat and placed it carefully on the nearest, least cluttered table.

"Following your calculations, our artillery, whatever their positions, could all fire at the same target directed by a single observer without that person even really knowing where the guns were located. To put it more simply, it's a mechanism that would allow us to have the best artillery in the world. The only question is: will it be ready soon?"

"Why such a question? Are you afraid storm clouds are gathering?"

As he said this, the general finally turned to face his unexpected visitor. Hollow-cheeked, with black, bushy eyebrows and an apparently frail physique, his oiled hair brushed back, his left eye wayward, Nenonen was not surprised by this visit: he had been expecting it since the previous day.

Airo handed him Mannerheim's envelope. The general read the single word.

65

"Mainila."

"Mainila," Airo confirmed.

"The bombardment of the Russian garrison? You want to know whether it's us?"

"According to the field marshal, you're the only one who can supply the answer."

With a sweep of his arm, Nenonen indicated a row of open-fronted cabinets filled to overflowing with plans, scientific treatises, leaflets and maps.

"I know people dismiss me. They think I'm slightly ... I believe my friend Gustaf uses the word 'original' to describe me."

"Crazy genius" would have been closer to the mark, but Aksel preferred not to correct him.

"I can understand it," Nenonen said. "What can one say about a man like me who spends his time studying all kinds of armament and munitions in order to make precise plans and user manuals for every possible kind of conflict for an army with equipment from Finland, Russia, Sweden, France, Great Britain and heaven knows where else, making ours the most disparate artillery in the world?"

"That this man is our trump card?" Airo told him sincerely. "Knowledge is everything."

"Ignored yesterday, trump card today. How fickle is esteem," Nenonen thought out loud. "However, I don't really mind the renewal of interest in me because yes, I have your answer. I worked on it all night. Indeed, I was expecting you even sooner."

He took out a map from one of his overflowing cabinets and unfolded it on top of a pile of others. Finland, the border with Russia, and countless red and blue dots.

"The blue dots represent the current positions of Finnish Army regiments," he pointed out with the tip of his fountain pen. "The red are the Russians. According to the reports I received yesterday evening, the shelling was observed from our lines and entered in the logbook of our frontier post. And it was two kilometres from our nearest artillery."

"Meaning?" Airo said, politely masking his impatience.

"Meaning, as yet we have no gun capable of firing that distance."

"Are you suggesting that Russia fired on itself?"

"Russia will never admit that. No country could allow itself to be seen to start a war, especially if it attacks an independent, neutral and relatively harmless one like ours. And Stalin may detest the West, but he is fearful of its opinion. He therefore needs a motive, a reason. So no, Aksel, Russia did not fire on itself, because it will deny it, even in the face of the most blatant evidence. Thanks to this manoeuvre that has killed its own soldiers, Russia becomes a victim, and to the rest of the planet we are the aggressors. But the result is the same: we are going to war with the biggest army in the world, that of a country whose capital city alone has more inhabitants than all of Finland put together. Which means you should start evacuating Helsinki. And the big coastal cities."

Mannerheim had already found it hard to persuade his government to double the defence budget, as both the president and his ministers still believed in their endless negotiations and a peaceful outcome to the impasse. To ask them to evacuate Helsinki was almost unthinkable. They would never agree to it.

If the worst-case scenario was already upon them, how long did they have? One week? Perhaps two. Airo had to protect Mannerheim, the commander-in-chief, since there was going to be a conflict. And more selfishly, he had to protect his own family. Wilhelmina, Aila and Anja.

18

Hotel Moskva, Moscow, Manege Square

A foreign visitor lost in the centre of the Russian capital might imagine it was inhabited by giants, or that it was where the Titans and Titanides of Greek mythology dwelled. The avenues were like huge rivers that an entire fleet of ships could sail down with space to spare, and each of the tall anthill-like buildings could have been a whole city. It was as if with these gigantic facades Russia was puffing out its chest to the world.

The brand-new Hotel Moskva, risen from the ground only four years earlier, was equally outsized. Vyacheslav Molotov, Stalin's right-hand man, usually had his breakfast there and no-one except the hotel manager was permitted to disturb him.

The hotel restaurant was bathed in light thanks to a series of high windows opening onto the nearby bulbous golden domes of the sunlit Kremlin. Knife and fork crossed on his empty plate, a copy of *Pravda* folded in four on his napkin, a still warm cup of coffee in his decorated china cup, Stalin's most faithful acolyte had summoned Tikhomirov to meet him.

With an obsequious gesture, the hotel manager invited the colonel to sit at the table, and then made himself scarce.

"He has asked me to inform you, He is very pleased with you," Molotov assured him, a broad smile on his fatherly face. "Have you made sure this is just between us?"

"The gunner Azarov took care of his men, and yours took care of Azarov, without knowing who he was or why he had to disappear."

Molotov nodded contentedly.

"So that's where the story ends. No-one could trace it back to us," Tikhomirov thought it worth adding.

"No-one apart from you."

The colonel almost choked. He felt as though he was breathing sand. A shudder ran across the back of his head. Evil deeds do not like witnesses; he recalled how the men in the shadows who had followed orders and eliminated most of Stalin's officers in the Great Purge had soon themselves been executed.

"But we have to stop at some point and decide to trust people," Molotov reassured him. "Otherwise we'd have to get rid of every-one, and in the end only He and I would be left – if He so wishes."

This was how Stalin ruled pitilessly over both his army and his citizens, thanks to a deep-rooted fear preferably referred to as respect, and complete submission preferably referred to as loyalty. In a country where people talked politics only if they were in complete agreement, with an army in which every military officer was supervised by a political commissar, where courtiers rather than those in the know spread real or imaginary denunciations in the hope of advancement, promotion or a small pat on the back, every single stone that was a part of the building of the Soviet Union was laid with a trembling hand. Every single word that history told about it was controlled, weighed up to make sure it satisfied the dictator's fantasies.

Even in the corridors of the Hotel Moskva what could be heard was the silence of closed mouths, of ideas not shared with anyone, of opinions suppressed. The original blueprints for the building were themselves a token of the fear of displeasing the Little Father of the Peoples …

Nine years earlier, the architect Shchusev had gone to show him the first sketches for the Moskva, destined to be one of the greatest hotels in Mother Russia, the showcase of a flourishing country for the detested West. Aiming to please, the architect had drawn two different designs on the same blueprint. Stalin signed in between them.

"He signed in the middle," Shchusev had confided to Molotov as he left the tyrant's office.

"Do you want to go and ask Him which he meant?" came the reply.

And since the architect did not have the courage to do so, he never discovered which of the two options had been preferred. As a result, both of them were built, and in 1939 the hotel presented a split personality, with one facade on the left that had high windows and was ornately decorated, and another on the right in more minimalist style with smaller windows.

The fear of displeasing Him was exactly the same whether one was an architect or a colonel returning from a secret mission.

"Now that the Finns are under pressure, I cannot see them refusing Stalin's requests, even if they have found them unacceptable until now," Tikhomirov suggested.

"Unacceptable?" Molotov chuckled. "But who told you we ever wanted them to be accepted? Our troops have been positioning themselves all along the Finnish border for more than two months now."

"While we were negotiating?"

"The negotiations have never been anything but a long fuse for a situation that was bound to explode. If Finland accepts our demands to annex territory and establish military bases, we'll only ask for more until we've taken the whole country, whether they agree or not. And if they refuse, which they seem determined to do, our only choice will be to take up arms."

"So the invasion of Finland has always been the plan?"

"And who could stop us? 'Ten days will suffice,' one general has told Him. 'Give me munitions for twelve, just to be sure,' he added. We may have to fire a few rounds for them to put up their hands and surrender, but I think it will be enough just to raise our voice."

"But we both know our army has been greatly weakened by the purges. Is this really the right moment to risk an armed conflict?"

"You sound just like Meretskov. Do you also think our officers lack training, that we have logistical and uniform problems, a complete lack of preparation for fighting in forests, and that we underestimate and look down on the Finns?"

"Is that what Meretskov said?"

"Word for word, but these things always have consequences. When Stalin tells you to dance, you dance. Meretskov will pay for what he said by being the first commander at the front. Stalin wants to celebrate His next birthday on the steps of the Finnish parliament. In other words, in precisely 20 days. We will be facing an army hastily thrown together, badly equipped, few in number and unevenly trained. And I'll make sure our regiments are accompanied by brass bands celebrating our victories one after another until we reach their capital … After all, it's only Finland."

"What about the reactions from the rest of the world? Europe? America?"

"Let me remind you that two days ago, at Mainila, we were the ones attacked. That's the conclusion of your inquiry, isn't it?"

"Without a shadow of a doubt," the colonel confirmed, his survival instinct asserting itself.

Fabricating a war: lies and diplomatic language

Extracts from the Note from Vyacheslav Molotov, the Soviet People's Commissar for Foreign Affairs, for the attention of the honourable Finnish ambassador Aksu Koskinen:

Your Excellency,

According to the communiqué from Red Army headquarters, Russian troops on the isthmus of Karelia close to the border with Finland, not far from the village of Mainila, were unexpectedly bombarded today, November 26, at 15.45 hours by artillery based on Finnish territory.

The Soviet government has no intention of magnifying this repellent act of aggression by troops of the Finnish Army [...] but it expresses the desire that such unworthy acts should not be repeated.

Extracts from the reply of the Finnish ambassador, as instructed by his government:

To the People's Commissar:

As regards the border incident that is said to have taken place, the Finnish government has undertaken the required urgent inquiry. This inquiry has established that the artillery rounds to which your letter alludes were not fired from the Finnish side.

The calculation of the speed and trajectory of the seven projectiles leads to the simple conclusion that the artillery pieces launching them were at a distance of between one and a half and two kilometres to the south-west. As a result, it appears that we are dealing with an unfortunate accident that occurred during firing practice on the Soviet side.

**Extracts from Vyacheslav Molotov's reply to Finland
via its ambassador:**

Your Excellency,

*The Finnish government's denial of the shameful fact that Finnish
artillery opened fire on Soviet troops, causing loss of life and injuries,
can only be explained by a deliberate intention to mislead public
opinion and to insult the victims of the attack.*

*Nevertheless, the government of the U.S.S.R. cannot permit the
non-aggression pact to be violated by one of the parties while the
other continues to respect it. For this reason, the Soviet government
finds itself obliged to declare that from this day forth it regards
itself as released from the pact of non-aggression between the Soviet
Union and Finland, which has been systematically violated by the
government of Finland.*

**Radio broadcast by Vyacheslav Molotov
on November 29, 1939:**

*The hostile attitude of the present Finnish government towards
our country obliges us to take immediate steps to guarantee the
external security of our State.*

*The Soviet government has given the order for the high command
of the Red Army and Navy to be prepared for any eventuality, and
to immediately forestall any hostile initiative the Finnish military
clique might embark upon.*

*Demonstrating its continuing hostility towards us, the foreign
press affirms that the measures we are taking are aimed at the
conquest or annexation by the U.S.S.R. of Finnish territory. That is
a despicable calumny. The Soviet government has not had, and will
not have, any such intentions.*

*The unique aim of the measures we have taken is to guarantee
the security of the Soviet Union and above all of Leningrad and its
three and a half million inhabitants.*

We have no doubt that the proper solution to the security of

Leningrad will provide the basis for an inviolable friendship between the U.S.S.R. and Finland.

While Molotov was promising the 171 million listeners to the radio in the Soviet Union that he only wished to restore peace, he decided to expel all the diplomats from the Finnish embassy in Moscow and have them thrown into a carriage on the Trans-Siberian express. At the same time, he ordered Soviet bombers to be made ready, for tanks and fighter jets to be filled with fuel, entire trains to be crammed to the roof with shells and mines, and to deploy almost half a million soldiers, weapons at the ready.

In the early hours of the following morning, with his expressions of "inviolable friendship" still reverberating, one of the world's greatest military powers launched an attack on one of the smallest nations on the planet.

19

November 30, 1939, first day of the Russo-Finnish conflict

On the morning after Molotov's declarations, you had only to read between the lines to understand that the storm was coming. Mannerheim had been whisked away to the centre of Finland, where, in the town of Mikkeli, Aksel Airo had requisitioned a cluster of buildings that were soon to become the main military headquarters. Aksel had genuinely believed he had more time, which is why he was now haranguing his daughters as they stood bewildered in their bedrooms with open suitcases and no idea what they should be packing.

"Hurry up, my darlings, I beg you, hurry up. I'll replace anything you leave behind, I promise."

*

A few kilometres away in Russia, in front of the brand-new S.B.2 bombers lined up on the aerodrome tarmac, a commanding officer was also haranguing his pilots in ringing tones. The words he was uttering were those of the dictator. "While their soldiers are at the front, their eyes fixed on the border separating us, we will bombard the cities they have left unprotected, their houses, their women and children. We will strike at the heart of the enemy, to terrorise, paralyse, root out their resistance, smash what they hold dearest. No war will ever have been so short-lived."

Stalin's ultimate weapon was psychological. He was convinced that the more ruthless he was, the quicker Finland would capitulate. And to achieve this, the Finnish civilians were in his sights.

*

Aksel wasted precious time trying to convince his neighbours to leave, knocking on their doors, even offering to send them a car with a driver if need be. Then he looked at the seemingly endless lines of buildings to his left and right, and realised what a hopeless task this was. Did he expect to evacuate Helsinki all on his own? So he loaded his family's suitcases into the boot of the car. His wife and daughters climbed into the back and he slammed the door, ordering the soldier behind the wheel to drive off as speedily as he could.

"The girls are scared stiff, Aksel."

"That's good," he said, without turning round. "They are right to be."

*

During the interminable negotiations and the sterile exchanges the two nations exchanged after the "attack" on the Mainila garrison, Finland had been rapidly preparing for war, without really believing it would come. The sites of public underground shelters were signposted on city streets, and a person in charge of evacuation had been appointed for each building. The anti-aircraft guns transported to the rooftops were primed, everything was ready, and yet doubt still lingered. Helsinki, the obvious first target, had been but half evacuated, and then only voluntarily.

Gazing up at the lowering sky through the windscreen of their car, Aksel could make out the bombers' menacing shadows high above the clouds. Their dark outlines seemed to him like those of legendary sea monsters gliding beneath the boat of some unfortunate fisherman.

When at precisely 09.30 the sound of sirens blared out all over the city, Wilhelmina covered her elder daughter Aila's ears. Aila covered those of Anja, her sobbing younger sister.

"It's begun," Aksel muttered.

All around them, the Finnish capital was plunged into Hell. Each of the twelve aircraft in the first Russian wave dropped 100 kilos of bombs – that is, more than seven tonnes of incendiaries. Whole neighbourhoods were swiftly reduced to ashes.

The car sped on, the fires reflected in its windows and on its bodywork, the driver swerving as best he could to avoid rubble and bodies. Inside the car, the family could feel the heat from burning buildings, and the air became impossible to breathe. Wilhelmina was praying softly; Aksel stretched his arm into the back for her to take his hand.

Rivers of fire ran down the streets of the Finnish capital. Where before there had been air, now there were flames.

The driver slammed on the brakes when part of a three-storey building collapsed in front of them, exposing here the interior of a dining room, the table laid for breakfast, there a bedroom with rumpled sheets and toys strewn around, a sign of the lack of con-cern that had reigned until only a few moments before. The thick clouds of dust from the collapsing building made it impossible for them to continue. Through the dense grey screen, the orange glow of explosions and the yellow of flames were still visible. Their car could be hit at any moment, and only luck could save them.

Aksel snapped the driver out of his daze, and he set off again at top speed, turning down the only clear street.

Broad strips of adhesive tape had been stuck on the windows of apartments and shop fronts to lessen the impact of the explosions. Everyone had imagined the war would be at a distance, not believ-ing that the Soviets would dare to attack the capital directly.

Their vehicle skidded round the corner of a street where stacks of newspapers had been bound together in two-metre-high barriers to create makeshift shelters that were about as solid as children's cabins.

The second Russian squadron was met with anti-aircraft fire that hit two aircraft and made the others turn back.

Whereas the cloudy skies were useful to conceal the Russian bombers' approach to the city, when it came to aiming properly they quickly became a hindrance. Almost guessing, a pilot in the third wave released his bombs and destroyed the Soviet Legation building.

Burnt-out vehicles, ruined buildings with smoke rising from them, craters seven metres deep: for 20 metres around the Aksel family's car, all that remained was the debris of things that no longer existed.

As the bombers turned back into Russian air space, the sky suddenly became calm again – too suddenly, leaving behind a city mute from fear.

Then cries of pain, calls for help, and desperate wailing rose into the sky together with spiralling black smoke. In the midst of this carnage, life reappeared in spite of everything, while elsewhere, even more terrifying, was the silence of soot-blackened buildings; noiseless, devastated streets where nobody had survived.

Weeping children were taken in by adult strangers until their parents could perhaps be found. Bewildered silhouettes with charred clothes and blistered skin wandered around, stepping over lifeless bodies.

Then, after no more than a few minutes, the sound of thousands of footsteps weighed down with luggage echoed round the capital in a muffled murmur. Helsinki had capitulated, and was fleeing. The bolder and more fortunate leaped on board cars and buses, and took the railway station by storm. The destitute loaded prams, horses, wheelbarrows and headed for the nearest forest, the nearest village, where cousins or friends would be waiting for them.

"What about them?" Anja asked as they passed a line of evacuees.

"Look straight ahead," her father told her.

Only families separated by the bombardment were still wandering the streets, hearts in their mouths. Kept in the city by the love uniting them, they searched for a son, daughter, husband, mother. Every silhouette they saw in the distance through the black shrouds of smoke became a hope. Lost children were collected by firemen and brought to a school that had been spared. The little ones became a list added to with each new arrival and read out over the radio. Their names were repeated one after another throughout the day like a litany. And when, thanks to a fortuitous stroke of good fortune, people who had accepted the worst occasionally found themselves being hugged or kissed by a loved one, there was an explosion of pure joy that was almost indecent, a joy never before seen.

When they reached the railway station, the stripes sewn onto Aksel's uniform allowed him to jump the queues and be escorted to the train, already being filled to overflowing. He helped his wife, Anja and Aila into carriage number 6, following them along the platform as they walked down the corridor. They settled into their compartment opposite a woman and her son, who was barely three years old. Wilhelmina lowered the window and Aksel took out a small cloth bag and handed it to her.

"I've collected everything of value. Money and jewels. Spend as much as you need. I'll write as soon as I can, *Mummo* is expecting you."[12]

They forgot to embrace and Aksel was swallowed up, as if drowning in a human wave.

∗

The boy in carriage number 6 had his face pressed against the window, staring at the crowds thronging the platform without really understanding what all the commotion was about. People were pushing and shoving, separating families to keep their own together, cursing one another as much as helping them. To try to make room, the station guards were refusing to accept suitcases, but some people sneaked their luggage in through windows on the left-hand side just as others threw it out on the right. Without being exactly frightened, the young boy could sense the anguish and panic all around him.

"Look at me," his mother said, to attract his attention. "Can you see all these people going on holiday with us?" She turned towards Wilhelmina and appealed silently for her support. "You're leaving on holiday as well, aren't you?"

"Of course we are," Wilhelmina said kindly. "It will soon be Christmas, won't it?"

The two women smiled at each other, pleased not to be alone any longer, already friends through force of circumstance. Wilhelmina put her hand on the boy's.

"These are my daughters, Aila and Anja. And you, what's your name?"

"Martti," his mother eventually replied when the boy said nothing.

She was fearful of what he would inherit from this war, how it would affect his life, his character, his thoughts, and what dark stain it would leave on his soul. She studied him, not knowing, of course, that 69 years later Martti Ahtisaari would win the Nobel Prize for Peace and be president of the same country they were now fleeing.

Leaving stranded as many people as it was able to save, the train finally pulled out of the station and left Helsinki.

"Do you know where you will stay?" Wilhelmina said.

"Do we even know which towns have been spared?"

"My husband's family lives only 50 kilometres away, we'll be happy to welcome you there."

"Yes, but ... what if ...?"

She glanced at her son and did not have the courage to finish her sentence.

"Well then, we'll go to yours," Wilhelmina reassured her.

"And what if …"

"In that case, we'll carry on looking."

*

This was the scene on November 30, 1939, in a bombarded Helsinki, attacked together with tens of other cities in Finland.

Along the 1,300-kilometre border, four main fronts were targeted. Petsamo, in the far north. The centre of the country, to cut it in two towards Sweden. And on both sides of Lake Ladoga: the Kollaa front to the east, and the isthmus of Karelia on the Mannerheim defensive line to the west (a mere 30 kilometres from Leningrad), which opened the way to Finland's coastal cities.

And since it now existed, it had to be given a name. This last day of November 1939 saw the Winter War begin.

20

Kollaa front, first day of war

There has to be a first death for you to truly believe in war.

A communiqué is not enough, or a radio message, not even the words of someone who has witnessed it. There has to be a dead person. Right in front of you. To see his blood. You have to see his blood.

It only remained to discover who, among the 15,000 soldiers on the Kollaa front, would be the one … Who, among the 15,000 soldiers, would be the first to be laid out in the big black tent behind the first-aid post.

*

In another tent, this one lit at the four corners, the floor covered in peat and lichen and a flag of Finland on the wall, Teittinen's twelve officers were waiting for him. When he entered, they saluted as one. Taking his place at the table, he refused a coffee as he too bent his head over the maps. The officers were standing shoulder to shoulder, packed so close it was hard to tell which of them was speaking.

"Do we even know if they're going to attack through Kollaa? All our big towns are in the west. Here there are only villages and forests. There's no valuable target, only one road, endless slippery granite rocks, and salt marshes. Where's the interest for them? It's no coincidence that we're the front with the smallest number of soldiers."

"The people of Helsinki didn't think they would be targeted

either," Teittinen retorted. "So if we're not sure, let's prepare for the worst. Has the first-aid post been strengthened?"

"Fresh medical tents have been put up and the companies have been given first-aid exercises, along with bandages and dressings. Four other tents will be used for the triage of the wounded. If the Russians ever reach us."

"Firing practice has been doubled, all the weapons checked, ammunition counted and distributed to the men."

"So as not to seem threatening, we have called off our reconnaissance patrol. We have no idea what is going on a kilometre beyond the border. Are there 10,000 of them, twice that? Are they even there?"

"Whatever the case, we have to evacuate the border villages in the Suojärvi region," Teittinen insisted, "starting with Hyrsylä. If the Russians attack Finland through Kollaa that will be the first village they overrun. Which company have we got down there?"

"The 6th. Juutilainen and his 300 lads."

"O.K., so I'll visit them today. Prepare two combat groups and a quartermaster unit to accompany me."

First day of war, forward post, Suojärvi region

Ever since the morning's announcement, tension had spread from one group to another. It even affected the horses in their stables, from where came the muffled sound of their hooves on the straw bedding and the thud of the wooden planks in their stalls as they made room for themselves. At the slightest sudden movement outside, the horses began to rear, and so they were tied up separately, each to a different manger, to prevent them injuring themselves. It was still several degrees above zero, a temperature that did not bother either animals or men.

Juutilainen untethered his horse to rub its hooves warm, handling them with greater care and with more tenderness than he had ever shown his soldiers. His four platoon commanders walked their horses behind him as instructed.

"There are no Russians until I see Russians. *Sissi* 1, you are to lead your men to the border to reconnoitre. Do not engage in hostilities unless you are fired on."

Karlsson nodded. Juutilainen laid his open hand close to his horse's muzzle to give him a biscuit, and continued:

"*Sissi* 2, your group will evacuate the village of Hyrsylä and the others on the way to Suojärvi. Make sure you leave behind nothing the *Ryssät* could use. *Sissi* 3 and 4, follow them and lay mines behind you. Do not forget to mark each one on a map; we don't want to blow ourselves up."

The three other officers nodded their agreement.

Juutilainen's horse lowered its head to the surface of the lake where they had come to a halt. It drank for a moment, its long mane trailing in the water, then raised its nostrils, sniffing the air. Its muscles rippled beneath its coat. It pawed the earth a couple of times, ears flattened.

The sun could not pierce the clouds in the overcast sky, and its yellow shadow was no more than a dull reflection on the lake's flat mirror. The forest was unusually silent around the soldiers.

Both men and beasts could sense the unseen danger in their own way.

"What if the villagers refuse to leave their homes?" Karlsson said.

"Then we'll have to convince them," the legionnaire said.

*

Hyrsylä, the furthest forward of the villages, was like a comma that protruded into the neighbouring country, a tiny punctuation mark between nations which a few hours earlier had become enemies.

It was no longer a time for doubts or hesitation, so the soldiers marched along the streets announcing that Finland was at war and giving the order to take only what was essential for the evacuation.

The villagers had barely been able to save their horses, a little food and some family photographs stuffed into their pockets before leaving their homes, embers still glowing in the hearths. Only the most stubborn stayed, the ones for whom the land was their blood, the ones who the soldiers would have had to shoot to uproot.

On the threshold of a farmhouse, Simo struck the storm match covered with sulphur stuck to a bottle filled with a mixture of kerosene, petrol and tar. He tossed it inside the open door. The flames spread in a scorching cloud, gaining intensity as they took hold of the wood.

Everywhere the soldiers were using the same improvised incendiary bombs, first used during the Spanish Civil War.

Perched on his horse, Juutilainen watched to see the evacuation was being carried out effectively, as if he was the enemy banishing the villagers from their lands.

They had to evacuate, and to leave nothing behind that the Russians could use.

"Make sure there's no bed left for them to rest in, no cow whose milk they can drink, no horse to carry their gear, no roof to shelter them from the rain," the Terror had commanded.

A long line formed for a painful exile. Time was short, so the soldiers could not wait for the evacuation to be completed before they set fire to the houses, almost in front of their owners. With the heat of this brazier on their backs, most of the villagers did not even turn round.

Simo went to look for Toivo, Onni and Pietari. He found them standing irresolutely outside a barn with eight cows in it. Hugo, the gentle giant from Rinkilä, was on the other side of the barrier, stroking the flank of the beast in front of him.

"Are we to shoot the cows?" he said anxiously.

"One bullet? In the top of the head so they don't suffer?"

They knew the technique, but didn't have the courage to carry it out.

They were startled by the whinnying of Juutilainen's horse. The legionnaire could not wait to be fighting again, and this mission was beginning to get on his nerves. Dismounting, he pulled a grenade from his belt, pulled out the pin, shouted, "Take cover!" and tossed it into the shed. Much too close, Simo and Hugo threw themselves to the ground, hands covering their heads, just as the cows exploded in a sticky cloud of blood and entrails.

"Follow me!" the Terror of Morocco ordered as he got to his feet. "I saw some pigs over there!"

The others obeyed reluctantly, certain their commander was taking pleasure in this new pursuit.

*

Scarcely a kilometre away, Karlsson and his combat group were scrambling the last few metres to the crest of a low ridge that rose in Finland and descended into Russia.

"Periscope."

The apparatus was passed from hand to hand to the first soldiers. Its twin lenses just topped the top of the ridge as Karlsson raised his head to the eyepiece.

"Well?" he was asked. "Are they there?"

"A thousand … ten thousand …?"

Karlsson lowered the periscope. The colour had drained from his face. It had quite simply been impossible for him to guess the number of Russians because the flood of men, horses, trucks and tanks moving towards them seemed to be endless. Like a thick fog clinging to the ground, the compact mass of the enemy was advancing irresistibly. Nobody had foreseen there would be so many of them.

"*Perkele*," Karlsson muttered. "Saddle me a horse and find a messenger!"

*

The column of evacuees from Hyrsylä left behind them a village in flames. They were soon joined by refugees from other villages, their number growing like streams forming a river, beneath a sky obscured by the black smoke from the fires. The exodus carried on in silence, escorted by the soldiers from the 6th Company.

Simo nudged Pietari with his elbow when he saw passing them the old man whose rifle had threatened his comrade the previous evening. With no horse to help them, his daughter was carrying everything they wanted to save on her back. Beneath her already dirty, mud-spattered skirt, her bare white ankles shone above a pair of men's boots.

Only a day earlier the two of them had been dancing, carefree. Pietari had put his arm round her waist, her cheek had brushed against his, they had felt their breaths mingle. Today, Pietari had set fire to her farm, reducing a lifetime's work to ashes. Pietari or someone else, it did not matter. Their eyes met sadly.

Juutilainen fired twice into the air when yet another village had been emptied, the signal to the two other combat groups to mine the roads behind them. But a lack of munitions made this defensive grid relatively ineffective, and the Russians would have to be extremely unlucky to trip over one of the buried traps.

*

First day of war, Mannerheim Line, Isthmus of Karelia, 400 kilometres from Kollaa

The new recruit had arrived 35 days after the others and, having avoided two months' training and forced marches, had earned himself the nickname Onnekas, the Lucky One.

"Welcome to the line, kid," he had been greeted by someone more or less the same age as him. "You'll see, there's nothing going on."

"I was hoping to be mobilised at Kollaa," the newcomer confessed. "I know somebody there."

"I'm sorry to hear that, but Mannerheim is sure everything will happen here, and almost all our forces are on this defensive line."

It was named after the field marshal, and if the Mannerheim Line were to be breached, Finland would fall within a week. In a week, but it would be no easy matter.

Along this bottleneck separating Finland from Russia were 132 kilometres of bunkers; the barrels of the machine guns poked out from the reinforced concrete like insects' stings. The bunkers were linked by trenches festooned with rolls of barbed wire, and protected further off by concrete blocks and minefields. The line was far from unassailable, but it was there. Whatever its short-comings, it was Finland's only rampart.

"Come on, kid, I'll take you to your company."

That had been a week earlier, since when the situation had changed dramatically. After Mainila and the false accusations. After the Soviet Union had cut all diplomatic ties with Finland. From one day to the next, they would perhaps be told that the two countries had patched things up. Or the opposite. No question as to which option they hoped for.

Leaning back against the wooden staves lining the trench his battalion occupied, a sheet of paper on his thigh, the Lucky One had heeded the advice of the non-commissioned officers, some of whom had already fought a war and knew that families in the rearguard always suffered from a lack of news. The boy's hand-writing was shaky, but it wasn't the fault of the cold. He did not have much time before his next guard duty to finish his letter. Signing his first name, he folded the sheet in two, slipped it into the envelope, and asked his officer for permission to go to the postal unit.

The officer read 06.50 on his fob watch, lifted his head, sur-veyed the sky, listened intently and finally agreed. The Lucky One climbed out of his trench and walked the 500 metres back to the main camp, exactly like the one at Kollaa.

He ran past the bunkers and crouched down to pass the half-buried machine guns and the loaded mortars, until finally he reached the small postbox nailed to one of the spruce trees. It was full to overflowing with envelopes, and so a jute postal sack had been propped against the tree. This too was soon full.

Sitting at the foot of a tree trunk, pen rolling between his fingers, a soldier who lacked inspiration was asking a colleague for help. They were supposed to send news and, without really lying, make no mention of the fear gripping their stomachs.

"What shall I write?" he wanted to know.

"Write that you're doing fine. They can't do anything for you back at home. You would only worry them. Write that you're fine. What else can you say?"

In front of them the Lucky One dropped his letter on top of a thousand others. He had considered every word so carefully he could almost recite it like a prayer. He hoped the person receiving it would be proud of him.

> *Dear brother,*
>
> *You're not expecting what you're going to read, because you did all you could for me not to write it. And yet after you left, more unbearable than the fear was our father's way of looking at me. You know him, he has no need to speak to make himself understood. And it really hurt me to disappoint him, to disappoint everyone, you included. "Why aren't you with the other soldiers?" Papa seemed to be saying every day. In Rautjärvi, the old people, the children and the women who were left behind were asking the same question, I'm sure. And with reason. If my country is being attacked, how could I simply do nothing? So I went to see the doctor, who gave my hand a splint, and within a month I was more or less restored. Sufficiently to present myself to the Civic Guard and sign up. I thought I was going to join you at Kollaa, but my posting*

turned out otherwise, and here I am on the isthmus, on the Mannerheim Line. That's good, we'll each have different stories to tell one another. You know, here they call me "Onnekas", so if this war really breaks out, I'll find you on the last day. Excuse my shaky handwriting. My hand hasn't completely healed yet, but although I write with my left hand, I shoot with my right, and it won't shake when it comes to killing an Ivan! Give our friends Simo, Toivo and Onni a hug.

Your brother who loves you,

Viktor.

*

At 07.00 precisely, the engines of the first air squadrons could be heard as a distant rumble, and soon they could be seen approaching, like a hundred or so dots in the sky. Viktor looked up.

At 07.03 the shadow of a bomber passed over the line. It dropped three incendiary bombs that whistled as they plummeted to their target. From the postbox 500 metres away, Viktor saw his trench take a direct hit, gaping like an open mouth and spewing out sand and earth. His entire company disappeared in a fiery mushroom.

Another explosion, further off, another one much closer, and as everyone around him started to run, he heard the stifled shout of someone yelling at him. The man was covered in earth as if it had rained on him.

"What company are you from, soldier?"

"The fourth," Viktor said, almost without realising he was speaking.

"*Perkele!*" The fourth no longer exists! Follow me, we'll find you a new one. What's your name?"

"Private Koskinen. Viktor Koskinen, from Rautjärvi."

*

First day of war, Petsamo, Finnish Lapland

Swathed in a black fur coat, mittens and a fur hat, Captain Salmelo had not left his post since that morning, standing motionless at the entrance to the bomb shelter on the border.

As the orders were the same for everybody, here too in the Arctic Circle the evacuation of villages had begun exactly four days earlier – that is, if you could call a few houses huddled together a village.

The same lines of refugees, the same overflowing suitcases, here loaded onto sleds pulled by domesticated reindeer, with the youngest children wrapped up against the cold riding on their backs.

The soil of the south of Finland was replaced by the northern snow of Lapland, along with ice and piercing cold. If the idea of attacking Finland at its harshest point might appear suicidal, Petsamo also meant access to the Arctic seas and their trade in nickel. Mannerheim had therefore posted two divisions here, and these were commanded by Captain Salmelo, who, eyes glued to his field glasses, was observing the endless white wastes in front of him.

Then came the distant thud of footsteps. Tens of thousands of marching feet, at first no more than a thickening of the horizon line. According to Salmelo's first estimate, there were twice as many as on the Finnish side. As this horizon line drew closer, he realised there were ten times as many. At first he felt a huge hole in his chest that was instantly filled with terror, although he did not allow any of this to show on his face …

"Have all the villages been evacuated?" he said calmly.

"Yes, they have, Captain, sir."

"And set on fire?"

"Yes, they have, Captain, sir."

"Then go and find Captain Pennanen for me."

The soldier saluted, turned on his heel and quit the shelter.

Left on his own, Salmelo took out his wallet and kissed the photo-graph inside. Then he drew his gun from its holster, pressed it against his temple, and fired a bullet that went right through his skull, sending part of it splashing against the wall. Hearing the shot, Pennanen came running. His boots slipped on the pool of blood already forming on the floor.

So Salmelo had just resigned his commission, and Pennanen had been promoted.

No-one knows in advance if they will have the courage to really fight. Not even a professional soldier.

*

First day of war, return to the villages of Suojärvi

They had left nothing behind them but scorched earth.

Their missions accomplished, the four *Sissi* had regrouped, and the entire 6th Company came to a halt beside Lake Suojärvi, halfway back to their camp at Kollaa. In the distance, the burnt villages hidden in the forests threw a ruddy halo above the tree-tops. Both halo and treetops were reflected upside down on the surface of the lake.

The men took off their knapsacks, drank with the horses, and while some were loosening their bootlaces, others were already falling asleep, heads on the cushions of brown moss at the foot of the pines. Some were soldiers, others villagers, and as the former did not all have complete uniforms, they were all mixed up together. A Russian spy could easily have slipped in among them and shared their meal without too much trouble, provided he kept his mouth shut.

A little further off on the top of a knoll, Karlsson raised his field glasses and surveyed the horizon. The distance they had put between themselves and the Russians meant they were no longer visible, and yet the vibrations from their marching still gave away their presence, like a distant earthquake. You had only to touch the ground to sense them approaching, or to place a hand on your chest to feel your heart beating faster.

On one of the rare stretches of flat terrain in the area, Karlsson spotted a moving dot. A man running. He whistled softly and the man next to him, also a combat group commander, imitated him and got out his field glasses.

"Is that one of our lads?" he asked.

Karlsson took his map out of its plastic cover and studied the red circles showing the areas they had mined as they retreated.

"I'm not sure, but he's in the middle of a minefield."

"Did we leave him behind? Or did he get lost?"

"No idea. Warn Juutilainen and count the men."

For some unknown reason, the missing soldier from the 6th Company had found himself separated from the others. He was now running towards them, waving his arms in response to the raised arms of his companions on the knoll who, 400 metres away, seemed to be saying: "Over this way, we're here!"

"*Perkele!* That idiot thinks we're waving to him."

"But he's not going to be blown up in front of our eyes, is he?"

Juutilainen snatched the field glasses from Karlsson. To return to the camp at Kollaa with their only trophy the first dead man in their division was unthinkable to him.

"Karlsson. Who is the best marksman in your unit?"

In response, Enso Friari was brought forward from the back of the company. This timid worker from the Rautjärvi timber mill had stood out during training, perhaps not having been able to benefit from the wise words of a father like Simo's, who had taken him in his arms to give him a farewell kiss and one last piece of advice:

"Up front you get slapped. At the back, kicks up the arse. Stay in the middle and keep your mouth shut. That doesn't make you a coward, but a survivor."

Enso Friari stretched out and calculated the distance between him and the lost soldier. Three hundred metres now.

"Shoot in front of his feet," Juutilainen commanded. "Let's hope he understands."

Enso controlled his breathing. He took into account the wind and the humidity, placed his hand on the trigger, hesitated, and then hesitated again. He was hoping he could hit the ground, but with a target so far away, especially a moving one, he ran the risk at best of shooting off a toe or two, at worst destroying a knee or shooting the man in the stomach. He was paralysed, unable to shoot, and the longer the soldier was left to advance through the minefield, the greater the danger of him stepping on a mine.

Toivo looked at Simo enquiringly. "What are you going to do, my friend?"

Two hundred metres. Simo pushed his way through the others, put a hand on Enso's shoulder, and asked to replace him. Enso did not object.

Simo had already done his calculations and surprised everyone by firing almost as soon as he had lain down. On the far side of the plain, the bullet sent a clod of earth flying in the air just in front of the soldier. He came to an abrupt halt, raised his arms once more so that they would recognise him, but then ran on again.

"He thinks we think he's a Russian," Karlsson decided. "Fire another shot."

By now, everyone in the 6th Company was crowded on the knoll, staring at Simo.

A hundred and fifty metres. A fresh report, and this time Simo's bullet brushed the leather on the tip of the boots of the soldier they were trying to save. He lifted his rifle high above his head to show he was coming in peace. He took another step forward ... only to disappear in a cloud of earth and stones that rose into the sky. When the cloud cleared, the ground was deserted once more. All the men fell silent.

War ... There always has to be a first death for people to truly believe in it.

"O.K.," Juutilainen muttered disappointedly. "He was asking to die. Do we know his name?"

"Janne," came Hugo's gruff voice behind them. "Janne, from the hamlet of Rinkilä."

Juutilainen turned towards the soldier and raised his head to look him in the eye.

"Was he your friend?"

Tears in his eyes, Hugo confirmed this with a nod.

"So why did you abandon him? Honour would have required you to croak with him."

Hugo would only have had to open his mouth to swallow Juutilainen without even chewing, but the giant's shoulders simply slumped like those of a scolded child, mortally offended.

"You can tell his family what a good friend you were."

Juutilainen barged past him and headed towards the marksman just getting to his feet.

"Your name, soldier."

Simo reeled off his identity and the Civic Guard unit he belonged to.

"A reservist from Rautjärvi!" the Terror of Morocco guffawed. "My best marksman had to be a reservist, not even a proper soldier!"

A snowflake drifted from the sky. The first snowflake of winter. Autumn had lingered patiently until now, throughout all the negotiations. The new season began precisely on the day of the first dead soldier on the Kollaa front, November 30, 1939. Spiralling down, the snowflake finished up on the still-warm barrel of Simo's gun.

"Simo Häyhä, from now on you are to march alongside me," Juutilainen roared.

As ordered, Simo moved up next to him.

When the company set off again, Hugo stood still, scouring the plain as though there could still be some doubt. Onni tugged at his sleeve.

"Pay no attention to the Terror. It's not your fault."

"But … don't … don't we recover our dead?"

"Yes, that's the spirit of our army. But there won't be much left to recover, will there?"

"What about his dog tag?"

"Do you want to look for it in a minefield and join him in Tuonela?"

Overwhelmed by a sense of guilt, Hugo stayed silent.

"I've discussed it with the others," Onni told him. "If you agree, we'd like you to join us."

*

The Russian patrol had returned from its scouting mission to the first villages in Suojärvi. Its shamefaced commander was reporting back to General Habarov, head of the 8th Army.

"We've gained a heap of ruins and a few metres. There's nothing left. No inhabitants, nothing."

"Go back and search more closely, dammit! Find provisions and warm clothes. And somewhere to set up camp."

A few months earlier, Russian soldiers had been mobilised from all over the country, and even before the war started some had had to travel almost three thousand kilometres to reach the front. They were cold. They were hungry. Already. And many of them had no idea why they were going to fight.

"I'm not refusing to obey," the commander defended himself, "but they burned absolutely everything as they left. They even blew up the pigs."

"Savages!" the general raged.

He turned to the *politruk*,[13] who was standing a metre away, taking notes. Stalin trusted no-one, especially his military officers, and so had appointed a witness at their shoulder, instructed to relay everything to him. Expert informants, they were his eyes and ears at the front. The victories, advances, feats of bravery, but above all the acts of betrayal, cowardice and possible mutinies. In certain situations, the *politruks* had the authority to put a bullet in the back of the head of anyone who brought dishonour on Mother Russia. It was also in their interest to rewrite history when it did not go in Russia's favour – if they themselves wanted to stay alive.

"So?" the general said. "How are you going to write that?"

The *politruk* looked at his notes, cleared his throat and suggested his version.

"It was at the mere sight of our Russian troops that the Finnish debacle began. Cowards, they preferred to cover themselves in shame by fleeing rather than face our 8th Army ..."

"Something of that sort. I'll add some high-sounding phrases, but a real victory would be good for both of us."

21

At the outbreak of hostilities, Field Marshal Mannerheim, the commander-in-chief of Finnish forces, had left Helsinki, where now snowploughs were clearing the streets of broken glass from windows and shop fronts and bodies were being loaded onto foul-smelling carts. Mannerheim had established his command centre in the town of Mikkeli, almost 200 kilometres from the capital and far from the battle fronts. A hotel, school and church had been requisitioned and turned into the main military headquarters.

Aksel Airo, who of necessity had become the quartermaster-general, entered the Hotel Seurahuone. He crossed the ballroom with its pale blue walls and fine lace curtains. Throwing his snow-covered coat and astrakhan hat onto the lid of a grand piano, he opened the door to a less grand but equally elegant saloon, its walls plastered with maps so big a stepladder was needed to add the coloured pins showing troop movements.

In the centre of the room at a long table also covered with a map so large it was like an outsize tablecloth dangling down to the floor, Mannerheim was listening to his generals' reports. Aksel went to stand beside him.

"Your children?" the supreme commander whispered.

"They're safe," Airo assured him.

"Good, let's get on then," Mannerheim said to the officer beside him.

The Russian strategy was simple but brutal. Bomb the cities in the centre of the country and keep continuous pressure on the

1,300 metres of shared border. Overwhelm Finland, cover it in molten lead from bullets and shells, turn over every square metre of earth and leave every ploughed field like a cemetery.

"It's an all-out attack. From north to south," the officer began. "Above the Arctic Circle at Petsamo, Captain Salmelo found himself facing the 14th Soviet Army from Murmansk, but took his own life even before the first artillery barrages. They have not stopped ever since. Fortunately, the ice and cold are preventing any infantry clashes."

"Lower down, around Salla, Suomussalmi and Kuhmo, the Soviet 9th Army is advancing. Their obvious intention is to cut Finland in two, opening the way to Sweden. We're awaiting confirmation, but observers have apparently seen Russian soldiers shivering in summer uniforms, and there are whole brass bands accompanying the troops. It's almost infuriating to realise they thought they could walk through our land like someone wiping mud off their boots on a doormat."

"If they die of cold, perhaps we'll have a chance. If they attack us with cymbals and trombones, an even better one."

"The main thrust of their assault is obviously against your line, Field Marshal, on the isthmus of Karelia. There we're up against the 7th Red Army. Nine infantry divisions, four armoured brigades and columns of artillery guns stretching as far as the eye can see."

"But the biggest surprise is here, on the Kollaa front," Mannerheim was told. "All of Habarov's 8th Army is moving up, even though there's nothing strategically important there. Endless forests and an Arctic winter that looks like being harsh. The Russians are probably trying to break through at Kollaa to attack your line from the rear. Unfortunately, whereas we have more than 150,000 soldiers on the line, we only have 15,000 at Kollaa."

"Well then," Mannerheim said, "the unimportant Kollaa could mean victory for them. And if Kollaa falls ..."

*

Mannerheim had asked them to excuse him a moment. Installed at the desk he had had especially transferred from Helsinki to Mikkeli, and which he had bought at the flea market in Paris during a visit to his daughter, he slipped a blank sheet of paper onto his blotter and dipped his pen in the inkwell. A stuffed Lapland owl, perched with spread wings on a glass-fronted case, surveyed him with its glass eyes as if, since it was just the two of them, it gave itself the right to read over his shoulder. Mannerheim wrote another letter to his eldest daughter Anastasia, taking advantage of what little time was left to him and his country.

I am 72 years old, and was hoping to end my days without having to go to war again, but superior forces have determined otherwise. And yet, even those dreamers who lived convinced peace would last forever are waking up and comprehending the twentieth century in all its brutality. It is not with declarations and speeches that we can defend the rights of nations, but with actions and the determination to sacrifice ourselves in the fight. Because they will be sacrificed, my soldiers, for their nation. The Finnish Army is not ready to face the Russian giant, and yet here we are. I have had to give the first order and, more a man of peace than a warrior, I wanted to speak honestly to the soldiers. "You know me," I told them, "and I know you. Confidence in a head of state is the first requisite for success." I hope to build this confidence as quickly as possible, and we will need it if we are to avoid them deserting one after the other, because I am sending them into Hell.

22

The 6th Company caught up with Colonel Teittinen and his combat groups on the outskirts of the last village evacuated in the Suojärvi region.

With the first snows of winter forecast, the quartermaster unit distributed pairs of skis. As Finland was covered in snow for half the year, for Simo, Toivo, Pietari, Onni and indeed every Finn, skiing was second nature, whether as children going to school, or adults going to work or church. With skis on, they would be able to get around silently and rapidly, three or four times more quickly than soldiers on foot.

The soldiers also received white camouflage suits that covered them head to toe, making them all look alike close-up, and almost invisible from a distance.

No doubt, they told themselves, the Russians were doing the same thing 40 kilometres away, and with better equipment.

Kitted out in this way, Juutilainen was summoned by Colonel Teittinen.

"An army advances 20 kilometres a day when it doesn't come across any obstacle or enemy forces. That means we have a day left to accompany the last civilians, and another day to return to Kollaa. But I need one company to remain here to keep an eye on the Russian advance."

Juutilainen saw this order as a reward: his only wish was finally to be able to use his rifle and down some Ivans. To say that his 300 men did not share his enthusiasm would be putting it mildly.

The decision taken, Colonel Teittinen called for a messenger to relay their movements to his superiors.

"Russian advance confirmed," his note announced. "All units withdrawing to defensive line at Kollaa. 6th Company staying in place to observe. Will rejoin us in two days."

The messenger folded the note, slipped it in his satchel, and mounted the horse saddled and bridled for him.

To communicate over short distances, radios were connected with cables. The radio itself was carried in a rucksack, and the fragile link was unrolled, sometimes over several kilometres and buried as best as possible. But Kollaa was too far away to be reached by cable, and so messengers had to be used to convey orders to other units. Too old or too young to fight, the walking wounded, or simply lacking in military training, these messengers were sent post haste, galloping unarmed through forests and marshes.

With his troops ready to move off, Teittinen wanted to have a final talk with the officer commanding the company he was leaving behind. He had not intended to broach the subject, but the smell was so strong it was hard not to reproach the man for it.

"You stink of alcohol, Juutilainen."

"I'm often told that, Lieutenant Colonel, sir," he replied solemnly.

In peacetime, a society does not want to know these animals, but in war they become necessary. Men who are only in harmony with chaos, as though they are calmed by discord. When guns are blazing, they are the first to leap roaring out of the trenches, laughing with Death as if it was their lover. And since not even a colonel knew of any muzzle strong enough to restrain these dogs of war, they were the ones given missions whose success was doubtful, because they were ready for any sacrifice, and therefore could be sacrificed.

"We are leaving you some mortars and a heavy machine gun. I stress that they are only to be used to defend yourselves or with-draw with honour. You are only to observe, is that understood? Do not engage the enemy."

"At your orders, sir," Juutilainen promised, even though he had heard nothing after "mortars" and "machine gun".

*

Kollaa front

The first evacuees from the Suojärvi region were finally arriving at Kollaa. Whole families retreating on foot, their lives on their backs, a few horses that had been spared, overloaded lorries where people sat on each other's laps, and cars for the better-off. These at least would be saved.

When a rusty old truck, roof bristling with skis, came past for a second time, one of the soldiers in the observation post on the edge of the camp signalled with his chin as it came to a sudden halt as though it had stalled.

"The third time," one of the others corrected him. "It's the third time it's been past."

As they approached the truck, the driver tried to restart the engine but only managed to send the wheels spinning in the muddy snow. He and the passenger in the cabin waved to the patrol. There was blood on the dashboard and bullet holes in the door.

"What village are you from?"

When the two men made no reply, the patrol raised their rifles.

The passenger was wearing a warm coat that was too big for him. The sleeves reached down over his wrists, and the coat had two bullet holes in it and was bloodstained. The driver smiled at them as he plunged a hand inside his coat, but had no time to pull out his pistol before sub-machine gun bursts from either side shattered windows and windscreen and sent ten if not 20 bullets through the two men's bodies.

The patrol searched the remains of the two Russian spies. On one of them they found a map sticky with fresh blood. A red cross had been marked on it. A runner immediately took the map to Lieutenant Teittinen's tent.

23

The next morning, after a sleepless night keeping an eye on the distant Red Army that never properly came into view, the faces of the men in the 6th Company were drawn and the mood was gloomy as they sat round the fire.

Daylight revealed a landscape covered in icy powder. Simo silently admired the shadows of the pine trees protecting the frost from the rising sun and casting their silver outlines onto the frozen grass.

An hour later, all this was wiped away by the spotless white of the first snows of winter.

At $-2°C$, the men's coffee quickly grew cold in their freezing mugs. Winter was upon them, and Juutilainen was furious at still not having put a bullet into any Russian's head. He had been raging a good part of the night at anyone, civilian or military, who crossed his path. By first light, he already had the look and the breath of his bad days. Suddenly the soldier in the observation post gave a loud whistle.

"Down there," he pointed, as Karlsson and the Terror joined him. He passed his field glasses to Juutilainen.

In the distance a silhouette on horseback was galloping towards them.

"It's a Russian," Juutilainen growled.

"He's coming from the west, and the Russians are in the east," Karlsson pointed out.

"The Russians are everywhere," the legionnaire insisted, picking up his rifle.

Twenty or so soldiers had joined them on the small ridge that served as an observation post. Some of them had different opinions.

"Yeah, he could be Russian, but it's more likely to be one of our messengers," Onni said.

Toivo and Simo agreed with him, while Hugo thought he saw in this distant figure the ghost of his friend Janne.

Russian, messenger; messenger, Russian … Juutilainen had heard enough, and raised his rifle towards his target. Karlsson tried one last time to dissuade his superior, but was rewarded only with a stream of insults and threats.

At less than a hundred metres, the Terror held his breath and slid his finger to the rifle trigger. At that instant, just before he could fire, his eyebrow was split open by a powerful blow from a rifle butt. His weapon fell into the snow. Groggy and blinded by blood, he turned and saw Hugo thrusting the end of his rifle at him. Beside himself with rage, Juutilainen grabbed his pistol from his belt and aimed at the giant, hell-bent on shooting him in the head. Ready for the worst, and above all ready to protect his friend, Simo had also raised his gun, when just at that moment the soldier observing the man through his field glasses shouted:

"Messenger! It's one of our messengers!"

The Terror paused … then burst out laughing as he lowered his pistol. Simo breathed a huge sigh of relief.

"Hugo from Rinkilä, you abandoned a friend, but today you saved a messenger," Juutilainen crowed. "You've wiped the slate clean!"

Then, still smiling, he turned to Simo.

"As for you. I saw you."

*

It did not occur to anyone to tell the lad who was now warming his hands at the campfire that he had very nearly died stupidly. He had the face and soft body of a child, because that is what he was. He was sixteen and his name was Pulkki.

The wound on his eyebrow dressed, Juutilainen was reading the message out to his officers.

Your position is known to the adversary. Return to Kollaa at once.

They all turned towards Pulkki.

"Do you know anything more?"

"Almost nothing, Lieutenant, sir. Two spies in a truck they must have stolen when the villages were being evacuated. They had a map with your camp marked with a red cross. The high-ups don't know if there were more than two of them, and if the information has already got back to the Russians. The general has ordered Teittinen to have you interrupt your observation mission and withdraw."

"If they were 40 kilometres from our position yesterday morning," Karlsson remarked, "they can be only 20 kilometres away today. By this afternoon we'll be in range of their artillery. Shall I strike camp?"

"Absolutely," Juutilainen decided. "Have the men ready in half an hour."

"At your orders. If we keep up a good speed, we'll be in Kollaa this evening."

But frustration was gnawing at the Terror. The Russians were there, closer than ever, and yet he and his men had to withdraw yet again. So the 6th Company would return having lost a soldier, blown to bits by one of their own mines, and without any useful information or war trophy to show for it.

On his map there was only one road that looked wide enough to allow the guns, lorries and tanks of Russia's 8th Army to advance: the road to Loimola. So he knew where to find them.

"Who says we're going back to Kollaa?" he told Karlsson.

While an icy wind swept along the ground, freezing the soldiers from ankles to waist, and the first storm of winter was brewing in the sky, the men of the 6th Company began their march east, the opposite direction to the order they had received, and straight into the jaws of the Red Bear.

24

The 300 men of Juutilainen's company positioned themselves on the edge of the forest bordering the road to Loimola.

The wind was blowing twice as hard and the snow it brought with it seemed to be falling horizontally, whistling in their ears, whipping their faces.

In the distance, like a black lizard crawling up a white wall, the column of Russian soldiers almost ten kilometres long advanced ever deeper into Finnish territory, tall pine trees looming over them.

By now it was past midday, and the throb of engines warned the 6th Company that the Russians were close. A group of skiers was despatched to observe as the first enemy unit appeared.

Leading the way was a tank, acting as a shield. It passed only a few metres from the observers: a deafening monster, belching smoke and clanking, its tracks crushing the ground beneath their weight. The Finns had no tanks, and this indestructible machine created a feeling of fear and unease. How could they destroy such a monster?

Behind the tank, three officers on horseback, followed by almost twice as many soldiers as the Finns had. To everyone's surprise, they were all wearing dark green uniforms. In the white-out, where every colour stands out, the Russians had chosen green ...

None of the enemy units contained the same number of men or the same kind of artillery, and there were gaps between them in the long column, which meant the second unit took several minutes to arrive. A few minutes later the skiers spotted the third one, and they counted more than thirty of them before they returned an hour later.

Speaking softly despite the noise of the engines, one of them gave his report, confirming there were important gaps between units along the whole length of the column.

"And we stopped before we saw the end of it," he said.

"Is there one unit that's more cut off from the others?" Juutilainen asked him.

"Yes, three kilometres behind us. An artillery unit that's slowed down because of the weight of its guns."

*

Taking advantage of the gap created between two units, Toivo and Onni were ordered to plant a string of mines across the road in order to slit the Russian column like a throat. Juutilainen told Simo to follow him.

"Here," the lieutenant ordered.

Simo stretched out behind a boulder facing the road, awaiting orders.

"Have you ever killed a man, little fellow?"

Simo shook his head.

"Well then, tell yourself that every Russian you don't kill could be the one who sets fire to your farm and butchers your family. But no man knows in advance if he is capable of shooting someone. Today you're going to find out."

*

They could hear the artillery unit's tank long before they saw it. Its long gun barrel was the first thing to appear as it rounded the bend where the 6th Company had taken cover.

Behind the tank came a truck with a green tarpaulin, then five officers on horseback commanding the infantry, who marched along shivering: the temperature had fallen again since morning, and it was now –5°C. The surrounding forest created a tall barrier that trapped the wind at road level, making it blow violently over them.

Reaching the trap, the tank track rolled onto a mine, which exploded in a cloud of snow, earth and fire. The Russian unit came to a halt; the soldiers raised their rifles and aimed blindly at the sides of the road, ready to repel any attack. As the explosion subsided, a disturbing silence ensued. Juutilainen dropped his hand softly on Simo's shoulder.

"Now."

Five horses, with five officers mounted on them. Five moving targets. A magazine with five bullets. Simo trained his gun on the first rider, finger on the trigger. Time came to a standstill. The Russian was red-cheeked, with a fur cap jammed down over his ears. Simo no longer regarded him as a man, aware that the more human he made him, the harder he would find it to shoot.

To kill. His country was demanding he kill. But he could not.

Simo was suddenly enveloped in a flurry of snow, and when it ceased a huge fox the size of a man was sitting beside him. He recognised it instantly from its fiery coat. The soul of his forest had followed him and was watching over him. His forest, his village of Rautjärvi, his farm, his parents, his sisters and brother, all scorched by the flames of war. The animal's tail wrapped itself round him before disappearing once more. Simo aimed at the officer's chest. Twenty metres away, the force of the bullet knocked the man backwards off his horse. There were four more rounds in the magazine, and in four seconds Simo downed the other four.

It was only then that his hands began to shake, and he retched from the pit of his stomach.

"Now you know," Juutilainen crowed.

Seeing their tank with its track shredded and their officers' hot blood melting the snow before freezing, the Russian unit turned tail, desperate to avoid blundering into any more mines. Only to discover that after their first salvo, the Finns had set up a machine gun in the centre of the road.

Its metal prongs embedded in the ground, one man on the trigger, another feeding the ammunition belt and a third ready to cool the gun down with water, the machine gun spat a constant stream of bullets. At the same time, from both sides of the road the soldiers in white hidden in the forest fired as well, until not a single Russian was left standing. Then the weapons fell silent. There was a moment of eery calm when all that could be heard were the death rattles of those unfortunate enough not to have died instantly.

Juutilainen whispered an order to Simo, another to Onni. The other Finnish soldiers stayed in position.

In front of them, the tank hatch popped open, and a head appeared cautiously.

Simo did not miss. Onni sprinted across, clambered up the enormous machine, tossed a grenade inside, and jumped back down. Seconds later, nothing remained of the crew, and a pink cloud rose from the opening.

"We have ten minutes to get our hands on their things before the next unit arrives," Juutilainen barked. "Steal everything you can."

The 6th Company's empty magazines showed that all of them had fired. But many of the soldiers had not succeeded in killing. In wartime, one shot in three is a deliberate miss, because even if history is written in blood, it's not made up of murderers, and taking a life is far from easy.

"Save your bullets. Use your *puukkos* to finish off the survivors. Collect their weapons and ammo."[14]

Nothing had prepared Onni or Pietari for plunging their knife blades into the body of a living man. And to judge by the way the soldiers around them were also hesitating, none of them had even imagined it would be demanded of them one day.

The tips of the *puukkos* rested against Russian necks or hearts.

Now they had to press hard, pierce the uniforms and then the flesh, hear the bones crack, press even harder, up to the hilt, without looking their victims in the eye so as not to engrave that image on their memories.

Some of them, like Onni, only pretended, stabbing their knives into the snow. Others like Pietari obeyed, shutting their eyes and grimacing with disgust. Hugo stayed on his knees, unable to finish off the wounded man begging him to do so.

"Leave it," Toivo told him. "In this cold, he won't need anyone to help him croak."

Juutilainen had fewer scruples, and shot four of the horses with a bullet between the eyes. He spared the last one, took hold of its bridle, and tugged it as best he could over to Hugo. Bearing no grudge for his split eyebrow, either because the blow was justified or because he had been punched so often he could no longer remember them all, he pointed to the terrified animal.

"We're going to steal a lot more than expected! Harness him to this cart, and we can take their machine guns and howitzers as well."

Hugo approached the spooked horse, which kept rearing and crashing back onto the lifeless bodies around it. He seized the bridle and pulled it down hard. As big as the horse, and like all Finnish peasants accustomed to this kind of beast, he steadily calmed it, leaning down to its ear and whispering to it.

Pietari remained astride his dead Russian, the blood still warm on his *puukko*. He had expected to be fighting monsters, but could see only men scattered around him. He turned to Simo, who was also contemplating the carnage. He too had killed for the first time. Six times.

"Now you know," Juutilainen had told him. And yet he had not learned a great deal. Could he do it again? What would he do about their ghosts? He peered into the forest, to the spot where he had taken up his position, searching in vain for his fox with the fiery coat. Instead, he thought he saw himself, the man he had been only a few minutes earlier. The one who had not yet killed. And he envied him that lost innocence.

Onni climbed into the back of one of the Russian trucks, three tyres blown out and its engine boiling over. He discovered a stack of ammunition boxes, but it was something else that caught his eye.

"Hey! Look at this," he said, holding up a two-metre-by-one portrait of Stalin. "Do you think they brought it because they're afraid they'll forget him?"

It was forced idolisation at work: every unit, no matter how small, had to have a picture of the Sun of the Nation, as He liked to be known. Onni threw the dictator overboard, and the Finnish soldiers continued their search.

"Look at their uniforms!" Toivo cried in amazement. "They're green! And some are wearing summer ones!"

"And town shoes!" Onni added. "The same as mine. I thought they would be more ..."

"... terrifying and better equipped?"

"Something like that, yes."

*

When the next Russian unit reached the bend on the road to Loimola, they had to toss the piles of bodies into the roadside ditches. Two soldiers to each body, eight for a horse.

They also stripped off the dead men's clothes to reuse. One group came to blows over a pair of boots.

"Take their dog tags," the military officer commanded.

A soldier bent down, groping round a dead man's neck to find the metal tag. He was about to snap it in two when he felt a pistol barrel pressed against the back of his neck.

"Don't touch it," the *politruk* warned him. "A dog tag means a dead person, and we didn't lose anyone here today."

*

Since they had pushed on a kilometre, a new Russian camp was established by the roadside. All the tents and the command post were erected in silence; everyone was gripped by a dumb fear as heavy as carrying a wounded comrade on their back. The white soldiers were invisible, and because of that could be anywhere. And so, without doing anything more, without firing a single extra shot, without even being there, the Finns were all around them.

"The general says they don't take prisoners," muttered one Russian soldier, carrying a heavy roll of canvas that would soon be a tent.

"He says they'll eat our balls," another man added.

"No, they just tear them off. The prick as well."

"No, I promise you, they eat them. The general said so. He also says we should put a bullet in our head rather than be captured. To avoid torture."

"For heaven's sake, what have we done to these Finns for them to hate us so much?"

25

Weighed down by all the new armament taken from the Russians, the 6th Company was now only ten or so kilometres ahead of the Red Army.

Night fell in the middle of the day, as sudden as an ambush. As winter progressed, the less daylight there would be, until eventually there were no more than five hours of light.

Juutilainen calculated the enemy would also halt to get some rest, and ordered his men to set up camp in the forest a few kilometres from where they had been that morning, the place marked with a red cross on a map. Trenches were dug in front, tents put up to the rear, machine guns and mortars placed strategically, and then they tried to sleep.

Around 20.00, the ground trembled beneath them. When the first shells landed, Karlsson threw snow on the campfires where the soldiers were warming themselves and signalled for total silence. The Russians had continued their advance and were much closer than Juutilainen had calculated.

Flares lit up the sky like a red sunset. More thunderous explosions. Here, there, far off, closer to, incessant.

"Who are they shelling?" Onni said anxiously.

"Is there another company besides ours near here?" Pietari asked Karlsson, who was staring into the black forest. Fifty metres from them, a flare slowly drifted down over the trees, casting their shadows like spears. Almost immediately, a shell flattened three giant pines at the same spot.

Pulkki, the young messenger, began to pray. Hugo wrapped an arm round his shoulders.

"We're in the middle of thousands of kilometres of forest," he reassured him. "They're firing at random."

"But they'll end up hitting us, even at random."

Lights in the distance; more muffled explosions, everywhere and nowhere.

"Imagine a grasshopper," Karlsson tried to reassure Pulkki. "Imagine it's hiding in a huge wheat field. Now imagine you are a hundred metres away from that field, with some stones in your pocket. How long do you think it would take you to hit it?"

"That's all well and good," Pietari agreed, "but just how many stones do the Russians have in their pocket to be throwing so many all at once?"

And yet, even though it seemed highly unlikely that the Russians would hit their target, a shell fell so close it filled with earth and snow one of the holes where the soldiers of *Sissi* 2 were on guard. When their colleagues went to clear it and help the men out, four of them were no longer breathing. They were put on a sled, their dog tags snapped in two, and Karlsson asked who in the 6th Company was close enough to them to write to their parents.

Sleeping was out of the question, and since to fire their artillery the enemy must have come to a halt, Juutilainen decided to strike camp and return to Kollaa under cover of dark.

The order was received without a murmur: none of the soldiers complained about collecting their gear to move out as quickly as possible and escape the unending bombardment.

And yet there was no such thing as proper night. The snow covered everything like a fine veil and reflected the full moon, bathing the entire forest in light from high in the sky. Even hidden in the depths of the trees, the soldiers could see as if it were twilight, a mysterious twilight where the only colours were shades of grey, white and blue.

26

Isthmus of Karelia, Mannerheim Line

The Russians had deployed the same tactic all night. They did not launch a frontal attack, but stayed in the rear and fired hundreds of shells hour after hour, as indiscriminately as they were doing on the Kollaa front.

To honour his father, his brother Pietari and the family name, Viktor was on the frontline, only a few dozen kilometres from Leningrad. Like many of the soldiers, he had trembled and prayed as the shells exploded around him. Others had laughed, panic-stricken, then burst into unstoppable tears.

It was only at daybreak that the barrage ceased.

The Finnish observers returned at dawn and announced that a division of 3,000 men was advancing towards them. In the command tent, a soldier pointed on the map to the positions the Russians held and the direction they were heading. The officer asked the observer to repeat it: if they continued the same way the Russians would be out in the open on a broad plain.

"Don't they have a map?"

"Maybe they don't know how to read it," the soldier said.

*

Opposite them, under the Russian flag, the information and questions were the same. In a freshly dug trench, the commanding military officer was so dubious about the strategy he even dared to challenge it.

"It's a flat plain. We'll be out in the open."

"We are simply following the strategy outlined by the Stavka," his political commissar reminded him. "This is definitely the route we must take."

Created by Stalin, the Stavka was a bureau of his most loyal followers who never contradicted their great leader. Half politicians, half bureaucrats, with a few military men thrown in. A bureau where decisions were made without any reliable information or precise knowledge, it was nevertheless required to establish frontline strategies. Despite being blind and in the distant rear, they were the ones who directed the troop movements.

"We're on the ground, while they are parading around in their suits. Couldn't we adapt to the situation and get round the plain?"

"The Stavka's voice is that of Stalin. Do you want to get round that as well?"

"But you can see for yourself. There are no ditches, no hills, nowhere to hide. It's senseless!"

"No, comrade, it's patriotic. And numbers are on our side, you'll see," the *politruk* insisted.

With the temperature at −10°C, a first line of 200 Russians stepped forward. When the order was given, they charged out of the trench, brandishing their weapons.

*

Facing them, Viktor Koskinen was hauling long munition belts out of a wooden crate. The metal was icy between his fingers.

"As soon as the machine gun clicks empty, you load another belt. Like this," the gunner demonstrated. "And always check there's enough liquid in the breech to keep it cool, otherwise it'll blow up in our faces."

A bonfire had been lit behind them. Next to it stood barrels of water that the flames kept from freezing. A 300-metre line of machine guns had been set up, but when they saw the Red horde charging towards them, at first the white gunners hesitated. They only had to fire at will, shoot straight ahead, to endlessly cut down the men in this suicidal attack.

When their enemy was so close there was no longer time to hesitate, the machine guns roared.

Under this sustained fire, bodies were stopped in their tracks, thrown backwards, torn to pieces by the volleys of bullets. A Russian soldier saw his neighbour die, trod on the remains of the one in front, and as he turned and realised there were no more than ten or so still with him, half his skull was blasted away.

As Viktor fed the machine gun, the Russian soldiers died as surely as if he himself had shot them at point-blank range. Inserting the next belt of bullets, he turned to one side and vomited.

Littered with bodies, the plain had become a cemetery open to the skies.

*

In the Russian trench, the political commissar brought up a second line of 200 men. He fired his pistol into the air to drive them on. But now war had become a reality for them, and they could see the carnage on the plain in front of them. Soldiers who had been promised a quick and easy victory had lost their lives on territory that had nothing to do with them, in a country that the Kremlin's propaganda had raised to the level of enemy, and against which only a week before they had felt no hatred. It was not an entire nation that had declared war, but a single man who had been intent on it.

Despite the pistol shot in the air, the terrified men refused to move. Furious, the commissar had to shoot three of them to make the others clamber out of the trench.

*

Seeing this second wave running at them, the Finns fired once more, scarcely able to believe this repeated sacrifice.

"Why …? Why are they …?" Viktor stammered.

"Shut up and keep loading!"

The bodies piled up, and Viktor's nostrils were assailed by the smell of blood and flesh.

*

When the second wave had been demolished, the *politruk* called up the third. Two hundred more men stood to at the bottom of the trench, ready to charge, willingly or not.

After the first 50 were cut down, the line faltered in the middle of the plain. In front of them, the Finnish machine guns. Behind them, certain execution by their officers.

"The soldiers have halted!" the *politruk* shouted. Glued to his field glasses, head above the parapet, he nearly choked.

"Now they're running back!"

Sliding down into the bottom of the trench, he warned the military commander:

"If ten of them turn tail, use the sub-machine guns on them. If it's 50, the heavy machine guns. If 100 appear, have the tanks punish them like the traitors they are!"

Bullets were flying in every direction, and soldiers were dying under enemy and friendly fire in a senseless slaughter.

One Russian soldier stood stock still as all around him bullets hit the ground and his comrades fell one after the other. He dropped to his knees, laid his rifle beside him, then calmly sat down. His lips moved in a silent prayer. Nothing was important any more, because he was already dead. Strangely serene, he sat still for a few seconds, and never knew which side the bullet that took his life had been fired from.

By the time the fourth and fifth waves had also been cut down, the plain was littered with 1,000 dead bodies that formed make-shift barricades. A thin layer of snow barely covered them, and, as if under a gauzy white veil, the pale tones of their green uniforms, the beige of skin and the black of their open mouths could be seen.

The *politruk* attached no more importance to these men than to the diesel that fuelled the tanks or the bullets fired from their rifles. He turned to the military officer, a demented smile on his face.

"In an hour the bodies will be frozen as hard as stone and will stop the bullets," he said almost proudly. "You were afraid of having no cover on the plain? You wanted protection? I've made some for you. Call up the next waves."

*

In that one day, the Finnish unit of 60 men with their heavy machine guns killed 2,000 soldiers, sent like cattle to the slaughterhouse. Of course, the Russian artillery would kill similar numbers on the Mannerheim Line, but firing a cannon from a distance does not produce the same shock as shooting a man when you can see his face. Still less killing 2,000 men in one day. The day before they had been simple farmers, fathers of families, friends and husbands. Now they were mass killers.

When night fell and Viktor returned to camp, head still echoing with the day's thunder, he lifted his eyes to the heavens, and when he imagined God's presence up there, he lowered his head in shame. It was no longer a question of trying to find out which side was right, but of knowing why and how things had reached this point, men killing one another as if lives no longer had any value.

Stretched out on his straw mattress, Viktor kept his eyes wide open until the next morning, afraid that if he closed them he would see everything again.

After this first day, a number of Finnish soldiers were evacuated to the first-aid post. Some had gone blind. Others were dumb. One had amnesia and seemed to have forgotten everything. An orderly was so troubled that he asked the doctor about these strange illnesses affecting the machine-gun company. The doctor told him:

"What normal man could have endured so much horror?

Traumas create their own defence. Blindness, to no longer see. Dumbness, so as not to have to talk about it. Amnesia so as not to remember."

"Not to remember," the orderly echoed him. "Perhaps they're luckier than I thought …"

27

Kollaa front

It had been ten days since the legionnaire's 6th Company had returned from the villages in the Suojärvi region. On the way, despite an order to retreat, they had carried out a lightning attack on an isolated company of the Soviet 8th Army, destroyed their first tank, and even stolen a portrait of Stalin that was burned amidst much merriment when they got back.

At army headquarters, when Mannerheim was informed by Aksel Airo that the general commanding the Kollaa troops had had the temerity to order Juutilainen to retreat, he dismissed the officer with a fateful letter:

Our officers should be steeped in the great mythology of the European armies of the First World War. They should consider attack as the very essence of their function. A moral obligation for glory and fame.

Return at once to headquarters at Mikkeli, where you will receive your new posting.

The general was thanked and replaced by someone more in tune with Mannerheim's philosophy of war: General Hägglund. Woldemar Hägglund.

Not only therefore did the Terror escape unpunished for his insubordination, but in view of the booty stolen from the enemy – machine guns, sub-machine guns, light artillery pieces and mortars – the newly appointed Hägglund encouraged him to carry on.

"Disobeying orders is a sickness that spreads quickly," his

second in command had nevertheless warned him. "A sanction, however small, could send a message."

"In wartime, morale fluctuates," Hägglund had objected. "We lack weapons and ammunition, and this legionnaire supplies us with more than our own factories! As long as disobedience is crowned with success, I prefer to consider it as initiative."

And so Aarne Juutilainen's lack of discipline at the outset of the Winter War became the spirit of the 6th Company. They stood out on the grounds of their courage and efficiency. Respected by all, they became known as the "war thieves".

Now, obeying Hägglund's orders enthusiastically, Juutilainen set out several times a day with one *Sissi* after another, and although he rotated them so they would not be completely exhausted, there was always one constant:

Simo Häyhä.

*

A heavy wooden box was being towed on a sled by a phantom horse, covered to its hooves in a white sheet, with holes for its nostrils and eyes. The rider had been sent to deliver his load from headquarters in the rear, for security reasons located several kilometres back from the Kollaa defensive line. It arrived therefore from behind the camp, passed the first-aid post and the field hospital, went along the lines between the labyrinth of tents, and came to a halt before the forward trenches and wooden bunkers.

Because of its difficult terrain and lack of strategic value, Kollaa had not been fortified to the same extent as the Mannerheim Line. Whereas that had reinforced concrete bunkers cased in armour-plating and topped by an observation post with a machine gun, at Kollaa the bunkers were made of long pine logs, their roofs like an upturned canoe, and walls alternating layers of wood and stones that were meant to be able to resist a direct hit from a shell. Possibly two. Time would tell.

It was only thanks to the handwritten inscription in chalk on the box that the rider found the 6th Company's tent, camouflaged for winter like all the others: *Lieutenant Aarne Juutilainen, 6th Company, 2nd Battalion of the 34th Regiment of the IV Corps of General Hägglund's Finnish Army.*

Seeing the loaded sled, the men tried to guess what was in the box.

"Weapons?" Toivo suggested.

"Too small," Onni said. "Petrol bombs or ammo, perhaps."

And since nobody was foolhardy enough to open a mysterious box addressed to the Terror, it remained guesswork on their part.

"Juutilainen is with Karlsson's *Sissi* 1. He'll be back before nightfall. There's not long to wait."

*

By one way of counting, the legionnaire and his *Sissi* were three forests, three lakes and two marshy swamps from the Kollaa front, the camp, Juutilainen's tent and the wooden box dumped in front of it.

Juutilainen and Karlsson were on either side of Simo. Invisible in the white of their snowsuits, protected on both flanks by granite boulders, for several minutes they had lain silent and motionless in the snow, observing their new targets 200 metres away. Russians around a campfire. Six men, probably reconnoitring or looking for the Finnish rear base. Next to them, a portable cable radio and some fine-looking sub-machine guns.

No snow had fallen since morning and the sky was a dazzling blue, but the temperature kept on dropping. At −20°C, breathing created clouds of vapour as thick as wet hay that refuses to burn. The clouds the Russians made gave them away even more than the smoke from their fire.

As with every new mission, Simo was learning and becoming more skilful. Two days earlier he had spotted a Russian observer thanks to the vapour from his breath. The Russian was a long distance from his lines, hidden behind a mound of snow. Seeing the small cloud rise in the air, Simo had estimated where to shoot without even seeing his target. On the far side of the mound, the Russian collapsed.

Every mistake the enemy made was a lesson for the young soldier. After this, Simo made small snowballs that he put in his mouth and allowed to melt so that his position would not be betrayed by his warm breath.

The Russians stamped out the feeble campfire with their boots. The thousands of square kilometres of forest separating the Red Army from the Kollaa front were haunted by patrols, observers and snipers from both armies. And it was in these forests that Simo learned the elementary rules of survival.

From the officer he downed when he saw the sun's reflection on his field glasses, Simo promised himself never to add a scope to his rifle. From the soldier he shot through the head when his shiny rifle barrel gave him away in the distance, Simo acquired the habit, just before leaving camp, of smearing a layer of ashes on his own weapon. From the sniper lying in wait who, suffering from the cold, abandoned his position and was shot after taking a single step, Simo learned to remain motionless for hours on end, whatever the temperature, controlling his body and slowing down his heartbeat.

"They're putting out their fire," Juutilainen whispered. "And picking up their sub-machine guns. They're leaving."

"It's an isolated patrol," Karlsson said. "There's only six of them. But at 200 metres they'll have all the time in the world to see us coming and radio for reinforcements."

Behind Karlsson, the 50 men of *Sissi* 1, all wearing their cross-country skis, were ready to move in, but Juutilainen touched Simo's shoulder and he nodded.

Five rounds in the magazine. Six targets. He would have to be quick.

For ten days now, Simo had stopped counting the kills he had to his name, even if his conscience did it for him. He had not become insensitive or inhuman, he had only had a dream, and that dream had changed him.

In the dream he was with his father. In his forest. And in front of them, a huge bear with dark fur and red eyes.

"Kill him," his father had ordered.

But Simo's finger was rigid, unable to pull the trigger. And before his eyes the bear kept on growing bigger, growling as it flattened saplings and broke branches as it lurched towards them.

"Kill him or watch him eat our animals. Look, his jaws are so big he could even swallow our farm. You know it's either him or us."

The shot finally rang out. Simo woke with a start. Startled, but at peace.

Ever since that dream, the Russians had become the predators, and Simo was not waging war on them, he was hunting them.

Five rounds in the magazine. Six targets. He would have to be quick.

"Kill them," Juutilainen ordered.

In five seconds, Simo hit five Russians in the chest before they even had time to raise their rifles. His magazine empty, Simo loaded another one as quickly as possible, but the sixth soldier had run away and disappeared before he could aim again.

"Pietari! Hugo!" Karlsson roared.

The two men stood up and, skis already fixed to their boots, pounded after the man running away through the deep snow. Meanwhile the other thieves in *Sissi* 1 swooped on the abandoned Russian equipment.

*

The machine guns, ammunition and two mortars were lined up as booty in front of Juutilainen's tent. Karlsson's men stacked their rifles upright in pyramids so that no earth would get into their barrels, and went off to the canteens.

"What's that wooden box?" the Terror wanted to know, seeing his name chalked on the side.

"A rider left it a few hours ago," Onni told him.

A bayonet blade prised it open. A letter lay on top of the contents.

"*The* Talvisotakäsikirja *has shown the way, and you are following it honourably.*[15] *Every stolen bullet is a bullet less in the chest of one of our brothers. Finland is watching you; you are already their hero. A mistake in ordering our supplies has left us with a spare box of* viina. *Share it with your men. General Woldemar Hägglund.*"

To fight and get drunk. Juutilainen could have wept for joy. He snatched up one of the bottles and disappeared into his tent, where Pietari and Hugo were guarding the runaway Russian soldier.

"Shall we have a drink, comrade?" the legionnaire proposed to the terrified Russian tied up on the ground.

*

Simo had not liked the way things had developed after that. Nor had his friends. The Russian soldier was blind drunk and gulped down each mug of alcohol forced on him.

Juutilainen was asking the prisoner questions he could not understand, his mind befuddled with drink. He replied begging for his life with entreaties that fell on deaf ears.

Around them, some of the soldiers were laughing at their prisoner's fate. Others remained sombre. One came from a frontier village and had some knowledge of Russian, so offered to interpret.

Juutilainen spoke, waving his arms in the direction of Simo. The makeshift interpreter repeated his words:

"You see this man? He is one of our snipers. He has killed

many of your comrades all on his own. He's not a soldier, he's Death dressed in white. The White Death."

Unimpressed by the compliment, Simo lowered his eyes and left the tent, followed by Onni, Toivo, Pietari and Hugo.

Tired of his game, the Terror had the drunken Russian soldier escorted to the edge of the camp. His bonds were cut with a *puukko*. In front of him, the dark depths of the forest, and, in the sky, a moon obscured by clouds.

"Walk!" they shouted at the Russian in Finnish.

Paralysed with fear, he did not move.

"Walk!" Juutilainen snarled, raising his rifle.

The prisoner took a few steps. Only a few more, then the first trees.

"He's going to tell them the exact location of our frontline," Karlsson said anxiously.

"They'll know it soon enough. A frontline is where wars are fought. He doesn't know where our rear base is, and that is what's most important."

He lowered his rifle and spat into the snow.

"He'll die of cold before he reaches them anyway. And I don't like killing a man I've shared a bottle with."

The freed soldier vanished into the forest. Juutilainen, who had drunk as much as him, staggered back inside his tent and collapsed into a deep sleep. That night, not one of the hundred Russian shells launched blindly and randomly in the forests managed to wake him. Not even the one that scored a direct hit on a 4th Company trench, killing three men. Their remains would not have filled a tin can.

They killed, they spared lives. Nothing made sense any more, and yet the Winter War was no more than a few days old.

28

In the morning sky above the camp, the thick flakes stuck to one another and fell in fleecy clouds. As the wind rose, the temperature plummeted, and the flakes whipped up by the blizzard became icy shards that glinted like razor blades. Through this luminous white curtain, a soldier had appeared, frozen to the bone, his face frostbitten, his fingers already blackened and dead.

Now wrapped in a warm fur coat inside the tent, he was shivering uncontrollably, slipping unconscious and being slapped awake again. Even when he came round his chattering teeth made his replies to Sadovski the *politruk* almost incomprehensible. Sadovski was hollow-cheeked, with eyes a little too deep-set that gave him the look of a perfectly preserved mummy, the outline of his skull clearly visible beneath the skin.

"A single marksman, you say?" he said, removing his cap with its red band and star.

"Yes. They … they call him the … the Death … the White Death."

"*Belaya Smert?*" Sadovski repeated. "And you? How come you aren't dead? You stink of alcohol."

"They … they made me … made me drink."

"So you know where their rear base is, soldier?"

"I … I don't even … know how … how I got back here."

With a grimace of disgust, Sadovski stood up and raised his hand to his belt.

"It seems to me you spent a very pleasant evening with your new friends," he said, firing a bullet into the soldier's head.

When Borodin the military officer came back into the commissar's tent he found him wiping his face with a bloodstained handkerchief. On the carpet of branches covering the floor lay the lifeless body of a soldier, his skull blown apart, its contents oozing out.

Borodin was superbly built, like an Olympic swimmer, made to last a hundred years or more. He had a smooth, high forehead, a lantern jaw and a broad chest. It was as if some secret Soviet programme had succeeded in creating the perfect Caucasian. The physiques of Sadovski the perfectly preserved mummy and Borodin the athlete were so contrasted they seemed designed never to appear alongside one another.

"A traitor?" the military officer said.

"He may have been," the political commissar said. "Let's just say it was preventative. I prefer a dead innocent to a living spy."

"Nobody is a spy at sixteen, comrade."

"Spare me your bleeding heart and tell me how we're going to advance. I have to report back to General Habarov and neither the gulag nor the gallows are part of my plans. We've been bombarding them for more than ten days, and yet they refuse to surrender. By now, Stalin was expecting us to have joined up with our troops on the Isthmus of Karelia to take the Mannerheim Line from the rear. And yet here we still are, better armed, superior in numbers, but blocked on this damned road!"

Advancing from one burnt village to another, the Soviet 8th Army had penetrated Finnish territory without ever reaching the Kollaa frontline. Having chosen a war of machines, artillery and tanks, the Russians were obliged to stay on the road to Loimola.

"What's happened to our air support, dammit?" Sadovski yelled.

"Our airmen are blinded by the snowstorms, and even if the skies were clear, the Finns are hidden deep in the forests, and our pilots would see nothing more than treetops. Molotov prefers to use them to bomb the towns, railways and military installations."

"So this road is all that's left to us?"

"Yes. Mined and infested with the enemy."

"Well then, let's send our men in small groups all over the forest to root them out."

"We're already doing that, but our soldiers haven't been trained for these conditions, or even for combat."

Despite the Russians' crushing superiority in numbers, the Red Army lacked experience. During his paranoid Great Purges, Stalin had imprisoned or executed almost three-quarters of his officers, and many of those now engaged in the Winter War had not even completed their training. For their part, the soldiers under their command had only had time to learn to shoot straight, throw grenades, dig foxholes and throw themselves into them.

Not having received precise instructions, the political commissar washed his hands of it.

"You make the decision, comrade. If it's a good one, you'll be rewarded."

The opposite was not spelled out.

The *politruk* tugged the sheet from his camp bed and spread it over the corpse of the supposed spy.

That was the limit of his concern for the life he had just taken. He went and sat behind the trestle table that served as his desk.

"Have you heard the news?" he said. "General Habarov was told by radio that an investigator from the Stavka is coming to the front to try to understand our lack of progress. He's arriving tomorrow on the supply train."

"What supplies have you asked for?"

"Arms and ammunition. Just like all our 140 units, I suppose."

"We have enough of those for several wars," the military officer said. "Did you at least ask for warm clothing and provisions?"

"What do you think? That I was going to complain? Tell the

Kremlin we're cold and hungry? Suggest discreetly that we arrived here badly prepared? No, thank you. What I did order were portraits of Stalin. Every unit has to display one out of respect for our Great Leader, and we are several short."

"A request like that will look good on your file. But here on the ground ..."

"I am more afraid of him we are fighting for than of those we are fighting against. And so should you be."

29

Helsinki, Hotel Kamp

In November 1939, journalists had flocked to Helsinki to cover the preparations for the Olympic Games due to be held the following summer, but the first days of December and the Winter War meant a drastic change in what they wrote. The Olympic champions and their medals would doubtless have sold newspapers and magazines, but the Games had been banished from front pages and headlines. Now it was time to write history, and rather than return to Paris or London the sports journalists became war reporters.

Over the next few days so many more journalists arrived that the Finnish government had to get used to the idea: the Winter War was news all round the world. But what was the world going to say about this tiny country previously so little talked about, and which remained a mystery for readers and listeners alike?

Somewhere secure had quickly to be found for the foreign press. The very chic and above all miraculously spared Hotel Kamp was chosen. Staying in its luxury and refinement could easily help the journalists forget that only three streets away other buildings had been reduced to rubble, while the blood of casualties of the Russian shelling had not yet been cleaned from pavements.

Luxuriously decorated, its ballroom flooded with light from 50 Berlin crystal chandeliers, and the bedrooms lined with silk wallpaper, the Hotel Kamp was the last word in modernity. The first lifts installed in Finland led to floors with balconies and terraces; hot water and radiators offered comfort. Inelegant but massive wooden beams had been brought in to make the Hotel Kamp a perfect air-raid shelter. The international press installed there on the second floor could spread across all five continents the news of the unjust aggression committed by the Russian bear against peace-loving Finland.

The more they portrayed it as beautiful and a victim the more the world would want to come to its aid and cherish it. This meant propaganda was vital to counterbalance the highly unlikely success in the fight against the Russian giant. So that the image of Finland and the careful use of language were respected, the government began to keep a close watch on the journalists, without ever employing the word "censorship", although that is what it was.

Whether they came from the Foreign Ministry or the Ministry of Defence, the hotel was full of propaganda officers, writers, university students, translators and local journalists, all eager to answer any questions about the war, or to fill in gaps about their country's history.

The entire planet was gathered together in the Kamp. *Time* from the United States, *La Tribune de Genève* from Switzerland, *Reuters* from Great Britain, the *Daily Express* from Australia, the *Telegraaf* from Holland, *Paris-Soir* from France and *La Stampa* from Italy, among others.

To a background of the incessant din from typewriters, the propaganda officers read and reread the fifty or more articles written daily before they winged their way to newsrooms all over the globe.

Snow, cold, night, the Arctic winter, the Northern Lights, the battle of a Scandinavian David against a Red Goliath: so many elements to awaken the novelist in these reporters and get their fingers tapping on the keys. The story of the Winter War was told on Remingtons and Underwoods. The telephone and telegrams created the legend of this unexpected resistance. If Finland could hold off Russia, then France, Belgium or Great Britain could succeed in defeating Nazi Germany. This was the mirror image of Europe's hope against the Reich, which had declared war on them more than three months earlier, even though nothing had really happened yet, leading to this period being called the "phoney war".

In the bar at the Kamp, where the red neon sign advertising Martini filtered the light and helped outline the black leather of the broad armchairs, journalists corrected one another and discussed stories and journalistic angles. Among the four men leaning on the zinc bar, the American ordered a White Horse whisky, but the Swede advised him to adapt to local customs.

"You should try the Marshal's cocktail. It was invented in honour of Mannerheim."

"And what would I find in my glass?"

"A kind of Finnish vodka, aquavit, gin, those three of course, plus a few other ingredients. No-one knows the exact recipe, but it has to be served up to the brim, almost to overflowing. The field marshal himself has said that."

Either narrow-minded or patriotic, the American nevertheless ordered his whisky.

"People say Martha Gellhorn is about to arrive," the Italian said, slipping into the conversation.

"And I say women will become good journalists the day I become a good dressmaker," the Frenchman said. "What are you working on?"

"The officials are still refusing to accompany us to the front," the Italian said, "so I do what I can. I'm writing about the 72-metre tower built for the Olympic stadium. It won't see many athletes, but it's become the main lookout post for air raids."

"As for me," the American said, "I'm writing about how pleased the Finns are that our president is supporting them."

"And what has Roosevelt said?"

"From memory: *The Soviet Union invaded a neighbor so infinitesimally small that it could do no conceivable possible harm to the*

Soviet Union. A small nation that seeks only to live at peace as a democracy."

The Italian raised an eyebrow. "'Infinitesimally'? How do you spell that?"

The American picked up his coaster and wrote the word for him.

"Don't ever be afraid to ask," he said, handing him the mat. "It stops you looking like an idiot."

This remark was aimed at the Frenchman, who took the bait at once. The two of them frequently swapped jibes, although only one really appreciated them.

"I'm sure he pronounced it badly," the Frenchman retorted, as if everyone there knew what the two of them were referring to.

"And I'm sure you're right," the American conceded diplomatically.

"Don't keep us in suspense," the Swede said. "Tell us what you mean!"

The American emptied his glass, and didn't need to be asked twice.

The French and British had declared war on Germany on September 3 following the Nazi invasion of Poland. But in the three months since then, none of the countries had taken action.

"The Germans call it *Sitzkrieg*, the seated war," the American began. "For the Poles, it's *dziwna wojna*, the astonishing war. But a few weeks ago, a French journalist heard an English one talking about this 'phoney war'. He didn't really understand the expression, but didn't ask, and dashed off an article where he called it a 'funny war', or *drôle de guerre*. And now all France calls it that."

"As I said," the Frenchman defended himself, "I'm sure he pronounced it very badly."

"How about you, then," the Italian asked. "What's your article on today?"

"Molotov," the Frenchman said. "Molotov and his way with

words. After the surprise attack on Helsinki, he dared to say – without the slightest irony or cynicism, I've been assured – '*We do not bomb civilians; our aeroplanes carry pamphlets calling for peace and breadbaskets. The rest is Western propaganda.*' He claims it is humanitarian aid, but you only have to leave the hotel to see the damage caused by his famous 'breadbaskets'."

By now considerably merry, the journalists finally plucked up the courage to try the field marshal's cocktail, intrigued by its secret ingredients. As a result, the copies of the articles they presented to the censors were covered with glass stains and cigarette burns. Never in the history of censorship had the task been so boring. Everyone here was already staunchly pro-Finnish. They were convinced the Soviet Union had committed an outrage, and the censors never had to change a word.

In the Soviet Union on the other hand, the only acceptable history was the one approved by the Kremlin, and following ten disappointing, not to say shameful, days, the Red soldiers' correspondence was being confiscated and then burned. Without victory, nothing was to leak out.

The barman in his gold-buttoned white jacket cleared the empty glasses and stood waiting for fresh orders, when an unusual silence spread across the second floor at the discreet arrival of a newcomer.

Joseph Kessel, a renowned French reporter, already an internationally renowned author and First World War pilot, strode in ahead of the porter carrying his luggage. Kessel combined the appearance of a respected combatant, novelist and journalist. He was accompanied by one of the propaganda officials, and to judge from their attitudes they were in the midst of an argument.

"No!" Kessel shouted. "I haven't crossed the planet to write about the rearguard. I'm not interested in the Lottas who are donning uniforms again. Still less in visiting the capital's ruins. What I want is to get close to the action, and I'm offering you a choice. The Mannerheim Line on the isthmus of Karelia, or the Kollaa front. That's where this war will be decided, and that's where I want to be."

The official was still searching for a polite way to refuse Kessel's demand when the sirens began to wail all over the city. Fearing chemical warfare, the journalists leaped for their gas masks and put them on before making for the windows. They stared out at the spectacle through their big black glass eyes.

A quarter of an hour later, the hotel staff and ministry officials went from table to table to announce that the alert was over and that there would not be any "breadbaskets" dropped on Helsinki that day. The journalists removed their masks and went back to work.

"What did you call this?" the American said, pointing to his empty glass.

"The field marshal's cocktail," the Swede said. "I'll get another round."

30

A column of trucks had been waiting for the supply train. Instead of the provisions and warm clothing no-one had dared to ask for, the ordnance unit had found itself unloading wagons filled with munitions and weapons. And to everyone's surprise, the trumpets, drums, trombones, tubas and saxophones of the brass band that accompanied Lev Mekhlis, the Stavka's emissary. As chief of the Red Army's political bureau, his mission was to find out why the 8th Army remained stuck only ten kilometres inside Finland, and why Stalin could not yet stroke his moustaches on the steps of the Finnish parliament, three days before his birthday, its people at his feet.

"I'll spare you a complete biography, comrade," Sadovski had said. "I'll just explain the reason why, in Moscow, Mekhlis is untouchable."

"And why is that?" Borodin asked anxiously.

"He helped plan the Holodomor," Sadovski said simply. "Even from a logistics point of view, to starve 4 million Ukrainians to death is no easy matter. Especially when you yourself are a Ukrainian Jew. What greater proof of loyalty could there be?"

"You seem to admire him."

"I acknowledge his efficiency."

"Well then, you'll have a great opportunity to tell him so. General Habarov informs me it's our unit he's going to follow on the frontline."

Hearing this, Sadovski had turned pale, but even if he found it hard to lie convincingly, he had made the attempt with remarkable aplomb.

"Wonderful. There are almost 240 units in the camp, and he chose ours. That's wonderful, really wonderful."

Equally dismayed, Borodin served two glasses of vodka. Before putting the bottle down, he poured one more for Sadovski, whose glass was already empty.

*

In Lev Mekhlis's honour, the Russian camp had been renamed Potemkin Village. Knowing that whatever he saw was equivalent to having Stalin see it, they had concealed the exhausted soldiers and the wounded in tents. Only proud specimens of *Homo Sovieticus* were on display: men as brave, strong and handsome as their propaganda portrayed. Mud was brushed off uniforms, the bodywork of the trucks polished, and, however ridiculous it might seem, even the trenches were tidied.

In General Habarov's tent, Borodin and Sadovski the *politruk* had demonstrated on a map the complexity of the situation in which the 8th Army found itself. They emphasised the problems without accepting the least responsibility, because when Mekhlis had asked on arrival "What's the problem?" they had clearly heard "Who is the problem?"

His black hair bristling like burnt stubble, the Stavka emissary's physique was a visible representation of the antipathy he felt towards them. And he wanted explanations.

"Finnish territory is completely vertical," Borodin had begun. "Therefore all their roads run north to south. We're attacking them horizontally, from east to west, so there is only a single road we can take, the one to Loimola."

"Well then, cut through the forests," Mekhlis had cleverly suggested.

"That would of course be the most appropriate strategy,"

Borodin flattered him, "but with tanks and cannon seven metres long ..."

"I see. And anyway, my band would find it hard to march in a metre of snow. So we have to advance along the road."

"That is what we are doing, following instructions from the Stavka. We bombard the forests, hoping to hit their rearguard. We send observation and combat units to the Kollaa front, and are advancing metre by metre towards Loimola."

"That is far from satisfactory," their guest from Moscow had observed.

Ever since the start of the conflict, the constant fear of failure – which inevitably ended with a bullet to the back of the head – had meant that army officers were unwilling to take any initiative. Ideology and obedience prevailed over tactics or realities on the ground. And so Borodin hesitated before declaring:

"If the Finns continue to resist on the Kollaa front, we could perhaps go round them to the north. We would meet no resistance and would be able to join up with the 7th Army fighting on the isthmus of Karelia to take the Mannerheim Line from behind, as He wishes."

Sadovski had looked at the foolhardy Borodin as though he already saw him sentenced to death, standing blindfold against a wall.

"Go round them?" Mekhlis had repeated with a tinge of disgust, as though the words left a bad taste in his mouth. "My car does not go round dead cats in the road. One only goes round an insurmountable obstacle. Do you think that is true of the Kollaa front for our army?"

A contrite silence ensued. Buoyed by the authority conferred by being, in his view, an exceptional strategist, Mekhlis had immediately outlined a plan of attack.

"Good. We will wear them out with constant night-time artillery barrages. In the morning, some of our units will attack

Kollaa so that the enemy concentrates its troops in that one spot. At the same time, we will advance along the road to Loimola, and the remaining units will protect our provisions, munitions and weaponry. And you'll see that thanks to me we'll gain more than a few metres!"

Once they had all agreed, and their "guest" was installed in a luxurious tent with a wood stove, furs and warm blankets, General Habarov had to decide which infantry units he would send out the next day. They were to march in close formation a hundred metres in front of Mekhlis's vehicle, so that they would be the ones blown up by the mines on the Loimola road. And as there was no question of sacrificing "true" Russians, he hesitated over which of the far-flung minorities in his army he could send: Ukrainians, Romanians, Siberians, Georgians, Mongols, Turks, Azeris, Kazakhs, Tadjiks, Uzbeks, Byelorussians, Armenians ...

Without a second thought, he chose the Ukrainians, as Mekhlis had suggested when he quit their meeting.

31

Hair and eyebrows frosted with ice, the Ukrainians advanced along the seven-metre-wide road towards Loimola. They were in a cluster like crab's roe, their rifle barrels sometimes prodding the men in front of them.

A hundred metres behind them came the remainder of the army, almost 10,000 men. Their column was led by two tanks, then officers on horseback, the infantry units and the artillery, ordnance trucks and finally an official car with two red flags fluttering on its bonnet. The car was escorted by ten soldiers, and behind it followed an incongruous brass band, the unarmed musicians stumbling along, frozen hands and stiff fingers stuffed in their pockets. Even if there was a crushing victory, it would be impossible for them to play a single note.

One of the Ukrainians turned round. Thanks to the blizzard that had not let up in the past three days and the wind that constantly raised opaque white curtains of snowflakes, all he could see of the troops behind them was a dense blurred outline.

"They're using us to clear the mines," he muttered.

"They're a long way back," his neighbour said. "They can't see us. Let's move off the road or we're done for. Pass it on."

"We're moving off the road. Pass it on … We're moving off the road …"

The whispered message circulated quickly, and the Ukrainians moved stealthily to the edge of the road, by the ditches lining both sides.

"Close ranks," their commanding officer on horseback shouted when he saw what they were doing.

None of them obeyed. A man alone would have submitted, but they were no longer individuals but a solid mass, and therefore less vulnerable to pressure. The officer immediately turned his horse and went to report to his superior a hundred metres to the rear on what he saw as a spark of rebellion.

In the official car with its red flags, Mekhlis saw the officer ride past and heard him talking to Borodin. He stuck his head out of the window and shouted above the storm:

"Is there a problem?"

Reprimanded by Borodin and forced to restore order at once among the Ukrainians, the officer on horseback galloped the hundred metres back to his unit and drew his pistol. He pointed it just below their helmets, at the back of their necks.

"Close ranks!" he yelled again.

As if they had all suddenly gone deaf, the Ukrainian soldiers did not budge an inch, but continued to avoid the centre of the road.

"I have the authority to use my weapon!"

One of the Ukrainians raised his rifle and surreptitiously fixed the bayonet. In the compact mass he slipped from one row to another until he was level with the officer.

"I'm warning you for the last time …" the officer threatened.

He did not even have time to catch sight of the bayonet as it pierced his chin, slid through the roof of his mouth, and penetrated his brain. When the bayonet reappeared, a spurt of blood drenched his saddle. He was yanked off his horse.

A hundred metres. The distance gave the Ukrainians time to tip his body into the roadside ditch, hastily cover it with snow, and help one of their own up onto his horse.

Ukrainians, Romanians, Georgians, Mongols, Turks, Azeris, Kazakhs, Tadjiks, Uzbeks, Byelorussians, Armenians … None of them had wanted to go to war, but all had been conscripted. And to force someone to fight means creating a rebel.

The murder concealed, the Ukrainians renewed their march.

No-one in the column of 10,000 men struggling forward noticed the muzzle of the cannon poking out from the branches of the trees lining the route. The gun roared, and the shell smashed into the first tank, which was sent toppling over, as if flicked by a Titan. Then the Finnish machine guns began to fire. One after the other the soldiers fell, the horses reared; one of the front wheels of Mekhlis's car hit a mine and leaped two metres into the air above the heads of the troops.

A dozen similar lightning attacks took place all along the column. The Russians had no idea where to fire at an invisible enemy. They began a chaotic retreat, whose sole aim was to save their lives. Nobody bothered about Mekhlis. In fact, none of them could imagine he had survived the explosion.

The Russians had advanced barely a kilometre, and were now straggling back to their original position.

*

All Mekhlis could hear was a loud whistling noise. With burst eardrums and blood pouring from his ears, he peered through the car's shattered window to make sure the road was clear, then hauled himself out of the smoking wreckage. Two metres from him, the second T26 Russian tank swivelled its barrel and sent a shell straight into the forest. The blast was so close he was almost knocked unconscious. Then the machine gun on the armoured vehicle began firing blindly in all directions, with no precise target, like someone desperately waving their arms to drive off a mosquito.

Reversing desperately, the tank crashed into the ditch. At once, Finnish soldiers swarmed round it, throwing petrol bombs. The tank caught fire at once. Mekhlis took advantage of the enemy concentrating on this target to crawl into the trees and hide in a shell crater. He covered himself in leaves, moss and snow.

He had been buried for a good half-hour when he heard the padded crunch of snow beneath soldiers' boots. When he realised they were speaking Finnish, his blood froze. Something fell just above his head and slipped through the layers of camouflage. It came to rest in front of his nose: a silver lighter on which the name "Natasha" was engraved. Mekhlis prayed its owner had dropped it by mistake, or thrown it away when it did not work, because discovering a high-ranking officer hiding like a child under a bed promised a truly dishonourable end.

When silence returned, he poked his head out of the hole. His black, bristly hair was covered in pine needles. Fearing there could be other deadly surprises on the road, Mekhlis blundered deeper into the forest. After 50 steps, he looked around him, but all he could see was the same tree everywhere, the same snow. He had lost all notion of distance or depth: everything looked identical.

He wandered about in a daze until nightfall. The waves of cold intensified until they were like blows pummelling the muscles all over his body.

Suddenly a flare rose in the sky, casting a reddish glow over the forest. Tree shadows turned into lengthy black phantoms. Glimpsing a metallic gleam in the distance, Mekhlis headed towards it, hope rekindled. He came upon the corpses of two men, limbs torn off by shells or machine-gun rounds. In their hands, a twisted, melted trumpet and the remains of a trombone, its horn reflecting the light from the dying flare. He looked around and saw another 50 bodies already covered with snow. He realised he was back on the road to Loimola, no more than a kilometre from the Russian camp. At the sight of his decimated brass band, he fell to his knees and burst into tears like a child.

*

Mekhlis had survived. They stripped off his clothes, leaving only his woollen long johns and his fur undershirt, and rubbed his skin to stimulate the blood flow. He recovered slowly, sitting beside a fire that brought colour to cheeks already inflamed with anger. Mekhlis had survived, and that wasn't good news for anybody, because it meant they had to face his wrath.

32

The Finns had lit several small bonfires to help ward off the morning cold in the trenches and the wind that slithered in like an icy serpent, coiling itself round their freezing bodies. As a precaution, the crates of petrol bombs and grenades were stocked a safe distance away.

By now the soldiers had become accustomed to the background noise of the bombardments, and the gentle warmth from the flames quickly overcame Onni's flagging strength. He drifted off for a moment as day broke, marking the end of their guard duty. He woke with a start, even though all Simo had done was touch his shoulder to warn him he had fallen asleep, his cheek resting against his rifle barrel. Since life was a matter of chance, the soldiers always woke with a start, and in so doing Onni tore off a strip of skin that had stuck to his icy weapon.

"*Perkele!*" he yelled.

An open sore could be as dangerous as a wound, so Simo suggested they go to the first-aid post together. They skirted the other trenches that criss-crossed the frontline like an earthquake splitting open the earth's crust with a hundred crevasses.

*

Coming out of the first-aid tent, his cheek freshly decorated with an impressive dressing by the Lottas, Onni slipped a piece of paper into Simo's hand.

"It's for Toivo," he said simply.

Simo pocketed the note without reading it. As they returned to their tent they passed in front of the rapidly expanding garden of unexploded shells.

"Look at this one," Onni called to him, standing in front of a shell as tall as him. "You could almost fit inside it!"

Whenever a Russian shell buried itself in Finnish earth and failed to explode, it was planted in this garden as a monument to the soldiers who had been spared. The garden was surrounded by a picket fence on which ribald jokes in charcoal or chalk were added as the days went by.

"Maybe we could show them how shells are made?" Onni joked.

Finland had only as many artillery shells for the entire war as Russia could fire in a single day. But to reach that number, Stalin had forced his factories to produce them at an impossible rate. To meet this target and avoid provoking his anger, a third of the shells delivered either had too little explosive or were faultily made.

Commanding through terror, Stalin created his own headaches.

*

Relieved of night guard duty in the trenches, the men of the 6th Company returned to their wooden bunk beds. As the days wore on and memories of their previous lives faded, these beds seemed less and less uncomfortable.

Unable to sleep, Juutilainen was brooding on his camp bed. Seeing only evil spirits whenever he closed his eyes, he decided to go and find out if any other officers suffered from the same daytime insomnia, and if they had a bit of *viina* they would share. He was just tugging at the fur collar of his jacket when he caught sight of Pulkki, one of the many messengers, returning from a forward observation post.

"You're not dead yet then?" Juutilainen greeted him. "I would have bet my pay on it."

"The Russians are advancing on Loimola," an out-of-breath Pulkki announced. "With a brass band," he added.

"A what?"

"A brass band," the adolescent repeated.

This news finally gave meaning to the legionnaire's day. He immediately roused his company, even though they had only just gone to sleep.

When Simo and Onni returned and saw their tents were empty, they ran towards the sound of Juutilainen barking orders at the ranks of their colleagues. Some were still putting on their white snowsuits, others had their rifles slung over one shoulder, a pair of skis on the other. Their efforts created little clouds of vapour above the unit as the two men took their places among them.

Simo barely had time to pass the message from Leena to Toivo before they moved off.

Toivo unfolded it and smiled. Now he had another reason to return safe and sound that night. Above him, a sky worthy of an inspired painter was in tune with his heart.

Unlike in the summer months, when the sun hardly sets and flirts with the horizon without ever really disappearing, this winter sun found it hard to rise, as though its journey ended at dawn. It merely helped spread sublime pastel colours through the hours of weak daylight. So, amidst a landscape that in times of peace would have encouraged contemplation and beatitude, the 6th Company set off for battle, to kill or be killed, or, today, to track down a brass band.

33

They had been joined by ten or so other companies. Even if it had been another hundred, Juutilainen would have suffered if he had not been able to lead them. Whether his life was to be cut short by alcohol as slowly but as surely as candle wax beneath a flame or by an enemy bullet, Juutilainen used every extra day God offered him to defy death. And he did not give a damn how many "comrades" he took with him.

After almost three weeks of organising them several times a day he had, together with the condemned men of the 6th Company, perfected one of the most successful techniques from the winter war manual: the *motti*.[16]

An attack *motti* to surround and destroy isolated Russian units on the Loimola road or in the forests. An attrition *motti* when larger or tougher units had first to be weakened and harassed before being wiped out.

The Finnish companies followed Pulkki's directions and soon joined the observation platoon. They took up positions in the forest at 200-metre intervals, behind the advancing Russians. The *motti* trap was laid.

Soldiers dressed in white in a white universe, breathing slowly, their minds utterly focused on the present and sharpened by a heightened sense of danger, they enjoyed this moment of silence as much as if they were listening to music.

From the first day of the conflict, the forest had become a battlefield. All the animals had deserted it, just as they do when faced with devastating fires. No birdsong, no cries, no barks from deer; even the wolves and bears had joined the exodus.

This desolate, mutilated world was alien to Simo. He could not recognise it. He marched through the forests with a troubled soul, as if he were at the bedside of an ailing loved one, across ground strewn with pine needles and leaves and branches torn off by the shelling. In this strange, silent nature swept by a glacial wind, the only sound was the voices of debased, sick humans.

Invisible in this silent forest, the 6th Company waited. It was linked by radio to the others by several kilometres of telegraphic cable. Finally, after a few short minutes, a black shadow appeared behind the curtain of snow, followed by the noise of engines. The swirling snow also brought the dense smell of diesel.

Patiently, they allowed the Russians to advance. Patiently waited until half of the soldiers had gone beyond them. When the core of the column drew level, Juutilainen waved an arm and the Finnish cannon roared.

The first salvo slammed into the side of the leading tank. It toppled into the ditch, and the legionnaire gave the order for the machine guns to open fire. In this mortal tumult, a car with two red flags on the bonnet struck a mine and was lifted high into the air before it came crashing to the ground.

Lacking precise orders and clear organisation, and often without any great desire to fight, the Russian forces scattered in all directions. They fired their weapons aimlessly, fingers on the trigger until they clicked empty, ignoring the vain orders shouted by their officers on rearing horses before they were inevitably unseated.

In this chaos of headlong flight and blind attacks, the second tank, hugely imposing as it advanced along the middle of the road, as black as the worst nightmare, swivelled its turret and aimed towards the depths of the forest. In a blinding flash, it launched a shell that exploded close to the Finnish line, claiming the lives of eight members of the 6th Company.

Taking advantage of the debacle, Simo carefully chose his targets, aiming infallibly for the upper body. A few days earlier, he had missed a shot to the head, leaving the Russian time enough to kill three men before he finally finished him off. Ever since, Simo had preferred to aim at the body, which offered a larger target. What was lost in panache was gained in efficacy. Sometimes, the shot was not immediately fatal, but in the merciless cold of this Arctic winter, in the midst of a Soviet Army that preferred to call up fresh soldiers rather than care for its wounded, even a broken ankle was enough to attract the attention of the Grim Reaper.

For Simo, the first kill of the day was always painful. The second anaesthetised whatever feelings of pity he still had, and by the third he was nothing more than a machine, mechanically adjusting each movement to increase his speed and precision. So as not to go mad, he forgot they were men, forgot however many fathers and brothers he was sending six feet under the snow, even if they were Russian invaders.

Bewildered by the commotion and blinded by the snowstorm, some of the Russians ran straight into the Finnish lines of fire. Others scrambled to lose themselves in the icy forest, while still more ran back along the road, often being knocked down by the galloping riderless horses. In the midst of this pandemonium, the second tank had got stuck in the roadside ditch, and was trying to reverse. Even in such a situation, the T26 Russian tanks were almost indestructible.

Ten tonnes of metal on tracks could crush everything they ran over into mud or dust. The tanks were protected by armour plating a centimetre and a half thick, and could attack with a gun firing shells as long as a forearm and a machine gun so powerful it could cut any tree in half with a single burst.

When Juutilainen gave the order, Onni and Toivo raced towards the T26 tank, ready to put into practice the theory outlined in one of the most debatable chapters of the Finnish winter war manual: *Tanks – their weak points, and different possibilities for destroying them.*

Page 59 read:

"*If the situation so demands, the infantry can prevail over a tank. They will need to have at least two petrol bombs and a log. The wood should be of thick forest pine, which cannot be easily compressed and is dense at its core.*"

For their reckless mission, Onni was the one carrying the log, Toivo the two petrol bombs.

Through the gunsight in the tank, the Russian gunner was struggling to follow the two soldiers with his machine gun. He kept firing, but failed to hit them. In the tiny hull, side by side with his gunner, the driver was desperately manoeuvring to get out of the deep ditch he had fallen into.

The machine gun almost brushed the top of Onni's head as he forced the log into the tank's left track with all his might. The wood split with the pressure and was squashed in half, but did momentarily bring the machine to a halt. Toivo lit the storm matches on the petrol bottles and threw them onto the body of the tank, level with the rear deck. The two fireballs were immediately sucked in through the air vents, roaring as they plunged down to the engine block. There the oil, grease and rubber also caught fire, giving off thick, choking smoke that seeped into the hull. On the Finnish side for a few seconds time came to a halt at the hypnotic sight of this metal monster engulfed by flames.

The crew would suffocate in two minutes. This meant they had to open the top hatch, at the risk of becoming targets. Even if the air had been breathable, it would not have been long before the tank became a modern version of the Bronze Bull, heating its occupants to boiling point until the fuel tank exploded. Dying inside or dying outside: the choice was the same, only the timing was different.

The hatch opened, to reveal a fist clasping a grenade. No doubt the idea was to throw it as far as possible to clear enough room for the tank crew to escape. At 705 metres per second, Simo's bullet struck the wrist. The hand dropped the grenade, and it clanked down to the floor of the cockpit. A muffled explosion signalled that its occupants had met a rapid death and avoided unnecessary suffering.

34

The 6th Company was recovering weapons and munitions on the road to Loimola, which was now strewn with dead bodies. They searched even in the dead soldiers' pockets, their fingers coming into contact with a photograph or a souvenir jewel they did not dare to steal.

Twenty-one-year-old Aksu, a simple cowherd, wanted his share. Seeing a pistol with the letters C.C.C.P. round a black star on the butt stuck in a Russian officer's belt, he quickly stuffed it under his coat. He began to go through the pockets and fished out a silver lighter with the name *Natasha* engraved on it. So somewhere far away, snug in the warmth of an empty house, a woman called Natasha was hoping to again see this lighter light the cigarette of the person who lay sprawled here, three bullets in his stomach, eyes staring at the sky, his body on the way to becoming frozen solid.

"Don't do that," Onni warned him.

"Who's going to use it now?" Aksu defended himself.

"There's too much love there, it will turn against you," Hugo said fearfully.

"Don't come to me with your superstitions," Aksu said darkly, pocketing the lighter.

*

Once Simo had estimated from his observation post that no more Russians would get up again, he rejoined the rest of his company. In the middle of the road to Loimola, he found Pietari and Toivo. Surrounded by the piles of bodies, they looked puzzled.

"How about you, Simo, do you notice anything odd?" they asked.

The marksman looked around him, and his eyes fell on the brass instruments.

"No, not that," Toivo forestalled him. "Not the trumpets or trombones; I still have no idea what they're doing here. I mean, can't you smell something strange?"

There was of course the smell of diesel, as heavy as a mantle of soot. And the metallic, disgusting smell of blood. But the most powerful smell that hovered over this scene of carnage was completely incongruous, both pleasant and astonishing.

"It's vodka!" Pietari assured Simo before he had time to respond. "Those guys all stink of vodka!"

"Either they were scared stiff, or they really have no wish to fight … Either way, they had to get them drunk to make them advance!"

Overjoyed at knowing their enemies were as terrified as they were, the friends soon had reason to feel even more confident. A few metres from them they saw Juutilainen raising a weapon high into the air, one that was far too long to be merely a rifle.

"An anti-tank rifle," he shouted, holding the P.T.R.D.-41 aloft despite its seventeen kilos and six-centimetre ammunition.

"But … we don't have any tanks," an astonished Toivo said.

"But they do! They're giving us weapons we don't have that they intended to use against our non-existent tanks. I'm surprised they're such idiots. We'll blow holes in them with this. It's as though they're being bitten by their own dogs."

No Christmas morning, had the legionnaire ever celebrated one, could have been more wonderful to him. And for the others, to realise at that moment that the Russians did not have the slightest idea of the weaponry the Finns possessed (that is, not a great deal, and especially not any tanks) renewed their hope.

*

That day, the Soviet Army lost close to 300 men. The Finns, fewer than 20.

In the shelter of the friendly forest, they laid the dead and wounded on sleds. When the state of the bodies permitted nothing else, they made do with taking their comrades' dog tags. A cousin. A neighbour. A friend. None of them was a stranger.

They were 20 kilometres from their rearguard camp. Even though the blizzard had finally abated, it left behind a layer of snow that was occasionally knee-deep, making cross-country skiing as laborious as swimming against a current. After a hundred or so metres, certain they could not be seen from the road, Juutilainen raised his gloved fist to allow his men a rest before they began a non-stop march back to Kollaa.

They stayed pressed close to one another so that their bodies would not grow cold and the sweat on their skin turn to ice. Onni took out a packet of cigarettes and offered it to the others. Aksu stuck one between his lips and lit it with Natasha's lighter.

"We told you to get rid of that," Onni grumbled.

"And I told you to get off my back," Aksu said.

Onni imagined himself in the place of the stripped Russian, his lifeless body searched by enemy hands, the wedding ring torn from his finger. Angrily, he slapped at the hand holding the lighter. Aksu was about to bend down to recover it when Pietari gave it a kick, and Natasha's lighter flew several metres before being lost to sight beneath some branches.

As with all the others, Aksu had gone from peace to war in a single day. Since then he had killed so often that his spirit, contaminated by the banality of horror, had been poisoned by it. The fruit had fallen to the ground, where it was bound to rot. Onni had just shown him up as if he was a child, and this public rebuke made Aksu seethe with anger, a red mist descending over his furious eyes.

But Simo could read Aksu even before he reacted, guessing

what he would do. First there would be a slight, imperceptible twitch of the shoulder, then the irate soldier would in a split second reach for his rifle or the stolen Russian pistol with its C.C.C.P. stamp. For now these movements had gone no further than an idea, but Simo had anticipated them. He clicked his rifle as a warning. As if frozen to the spot, Aksu halted and swallowed his bile. He had not had time to move a muscle.

"Good," Juutilainen scoffed. "You three seem in good spirits. We can take advantage of that."

Simo, Onni and Aksu were ordered to make ready to go ahead as scouts a kilometre in front of their companies and keep an eye open for any possible danger.

Even though his name was not called, and without even thinking about it, Toivo stood up, slung his rifle over his shoulder, checked his ammunition, and did up the hood of his snowsuit. Juutilainen let him do so. Simo and Toivo had said they were childhood friends, and it was best not to separate friends, because they were bound to be courageous. Courageous for each other. And that made them good soldiers.

35

Forests of Kollaa, −35 °C

The four soldiers struggled to make headway. Night was falling
before 16.00. If the clouds allowed it to shine, in a few minutes' time
the only light would be from the moon. As they marched, their legs
began to freeze, flesh and skin anaesthetised by the cold. They were
skiing on an invisible cemetery that had no regard for uniforms
or nationalities. The superstitious Onni wondered whether it was
the depth of the mantle of snow that was impeding their progress
or the corpses' phantom hands clutching at their ankles.

In the lead, Toivo raised his fist for them to be silent, and they
came to a halt. He tilted his head, and Simo came to lie beside
him. He saw the makeshift camp: a canvas tarpaulin hanging from
one tree trunk to another for protection from the wind. An extinguished fire, with seven hunched figures around it. Next to them,
a dead horse on its back, its belly slit open, hoofs pointing at the
sky. Onni stood his wired radio on the ground, ready to warn their
company of an enemy presence. Simo checked his lines of sight.
Seven targets, a maximum of seven seconds, plus two more to
reload. Their bodies stiffened with cold, the Russians would not
have time to understand what was going on, or to defend themselves. Simo controlled his breathing. Then, after a moment's
hesitation, he lowered his rifle as though he had changed his mind.

"*Perkele,*" Aksu whispered. "Why don't you shoot?"

*

Simo prodded the first Russian in the back with his foot, and the
body toppled forward, the face smearing with black, frozen ashes.

On guard duty, he must have forgotten to wake the others, letting them sleep until death overtook them. Alongside them lay the disembowelled horse, hacked to pieces with their knives. To judge by what little was left of the animal, they had obviously stuffed themselves as best they could.

Unhooking the lamp from his back, Simo slid the red plastic filter out and put the green one in. He waved it high above his head to signal to the others they could join him.

*

"Look," Onni whispered. "This one still has his arm outstretched, a stick in his hand."

In a last desperate effort to keep the fire going, the soldier on guard had ended up as an ice statue as white as salt.

"And Lot's wife, despite the advice from the angels, turned to look back at Sodom …" Onni quoted from memory.

"Let's search them and go," Toivo said.

Seven Degtyaryov light machine guns and their ammunition, fortunately compatible with Finnish weapons. Rich spoils they could not ignore, but which they would have to seize by force.

While Toivo held on to one soldier's rigid body, Simo pulled on the frozen arms locked round his rifle. In vain. Behind them, Aksu had shown less respect for the dead, and stuck his bayonet between their elbow and body, using it as a lever to free their weapons.

Nauseous at first at the sound of frozen flesh being ripped apart, the Finnish soldiers decided this was the only solution, or at least the quickest, unless they made a fire and allowed the bodies to thaw. They had to prise the fingers of the last Russian from the butt of his rifle, jabbing at them with their *puukkos.*

They walked away from the frozen men, whose petrified features were not twisted by the usual pain or fear, but simply extinguished, almost at peace, eyes closed.

36

Night had fallen by the time the four scouts reached the Kollaa frontline, with Simo in the lead. They were half an hour in front of the remainder of the 6th Company, so to avoid being hit by friendly fire, Onni raised the lamp with the green filter and shouted the day's password.

"*Kettu!*"[17]

In the distance another green lamp flashed. Reassured, they covered the final hundred metres, hoping against hope the Russian artillery directed at the Finnish line had not hit their tents. Fortunately, they found they were intact, and dropped their booty of machine guns and ammunition in front of one of them.

None of them flung themselves down on their beds, preferring to warm up by the stove. They knew that violent spasms of cold would prevent them getting any rest. They would have to wait patiently until the shivering lessened, no longer hammering at their stomachs and chests. Only Toivo dropped his rucksack on the ground and left the tent without a word.

The 34th Regiment to which the 6th Company belonged had lost men. Many dead, even more wounded, and it was in the first-aid post, nestling in the shelter of a hill to avoid direct artillery strikes, that they were screened.

If it was a question of fresh bandages, splints, or of stopping bleeding or administering a strong dose of morphine, they were attended to in the first-aid post. The most seriously wounded, who needed to be operated on, were evacuated in a medical bus to the field hospital 20 kilometres away – if they survived the journey.

Then there was the big black tent, concealed from the soldiers, that took in the dead, at first lined up and more recently stacked on top of one another, awaiting their return home.

Taking advantage of the lull, the short respite between the daily clashes and the start of the deadly night-time rain of artillery shells, Toivo walked over to the first-aid post.

Before joining Leena, he studied her for a few moments. She looked incredibly sweet as she bent over the wounded, giving them all her attention. They were Finnish, but Toivo was convinced she would have cared for Russians in exactly the same way. It seemed to him that at all times and in all circumstances, Leena was inspired by a universal compassion.

When she raised her head and their eyes met, they smiled at one another, and the Winter War stood still.

"I got your message," Toivo said, slightly embarrassed.

"Are you wounded?" she asked, spotting the dirty bandage on his arm.

"No, but I have to pretend I am to see you."

"You can stay a few minutes, no longer. Everyone is asleep. The night-time racket hasn't started yet."

Beyond a row of beds with bloody sheets, Leena raised the canvas flap dividing the tent in two. Behind it was where she slept. Toivo stretched out on the narrow bed, and Leena squeezed in next to him. At last they were one.

"Would you like to …?" she suggested, hardly daring to finish the sentence.

"I'm not sure."

"Then we can just stay like this. The two of us together. I enjoy that as well."

Toivo held her gently, trying to imbibe her breathing and her skin, the vestiges of a previous life. When all this was over, he had plans for them. He only wished she would agree to share them.

They embraced again, their hearts beating obstinately as one, come what may.

*

Toivo found it hard to wipe away the silly grin on his face. He was the only one who knew about the small scrap of Finnish-blue cloth Leena had quickly sewn inside the collar of his uniform jacket. This simple secret would give him the strength to carry on. He returned to the company's tents in a buoyant mood, expecting to find his friends asleep. He found them alright, but not there: Juutilainen had kept them awake, parading them in front of their commanding officers.

By the light from oil lamps and pocket torches, the legionnaire was displaying all the munitions pilfered that day in order to impress Teittinen, the commander of the 34th Regiment.

"One light cannon, twelve machine guns, 24 sub-machine guns, and five P.T.R.D.-41 anti-tank rifles, Colonel, sir!"

Pietari corrected the total:

"Thirty-one sub-machine guns, in fact. We stole another seven from an isolated unit. And the ammo that goes with them."

"The more we attack them, the more weapons we get!" Juutilainen boasted. "And we smashed two of their tanks, one with a log, the other with petrol bombs."

Teittinen looked delighted as he observed the 6th Company. Three weeks earlier, he would not have bet a penny on them. The more so with the Terror at their head.

"Gentlemen, you bring honour to the Finnish Army. And you give the word 'guerrilla' all its nobility."

The lieutenant colonel began to pace up and down in front of the men.

"The guerrilla is the poor man's military strategy. Our war manual can teach you the theory far better than me. Above all, it is 'an asymmetrical balance of forces, in number as well as in weaponry'. That is a good description of this war. 'Rapid surprise attacks': you are without equal in that regard. 'Over extensive territory of difficult access' – how better to describe our beautiful Finland? 'With ultra-mobile and flexible units': exactly like our *Sissi*! But in the end, those are not what's most important. We'll die just as surely in our rapid attacks as in an exhausting long-drawn-out defence. But rest assured that when those attacks are carried out by an army considered defeated from the outset, they terrify our adversaries. And you do terrify them, I promise you that. Morale is a weapon, and you soldiers are sapping theirs day after day!"

37

Mekhlis had gone to ground like a rat. He had soiled himself when he heard the Finns prowling round his hiding place. He had almost crawled back to the Russian camp: Stalin's man, the Stavka's prestigious emissary.

The day after their ill-advised advance on Loimola, an advance dictated by a politician who knew nothing about warfare or military tactics, the units who had taken part were drawn up in front of Mekhlis. His rage had only grown since the previous day.

Borodin and Sadovski were escorted to him and made to kneel in front of several thousand men standing at attention.

Mekhlis walked behind the two men, glared at the army facing him, then shot them in the back of the head. Hands tied behind their backs, they toppled face down in the snow. The guilty had been punished. The day could begin.

*

In General Habarov's tent, the officers of a new unit – new Borodins and Sadovskis – had listened devoutly as the bungling Mekhlis gave them a fresh lesson in military strategy.

"Go round it! We must go round Kollaa to the north to avoid them. And avoid that damned road!"

Impervious to any notion of bad faith, his anger sated by the morning's double execution, Mekhlis had swiftly recovered his arrogance. He made for his tent to pack his bags, only to encounter Habarov, whose rank and record shielded him from a bullet to the head.

"You're not staying?" the general asked sardonically.

"I've given you your tactics. I don't have to do the fighting for you as well, do I?"

"And your remaining bandsmen? Are you taking them with you?"

"Give them rifles. My musicians can become your soldiers."

Throwing his full suitcase to the floor beside his camp bed, Mekhlis turned towards Habarov, ready to leave him with a threat. But, thanks to his unrivalled experience in diplomacy and subterfuge, the general was quick to defuse the situation.

"In my report, I shall say you did not hesitate to venture to the frontline, demonstrating the remarkable courage of a true warrior in the service of the Mother Country and its Supreme Leader."

Mekhlis swallowed his anger as if it were bile. The "remarkable courage of a true warrior" was better than having to report the defeat he himself had provoked, and of which he had had a front-row view, before he had got lost in the forest like a baby rabbit separated from its mother.

"Then I will say that you command your men competently," Mekhlis retorted, "and that the unexpected and extreme wintry conditions are the only reason for your delay in carrying out his plan of conquest. It is possible he will be merciful."

The two men shook hands. After accompanying Mekhlis to his vehicle, Habarov asked to be given Borodin and Sadovski's dog tags.

The orders were clear. No bodies were to be returned to the Soviet Union, in order not to undermine the propaganda boast that the powerful, indestructible Russia would not lose a single man during the Winter War.

So Habarov had a pit dug for the two officers. With no cross and no prayers.

Leaning over their grave, he reflected on the two intertwined bodies tossed there carelessly, dishonoured even in death. He told himself there was room enough for a third corpse, and it had very nearly been his.

Mercy, however, was not one of Stalin's strong points, and the following day a simple telegram arrived "inviting" Habarov to pack his bags, sacrificed like a pawn. At least he was alive. Two days later, he relinquished command of the 8th Army to take on that of a quartermaster unit without even meeting his replacement.

When Grigori Shtern, hero of the Soviet Union during the war with Japan a year earlier, arrived in his quarters and took command of the 8th Army, there was no change to either orders or strategy: to advance at any cost and annihilate this insolent Finland which refused to surrender. Shtern had to succeed, or find himself in a pit as well.

New leader, same war, same chaos.

38

Kollaa front, mid-December 1939, −30°C

On the road to Loimola the Russians encountered one attack after another and minefields, and they still had not located the rear base where the Finnish commanders planned their campaign. They had, however, located the Kollaa frontline, and that was where they concentrated their heaviest artillery bombardments.

As usual, the furious storm of shells had ceased an hour before dawn. The silence that followed still echoed from its blasts.

Thanks to this lull, Simo had fallen asleep, hunched on the trench floor covered in brown snow and sheltered by Hugo's broad back. Next to him, light shone from Arvo's head torch as he pored over his book of recipes. Arvo was a young apprentice chef who had enrolled in the Rautjärvi Civic Guard less than a year before. He was in the bad habit of describing the ingredients of his favourite dishes to Hugo, who salivated painfully on hearing them and begged him to stop.

When two of the men were sleeping, the third kept watch. Now it was Arvo's turn.

As he dozed, Simo was disturbed by a sudden movement, as if nudged in the ribs by an elbow. Straightening up, it took his eyes several seconds to get used to the half-light. In those few moments, he thought he saw Hugo and Arvo fighting, for some as yet unclear reason. Arvo was flat on the ground, and a huge dark silhouette appeared to be punching him in the stomach. Grasping his torch, Simo shone it in front of him. Its beam lit up the Russian who had infiltrated their trench and, almost astride the youngster, was raining knife thrusts on him, gagging him with his hand to prevent him crying out.

Half a second later, Simo had plunged his bayonet up to the hilt under the attacker's armpit. All along the trench, other torches snapped on, revealing the murderous intruders and their victims' dead bodies. Behind Simo, Hugo buried his *puukko* so hard into the throat of a Red soldier that the point emerged from the back of his head. Bewildered, Simo and Hugo stared at each other, the two enemy bodies at their feet.

Shouts, confusion. Raised high in the air, anonymous knife and bayonet blades flashed momentarily in the moonlight before disappearing into flesh, slitting stomachs open, obscenely red intestines pouring out. Soldiers ran blindly along the bottom of the trench, grabbing uniforms and helmets to distinguish the enemy from their brothers-in-arms, to decide whether or not to kill. Gunshots rang out in all directions; some wept with fear as they fought; others were pleading, or shouting with the rage that bolsters a soldier's courage, killing with bestial savagery. The rest of the Finnish camp was finally waking up, men running towards the endless indistinguishable lines of trenches zigzagging along the front.

Never before had the enemy come so close.

Oblivious to the tumult, Simo sat in front of Arvo and pulled his body until his head rested on his legs. The youngster breathed his last in Simo's arms. Beside him lay the recipe book, stained red with his own blood.

The noise of the Russians pulling back from this lightning attack could still be heard. Simo crawled towards a box of petrol bombs. He took hold of one of the glass bottles, scraped the storm match taped to it, and threw it out of the trench. As it burst on the snowy ground, the flames did not hit anyone, but illuminated a wide area. He threw several more, which gave Hugo the chance to shoot at the Russians' retreating backs.

Only a hundred metres away, without bothering to await the return of their suicide unit, the Russians began to fire their mortars. Despite the roar of the explosions and the blinding flashes, Simo now had only one thought in mind: to find Onni, Toivo and Pietari. The trench snaked over more than three kilometres, but two of them were posted at one end, while Onni was at the other.

"Run!" Hugo shouted. "I'll look for Onni!"

To avoid a granite outcrop, the trench made a right-angled turn. Just as Simo was about to enter it, a shell exploded in front of him. The blast flung him several metres backwards until he hit a pile of logs. When he came round, his body buried in earth, Simo struggled to his feet and ran round the bend. The intense heat had melted the snow, and the trench was now covered in a layer of sticky scarlet organic matter. As the cloud of smoke gradually dispersed, he caught sight of Pietari and Toivo. Ignoring the chaos all around them, the three men fell into each other's arms.

The Finns responded to the attack at once. Leaping behind their mortars, light cannon and machine guns, they fired continuously straight ahead of them. Soon though, anxious to save their scarce munitions, the firing stopped.

As silence returned, a voice could be heard, calling for help in the distance on the Russian side.

"*Auta! Jalkani on rikki!*"

"That voice …" Pietari moaned.

"It's Hugo," Toivo said.

They were overcome by indescribable horror, like a landslide tearing at their insides. Simo loaded a clip into his rifle; Pietari grabbed two petrol bombs. Toivo pulled a pistol out of the belt of an officer who had lost part of his torso and left shoulder, as though bitten off by some gigantic animal. All three were about to go and recover Hugo, whatever the danger, when Juutilainen's shadow appeared in front of them, blocking their way.

Hugo's voice could again be heard faintly from somewhere at the forest edge.

"*Auta! Jalkani on rikki!*"

"What is he saying?" the Terror wanted to know, eardrums still ringing from the deafening combat.

"He's saying: 'Help me, my leg is broken,'" Toivo told him.

"How long has he been shouting?"

"A minute. Perhaps a bit longer."

"Then it's a trap."

In spite of this, it took all of Toivo and Pietari's strength to prevent Simo jumping out of the trench to run towards the cries.

"The lieutenant is right!" Toivo tried to convince him, gripping Simo's shoulders even more tightly. "If he's been shouting for so long, why haven't the Russians finished him off?"

At that they heard a single gunshot, just one, and the cries for help came to an end. The enemy's clumsy trick had not worked, so their lure was no longer any use to them.

"They can't stay so close after daybreak," Juutilainen assured the three friends. "We'll recover his body and tag in the morning. Go back to your positions."

The legionnaire searched in his pockets and pulled out the cigarettes he had, as well as a box of matches and a bottle of *viina*. He handed them all to his men.

"Simo, Toivo and Pietari," he named them, looking them in the eye one by one. "We'll get our revenge tomorrow."

As he was leaving the trench, he bumped into Onni, whose heart began to beat again when he saw his friends. Then he realised someone was missing.

"Where's Hugo?"

By tacit agreement, none of them told Onni that the giant had gone looking for him. And for the second time in his life, in Tuonela the black swan welcomed Hugo to the land of the dead.

39

When calm returned in the morning, the Finns counted their casualties. The wounded were put on sleds to be towed to the first-aid post or, for the worst cases, back to the field hospital at the rear.

At night, the Russian artillery was in action along all 60 kilometres of the Kollaa front, the first half of which followed the meanders of the river that gave it its name. By day, their infantry roamed the surrounding forests, and at twilight carried out attacks on the nearest Finnish positions. War had come to stay, and the daily butchery had become a familiar routine, although never before had there been hand-to-hand fighting.

*

No one man was more precious than any other, and so Hugo's body was loaded without ceremony onto a cart pulled by a slow horse. An elderly chaplain led it without even needing to hold the bridle: the animal knew the way.

Four soldiers lowered their heads as the cart passed by.

Karlsson, the commander of *Sissi* 1, went over to them, half a dog tag in the palm of his closed fist.

"Do you know where he came from?"

"From Rinkilä village," Onni said.

"Do you know if he had a friend? A neighbour?"

All four thought of Janne, killed by a mine on the first day of the conflict. The only one from that village apart from Hugo.

"We're his only friends," Pietari said.

Karlsson opened his hand above Toivo's and dropped the tag into it.

"If one day you're passing by Rinkilä, tell them about him. They should be proud."

*

In Hugo's honour, the four lads from Rautjärvi had attended the short Mass said by the chaplain. In his prayer for the dead, for the children of the staunchly Christian Finland, he had as usual made the comparison with the heavenly struggle between Good and Evil, which was continuing on earth with the fight between the Just and the Wicked, Finland and Russia.

The chaplain had let them gather their thoughts for a short while before they returned to their earthly concerns. He was also the commander of a machine-gun company and, as everyone knew, a very good shot. War forces people to make many moral concessions.

For his part, Juutilainen had stayed in his tent to drink. He had always denied himself any grieving or regret. Not because he was devoid of emotions or sensitivity, but as a career soldier who lived from war to war, he had lost so many men he could have spent a lifetime shedding tears for them.

He had, however, the taste of fresh blood in his mouth, and the unsated desire to enjoy more. Only a few days earlier, Hugo had smashed a rifle butt in his face, and, however absurd it might seem, he had appreciated that. Hugo's humanity, and the courage that gave him. The humanity that was slipping through his own fingers, bottle by bottle. It had impressed him.

An adjutant raised the tent's canvas flap without daring to enter. Thanks to a simple message from Hägglund, he saved the legionnaire from his idle reflections before he could start on a second bottle.

*

174

As Simo, Pietari, Toivo and Onni passed by the trenches and rows of tents on their way back to the 6th Company, they discovered that now it was daylight the shell-scarred earth had vanished. So too had the blood, and the trees uprooted by the bombardments. Everything was covered in a carpet of soft white snow, as if yesterday had never existed, like a fresh blank page waiting to receive the next chapter.

When they clustered round their stove, it was as if Hugo was still there with them. It took Karlsson's voice to rouse them from their silent introspection.

"Juutilainen has been called with the other officers and with Teittinen to meet Hägglund. All the companies are to be ready to move out!"

40

"Operation Talvela," Hägglund, the commander of the Finnish Army's IV Corps, announced solemnly.

At the back of the tent, so far from the others that the light from the oil lamps did not even reach him, a young man, hair tousled as if blown by the wind, was respectfully listening as the officers laid their plans for the coming days.

"Ever since the start of the conflict, the Russians have been blocked on the road to Loimola," Hägglund said, "and whenever they attack our defensive line at Kollaa we have been able to keep them at bay. But we have learned from a trusted source that General Habarov has been sacked as commander of their 8th Army. He has been replaced by a certain Colonel Shtern. We don't know much about him, but we do know his plans."

Hägglund turned the wheel to make the lamp brighter, and a strong light shone on the map in front of him.

"The Soviet 8th Army is going to be divided in two. One half will continue to concentrate on Kollaa, but the other, a good half of their men, will go round us to the north, as they have wanted to from the outset, to try to take the Mannerheim Line from behind. Can you see Lake Tolvajärvi, 200 kilometres north of our position on the map? That's where they'll go."

A shiver of anticipation ran down Juutilainen's spine. He already pictured himself on the shores of the lake, machine gun in hand, unleashing a storm of fire and lead. He was simply awaiting the order that would unleash him.

"And it is Colonel Talvela who will carry out this mission with his men," Hägglund told them, presenting the colonel.

Juutilainen detested him on the spot.

"How can we be sure about the information?" the legionnaire said bitterly. "How do we know the Russians will go all of 200 kilometres north to avoid Kollaa?"

"Thanks to Private Antero!" the general said, proud of his secret weapon.

The tousle-haired blond youngster emerged from the shadows and began to give his report.

"Yesterday, when you went to Loimola, I was sent with others to the enemy lines to cut their radio wires and prevent them communicating. In civilian life I was a technician with *Yle Radio Suomi*.[18] I told myself that, instead of simply cutting the wire, I could divert it. In other words, listen in to them. But it didn't last long. A patrol came close, so I restored the line, so that they wouldn't know that we know."

Juutilainen knew how to acknowledge courage and initiative, but that did not stop him revealing his obnoxious side.

"So bravo, Antero, and good luck to Colonel Talvela, but what the devil am I doing here, if nobody needs me?"

Hägglund could not help but smile. He had of course been told about the legionnaire, but seeing him for real allowed him to appreciate still more his coarse, repellent character, with his wild eyes that opened as wide as windows to give a glimpse of the tormented spirit within.

"On the contrary, Lieutenant. You are certainly wanted. You will be at the heart of everything! Carry on, Lieutenant Colonel Teittinen."

"A large proportion of our forces will be deployed on Operation Talvela," Teittinen explained. "We are therefore going to cut back on the front at Kollaa so as not to be taken by surprise further north. We will leave only the 34th Regiment, that is, nine companies. A total of 3,000 men. Obviously, I shall be in overall command, but you, Juutilainen, will take the lead on the ground.

If we are right and half the Red 8th Army moves north, that means we will still have to face ten times more Russians than we have troops to defend Kollaa. But if we are wrong, and the enemy focuses on Kollaa, then we will be on our own fighting the entire 8th Army and ..."

"And finally ..." Hägglund said, "let's just say I'll be busy writing your obituaries. But that's enough loose talk. Lieutenant Juutilainen, I have only one question to ask you. However many Russians you face, will you hold out? Or more simply ... *Kestääkö Kollaa?*"

"Kollaa will hold, General, sir."

*

Accompanying Juutilainen back to their camp, and taking advantage of the calm night and the few minutes before the bombardments began, Teittinen responded to the legionnaire's questions.

"Why me?"

"Because Hägglund likes you. Between you and me, this war is nothing more than a huge national suicide. We cannot possibly win it: we have merely thousands of soldiers against their million. Our only allies are our knowledge of the terrain and a winter that only a Finn can withstand. We are bound to lose, but it's the way we do so that is crucial to Mannerheim. Either we capitulate quickly and the entire country becomes Russian, or we hold out long enough for the war to become a burden for them. In that case, we could oblige them to enter peace negotiations – but every metre we have lost will be annexed by the Soviets. Every metre the Russians occupy today will be Stalin's tomorrow. And Hägglund knows you hate to retreat."

"Is that the only reason?"

"No," Teittinen said, after giving it a moment's thought. "It's also because making war is probably the only reason why your mother took the trouble to bring you into this world."

The Terror accepted this point without taking offence.

"What about Sweden? Will they end up helping us?"

"No. They won't budge. They're far too busy selling their iron to Hitler and counting their gold."

"What about Europe?"

"They've kicked Russia out of the League of Nations, but that's all. It's a symbolic gesture that barely conceals their cowardice."

"And our air support?"

"What few planes we have are concentrated on the isthmus, above the Mannerheim Line."

"And the navy?"

"Our ships are stuck in the ice. As you know, this is a harsh winter. We're on our own, and we'll fight to the death on our own, because if we give in, we won't even have the honour of calling ourselves Finnish. So tell me … What do you need?"

By now they had reached the 6th Company camp, and Juutilainen dived into his tent, only to reappear with a bottle of *viina*. He downed half of it, as if all this time he had been starved of air and it contained oxygen, before finally offering it to the lieutenant colonel, who did not need to be asked twice.

"I need men. I have already lost a third of my company in less than three weeks. As far as weapons go, I'll make sure we steal even more. But against tanks we need more grenades and more petrol bombs."

*

Three tents away, looking at the half-empty crates, Onni was saying the same to the ordnance officer, who was chewing the end of his pencil as he bent over his little notebook. It was past 20.00, and time to prepare for the night attacks. So the weapons and munitions were being checked, and the lack of petrol bombs was becoming a real problem.

"We're going to run out!" a worried Onni said.

"What do you do, drink them?"

"It's possible Juutilainen has already tried to. But mostly we prefer to throw them at tanks. We also toss them into their trucks when we can't steal everything from them, and their cars, so that we leave nothing for the Ivans. We also throw them on the road, into their trenches when they have time to dig them, and—"

"*Selvä, selvä* …" the munitions officer interrupted.[19] "I'll order some new crates, seeing you're so fond of them."

"So much so that we call them Molotov cocktails."

Seeing the surprise on the other man's face, Onni said:

"When he bombarded Helsinki on the first day of the war, Molotov reassured international opinion by saying that they were not shells, but breadbaskets dropped for the starving populace. So if he's providing the food, it would be rude not to bring a nice bottle or a small cocktail, wouldn't it?"

"Of course, if it's a question of being polite," the officer admitted, "we shouldn't seem uncouth. In any case, don't expect to receive your Molotov cocktails any time soon. The Rajamäki factory hasn't delivered any for days now. Don't ask me why, but their bottling lines have halted. While you're waiting, the best thing would be to go and scrounge them from the other battalions. As you may know, not all the companies are as spendthrift as you."

"Not everyone is lucky enough to have someone they call 'the Terror' in command."

Before he closed the crate once more, Onni checked the storm matches were solidly attached to the bottles. A small detail caught his eye. A detail that could explain why production at the Rajamäki factory had slowed down. He invited the officer to see for himself, before the two of them understood.

"*Perkele!* How stupid can you get?"

41

Rajamäki Factory, outskirts of Helsinki

The official from the Ministry of Defence could not take his eyes off the new hole in the factory roof. It was big enough for a train to pass through, the wooden beams open to the sky, and gigantic ragged slats hanging down into the interior.

"Two hundred and seventy-one shells?" the official exclaimed, as exasperated as if they had landed in his own garden. "And yet you insist on telling me this isn't the work of a spy? How can the Russians know which factory we bottle our petrol bombs in?"

"We have no idea, sir. All this operation is classified 'Top Secret', and if there were a traitor to Finland among my workers, I can assure you: I would have unmasked him."

"Is that so? And how would you have done that? By his traitor's looks? His traitor's clothes, or his traitor's laugh?"

Humiliated in his own factory, the manager lowered his eyes.

High above their heads, a muffled metallic clang made the building vibrate. A crane had just lowered a two-tonne Bofors 40 mm. anti-aircraft gun onto an undamaged part of the roof. Three more installed on the ground in front of the factory were also pointing their five-metre-long barrels into the sky. In the distance, men were laboriously dragging up 40-kilo crates full of ammunition for the guns.

"Let's hope that the two hundred and seventy-first Russian shell will be the last," the government official said. "Now you have four Bofors guns, you're the best protected alcohol factory in the world, and no longer have any excuse. You must resume production and even double it. The defence of our frontlines all over the country is at stake."

The factory manager seized the chance to regain his authority.

"Our 90 men are working 24-hour shifts, sir. More than 200,000 bombs have already left our production lines."

"Kerosene, petrol and tar?"

"Our mixture is slightly different. We are a state alcohol factory, so we have replaced the kerosene with ethanol because we had quite a lot in stock. But that doesn't lessen the effect of the bombs in any way. One of them releases fifteen times more energy than gunpowder. And if you would care to follow me …"

The little committee moved on past the huge steel vats, around which a series of conveyor belts transported the merrily clinking glass bottles. The factory manager came to a halt in front of a crate on a table. It contained the new prototypes, for which he was expecting to be congratulated.

"This is the future of our factory, sir. There's no change in the mixture, but in how the bomb is lit. As you know, at the moment there are two storm matches that have to be struck. But when our soldiers are fighting at night, those two sulphur matches can be seen a hundred metres away, which means our heroes are at the mercy of marksmen. So we have invented replacing them with a sulphuric acid capsule that sets fire to the contents only once the bottle is smashed. Even in the darkest night there will be no risk of being spotted!"

It was an ingenious idea, and the government official, spinning one of these prototypes around in his hand, was already enjoying his moment of glory in front of Mannerheim or Aksel Airo. All of a sudden he stopped, a bemused look on his face.

"Are all the bottles sealed with this same metal cap?" he said.

"All of them, sir."

"And what does it say on them?"

He handed the manager the glass bottle. On its top was written

"Alko", the name of the factory, and "Rajamäki", the town where it was situated.

"So that ends the mystery and explains why you are constantly being bombarded. I was looking for a spy; I've found a numbskull. I'd throw you in jail if the nation didn't need you so much."

The Ministry of Defence official left the factory with his minions following in his wake, leaving a contrite silence behind them.

42

Winter had December in its grip.

If in its early days it had been content to sprinkle the trees with snow, now their branches drooped down almost to the ground under heavy drifts, like weary soldiers lowering their arms. Winter had frozen the heart of the forest, turned tree trunks to stone, pine needles to shards of glass.

For the first time in his life, Simo was walking on a pure white sheet, with no animal tracks to read on the ground. But the Russians were also animals, and Simo had learned to hunt them. He studied their habits and the speed at which they moved, in order to anticipate their every move, as he would have done for any quarry.

Every kill cost him more than it would have a simple infantryman or gunner, because in order to be sure of a perfect shot, Simo had to observe his adversary for many minutes, until he understood him, until he had penetrated his skin and his brain, until he became him, and then killed him. A gunner fires into the distance. An infantryman often fires at random, or with a machine gun when the enemy is charging towards him. For a sniper, it is almost personal.

With every mission, Simo had improved his technique. He had learned that if a marksman does not hit his target with the first shot, he himself becomes a target. He had also acquired the habit of piling snow up in front of him under his rifle so that none flew up with the rush of air from the gun barrel, creating a treacherous little cloud that hung above it for far too long.

And again, even though his white snowsuit gave him perfect camouflage, it stood out perilously when he was in front of a tree trunk, whether it was striped like a silver birch, the beige-grey of spruce, or the red of pine bark when it catches the rays of the setting sun. So, as soon as he found a good shooting position, Simo created a little mound of snow behind him so that he could blend in with his surroundings.

At almost 150 metres from a makeshift Russian camp, Toivo had made sure the sun was behind him before taking out his field glasses. Fifteen Red Army soldiers round a fire looked as if they were right in front of him. Stretched out alongside him, Simo laid down two clips with five cartridges each. He already had another one attached to his rifle. Fifteen rounds, fifteen enemy soldiers.

"That's taking a big risk, don't you think?"

Simo's only response was to pile snow under his weapon and put a handful in his mouth.

"Alright then," Toivo conceded. "So the officer is on the right. The others have sub-machine guns. There's a bigger machine gun, but there doesn't seem to be anyone manning it. I can't see a marksman."

The spotter's role is to accompany the sniper and among other things to estimate the wind speed and the distance to the target. Simo had no real need for any of that as he was better than anyone at this kind of calculation. Toivo was useful for a very different reason: while Simo was completely focused on his target, on his own in a tunnel of concentration, his friend was keeping an eye on everything around them, because it takes a sniper to kill a sniper, and the Russians had excellent ones.

Timo swept the area in front of them with his field glasses, then studied the enemy unit once more.

"They're trying to start a fire," he whispered. "They look frozen stiff. The officer has moved away from the group. To the left. He's leaning against a pine. Fire whenever you are ready."

Simo loaded the first cartridge into the breech. Then he hesitated, intrigued by the officer's attitude and gestures. He held out his hand to Toivo, who passed him the field glasses.

In the two magnifying circles he saw the abhorred Ivan, the unjust invader, the bloodthirsty, monstrous aggressor sit on a rock and open a small notebook. In it was a sheet of paper he was now unfolding. A letter, perhaps … As if it had been made from the skin of its writer or still bore that person's smell, the officer kissed it twice before putting it away. Then he lowered his head and buried his face in his hands.

Simo handed back the field glasses. Toivo looked through them again at the group.

"It's almost night," Toivo said. "And we've already killed eleven of them today. What do you say we go back to camp?"

There is a difference between being able to kill and having to kill. And for every believer, accounts to be rendered some day or other. Simo turned away from his lines of sight. Day after day, with his humaneness and rectitude, Toivo justified the unshakeable friendship Simo had for him.

43

The previous night Colonel Talvela's troops had left by the light of the stars. On their cross-country skis, they hoped to travel more quickly than the Russians and arrive in time at Lake Tolva-järvi to await them there and, as far as they were able, block their passage.

With Talvela's men heading north, the front at Kollaa had lost a sizeable proportion of its forces. They could no longer wait to be attacked, but they had, if possible, to anticipate them. So every day, ten or so scouts were chosen and sent into the forest to watch the enemy. And every day, Simo stepped forward to be one of them. This became such a routine that, with Juutilainen's approval, he would leave before dawn with his *tarkkailija*,[20] some sugar cubes and biscuits in his pockets, and disappear before even the first soldiers were awake. He chose his spotter at random from among his brothers-in-arms – Toivo, Onni and Pietari – and at random the choice almost always fell on Toivo.

Their mission was to observe and report back, but whenever Simo had the opportunity he decapitated enemy officers, making orphans of the troops he saw in the distance. With nobody to force them on, it was rare for them not to turn tail.

Stalin had promised them an easy, short war against an adversary they would crush within a fortnight. This was a monumental strategic blunder, because the soldiers were being promised certain victory, and in the very first letters from the Red Army, they vowed to return home.

"*We will swallow Finland whole, and if I'm not among the first on the frontline, I'm not even sure I'll get the opportunity to fire a single shot."*

"It won't be long before I hold you in my arms again."

"I'll return with our victory."

"Two weeks, no longer. That's what they've promised us."

But a month later, as Christmas approached, the first doubts began to appear in the enemy lines. And it was because of these letters, these simple pieces of paper that weighed as heavy as lead in their hearts, that the Soviet soldiers found themselves paralysed at the moment of attack when they had to leave their trenches under deadly fire. How could they run towards death when they had sworn to return?

Whether they were convinced or forced to fight, aggressors or aggressed, the Soviet soldiers always fell into two groups. Those who embraced death in the same way as the Finnish soldiers who could be seen during the lengthy artillery bombardments waiting for the storm to pass by playing cards or writing their letters. And those who feared death, like the soldiers who shot themselves in the hand or the flesh of their thigh, hoping to be demobilised.

Simo found it easy to recognise the lost ones, the terrorised ones, the ones forced to fight, and sometimes he spared them. Did he really spare them, or was he simply trying not to burden his soul with more senseless deaths?

"So, how many?"

This inevitable question awaited him each time he returned to camp. No-one would have detected the slightest sense of pride in his reply.

"Eleven," Toivo said in his stead.

The others whistled. They applauded. But Simo remained stony-faced.

When he was on his mission as marksman, Simo slipped right up close to the enemy units. He came to know their camps better than his own. He spent more time close to his targets than to the companions he was protecting. And above all, he fired from a distance. In short, he was every day saved from any hand-to-hand fighting, from pure violence. At least he was spared that. But every time he came back, the number of deaths he had caused wounded him like a reproach.

"We lost about thirty men, but I'm sure we took down twice that many," boasted someone Simo had never seen before.

New men were arriving all the time. New career soldiers, new conscripts, reservists or Civic Guardsmen. A fresh batch each week to replace those stacked up in the black tent behind the first-aid station. They never altogether made up for the losses: Finland was already running short of soldiers, and the recruits were called up even before they finished school or the ink had dried on their enlistment forms. A rifle was thrust at them, a rifle someone else had already held.

"My name is …" the newcomer said, holding his hand out to Simo.

Simo refused to listen. There was no guarantee the lad would be alive the next day.

Onni arrived, out of breath. He had run through the whole camp, and was smiling as if the armistice had been declared.

"You're never going to believe me, Simo! Lapatossu is here!"

44

Every so often, a Russian plane flew over the Finnish lines on the Isthmus of Karelia, Lapland or the Kollaa front. It would drop a load that did not explode but burst open in the sky, releasing a sheaf of propaganda leaflets, printed on red, yellow or green paper so that they stood out in the snow. On them were slogans designed to undermine the morale of the Finnish troops.

"*You will lose this war. Surrender if you want to survive.*"

"*Rise up against your officers. You will be heroes in our land.*"

"*If you are here, that means we're taking care of your wives at home.*"

The Finnish soldiers had read the first of them out of curiosity. When they saw just how many leaflets there were, they collected the paper for other less political but more hygienic purposes.

Occasionally as they patrolled or were on scouting missions, the units came across cloth banners slung between two trees. On them were scrawled in their own language:

"*Lay down your arms here, put your hands up, and come and join us.*"

"*Is it worth dying to defend a government subservient to the imperialist West?*"

"*Helsinki has already fallen. Mannerheim is dead. Why go on?*"

So within the Winter War another battle was being fought, one of fake information and manipulation. To fight it, Finland had created a new unit: the Anti-Depression Brigade, also called the "Anti-Homesickness Brigade". It was headed by the Truth Officer. This officer travelled from frontline to frontline all over Finland, supplying the soldiers with the latest news from towns and cities, demystifying the rumours, chopping the head off the "It's said that …" and adding a few amusing anecdotes. No-one was astonished at this, because many of them knew this Truth Officer by another name: "Lapatossu", the clown star of cinema comedy who had won Finnish hearts for almost a decade.

No red nose or funny outsize shoes, but a lopsided, oblong face like a smiling potato, thick eyebrows that lent themselves well to grimaces, sparse hair scraped on the top of his skull, a kindly, open smile. A buffoon without any military training who no-one had forced to go to the front, but who was now making his three hundredth appearance.

Onni more or less dragged Toivo and Simo to the truck where, loudspeaker in hand, Lapatossu was haranguing a uniformed crowd of thousands.

"The Russians are promising to treat you well if you desert," he cried, "when they don't even look after their own wounded. Don't believe them! The Russians claim you can't win this war, when they start to tremble at the idea of leaving their trenches. Don't believe them! The Russians say that Helsinki has fallen, when it is still being defended. Don't believe them! They tell you Mannerheim is dead, but I promise you that from the headquarters in Mikkeli, our field marshal is directing this war day and night. He'll use his baton to crush every last Russian skull!"

"But they say there are ten times more of them than us!" Pietari shouted, anonymous in the crowd.

Without attempting to identify the heckler, Lapatossu burst out laughing. He dropped his hands to his round belly before responding:

"Oh yes, there are lots of them, I can guarantee that. And there'd have to be a lot more for them to … But wait … would you like some good stories about that?"

191

As delighted as kids at the fair, the earth- and bloodstained soldiers roared their approval.

"Rumour has it …" Lapatossu always began with this catchphrase. "Rumour has it that Stalin has gone as far as Crimea for conscripts. Do you know that in summer the temperature in Crimea is close to 30°C, and that in the harshest winters it rarely falls below zero? And do you know what remained of them when the train doors were opened in Lapland? Ice cubes! They were all dead, frozen in their summer kit! Whole carriages filled with Russian ice! Who would like one?"

Ever since death had become so familiar to them, the soldiers laughed at horror stories like this. They begged the clown to tell them another story, so he embarked on one more joke.

"Rumour has it … Rumour has it that the Soviet high command only has incomplete maps of Finland. Do you know they fired 7,000 shells at the same spot? They thought they were flattening a town, but in fact were aiming at a hamlet that had only one house, and a farmhouse with a red roof. And after 7,000 shells, do you know what is left of the hamlet? A house and a farm with a red roof! Are they shooting with their eyes closed?"

It was true that, however wounding his jokes were, Lapatossu never killed any Russians, but for a while he brought a pause in the war. He gave the men courage and hope, and the Anti-Depression Brigade bandaged souls as effectively as the Lotta nurses treated wounds.

They were all waiting for more stories, when Simo felt Juutilainen's hand on his shoulder.

"Follow me. The 4th and 5th need you."

*

The legionnaire poured two mugs of *viina*, drank the first and then the second, before filling it again and offering it to his soldier.

No long speech. Simply the facts. There were Russian snipers a few hundred metres from the frontline. They were good and accurate. Accurate enough to have killed three patrol commanders from the 4th Company, one of their N.C.O.s, and half a platoon from the 5th Company who had come to their aid, but had been forced to withdraw. Adding up to 20 men in total. Or rather subtracting. There were good, accurate Russian snipers, and the companies had no-one who could deal with them.

The Terror slipped the map of the Kollaa frontline and the forest concealing it into a transparent plastic folder. On it were red crosses where the surviving observers had marked the positions of the Red marksmen.

All Simo asked was when he should leave. Night had fallen on the camp, and Juutilainen told him that daybreak would be a good time.

*

At first light Simo left his tent. Toivo was already outside, rucksack on his back, biscuits and sugar cubes in a cloth bundle, an eager smile on his face. The first rays of the sun struck his hair, which shimmered in blond waves.

"Where are we going?"

Simo hugged his friend and told him that this time he would go alone.

45

A temperature of −30°C was already exceptional, but that day it had dropped to −40°. To locate the sniper more precisely than from the crosses drawn on the map, it was enough to find his victims.

Simo kneeled next to the N.C.O. the Russians had hit in this spot. His face frozen stiff as a statue, his skin chalky-white, only the black of his eyebrows and the yellow of his teeth in his open, twisted mouth stood out against the snow. This was where the Russian had shot him. Simo could do as much.

He crawled forward 20 metres, looking for the best firing position. Shielded by a rock, a clear view so that he could see everything, and flat ground behind him if he was forced to withdraw. The place found, he lay flat and waited.

He stared straight ahead at the top of a young spruce in the distance, at the same time taking everything in out of the corner of his eye. An hour went by. His heart slowed to the rhythm of his breathing. Until now the morning had been dark, with snowflakes stinging like iron filings, but finally the sun reappeared. Another hour went by, and Simo was dangerously close to the limits of his resistance. He felt his body loosen and a gentle warmth enfold him. As with the disturbing call of the sirens that led sailors onto the rocks, or the pleasant smell of bitter almonds that comes from cyanide, this feeling of well-being and warmth was deadly. The hand of Death had touched him on the shoulder, promising that all was well, that it would be even better as the hours went by, if he did not move. Behind him, the dead N.C.O.'s milky eyes stared at him, waiting for him.

Simo crawled backwards until he was hidden behind the rock and rubbed his body briskly until it responded. A little sugar, a little frozen bread that he had to soak in saliva to be able to chew, and Death sloped off. Taking up his position again, another hour went by.

The top of the spruce. The silence. The cold.

Then in the distance, a flash. The enemy sniper's gunsight had caught the sun just before the sky became overcast again. That did not matter: Simo had discovered where his target was. Two hundred and twenty-three metres. Because freezing cartridges are heavier, affecting the arc of their trajectory, Simo kept his ammunition in his trouser pocket under the snowsuit. He took the rounds out and loaded them into the magazine.

Several minutes went by.

After which, less experienced than his adversary and vanquished by the cold, the Russian stood up. The bullet hit him in the side of the head, even though Simo had aimed lower down.

There were still some hours of daylight left, and Simo looked for the next cross on the map open in front of him.

*

Simo reached the outskirts of the camp, leaving the cover of the trees and calling out the day's password. After warming himself and eating, he handed the map to Juutilainen, who was watching him silently. Two red crosses had been circled: two fewer Russian snipers. Many more crosses had been added, each of them showing the position of the bodies of Finnish soldiers to be recovered. A copy was traced and given to the lieutenants commanding the 4th and 5th companies so that one of their teams could go and find them at night. That way the Finns could continue proudly to say that the White Army never left anyone behind.

That might seem audacious or suicidal, or even ridiculous, but the respect the Finns showed for their dead was enough to keep them from the abyss. At the bottom of it, madness lay in wait, and monsters howled for them to come and join them. And those monsters had their own faces. The soldiers were only one step away from plunging into the void. Each day they came a little closer; and each day the irrepressible desire to go over the edge grew. It was as if they were enchanted. To kill would become a habit, and with their souls finally condemned, anything would be permitted.

As night fell, the camp took precautions. It was no surprise when the Russian artillery began its hammering, and Simo slept a while. There were more crosses on the map.

*

In the other camp, they whispered about the ghost. That was what some of the Russians called him; others had different names. There was even more talk of him that night as they stood in the interminable lines for food. Two of their best snipers had been shot in one day.

"Borodin confided in me," one of the soldiers said. "They call him the White Death."

The whisper spread along the line like a shiver through a body. *Belaya Smert … Belaya Smert …*

"He made a unit of 200 men retreat all by himself," another soldier said. "A bullet in the heart of the very first soldier. Then another in the heart of the next one. Another and another. By the eighth, unable to tell where death was coming from, the whole unit turned back."

"They say six of ours were found around a fire. All six of them killed before any of them had time to pick up their weapon."

"They say he lives in the trees and leaps from branch to branch. That's why no-one can ever spot him."

The poisonous rumour, growing each time it was repeated, spread from campfire to campfire, from tent to tent, until eventually it reached that of Grigori Shtern, the colonel now commanding the Soviet 8th Army.

*

Shtern had the square face, plump cheeks and amiable look of a well-fed trader. But nobody in the army was fooled by his affable appearance, and when he thumped his fist on the table, his officers turned pale.

"You don't kill a rumour, still less a ghost," he snarled. "I want this *Belaya Smert* nailed to a tree, slaughtered like a pig. With his guts round his feet, everyone will see he is nothing more than a man."

"If he is tracking down our snipers, perhaps we should change their positions?"

The colonel thought about it. The idea was simple, obvious and appealing, but Shtern was not so concerned about protecting his marksmen as wanting to see the ghost's white sheet gashed by a thousand holes.

He had a different idea, one that amounted to using a sledge-hammer to crack a nut.

46

Simo never knew he had fired at a dead body.

In this part of the forest, the level ground came suddenly to an end, leaving only a jumble of flat granite boulders among which he found a hollow big enough for him to lie flat.

A hundred metres away, the Russian was more or less on a spot marked by a cross on Simo's map. He was standing motionless as every marksman should, hidden behind the broad trunk of a pine tree, his long rifle barrel covered in white gauze resting on a branch to avoid fatigue. When the bullet struck him in the middle of the chest, he did not budge an inch. The projectile did not even go through his frozen body.

Simo had hit his target, but in doing so had revealed his own position. And the sledgehammer descended on the nut. Dark silhouettes began to move everywhere. With a terrible roar, a barrage of mortar bombs rose into the sky. The trap was closing around him. Concealed under white camouflage, five rapid-fire anti-tank rifles spat continuously in his direction.

Simo's stone refuge became a tomb as the shells hit the granite, shattered it into a thousand deadly fragments. All he could do was to flee. He ran from the rocky outcrop into the heart of the forest, bullets whistling round his head, ricocheting off rocks with a loud hissing noise, or tearing chunks off trees in a cloud of sawdust that smelled of burnt wood. In front of him, an explosion uprooted a tree, which cracked mournfully as it toppled. The tangled earth-covered roots formed what looked like a big crown. Simo gathered his breath under it for a moment, fists clenched, eyes closed. His parents' farm. His forest. Rautjärvi, his village. Toivo and the others ...

Today, as at every second since the start of this war, he should have died. His parents' farm. His forest. Rautjärvi, his village. Toivo and the others ... With them, or for them, he found the courage to take a leap onwards. He had gone a few metres when the blast from a shell lifted him in the air and pounded him against a tree. His rucksack softened the blow, but he blacked out for a moment. When he came to, he was face down in the snow. All around him, the detonations sent earth and a shower of snow into the sky. Simo plunged through this protective curtain and disappeared.

*

The Russian soldiers searched the forest for almost an hour.

"No-one can survive that," their officer swore at them incredulously.

Seeing dark clouds looming in his future if he returned to camp empty-handed, without a corpse to present, the officer shouted:

"Carry on searching! Find him, for fuck's sake!"

They had attacked a man on his own with mortars and anti-tank rifles. They had attacked a man on his own with the same firepower as if they were facing a whole army unit, and yet around them found only a wounded forest, its trees splintered by their assault.

"*Belaya Smert ...*" the soldiers whispered to one another.

*

The noise of the storm unleashed on Simo had been heard as far away as the Finnish camp. Juutilainen had laughed, repeating to everyone: "Listen to the Russkis applauding Simo!"

Now, as if confronted by an incomprehensible phenomenon, Toivo was searching in vain for the slightest tear, the slightest hole in his friend's snowsuit.

"They tried their best to kill you," an astonished Onni said, "but you look as though you're returning from a stroll."

"It seems Death doesn't want anything to do with you," Toivo said.

"No, I think Death is happy with things the way they are. She will never have such a willing collaborator, or such a rich harvest. Why get rid of her best employee? Lapatossu will make a good story out of Simo and Death hand in hand!"

Simo still had his rucksack on his back. Onni helped him ease it off, while Toivo bustled him into their tent. They could hardly contain their excitement to tell him the day's good news. This didn't happen often, so they had to make the most of it.

"Alright, you tell him!" Onni said impatiently.

Many of the men from the Kollaa front had been despatched to Operation Talvela, and messengers had brought back news of their exploits 24 hours later. Toivo added two more logs to the stove and filled their mugs with coffee before sitting down.

"The Talvela soldiers were quartered ten kilometres upstream from Lake Tolvajärvi, convinced the Russians were still a whole day's march away. So they made a soup. A soup with sausage, the sort we're so good at making, heavy and tasty. No sooner was it ready than a sentinel came running. He was in a panic because four Russian reconnaissance patrols were only a few hundred metres off."

"As you can imagine, none of the Finnish soldiers was prepared," Onni said, thinking the story was being told too slowly. "So Colonel Talvela gave the order to abandon the camp and withdraw to the shelter of a nearby forest. By the time they had gathered all their gear and left they could already see the first Russian infantry. In the chaos, the Ivans could have easily shot our men in the back. But when they came upon the camp deserted only a few minutes earlier, the soup's aroma filled their nostrils as if a spell had been cast on them."

"And nothing else mattered to them," Toivo butted in, keen to provide the conclusion. "They threw down their packs and weapons and rushed on the mess tins. They even fought one another, they were so starving. They didn't notice that Talvela had surrounded them. Four hundred lads. All killed. Yeah, all of them. For a bowl of soup ..."

*

In the course of the evening, Pietari joined them in the tent. He did not even greet them. He sat apart from the others on the edge of one of the bunks lined with straw and leaves. Simo looked enquiringly at Toivo.

"He's received a letter," Toivo said simply.

Pietari, with the jet-black hair almost unknown in Finland, stern features as if hewn from badly chiselled stone, sat with a distraught expression, eyes moist with tears.

He was clutching a letter that was crumpled from being read so often.

Simo sat next to him, their thighs rubbing together.

"My little brother Viktor is on the Mannerheim Line," Pietari confessed with a sob.

He held out the clumsily written letter he was weeping over. Simo read it slowly. Pietari turned and fell into his arms.

Simo thought his day had been dreadful. But at that moment he realised that in war the worst thing was not to die. In war, the fear of dying is never as bad as the fear of seeing one's loved ones perish.

47

Isthmus of Karelia, Mannerheim Line

No-one could say Viktor Koskinen was not courageous, pig-headedly so, but he was a dreadful soldier. He often missed his targets – purposely or not, nobody could read inside his head – he struggled to understand military orders and was often embarrassed when presented with a map.

Viktor was the only survivor from his original company, decimated on the first day of the war. The new one he joined lost so many men in such a short time it was disbanded and its soldiers redistributed according to need. So he found himself in a new "new company" which a few days later suffered from the disastrous combination of a heavy blizzard, terrible organisation and faulty radio communications. As a result, the company became separated, and then so lost they began shooting at one another in a slaughter that lasted an entire night. Sixty-two dead. But yet again no bullet claimed Viktor.

And so, despite being such a useless soldier, the Koskinen family's youngest boy enjoyed extraordinary good luck. Two new incidents reinforced his legend, which would never be mentioned in any history book.

The first was the mine he stepped on, whose mechanism refused to function. That night, to celebrate his lucky star, for the first time in his life Viktor got drunk and spewed his guts up under a magnificent clear sky. Then, one day when they became engaged in hand-to-hand combat, there was the Russian who jumped into his trench and pressed the rifle to Viktor's forehead, finger on the trigger, only to change his mind, fall on his knees with his hands in the air and beg Viktor to take him prisoner.

As a result of this series of miracles, the others began to touch his shoulder or back whenever they met him. Rabbit's foot? Four-leafed clover? On the Mannerheim Line, they liked nothing better than to rub Viktor's uniform or pat his skull twice.

They even swore that Viktor Koskinen could have sat at a table, fill a six-gun with five bullets, spin the drum, press the revolver to his temple and pull the trigger – without anything happening. He could have repeated the gesture a thousand times and despite the odds the hammer would strike the only empty chamber. Yes, Viktor was so lucky that would not have surprised anybody. But even though they never played Russian roulette, the effect the war had on him was not dissimilar. His brain was scrambled, a mass of entangled nerves full of horrors and unbearable images, smells and sounds, cries and sobs. He found it impossible to sleep, and when his eyes occasionally closed from exhaustion he would wake up screaming, chasing the screams he heard in his nightmares. From time to time he was even seen talking to his brother Pietari as he sat in front of a tree or boulder.

For all these reasons, aware that Viktor's sanity was fracturing, the doctor at the rearguard base had him enlisted on a less stressful mission 200 kilometres from the Mannerheim Line, before his mental defences could give way and he sank into madness.

"What mission?" Viktor had said.

"There are children to be collected and escorted," the doctor told him. "From Viipuri to Turku, passing through Helsinki, Kotka and Porvoo. And we need men to guard them."

"But who are these kids? And where are they being sent?"

"I've no idea. All I know is that you'll be away from the Line for a few days."

This left Viktor with a painfully guilty sensation, like a prisoner facing a firing squad who is pardoned at the last second but abandons his companions facing the cocked rifles.

*

As the Russian bombers approached Helsinki, the air-raid sirens rent the sky as though all of Finland were howling with terror. None of the big cities was safe, and whereas the adults resigned themselves to going to ground in the basements of houses that had been spared or in underground shelters, afraid they might die at any moment, their stomachs in knots, fear clinging to their souls, they could not accept exposing their little ones to the same ordeal.

All over the country, the children had become a problem, because, in war, the fear of dying is never as bad as seeing one's loved ones perish.

Unconditional love had turned into an unbearable mental burden. The question was no longer how to protect one's children, but how to separate from them. To guarantee the new generation a future, many families decided they must leave. And Sweden, which had refused to involve itself militarily in the conflict devastating its Finnish neighbour, did offer to receive its sons and daughters.

*

For three days and nights Viktor and 300 other men were tasked with travelling from city to city to put these children on board trains. Often they would cling fast to their parents, desperate not to be parted from them, and the soldiers had forcibly to separate them, like tearing a paper heart in two.

From the platform of the last railway station before Turku, a defaced, partly destroyed hospital was visible. The wing containing supplies had been blown up, and thousands of sheets and white coats had been flung into the air. They came to rest on the branches of pine trees as if heralding some ceremony or other.

The flimsy material billowed in the breeze.

The train began to pull out. Only a few of the strongest or saddest of the children managed to find room at the windows, press their faces up against them, and retain one final image in their memory. Hands raised in farewell, the ranks of mothers smiled, inconsolable.

From the corridor inside the carriages, Viktor reluctantly had to shout to restore order, and the tiny dresses and pairs of trousers obeyed and returned to their seats. Tears were held back behind fingers or beneath pullovers, eyes sought friendship from someone new, a comrade to give them courage. A hand plucked at Viktor's uniform.

"Why are they abandoning us?"

He sat opposite the child, felt in his pocket for a biscuit, and broke it in two.

Viktor thought: "They're not abandoning you, they're saving you. Three million Finns can't leave their country, so they're protecting what's most precious to them, because if I'm honest, not everyone is going to survive." But obviously he could not tell the boy the truth; the biscuit was better than a lie.

"Here, half for you and half for me."

Instinctively, the boy smiled as he took his share from the hand held out to him. His half-whispered "thank you" pierced the heart of a man no bullet had ever managed to graze.

*

Hundreds of trains and lorries converged on the port of Turku where the *Arcturus* was moored. Eighty-eight metres long, and so white it melded with the horizon, the presence of the ship was betrayed only by the black smoke pouring from the huge funnel amidships.

Viktor was carrying the young boy from the train under his arm, the boy's fingers digging into his skin in their anguish. Alongside him, all round him, 80,000 others made up the biggest evacuation of children in the world. An ocean of bewildered blond heads, eyes brimming with tears. All of them clad in white like the soldiers, camouflaged to avoid being spotted from the sky. Around their necks, a brown cardboard label hung from a cloth ribbon with their name and age written on it. Whether three or thirteen, they felt the same fear at the thought of being sent to a strange country, into strange houses and the arms of strangers, having to deal with a strange language.

"You see that long ladder running up the side of the ship?" Viktor said, trying to reassure the boy. "That's where you have to climb. And then you'll cross the Baltic Sea to Sweden."

"When will I come back?"

"Let me take care of the Russians. As soon as we've sent them packing, you'll be able to return. I promise."

They heard a young girl sobbing, alone in her white dress and shiny shoes, hair unkempt, nose streaming.

"I think she could really do with a friend like you," Viktor said, depositing the boy on the ground.

The boy went over to her, read her name on the label, and told her his. By the time he turned round again, the soldier had gone. But the instant he took the little girl's hand, he grew up, became almost adult.

"Stay with me, alright?" he told her. "You see that long ladder running up the side of the ship?"

*

When Viktor rejoined the other men in the escort company, they had uncorked several bottles of *viina* and were drinking it in secret inside a hangar.

"O.K., shall we be off?" Viktor said impatiently.

"Don't you want to see the *Arcturus* set sail?"

"No, I don't. I'll wait for you at the trucks."

Finland had already been forced to separate from its soldiers and Lottas. Now that Christmas, usually devoted to children, was fast approaching, it was losing them too.

The evacuation had lasted seven days. The doctor hoped that during this break Viktor had been able to get some rest and regain some emotional stability. But in the lorries taking the soldiers back to the front, Viktor's heart had been replaced by a shattered old pump that no longer beat for anyone.

"So? How were your holidays?" they greeted him sarcastically on the Mannerheim Line.

Viktor didn't reply. He took his share of munitions, slung his rifle over his shoulder, and jumped down into the trench. His thoughts turned to his big brother Pietari, the only person in the world who really mattered to him. The only one keeping him going.

48

December 21, Kollaa front, twenty-second day of the conflict

It was a duel between snipers, concealed by the start of a snow-storm. They had both fired once at each other; both had somehow missed. The next shot was very likely to be fatal for one of them if they did not change position. Simo, however, trusted his skill, and checked his lines of sight, his cheek almost touching the stock of his rifle as it lay on the snow. The Russian pressed his eye to his gun sight, which meant he raised his head a few centimetres higher than the Finn's. That was enough.

The gunshot resounded through an impassive forest that no longer paid any heed to mankind.

*

When he returned to camp and found that another soldier had taken over his bunk, Simo realised there had been changes while he was gone, changes that had left Toivo sulking. He pointed his chin to the Terror's tent. In front of it, Juutilainen was in a battered arm-chair, smoking a cigarette. The chair, its stuffing sticking out of the arms in little tufts, had been stolen from a nearby abandoned farm. Next to him, Karlsson was making coffee as black as the legionnaire was drunk, hoping to keep him awake to the end of the day.

"Simo Häyhä! I've had you moved," Juutilainen informed him. "No more lice or foul smells for you. You're sleeping in my tent now, with the *Sissi* commanders. No more trenches or guard duty for you either. You're under my orders and those of the other company lieutenants for autonomous missions."

His father's words came back to Simo. "Up front you get slapped. At the back, kicks up the arse. Stay in the middle and keep your mouth shut. That doesn't make you a coward, but a survivor." Discreet and humble, Simo had never sought to stand out, but his exceptional talent as a sniper had done it for him. He was called upon by company after company, regiment after regiment.

His mind as foggy as an early morning in England, Juutilainen searched all round him on the ground before he discovered the plump folder under his own backside. He began rummaging in it. Karlsson tapped the handle of his knife against the frozen lump of sugar and served the coffee, with an extra mug for the young soldier.

"It seems the Russians call you the White Death," Karlsson told him. "For the enemy to give you a nickname is almost like a medal, you know."

Simo shrugged. A medal for being a good shot, a medal as a killer: he wondered who he could boast to about that.

"Don't think you're a hero, little Simo," Juutilainen thought it necessary to add. "Take this: new maps, new crosses. It's all in there."

Simo took the folder and studied his new hunting grounds. Then, after casting a glance towards his old tent, where his friends offered him just enough comfort for him not to sink into the abyss, he reluctantly entered Juutilainen's tent, unloaded his pack and settled in.

"Well … it's not his endless chatter that's going to buzz round my skull," the Terror said.

"I think it's just that he's exhausted," Karlsson said. "You'd be a poor strategist if you didn't use someone as valuable as him, but equally it would be a mistake to put him under too much pressure."

"That depends on how you look at it," the Terror belched. He drank a mouthful of disgusting coffee, stained the snow with the rest, and refilled his mug with *viina*.

"Yeah," he went on. "Sometimes pressure is good. It converts coal into diamonds."

*

Simo told everyone that he did not count his kills. Some said it was already a hundred Russians with his precision rifle alone. Others claimed he had killed as many with his sub-machine gun: almost 200 men to his name, in 20 or so days. No-one knew the exact total. But Simo did: during his sleepless nights, the spectres of every one of them, their icy breath, came back to him in shudders. Yet each morning, without fail, Simo left the camp to go to add more, ghosts who would haunt his spirit further still.

The different companies would leave their maps outside Juutilainen's tent, and he passed them to Simo. Two snipers here. An observation unit there. More snipers in different positions. Two red crosses similar to those on the trunks of trees to be felled, destined to meet the White Death. Simo killed as often as he was asked to. He did so without anger or hatred, for his country, simply because he had to, and because everyone did so.

And every evening after returning to the camp he went to see his friends. He was always fearful there might be one fewer, because on the other side of the frontline the Russians also killed as many soldiers as they had to, in order, they were told, to protect their own country.

Whenever Simo prayed, he demanded only one thing of heaven. That every evening, when he entered their tent, the count would be the same: Onni, Pietari and Toivo.

49

Two kilometres from the Kollaa frontline there was a surveillance post, close to a granite outcrop. All around it were waves of "snake pines", their gnarled trunks rising into the air a metre at most before plunging down again into the earth, to reappear further on. Sometimes this happened two or three times, making the tree look like a coiling snake. Because of this the surveillance post soon became known as the Snake Post.

There was no dense forest or marshes in front of it, only open ground that could be a way through for the Soviet Army. As a result, the spot was protected as the threat demanded: a double line of trenches, barbed wire, some concrete blocks, three heavy machine guns, and in front of them a broad minefield.

Despite being unconcerned by his losses, after seeing his soldiers repeatedly mown down or blown into the air, Colonel Shtern had decided to place a sniper there. And he had killed twice before the sun was properly in the sky.

Simo had left camp before first light on another mission. Juuti-lainen had therefore decided to send his second-best marksman to resolve the situation. Later that morning, a team had brought him back on a medical sled, a bullet in his head. An hour later, and probably on the exact same sled, a second, equally dead marksman was recovered.

Karlsson refused to send out a third soldier, preferring to await Simo's return. For once Juutilainen did not see this as a sign of weakness. He had lost two good marksmen. He still had a few others, but unlike the Russians, who had only to put new recruits in the same helmets, Finland had been short of men from the start of the war, and they became more precious as their numbers dwindled.

"Send two spotters," the legionnaire ordered. "When that *Ryssä* is a cross on a map, I'll know who to send, and I don't rate the man's chances."

*

The two chosen spotters caught up with the soldiers at Snake Post. They crouched down to untie their cross-country skis, then crawled and dropped into the trench.

"What the fuck are you doing here?" came the greeting.

"The Terror's orders," Pietari told them.

"Whatever you do, don't raise your heads! The *Ryssä* is 300 metres away at least, just beyond the minefield, and he never misses. We'll need heavy artillery to get him, not our rifles. That's what we told the messenger. Don't you receive our reports?"

"Don't take it out on us," Toivo protested. "Do you really think we're glad to be here? We've simply been asked to pinpoint his position for Simo."

The River Kollaa ran in front of the surveillance post. Too wide to be crossed on foot even in summer, its 30 kilometres of meanders narrowed in several places so that you could leap across its narrow bends. In winter, it made more sense to walk across where the ice was thickest.

"Can you see the river? Follow it to the dark wood. See those pines with red bark at the edge? He's been somewhere there since this morning."

"That's not very precise," Pietari said.

"We're here to correct that," Toivo reassured him.

Despite their obvious enthusiasm, the soldiers from Snake Post wanted to be certain it was worth the risk.

"Are you sure? Because we can perfectly well stay in the trench, nibble a few biscuits until nightfall, and say we didn't see anything."

Both Toivo and Pietari knew this was their chance to help Simo. Nothing else mattered. They made no reply to the soldiers' suggestion.

"*Perkele!* Alright, follow us."

*

Whenever Simo prayed, he demanded only one thing of heaven. That every evening, when he entered their tent, the count would be the same: Onni the husband, Pietari the big brother, and Toivo, his lifelong friend. But that evening he came across Leena, because one of them was no longer there. And it was she who gave them the courage they needed. She took their hands one by one and forced them to get up.

Outside, the cold had made of the snow a sheet of ice, which, like an empty canvas, reflected the spectral glow of the Northern Lights. The sky was lit by green curtains swirling in slow motion, merging with the countless twinkling stars in the heavenly canopy.

Above their little cortège, Tuonela, the land of the dead, was opening its gates.

The crunch of their heavy footsteps on the green-tinged white snow seemed to be the only noise that existed. With Leena at their head, they walked to the field hospital on the frontline.

Toivo was lying there on blood-soaked sheets. His eyes were closed, and there was a black hole in the middle of his chest. Around him, three friends and his love, fists clenched.

At both ends of the tent, two wood stoves provided a warmth that lifted the temperature a little above freezing, but was enough to give the impression of dying of heat. Leena slipped her slender fingers under the back of Toivo's uniform to feel the small Finnish-blue square of cloth she had sewn there. Then, choking back her tears, she turned to Simo.

"The doctor authorised me to keep him here so that you could

see him one last time. But he can't stay much longer. The heat …
his body will …"

Simo raised the edges of the sheet and softly, sadly wrapped
them round his friend. He put one arm under his legs, the other
beneath his shoulders, and lifted him in one smooth movement.
Behind the field hospital stood the black tent where the dead
bodies were laid. Many of the soldiers could not bear to look at
it. Despite regular repatriations, the war devoured so many that
the orderlies were obliged to make a stack of the bodies. Faced
with more than 500 sightless soldiers, Simo lacked the courage to
add Toivo's body to the pile.

Instead, he propped him against a tree. As nobody had as
yet dared to do so, he snapped Toivo's dog tag in two and kept
half in the inside left pocket of his jacket. Then he knelt down
and prayed. Prayed until he began to tremble.

"Come on, please," Onni whispered. "You'll freeze to death."

From the way Simo looked at him, Onni understood he had
made him the most sensible and simple proposition imaginable.
To stay there and freeze to death. The others almost had to carry
him away.

*

Simo found Juutilainen slumped over his table, empty mug by his
feet on the floor strewn with branches. By the light of a guttering
candle, he read the start of the letter which had meant the legionnaire had needed to get even more drunk than usual:

"*Dear madam, it is my sad duty to inform you of the death of
your son. I had the honour of fighting alongside him, and am proud
to have been his officer …*"

"He had never written to any parents before," came the voice
of Karlsson, invisible at the back of the tent.

And he would never do so again throughout the war.

The following morning, robbed of Toivo's light, all the soldiers of the 6th Company would shine less brightly. Simo sat on the edge of his bunk. He should have cried out, he should have sobbed, but the grief and pain were so great he did not even move. He barely breathed.

Karlsson concluded that, like a lot of men before him, Simo had simply lost his reason. But Karlsson was not inside Simo's head.

In his head, the White Death was going over his movements.

Load. Aim. Fire.

Load. Aim. Fire.

Load. Aim. Fire.

The Winter War no longer existed. Nor did Finland. Or the Soviet Union. There was only one thing left: him and the Red sniper.

*

Simo had dozed off. Or rather, his body had succumbed to exhaustion. When he woke up, his rifle was not where it should have been, and the ammunition had gone from his bag. Leaping up, he threw open the tent flap and discovered there was a howling storm outside. All the campfires had been blown out, and snow had filled the deserted trenches. Beyond the noise of the raging wind, there was no sound of artillery. Up against this wild weather even the Russians had stayed silent.

"Is this what you're looking for?" Karlsson asked him. He had a rifle in his hands.

Simo took a step forward and reached for it. Karlsson did not move.

"I know what you want to do. And I'm ready to go with you. I'll be your spotter. You'll be in charge. Just you and me. I promise. But not today. Today, winter is stronger."

*

From the 6th Company's tents, they could see Juutilainen's, perched slightly higher than the rest. In front of the legionnaire's tent was a big rock. On it sat Simo, wrapped in his white snowsuit and a heavy coat. His icy eyes were staring at the horizon. Snowflakes settled on his shoulders. Within a few hours he would disappear entirely. "He's waiting for the storm to end," Onni said.

"We should make him come in, shouldn't we?" a worried Pietari said.

"No doubt. But I'm not going to risk it."

Simo had wiped the camp from his field of vision. There was nothing more than a straight line between the barrel of his rifle and the heart of the forest. The fox came to sit beside him. Its fur rubbed against him; he was bigger than Simo. Slowly, its magnificent long black fiery tail wrapped itself completely round him. The animal lowered its warm muzzle to his ear.

"Soon," the fox murmured. "Soon."

50

There was a huge row when the cemetery was discovered. In the middle of a marshy area a kilometre from the rear base on the Kollaa front, members of the 4th Company stumbled upon a row of a hundred deep pits, in each of which ten bodies could have been buried. Yet none of these graves should have existed: the Finnish high command had sworn that every soldier killed at the front would be returned to their village, to their doorstep, into the arms of their family. Not left there in the middle of nowhere, in a marsh, piled one on top of another in a jumble of guts, to the sound of a collective funeral oration muttered through the chattering teeth of a freezing chaplain.

In General Hägglund's tent, Colonel Teittinen relayed the men's anger, which had to be quelled before it spread too far.

"They can't be taken to task for what is our strength: their loyalty to our country, our land and their brothers-in-arms. Every child of Finland must be returned to his family."

"No, they certainly can't be taken to task," the general conceded, aware that this makeshift cemetery had been a terrible mistake.

As a result of this brief conversation, the transfer of the dead bodies to the field hospital 20 kilometres behind the frontline was accelerated. There they would be classified by region, then by village, and returned to their families.

The medical bus transporting the bodies was not very large and so had to make many return journeys. It was decided that the Lottas should accompany them. Leena was the first to apply for the task, using the back of a companion to rest the form on. For an entire night and a day, she and the others loaded up the bodies.

On the final journey, Leena pointed to a soldier propped against a tree some distance from the black tent.

"He's the last," she said.

"There'll be more tomorrow," the doctor said.

"Then he's the last today."

With that, she climbed on board the bus, not once taking her eyes off Toivo.

*

The field hospital was in fact a requisitioned school. It was further from the frontline, sheltered from the fighting without being entirely safe. The medics had pushed the desks and chairs aside to create operating theatres. Old maps on the walls showed the contours of Finland and the borders over which two countries were now at each other's throats. In the centre of the building stood a big hall where the children could play if the weather was bad and the playground deserted. All that remained of the children was the distant echo of their laughter and the drawings they had painted that were stuck to the windows. Now the centre of the hall was filled with a mound of dead bodies that almost reached the high ceiling. Infinitely small alongside death, Leena peered up to see the summit.

"The bus is about to leave, sweetheart," another Lotta warned her. She was as round as Leena was slender, as rosy as Leena was pale, and as cheerful as Leena was miserable. "You mustn't miss it."

"Can I stay? There's a soldier I'd like to make sure is sent home to the right place. To Rautjärvi. His friends asked me to."

The Lotta dropped her fist to her hip, making the outline of a jolly teapot. She was moved by the young girl's white lie.

"Well … if it's for his friends. But I'm sorry, you'll have to wait. The triage is the last thing that's done, before they are put in a coffin. First we have to let the bodies thaw. Look, some are stuck to one another. We also have to be able to bend their limbs to strip off their uniforms. We know that at the front there's a shortage of weapons and munitions, so the least we do is give them whole uniforms. And before they go into their coffin, they have to be made presentable. For their families. We have to find civilian clothes for the ones in uniform, conceal the wounds with bandages, stuff newspaper down the trousers and jackets so that it's not so obvious there are missing limbs. All that takes time."

All this had become a sorrowful habit for her.

"If I miss the bus, can I sleep here?" Leena said. "Just here, I won't take up any room."

As she brought her knees up to her chin to show how small she could make herself, four Lottas came in to install wood stoves in the corners to create some warmth.

"You're out on your feet, sweetheart. But you won't be able to stay here. In less than an hour … How shall I put it politely? The cold stifles the smells, but in an hour it will be so unbearable you'll be sick. Come on, up above there's a classroom we've turned into a dormitory. And I promise to keep an eye on your soldier. I know which one he is because you can't take your eyes off him."

"Thank you …" Leena stammered. "I don't even know your name."

The Lotta looked up in the air seeking inspiration, as if she had to scour her memory for her name.

"Here or at the front our days are numbered, so I decided to change my identity whenever anyone asks me. As if I had several lives. So for you, I'll be … I'll be Greta. Like Greta Garbo. She's an American actress, but she comes from Sweden. You see, anything's possible!"

Who could have imagined that two young women, in the midst of a particularly bloody war, only centimetres away from a thousand dead bodies, could laugh so heartily.

"Well then, hello Greta. I'm Leena."

*

A bombardment flattened the field hospital. From the ashes of its ruins grew black roses, their thorns so sharp they tore at her thighs as she passed by. Even her blood was black. Her father appeared and took her in his arms for her to shelter and weep. He said to her softly: "Your soldier has gone ... Your soldier has gone ..."

"Hey," Greta repeated more loudly. "Wake up. Your soldier has gone."

Leena got up with a start, a lock of hair sticking up and the imprint of the folds of the blanket she had used as a pillow lining her cheek. Even so, her loving concern made her look very pretty.

"Everything is fine," Greta promised. "The bodies left on the train this morning. And I checked the name of his village on the coffin. It's Rautjärvi, isn't it?"

"How long have I been asleep?" Leena fretted, rubbing her face.

"Fourteen hours! You almost hibernated!"

Leena huddled up in the corner of her bed. She was preoccupied with a small square of Finnish-blue cloth.

"What's wrong, sweetheart?"

"His uniform jacket. I wanted to recover something from it ..."

"Oh, I'm sorry," Greta apologised. "All the clothes have been sent to the menders. They're in the neighbouring village. It's not very far, but trying to find one jacket among thousands of items of clothing ..."

Regretfully, Leena admitted defeat. She had many other treasures to keep for herself. The memory of Toivo's smell, the touch of his skin, his tone of voice, his smile, his gaze, his promises. All of that was far more valuable than a square of cloth.

After a while, Greta gave her a black coffee. The hall doors had been closed and the windows opened to let the stench out. They sat outside and drank in a leisurely way, snow halfway up their legs.

"An ambulance is leaving for Kollaa this morning. It seems yesterday's fighting was even more intense than usual. They're sending surgeons there. But there's nothing forcing you to leave, Leena. There's plenty of work here, and I get the feeling you have suffered a lot at the front. I can arrange it, I know the doctor well. I mean, I know him really well … He can't refuse me anything."

Leena took her in her arms. Faces pressed together, they sat huddled in the snow.

"Do you know the legend of Lotta Svärd?" Leena whispered.

"Yes … of course. When her soldier love is killed in a war, Lotta stays on to care for the others, risking her own life."

"So you know what I must do."

Friendships are formed more strongly and more quickly in times of fever, exhaustion, fear and violence. Greta gently pulled away from their embrace.

"We don't know each other very well, but do you think it's stupid if I tell you I'll miss you?"

*

Here, a school had been turned into a hospital. One of its classrooms had become a dormitory. Elsewhere, at Kemijärvi in Lapland, a cinema had been turned into a stable, and the white screen was no longer exactly that. In Helsinki, the Hotel Kamp functioned as an international press centre, while in Turku a radio communications command post had been set up in a restaurant whose black-and-white chequerboard floor and neon lighting recalled the American roadside diners seen in foreign magazines. Nothing had retained its original usage; each building, but also each gesture, each thought was now dedicated to the Winter War. No surprise then that in the village close to the principal medical post the menders had been installed in the tiny church where the benches had been stacked up on the sides of the nave.

Bathed in the strange sunlight filtering through the stained glass, heads bowed over their work, the menders sewed up tears made by bombs, or holes made by bullets. They patched up death by almost getting rid of it for the next soldiers who would wear the uniforms.

Sitting in a circle, they reached behind them to pick up a jacket, shirt or a pair of military trousers, searching in the material for what the bodies had suffered.

On the table one of them spread out a white cotton camouflage suit covered with a black bloodstain. One sleeve and leg were missing, and the whole of the right side was scorched.

"This one must have trodden on a mine," she said. "Nothing can be done with it."

Another held up a shirt, the back of which had a regular line of small holes all the way up. They had already seen a hundred, perhaps even a thousand of these by now, and could all recognise a burst of machine-gun fire.

Her neighbour picked up a jacket with a single hole in the chest. It was repaired in a few minutes and thrown onto another pile of clothes ready to be sent to the huge steel vats and washed for many hours in boiling water. Occasionally, once the garment was clean again, one of the women slipped a poem at random into one of the jacket or trouser pockets, hoping to offer a little warmth to the person reading it. Others put in a photo. A pretty face smiling at you. Sometimes, when these simple gestures were discovered deep in a pocket, deep in a trench, they could move a soldier to tears.

The jacket with a hole in the chest whirled round the boiler.

His body repatriated, his uniform soon to be worn by somebody else, nothing now remained of Toivo on the Kollaa front.

51

Leena almost jumped down from the ambulance and ran to the 6th Company's tents. She did not even say goodbye to the two surgeons she had made the journey with, who looked at one another in surprise. The storm had petered out soon after dawn, and the sun was brushing the tops of the trees, colouring the forest with flaming red and orange tints.

Leena had watched over Toivo and made sure his body was returned to the village of Rautjärvi. That would in no way lessen his friends' pain, but certain things have to be done for peace of mind, for honour, out of respect or love.

The only person she found at the tents was Pulkki, who was scraping the bottom of a mess tin and finishing the morning's hot tea. The messenger boy did not belong to any specific unit, but was used by the different companies as the need arose, and pilfered food wherever he could.

"They're not here," he said, still chewing. "Went on their thieving patrols with Juutilainen."

"What about Simo?" Leena said.

*

An hour after daybreak, Simo had watched the last snowflake of the storm spiral away before melting above the campfire's feeble flames.

He had let his company leave without him. He had not said a word to the others since Toivo's death. As they passed by him, Pietari and Onni each put a hand on his shoulder, but neither could be sure he had even noticed.

Left on his own, Simo put his mess tin down without even touching the food, knowing Pulkki would make short work of it. Then he spread ashes all along the barrel of his rifle and buttoned his white snowsuit to the top. Bound to the young sniper by a promise, Karlsson followed his every gesture.

The two of them raced off into the forest, their skis leaving behind deep parallel tracks in the snow.

For Simo, the entire conflict had been reduced to just one duel. Today, there would be just one death.

*

In the fighting on the Kollaa front, the Finnish Army would gain 50 metres and leave their trench to dig another one and settle in it. Then the Russians would push them back and take advantage of the new trench, until another ferocious clash forced one or other adversary to retreat. This made every victory almost point-less, winning back what had been lost the day before, or losing what had been conquered that same morning. Things seemed likely to continue this way until there was nobody left to kill on either side.

At Snake Post, protected by the minefield and heavy machine guns, the Finns and Russians fought the battle at a distance, employing heavy artillery, mortars against cannon, not seeking to advance or gain territory, simply to kill and kill again, as often as they could. And when someone's head was carelessly raised too high, the Red sniper reminded them that they were there.

As Simo and Karlsson were unlatching their skis, the post commander crawled over to them. He asked them to follow him into the shelter of a trench, which they followed for several minutes until they came to a halt at the best observation point. They made themselves room among the usual jumble of crates of Molotov cocktails, grenades, munitions and piles of pine logs, especially chosen to jam the tracks of armoured vehicles.

The periscope passed from hand to hand. The Snake Post officer outlined to Simo the probable position of the enemy: the dark wood of pines with red bark where 300 metres away the object of his revenge was concealed. But to locate the Russian precisely, he would have to reveal himself, and there had to be a reason for him to do that. Simo found one.

"What's that?" the unit commander asked him to repeat, eyes wide open with astonishment.

"He's not mistaken," Karlsson said. "We need a diversion. The Russian is at least 300 metres away. To hit a non-moving target at that distance would already be extraordinary, so if I run for it ... I'm not risking anything. And it will give Simo a window to shoot when the Ivan is concentrating on me."

"Would you prefer me to send a soldier?" the commander said.

Karlsson looked him up and down disdainfully, hesitating for a moment whether to send the man himself. He studied the terrain in front of them.

"Look," he said to Simo. "Twenty metres away there's a shell crater. I'll dive into that and be safe."

There were only 20 metres to cover, but even wearing his skis, he would be slowed by the deep snow.

"I'll await your signal," Karlsson said. "And if in this entire war there's one shot you mustn't miss ..."

If the Russian fell for the diversionary tactic, he would shoot at Karlsson. If he was wilier, he would suspect that no-one could be so suicidal as to ski across open ground in front of him, and that a Finnish sniper already had him in his sights. In that case, he would seek that sniper out. Which meant Simo had to become almost invisible. He decided to leave the trench and pull back. Followed by a spotter, he crawled another 50 metres, sheltering as best he could in the available cover: a heap of snow, a clump of thorny junipers, or a granite boulder. Then a further 50 metres.

Panting, the two men paused for an instant at a place where

the spotter thought Simo would want to fire from. They were already 400 metres from the Russian, so that hitting his target would depend more on luck than accuracy. But once Simo had got his breath back, he moved even further away, another 50 metres. Then almost 50 metres more.

"Five hundred metres," the spotter estimated. "No-one can ..."

In fact, it was 490 metres, but Simo did not correct him, and settled down without saying a word. At this distance, the dark wood itself was little more than a tiny black dot, and he was supposed to hit a man hidden somewhere there.

The spotter raised his green lamp. Karlsson saw the signal, took a deep breath, leaped out of the trench and skied straight ahead, completely out in the open.

A first detonation sent a small cloud of snow flying less than a metre from him. In the grey morning, Simo could clearly make out the brief flash from the enemy's rifle. Everyone in Finland knew exactly where they were and what they were doing when war broke out, because some things stay in the memory forever. And for the rest of his life, with utter clarity, Simo would remember that tiny flash of light, identical to the one that had ended Toivo's life.

Toivo. Simo swore he felt his friend's hand on his.

Karlsson felt the rush of air from the second shot inches from his face. The sniper was getting used to his rhythm, his strides: he was becoming Karlsson.

It was at this second flash, this tiny glittering point, that Simo took aim.

Just as the Russian was getting ready to shoot a third time, holding his breath and with his finger on the trigger, he saw Karlsson disappear into the ground, into a crater where he could no longer see the white uniform.

Then he could see nothing more at all.

The bullet that had left Simo's rifle had travelled the 490 metres in half a second. The sniper's skull was smashed by a few grams of burning metal, and he toppled backwards.

"Are you sure you got him?" the spotter said, hands still covering his ears.

Simo stood up, strapped his gun on his shoulder, and calmly walked back to the trench, and then on to the shell crater where Karlsson was still hiding, convinced the duel was still going on. Simo's black silhouette above him made him peer up.

"Did you get him?" Karlsson said.

His soldier was standing there, on the very spot where others had lost their lives.

"Yes, you got him," Karlsson concluded.

The Winter War was not the last conflict on the planet, but this shot was never matched by any army on any continent. In fact, in those conditions and without a telescopic sight, it would never even be explained.

Only one answer was possible, but first one had to give up all sense of reason. Simo was certain he had fired guided only by his heart, his anger, his love and grief.

"Four hundred and ninety metres!" the spotter told every soldier he came across. "Four hundred and ninety metres!"

"That's impossible!" they all said.

"I know, but I saw it!"

Four hundred and ninety metres. Thunderstruck, Karlsson also heard how far it had been. He saw then what Simo would become. The legendary Simo Häyhä, the White Death.

But revenge does not resolve anything, does not bring anyone back to life. It fills the void of absence, offers a goal to prevent someone succumbing, it retains sadness and anger. Once it has been satisfied, it releases everything in a single devastating rush, although nothing has really changed. So the White Death was neither satisfied nor appeased, and the fire of his rage was in no way extinguished.

Instead of his bullet, Simo would have wished he himself had travelled those 490 metres, taken the Russian's head in his hands and slammed it a hundred times against a rock until it cracked, split open and poured out between his fingers.

This was December 23, 1939, the night before Christmas Eve. For the first time, in the pit of his stomach Simo had an unquenchable thirst for blood, an irrepressible desire for violence.

Two days to Christmas, and Simo was ravenous.

52

"I don't recognise him any more," an anxious Onni had said.

"Finally we see the soldier I always knew he was," Juutilainen congratulated himself.

"How many kills did you say?" an astonished Colonel Teittinen said, when told of that day's exploits.

*

On the morning of December 24, the chaplain had decided to immortalise the Finnish resistance which the largest army in the world could still not muzzle, however many tons of shells it pounded them with. Close to 20,000 bombs furrowed the earth of Finland every day. Fourteen every minute for almost a month already. There were days even the Devil would have baulked at, when the Russians could increase the rhythm to reach 200,000 shells. And yet Finland was holding out.

And so, since the man of God was also a photographer, he spent the day taking photographs of the soldiers and Lottas from the companies holding the line at Kollaa.

In peacetime, which unfortunately is only remembered during a war, Toivo had never missed the opportunity to make fun of Simo's small stature. He would swear that to find him in a photograph you only had to look for the smallest person. One metre fifty-two was not exactly impressive. But Simo did not appear among the chaplain's photographs that day. Nor did Onni. Only their brothers-in-arms posed humbly with resigned, sometimes forced smiles, their eyes on the sky which so often rained shells, for these odd photographs in which none of them was looking at the camera.

Juutilainen also refused to join in, dismissing the chaplain with a curt excuse:

"Photographs are full of dead people."

*

As usual, Simo had collected from outside the Terror's tent the maps the companies had marked with crosses that would guide him. Then, in the tremulous pre-dawn silence, he had disappeared, taking Onni with him as spotter. But that day, as well as his M28/30 rifle, he slung over his shoulder a Suomi sub-machine gun – an entirely Finnish product that was exceptionally durable. He weighed down his pockets with magazines, and hooked grenades onto his belt.

From everywhere in the forest came the clatter of automatic weapons, the crack of marksmen's rifles, deafening blasts as bombs exploded, and a dull rumble as the earth trembled.

After weeks roaming them, Simo knew every inch of the kilometres closest to their camp. And the slightest change could conceal a threat. An uprooted tree recently moved became a possible shelter for a concealed sniper. A pile of branches strewn over the ground could hide a foxhole dug by the enemy, in which a soldier could wait patiently for hours until a Finnish unit passed by. And now a mound of snow like a low wall attracted his attention: it had not been there the day before.

Of course, the nine Russians who had wanted to set an ambush never heard Simo arrive. He swept away five with one burst from his machine gun, while Onni killed three more, letting the last one escape. Simo put a bullet in each of them as a precaution. Onni waited for him.

As they prepared to search bodies that were still warm for a few minutes longer, searching for ammunition, maps or mission orders, they were perplexed at the sight of the skis on the Russians' feet.

"Look, they're ours. They must have taken them from our men."

Examining them more closely, Onni discovered that Russian boots were not equipped to fit on the skis, which instead had quite simply been nailed to their shoes. Although this meant they could move two or three times quicker than on foot, the middle nail pierced through the leather on the sole and must cause them a great deal of pain as they went along. This explained why there was a pair of skis on its own on the ground. One of the Russians must have wanted some respite from the pain, and had had to take his boots off at the same time.

"Our runaway is barefooted," Onni surmised. "It's not worth following him, he'll freeze to death in less than half an hour."

Simo did not care whether the −40°C that gripped the skull like a migraine and burned fingers and face would soon finish the Russian off, or if a Finnish patrol would come across him and put an end to his suffering. Simo wanted to kill him himself, to watch him croak. There was no longer any thought of differentiating between being able to kill and having to kill. He wanted to kill.

The Red soldier struggled to make his way through the freezing heart of the forest. His frozen legs were plunged thigh-deep in snow; after several minutes fleeing laboriously, he heard his executioner gliding behind him, striding along rhythmically, breathing like a metronome. He stopped and turned round to beg for mercy, ready to surrender, unaware that any idea of mercy had long since forsaken the White Death.

From a distance Onni heard a single shot. Moments later, Simo reappeared, neither more satisfied nor more appeased than before. Without even searching the dead bodies, he set off hunting again.

His next five victims offered greater resistance, making a defensive redoubt that only two grenades succeeded in obliterating.

Their blood poured out, soaking the layers of snow until it reached the ground beneath.

After that, with three shots from more than 200 metres, Simo reduced the Soviet forces by an equal number of soldiers. Even at that distance, the desperate enemy cries could clearly be heard: "*Belaya Smert! Belaya Smert!*"

At sunset, they came across seven Russians by a campfire. And since campfires blind more than they illuminate, none of them saw their death arrive. Simo killed another seven times.

Twenty-four Russians in a single day. More were within reach, but Simo appeared to have had enough, or to have achieved his goal. A goal Onni understood on the way back.

This was December 24, and the Finnish sniper wanted, in his own manner, to celebrate Christmas with the macabre present of 24 dead bodies.

"I don't recognise him any more," Onni had said in confidence to Pietari when he returned to camp.

"Finally we see the soldier I always knew he was," Juutilainen congratulated himself again.

53

In the officers' camp some distance behind the soldiers' tents, a modest pine tree had been decorated. White bandages for streamers, bunches of lingonberries hanging from its branches, and the Finnish flag draped round the trunk: together they created a festive air. Here and there it brought a smile to the faces of the nurses in their bloodstained aprons and soldiers with eyes scorched to the depths of their souls. Even so, no truce was expected this Christmas: the Russians would celebrate their Orthodox festival on January 7.

In the canteens, the Lottas had prepared a special porridge, adding apples, raisins and honey to the usual oats and milk. There was also white bread, buns, sweets and schnapps for everyone, and for dinner pea soup with sausage. It was simmering already, and its warm aroma drifted like a wispy mist along the rows of tents and stables. Unlikely bursts of music drifted with it.

Protected and installed in an empty ammunition crate, a crackling gramophone was playing carols, and on every hour, the Finnish national anthem, "God is our Fortress". Whenever there was an explosion nearby, the needle jumped from one song to another, scratching the record with a sound like that of a car skidding off the road. These few nostalgic songs took the soldiers to Christmases past, only for them to be rudely brought back to reality by the cries of the wounded from the medical tent.

For Christmas there was an avalanche of letters. Mostly these were from families, although some came from strangers, women who tried in a few affectionate sentences to raise the morale of soldiers who had neither family nor loved ones. There were also thousands of parcels, filled with mittens and pullovers knitted by Lottas who had stayed behind in the rear.

Nearby, in a jute sack that soon filled up, were all the letters that arrived too late.

"Antti Armas?" Pulkki cried out. He was in charge of handing out the post. He waved an envelope above his head.

"He died two days ago," one of his friends said softly.

"What could be sadder than a letter that doesn't reach the person it was intended for?" Pietari lamented.

As they pored over their handwritten sheets, the entire universe gradually faded away. The soldiers once more became brothers, husbands, sons, almost children. Simple words they no longer paid any attention to regained all their importance as they called to mind some anodyne happy memory, and they cursed themselves for not having appreciated how precious that moment had been. Every kiss planted on the paper became a treasure. Tears welled up as they read the news. Kids were growing, parents were worried, fields languished without the men, and beds were cold. The soldiers were reminded that life went on elsewhere, and that was what they were fighting for.

Pulkki plunged his hand again into his Father Christmas sack and pulled out another letter.

"Onni … Onni Verner?"

*

The constant bombardments had led civilians to flee the big cities and the Gulf of Finland; they had found a semblance of refuge in the interior. Linked by the radio to the fate of their nation, they had all heard the announcement, one that Mannerheim feared might be poorly received. Had he not already asked too much of his people?

After 30 days of conflict, Finland had realised it would be

fighting alone. So it had to buy more and more weapons and munitions, and to find more and more funds. Of course, there was gold everywhere, but it was worth far more than its market value. There was gold, but would Finnish women agree to relinquish it?

And yet against all expectation, from the morning after the radio announcement long lines began to form at every collection point, growing as the day progressed. Lines of women; only women. Among those waiting their turn was one obviously exhausted lady in a black shawl with a child in her arms and another impatiently clinging to her leg.

"Would you like to go in front of me?" said her neighbour, a pretty young woman with a stocky body and kindly expression.

"I didn't dare ask ... I gave blood this morning for the hospitals at the front, but I never thought it would tire me out so much."

"Would you like me to carry her for a while?" the young woman said, pointing to the little creature hugging her mother's neck.

"I'd be delighted, but I'm not sure she ..."

Passed from one pair of arms to another, the little girl hesitated a moment, then immediately snuggled up against the stranger. Perhaps she had just eaten or baked some, but she smelled of warm bread, and it was enough for the child to close her eyes to imagine she was close to a comforting stove.

"Next!" shouted the official in military uniform. He had a notebook filled with names and addresses on his trestle table, lined up parallel to a big iron box with a heavy padlock hanging from its lock.

The woman in the black shawl gave one last look at her wedding ring, then had to prise it off her ring finger. With these few grams of gold she was saying goodbye to the "I do" she and her husband had exchanged many years before. Together with another 200,000 rings, this one would be melted down to make ingots and sold to permit Finland to carry on with the war. A reverse alchemy that saw gold transformed into lead.

The official dropped the ring into the box, wrote down the

identity of its owner, handed her a receipt and in exchange gave her a new iron wedding ring, engraved with the white rose of Finland.

"Thank you for your contribution. Next!"

All those who had responded to this call were offered a pastry and a cup of coffee. Protected from the wind and snow under a big wooden shelter, the two women caught up with one another.

"Where is yours?" said the woman in whose arms the little one had by now fallen asleep.

"In Mikkeli. He works at army headquarters."

"An important man, then …"

"That's true. And yours?"

"He's simply a recruit who didn't even have the time to marry me. So that wasn't a real wedding ring. Well, that's what I tell myself so as not to cry in front of you."

The smell of pastry gently woke the child. The stranger broke her bun in two for her to share.

"I don't think my husband, protected from the fighting in his office in Mikkeli, is any worthier than yours. No-one is simply a soldier, they're more like simple heroes. So be proud of … What's his name, by the way?"

"Onni. Onni Verner. And yours?"

"Aksel. Aksel Airo."

*

Pulkki plunged his hand once more into his Father Christmas sack, and pulled out another letter.

"Onni … Onni Verner?"

Onni tore impatiently at the envelope. He always skimmed his letters first, then began again at the beginning, savouring every word. But at the first glance of this one, his face darkened a little.

"Your wife to be?" Pietari asked. "Good news?"

"Neither good nor bad. Just a bit sad," Onni said, twisting his orphaned ring round his finger.

236

Pietari waited patiently for the post bag to be emptied, hopeful until the very last letter. His younger brother Viktor had written to him several times, but after the missive telling him about the heart-breaking evacuation of tens of thousands of Finnish children to Sweden, Pietari had heard nothing. Faced with the two options that could explain his brother's silence, he refused to accept the first, preferring to convince himself that on the Mannerheim Line they had little free time and even fewer chances to write.

For his part, Simo had shown no interest in this distribution of letters. He loved his family, they loved him, and in the Häyhä family, to know that was enough; they did not need to express it. So he was surprised when Juutilainen asked him to follow him to the tent of the commander of the 34th Regiment, Lieutenant Colonel Teittinen, who, he told Simo, had a present for him.

The ever-present cigarette in the corner of his mouth, the lieutenant colonel was sitting on the edge of his camp bed. He was gesturing earnestly to rid himself of the nurse changing the bandage on a healing arm wound.

Two days earlier, Teittinen had accompanied a platoon of scouts to a nearby area they thought was occupied by Russians. One of the soldiers had discovered a small case of vodka apparently left as a present. This kind of trap was an age-old trick, but it still worked: only the lure changed. The soldier had lifted the lid, setting off the grenade hidden inside. Fortunately his body acted as a shield for the rest of the unit, and only Teittinen was wounded by a piece of shrapnel. The arm that a Lotta was stubbornly trying to attend to despite her patient's resistance, treating him exactly as she would have done an ordinary soldier or Mannerheim himself.

"There's a package for you on the table, my boy," the lieutenant colonel told Simo.

Simo went over, tore open the wrapping paper, and turned a pair of blue-and-white woollen mittens over in his hands.

"Knitted by my wife. They'll keep you warm. I told her about you in my letters. Our best sniper. She wanted to thank you. They're even nicer than the ones I have. And I have this for you as well. A gift from headquarters. A gift for our most valiant soldiers."

Teittinen rummaged in his pocket with his good arm and took out a fob watch.

"Tissot. Made in Switzerland. They don't make war, but they do make fine timepieces."

Simo held the watch up to his ear and closed his eyes to listen to its mechanism. He left the tent, thanking the lieutenant colonel with a nod of the head. Teittinen looked a little perturbed.

"Your lad isn't in good shape, Juutilainen."

*

In spite of everything, the soldiers sang and drank themselves senseless. But for Simo, Christmas was just another day.

He left at first light, and did the same the following two days. He killed another 51 Russians, some from a distance with his rifle, others at close quarters with his sub-machine gun.

*

In the enemy camp, Borodin and Sadovski had had to be replaced. They now lay frozen somewhere beneath the snow, a bullet in the back of their heads.

Despatched directly by the Stavka on the supply train, Comrade Commissar Fiodor Komarov arrived. He was the new political officer, whose letter of recommendation and proof of competence lay in the fact of his having been responsible for organising the gulags and the almost one million forced labourers incarcerated there. He was going to appoint his military officer that afternoon, but first and foremost he wanted to assemble his unit commanders.

"Don't imagine I'm ignorant of the situation. During my journey, the soldiers on the supply train talked, and I listened. I know. He knows as well. And neither He nor I are satisfied."

With the expression of an implacable judge and the hands of a butcher, Komarov looked capable of delivering the verdict and of carrying out the sentence himself.

"First of all, I want to put a stop to the poison spreading through your ranks. The person who brings me the body of this White Death will earn the right to return home. Pass this on to your men, and the reward."

He leaned over the map tacked to his wooden table and followed the road to Loimola with his finger.

"To avoid the forests and marshes, this is the road you're struggling to advance along?"

Nobody dared to respond, aware that this was a rhetorical question.

"And here, a kilometre below, this is a railway line, is it not? Couldn't we send our men, our tanks, our artillery and our trucks along it?"

When this was met with a lengthy silence, he raised his head and stared at them all. One officer offered himself like a lamb to the slaughter.

"Yes, Comrade Commissar. It also leads across the Kollaa front, but transferring everything would slow us down."

"You're afraid of getting slowed down when we're not even advancing?" Komarov snorted. "So, we will abandon Loimola, and travel along the tracks. Make sure that this is carried out immediately; I require to be kept regularly informed. And you, step forward and identify yourself. You'll be the one in charge."

The unit commander turned pale, now less afraid of enemy bullets than of his new *politruk*'s ire.

"Anikine, Commissar. Captain Anikine."

"Well then, Anikine. I'll be your political officer, and you'll be my military officer."

54

The Russians had not been discreet – far from it – and the Finnish observation patrols all reported back with the same information.

"Here," Juutilainen pointed. He had watched the manoeuvres with his own eyes. "They're sweeping the snow off the railway tracks and moving their men and equipment."

Teittinen turned up the oil lamp. The faces clustered around the table appeared more clearly.

"They're abandoning the Loimola road," he told them. "They're taking a route we haven't covered or mined. If they get past Kollaa, they won't meet any resistance until they reach north of the Mannerheim Line, which they can then take from the rear. That will be the end of the war and the end of Finland. Whatever happens, Kollaa must hold out."

"*Kollaa Kestää!*" Juutilainen shouted.

"*Kollaa Kestää,*" the other officers replied as one.

These were not empty words: they knew their lives were at stake when they protected a line of defence as fragile as it was crucial.

"What if it is only a trap?" an N.C.O. proposed. "The Russians know we're observing them. Could all this movement be nothing more than a diversion? Perhaps they're trying to get us to abandon Loimola so they can take it?"

"To find out if it's a trap, you sometimes have to fall into it," the Terror advised him, confirming his chronic inability to avoid danger.

Teittinen looked again at the map, then smiled as he had an

idea, even if it seemed to him extremely audacious, to say the least.

"Gentlemen, do you know what's missing from that railway line?"

*

Erect in the saddle, Komarov turned to look back at the 10,000 men he had confronted on parade that morning and divided into three columns that disappeared into the distance as far as the eye could see. Twenty tanks were at the head, and 50 artillery pieces brought up the rear. From this dark, menacing mass rose the regular breathing of 10,000 men, like the undertow of a stormy ocean about to form a huge wave that would crash down on the Kollaa front. Brandishing his sword above his head, Komarov urged them forward.

It had taken the Russians only 24 hours to redeploy part of their army a kilometre to the south, and then to follow the railway tracks. And they were advancing more rapidly and more securely than on any previous day. Komarov's stern face almost softened into a smile.

"Praise for this strategy of yours is bound to reach as far as Moscow, Commissar," Anikine flattered him. "If we make this kind of progress, the entire 8th Army will have to follow us."

Komarov was thoroughly susceptible to such boot-licking. Puffed up with pride, back as straight as a Tsar reviewing his troops, he dug his spurs into the steed's flanks. "Komarov," he said to himself, "now there's an officer whose exploits and intelligence will satisfy the Kremlin." And when at last this ridiculously protracted war came to an end, with the ashes of Finland under his boot heel, he would return garlanded with victories.

Three days earlier he had presented this plan to Colonel Shtern, who had sanctioned it but was reluctant to commit all his forces to it. What a cold fish! What a lack of panache! What would he say now, confronted by the undeniable success of the operation?

They had advanced almost a kilometre, without any attacks or resistance …

"Look over there," said one of the leading soldiers, not entirely sure what he was seeing.

"What the …?" his neighbour queried, unable to finish his sentence.

In the distance, above the railway tracks vanishing towards the horizon, a thick cloud as tall as ten men had formed. The cloud was growing, which meant it was heading towards them. It was growling as well, like some kind of animal. The leading soldiers slowed down, jostled by those behind them who had still not seen anything. When they did, all three columns came to a halt.

Komarov raised his field glasses. The cloud was not advancing, it was charging straight at them. Impenetrable, but what it concealed must be immense, spraying tons of snow and ice on all sides and into the air. The Finns already had as an ally *Belaya Smert*, who the feeble-minded were convinced was immortal. Could it be that they were also aided by a prehistoric forest monster, a previously unknown beast they had managed to recruit?

Turning round 10,000 men, 20 tanks, and 50 pieces of artillery demanded very special logistical skills and an unimaginable length of time. Komarov did not have that much time, and so remained paralysed, a mere spectator of an inexplicable phenomenon. Then, 100 metres from them, the cloud began to shoot out sparks as if an intense storm were raging inside it. Twenty soldiers in the front rank were literally chopped in two, their legs stuck to the ground while their upper bodies toppled over, spattering the faces and uniforms of their closest colleagues with a scarlet, viscous spray.

Ten thousand breaths were held.

The insides of the cloud became even brighter. Now the flashing sparks not only shot straight out, but also up into the sky, tracing arcs that ended on the tanks, which exploded one after the

242

other. Many soldiers were mown down as they tried to flee. Others were so terrified they urinated on themselves. What was this magic, this creature with thousands of lethal bolts that had sworn allegiance to Finland?

*

Two days earlier, Teittinen had asked:

"Gentlemen, do you know what's missing from that railway line?"

And so the Finnish supply train was requisitioned. Not without discussion, because that meant going short on food, and Wilhelm Teittinen, commander of the 34th Regiment, had been obliged to promise headquarters that this would be a unique, short-lived operation. Twenty-four hours to transform the train into a war machine, and as many to send it to demolish the enemy.

Throughout that day and night, Finnish Army engineers set to work. By the light of the sun and lanterns they fitted sheets of bulletproof steel to the sides of the locomotive and its carriages, leaving only gunports open. Finally they screwed the feet of ten machine guns and 20 mortars onto the carriage roofs.

At daybreak, the heart of the beast was fed with coal. It came to life, bristling with artillery and carrying soldiers in its eight carriages, the barrels of their sub-machine guns poking out of the loopholes. Each man was allotted his place, and the three friends Onni, Pietari and Simo used their elbows to push their way through and stand next to one another, automatic weapons filled with venom.

To celebrate, and because curiosity had spread all over the front more quickly than a fever, Hägglund, the commander of the Finnish Army's IV Corps, had come to drink a coffee with Teittinen and the exhausted engineers. Delighted with the result, he twice slapped the indestructible metal lance that was going to pierce the Russian forces.

"A weapon like this," Hägglund said appreciatively, "absolutely deserves a name!"

"It already has one. We've christened it '*Hyöky*'."[21]

*

Like the prow of a ship slicing through the ocean, sending up a wall of water and spray as it advances, *Hyöky* plowed into the high white curtain and threw up millions of tons of snow, billowing around it like a protective screen.

First it was the heavy machine guns, their barrels glowing red, which mowed down the enemy troops like scythes harvesting in summer. Then the mortars launched a sustained barrage into the air. The Russians still had no idea what had hit them.

It was only when *Hyöky*, the tsunami, penetrated their columns and they had to scatter in pure confusion, flinging themselves on top of one another or simply treading on others, that they saw the flanks of the train protected by steel plates and the gunports, out of which spat 300 machine rifles for two interminable minutes.

Then, in the chaos, silence.

Trembling with fear just like their men, none of the Russian officers had the courage to give the order to counter-attack. Soon, as effortlessly as it had finished off almost 1,000 men, *Hyöky* went into reverse before it could be surrounded and vanished in the storm of snowflakes it had created and which the howling wind kept aloft.

The sun disappeared beneath this white covering, plunging the battlefield into a *kaamos*,[22] dulling the bright red of blood and the shiny spilled guts. Breathless and bemused, Komarov stood with his rifle lowered, slumping as he contemplated the carnage all about him. Wherever he trod, he was stepping on the remains of his men. Further off, he could only recognise his torn-apart horse by its hooves and its saddle.

He turned to Captain Anikine, who had fled with him out of

reach of the beast into the shelter of the nearest wood. The captain could read the concern and anxiety on his face.

"You're the political officer," Anikine reminded him. "You are the one who is writing the history of Russia. If this operation never existed, you have only to tell me. And Shtern. No-one would benefit from remembering what happened on this day."

Unaware that the Finns only had the use of *Hyöky* for two days, the Soviet 8th Army never again ventured anywhere near the railway.

And so, for all that remained of the conflict, the road to Loimola was their only viable way into Finland, and the most costly.

55

Thirty days of intensive combat had so far produced no victory to fictionalise, nor any significant advance on which the Russians could congratulate themselves. For Stalin, the Winter War was becoming a bitter defeat. Bitter and shameful.

Even among his own people, despite their being protected from a conflict on their own land, there was a growing, if muffled, rumble of discontent. Although the soldiers' letters were burned and propaganda was redoubled, rumour filled the gap left by the lack of information from the Kremlin. In spite of the wish to suppress gossip and opinions, news circulated in secret, under cover of laundry drums, in the grating of tram axles, whispered in the queues for the state-run stores. Russia was divided between those who kept the faith and those who were beginning to doubt. Caution was the watchword before you voiced your opinion in this nation where the least unfortunate slip of the tongue could cost, at best, years of forced labour.

The Soviet Union was looking ridiculous. That had to stop, and at once. Its all-powerful army was sending its legions to crash against a Finnish wall which they were chipping away at as gradually as waves eating away at a cliff century after century. So the army had to be rethought, reinvented.

The man to do this was quickly found. His name was Simeon Timoshenko. Not only did he have Stalin's trust, he had his friendship, born on the frontline of the civil war more than fifteen years earlier. Faced with the fiasco of the Winter War, the Sun of the Russian Nation had in a few words granted him full powers:

"If we don't resolve the Finnish question very quickly, it could receive the support of a West fundamentally hostile to the Soviet borders and its soul. Comrade Timoshenko, I put my faith in you, Molotov will give you the means."

Molotov therefore hastened to receive this imposing officer. Timoshenko was two metres tall, he had a polished, shiny skull and he wore a long black cape.

The two men strolled along the avenues of the Alexander garden next to the Kremlin, watched over by a very visible guard and some more discreet intelligence agents. They sat on a stone bench opposite the obelisk to fighters for freedom.

"Karl Marx, Jean Jaurès, Édouard Vaillant …" Molotov read, his accent massacring the two French names. "Do you know what the nineteen names engraved on this monument have replaced?"

"Those of the tsars of the Romanov dynasty," Timoshenko replied, as if this was self-evident.

"Exactly so. The tsars have given way to the republic, and their history has been effaced by chisels. Some things never change. What do you think will remain of our names if this war drags on forever?"

"Longer than it has done already? Not much, obviously."

"So tell me, comrade, what do you need to ensure our names survive?"

Timoshenko tapped a cigarette on his silver case, then, after a first long pull, searched in his uniform pocket and pulled out a bundle of dog-eared sheets of paper.

"I've taken an interest in the reports from the front," he said.

"As have we all," Molotov assured him.

"No, comrade. I'm not talking about the lying reports glorifying an indestructible Red Army … My interest was in those no-one dared to show Him. Those which tell how every other military operation makes no sense and is launched with no knowledge of the terrain or the enemy."

"You don't mince your words, do you? To hear you, we're simply incompetent. I doubt you allow yourself to speak to Him like that, however close you are. It's easy to criticise; I won't hide the fact that it was solutions I was hoping for from you."

Timoshenko's self-satisfied smile told Molotov that he did indeed have some.

"Our first problem is rivalry. Denunciations, intrigues, deceit, all kinds of accusations. At all levels of our army, and even in the Kremlin, there's not a single man who would hesitate to crush someone else if that brought him into the limelight. It's the same in the field. Our artillery and infantry are commanded by officers desperate for the slightest victory to help them shine. They do not communicate with one another; they even fire at each other. I'm going to bring them to heel and force them to collaborate rather than compete with one another."

"Could it be that easy?"

"Obviously not. A hundred other weaknesses are undermining His army. For example, thousands of our soldiers are dying as they attack the bunkers on the Mannerheim Line. I want to equip them with flame-throwers. I also want new, more robust armoured vehicles. The tanks we have now are vulnerable: the Finns can stop them with nothing more than logs and Molotov cocktails."

"What kind of cocktails?" asked the person whose name had been taken in vain like this.

"Didn't you know? Don't worry, I'm sure your name will survive for other reasons. Shall I go on?"

"Please do."

"Then there's the climate. Our men are dying of cold. Literally. And apparently the Finnish winter can get even harsher. We must clothe them properly. And feed them properly too, so they don't eat their horses. There's also the problem of the impenetrable forests. How can we direct our artillery fire if we can't see any-thing? I need helium balloons so that we can spot their positions from the air. And finally, since the Finns get around more quickly on skis, I want our soldiers to be taught how to ski."

"Is that all?" Molotov enquired ironically.

"No. I want a limitless supply of munitions and weapons. I want the whole of the Soviet Union's productive capacity at my disposal. I want to smother Finland under a blanket of explosives before a final attack I'm planning for mid-February."

"In 45 days? It's difficult enough to reinvent one's army in peacetime; to do it in the midst of war seems not only audacious, but foolhardy. Do you think Mannerheim will wait patiently for you to finish?"

"But I don't intend to let Finland rest, quite the opposite. We're going to exhaust them, bombarding their frontlines non-stop. Day and night, without respite, until our cannon fall apart! A war of attrition where no-one will gain a metre of ground, but which will give us time to restructure our army."

Hearing the sombre prospect in store for the enemy, Molotov felt glad to be Russian.

"All the same," he said with astonishment, "who would have thought that this tiny Finland would put up such resistance? We're made of the same flesh and blood, so why have they not yielded already?"

"There's something I believe, and something I'm sure of," Timoshenko said. "I believe this war has unified Finland as never before. If it has become a fortress, we have supplied the mortar. And I'm certain that we've awakened their damned *sisu*."

"I don't speak their language, comrade," Molotov said apologetically.

"And I don't know how to translate that word. *Sisu* is the soul of Finland. The spirit of a people that lives in savage nature, in biting cold, with only rare sunshine. An austere life in a hostile environment has forged their mentality into a steel that still resists us today. It also points to their courage, but it would take a lot more to define everything that *sisu* means. You need to add stubbornness, pluck, inner strength, tenacity, resistance, determination, willpower … and the character – complex to say the least – that comes from all that. They are as cold and savage as the heart of their forests."

"That must mean it's just as complex to command their army."

"Not really. To our misfortune, we're the ones who trained their commander, Field Marshal Carl Gustaf Mannerheim. And that should concern you more than anything else."

"Do you think it's enough for him to have learned a few of our techniques and strategies to make us quake in our boots?"

Timoshenko's heart sank at hearing in a single sentence the very reasons for all Russia's failings in this war. A lack of knowledge and smug self-satisfaction: they were at the root of everything.

"Did you know he was a cadet at the Saint Petersburg cavalry academy under Tsar Alexander II, when Finland was still a Russian grand duchy? Did you know he was a guard of the Empress, because he married the daughter of a Russian general and became an imperial officer? Are you not aware he also took part in the war we waged against Japan, and that when Tsar Nicolas II had his eyes on Central Asia, it was Mannerheim he chose as a spy?"

"What on earth could he spy on there? Rice paddies?"

"Yet again you make a joke of it, but unlike us, Tsar Nicolas II refused to launch any kind of attack without first learning all he could about his future adversary. You might be sceptical about what came next if it were not the exact truth. With his mission credentials in his pocket, the spy Mannerheim left by himself. He bought a horse in Samarkand and named him Philippe. He rode 14,000 kilometres on the same steed throughout Asia over two years. He passed himself off as an ethnologist, learning and studying the culture of those peoples whose land and riches Russia coveted. Can you see now what our enemy is made of? As it turned out, the First World War put an end to the Tsar's ambitions, and in that same war Mannerheim fought alongside us on the Austro-Hungarian front. All those battles and positions of great responsibility have given him a perfect knowledge of how we function and our ideology. So now, comrade, do you understand why it is no more than common sense to be concerned?"

Timoshenko allowed Molotov to digest the meaning of a conversation he had not been enjoying for some minutes.

"So he's an adversary who knows everything about his enemy?"

"Yes, and that is our greatest weakness. We are almost fighting against ourselves."

56

At −51°C – a temperature never before registered in Finland – it was enough simply to stop moving or to move away from the fire for a moment to freeze in a few seconds. The Lottas went from tent to tent handing out sheets of newspaper that the soldiers wrapped round their legs and bodies before they put on their snowsuits. Fighting against the cold, and suffering from it, took up a large part of their thoughts. They huddled together, relegating the stench, the dirt, the infestations of bed bugs, the lice and the itching that left their skin red raw to the level of slight discomfort. In this Arctic climate, even the hardiest units only allowed themselves one hour out on patrol before returning, to avoid catching frostbite. During those first days of 1940, even though he was accustomed since childhood to the rigours of winter, two hours outside was Simo's absolute limit.

Every day in the field hospital, surgeons amputated fingers, toes, ears and noses. These were regarded as only minor wounds; the soldiers were sent back to the front to risk the rest of their skin.

With this cold, even sleeping was dangerous – if sleep had been possible, that is, because the enemy was bent on exhausting them. Across forests and blizzards Russian military songs poured from loudspeakers aimed towards Kollaa, their volume at maximum so that the drums and choirs of the Red Army drilled right into the Finnish soldiers' skulls. At night, like beguiling nursery rhymes, the same loudspeakers endlessly poured out propaganda messages in Finnish, to eat away at the troops' morale:

"*Your families have been forcibly evacuated from their homes.*

They are wandering the country without refuge. Your children are starving, and you will die in your turn just to protect capitalists. Enough blood has been spilled that only benefits the imperialists. The Finnish people do not want war. Rise up against your officers. Kill them and come to join us: you will be treated as heroes. Your families have been forcibly evacuated from their homes. They are wandering the country ..."

On top of that came the noise from the engines of thousands of Russian vehicles – lorries, tanks and cars, that had to be kept running day and night to avoid freezing. A monotonous, droning noise. Along with it came thick waves of petrol fumes, so dense they seemed to settle on the tongue and the back of the throat, making the soldiers gag and vomit.

At the end of their tether, the Finnish soldiers clamped their hands over their ears as if a deafening swarm of hornets had nested there. They shouted as loudly as they could to drown out the noise, preferring to hear their own voices rather than anything else, cursing the Ivans without realising they were thereby inflicting the same torture on themselves.

Accompanying the songs, the propaganda and the engines, this unbearable orchestra was completed by a third instrument that was the loudest and most deadly of all. The sound of artillery fire, its thousands of shells on even the calmest days.

No respite, no rest. Not a single minute. After nightfall, flares warded off the darkness. Reflected on the snow, their bright red glow covered the landscape with a fresh layer of blood. Together with the maddening racket, it offered glimpses of Hell such as those in ancient icons.

This was how January and February went by.

Of the 300 men in the 6th Company at the start of the conflict, only 91 were left. The numbers were made up with soldiers from other equally depleted companies. In the rear, the Lottas patched up uniforms in the same way as the generals patched up their units.

The Russians were trying to wear them down rather than win ground. However, when all they had to do was wait and pray, Juutilainen – in whose blood the percentage of alcohol was inversely proportional to that of the thermometer – could not bear to do nothing. His relations with Karlsson, who was more measured and more concerned about the fate of his men, were frequently strained, and the two officers often almost came to blows. Juutilainen sent out his patrols, whatever the cost, and even though he lost many men, every day he sent out more. It was only one morning in mid-January when he had really overstepped the mark that Teittinen, commander of the 34th Regiment, began seriously to doubt his sanity.

*

On Juutilainen's orders, Karlsson had led a small group on an observation mission to the edge of the endless Russian tents. Pietari and Onni crawled to the top of a low rise beyond which they could hear Russian officers barking commands. When they took a cautious look at the other side, they were stupefied to see a huge lesson in the basics of skiing taking place. Like awkward children, the Russian soldiers were trying to keep their balance on the long ski tips, backsides sticking out, sticks flying every-where, holding on to each other as they slid for a few metres before invariably falling over. Karlsson's men were thankful for the con-tinual din from the engines and the songs booming from the loudspeakers that covered their hoots of merriment. Pietari was only sorry that Simo was not there to witness the scene. To Finns who could ski from earliest childhood there was nothing more ridiculous than these clumsy, flailing adults, constantly repri-manded by their officers as surrogate parents, unhappy with their offspring's lack of progress.

Karlsson motioned to assemble his group and return to their camp. They could have thrown Molotov cocktails, a dozen or so grenades or fired their machine guns indiscriminately into the Russians, but oddly, the absurd, grotesque spectacle they had seen had robbed them of any great desire for killing. The three heavy machine guns and two howitzers firmly installed around the skiers had probably also played their part, but there was no knowing exactly why Karlsson had taken the decision to withdraw.

At first, they made the journey back to Kollaa in silence, but when on his skis Onni imitated a Russian as wobbly as a fawn rising to its feet for the first time, they laughed all the way to camp.

*

Halfway between the soldiers' tents and those of the officers, Pietari caught up with Simo, rucksack at his feet as if he had just moved out. Standing there with his rifle reaching to his armpit, he looked the opposite of redoubtable. His vision obscured by the whirling snow, it took some time for Pietari to see what his friend and the others around him were staring at.

Juutilainen and his men had returned safely from a reconnaissance patrol. Although they had met a Russian unit, they had not brought back any booty: no weapons or munitions. Instead, the Terror had preferred to bring trophies, with which he had mounted a macabre display. He had impaled the bodies of three frozen Red soldiers on wooden stakes planted round his tent. Two of them were hanging from their pierced chins, their eyes still open. The third had a label round his neck, dangling above his rib cage, with the word WELCOME written on it in capital letters.

"*Perkele!*" Pietari gasped. "What is this nonsense?"

An incensed Teittinen gave the order and, as Juutilainen, who still could not comprehend what he had done wrong, scowled at them, some soldiers began trying to lever the bodies off the poles. They soon gave up and instead pulled the stakes out of the ground. No doubt the Russians would be buried like that.

"Lieutenant Juutilainen," the commander of the 34th Regiment lamented, "you do this just when I was about to promote you to captain? You do not make life easy for me."

"Whether they're left abandoned in the forest or guard my tent, they're still dead *Ryssät*, are they not?"

Teittinen gave up on the idea of educating his officer, of trying to discover what morals he still had. Instead he drew a veil over this unsavoury incident.

Simo, meanwhile, had not budged. He had witnessed all this with a different kind of emotion. Not disgust or horror. Simply a profound, invisible fear. Ten days earlier, when he had shot Toivo's killer, he had been almost disappointed not to be able to lay his hands on the Russian's body. The Devil only knows what he would have done to him. After that, Simo had toppled into the abyss, feeding off violence and hatred to lend him inexhaustible energy. Now he had to climb out, before he encountered Juutilainen there.

"You're coming back with us, aren't you?" Pietari begged him.

Simo nodded gratefully, his rucksack still at his feet.

"Don't worry, I'll carry it," Onni said.

As he settled back in the soldiers' tent, Simo discovered some new recruits. He did not know them, but they knew who he was. So did everybody on both sides of the front: here at Kollaa or as far away as the Isthmus of Karelia protected by the Mannerheim Line. Simo: *Belaya Smert* to the Russians, and *Taika-ampuja* to the Finns.[23]

He asked each of them for news, as if making up for lost time. The time spent at the foot of the abyss that someone else's sinister delirium had delivered him from before it was too late.

Onni and Pietari rejoiced to see in their friend's face something other than the murderous fever that had poisoned his soul. Now it had been replaced by a kind of calm that had been absent for more than ten days.

57

Four hundred and forty kills led to Simo being offered an unprecedented reward.

A rider on a phantom horse covered completely in a white sheet pierced only around the eyes and nostrils had appeared at the entrance to his tent.

"Leave your weapon here, soldier," the emissary told him.

He had waited for the 6th Company sniper to get ready, then led him to the rear base on the way to Lake Loimola, where he had been summoned by the divisional commander. In front of a small committee under a magnificent blue sky and a dazzling sun that set the snow aflame, Simo was congratulated for all he had done.

"*This rifle of honour made in Sweden is awarded to Simo Häyhä in recognition of his achievements as a marksman and combatant,*" the colonel read. Dressed in a snowsuit and wearing a fur cap, he was surrounded by his officers, a pastor and the official photographer, all lined up to face the recipient.

"*His actions, with 219 of the enemy killed with a precision rifle and an equal number with a sub-machine gun, demonstrate what a single Finn with a keen eye and steady hands can do when he is determined and fearless. This rifle of honour should be seen as being as valuable as a medal, and should be passed down from father to son as a reminder, for generations to come, of Simo Häyhä's courageous acts in this war, in which the soldiers of Finland have bravely and successfully fought for the liberty of their country, the future of their nation, and humanity's most precious ideals.*"

The photographer positioned his tripod in the snow and

prepared to keep alive the memory of the ceremony. He was waiting for a smile from his subject, but when this did not appear naturally, the pastor gestured for him to be patient and went up to Simo.

"What do you see, soldier, when you take aim?"

The answer was so simple that Simo hesitated.

"A Russian!" the pastor chuckled. "Obviously, that's what you're going to tell me. But you don't see the whole picture. There is you, at one with your rifle. Right behind you there is your company, then your battalion, your regiment, your division. Then there's your family, your village, the whole country, and an entire people holding their breath with you. You are not alone; you never have been. You are three and a half million hearts swelling with pride. This photograph is more important than you think. This photograph is Finland resisting. So please smile."

And since everyone else was smiling, Simo imitated them, the rifle of honour clasped tightly in his mittens.

After that there was a good lunch. Then the phantom horse reappeared, with the same rider.

*

The rifle of honour was passed from hand to hand around the fire. Its shiny steel and unblemished wood proved it had not yet been used, but when it was returned to Simo he slipped it under the bunk bed and recovered the one that until now had never failed him.

He knew the weaknesses of his old M28/30, and because he did, they became its strengths. Using a new weapon would have obliged him to readapt, to get to know it, and in the midst of the constant combat this did not seem the right moment. And besides, who would abandon his friend just because he's growing old? He had too much affection for it. Just as he was about to check the loading mechanism and clean it from top to bottom, loud noises outside the tent attracted his attention. Before he could even step outside, he heard a panicked voice:

"It's Juutilainen!"

"It's the Terror! He's been wounded!" another shouted.

*

Stretched out on a medical sled surrounded by soldiers, with Karlsson carrying his weapon, Juutilainen was struggling like a nag resisting being harnessed. He held up his hand, wrapped in a white bandage that had turned a sticky red, grimacing with pain and cursing both the Russian who had shot him and the Finns who had prevented him from taking his revenge even though he was wounded.

Kicking aside the Lotta who had come up to him, he unwound the bandage himself.

"Look, little one, it's nothing! Nothing a good bottle of alcohol can't cure."

With that he peered straight through the round hole the bullet had drilled in his hand. Through it he could see his unit staring at him, wide-eyed.

Simo and his two friends approached Karlsson. They had a hundred questions: the legionnaire had been wounded, which they all thought was impossible. Obviously Death herself would not know what to do with such a burden.

"Was it a sniper?" Onni said.

"Yes, yes," Karlsson eventually responded.

"But it was a Russian, right?" Pietari said, to make sure.

"Yes, yes," Karlsson repeated. "Who else?"

"So who is going to command us now?"

"First things first. Start by warning the first-aid post. Get them to radio for an ambulance from the base hospital. Our lieutenant needs to be operated on as rapidly as possible."

No-one needed to express out loud the relief the whole

company felt at the idea of getting the Terror off their backs for a few days. They watched their tyrannical officer being taken away to the first-aid post. Wounded by a Russian. No doubt about it.

Informed of Juutilainen's injury, Teittinen came at once to their camp to announce the appointment of his temporary replacement.

"Karlsson!" he roared. "Come here!"

58

Main headquarters, Mikkeli, Finland

Aksel Airo found Mannerheim in the church next to the hotel where their headquarters was based. It was here they had lunches and dinners; to make room for their long tables, the pews had been stacked in front of the stained-glass windows in the nave.

Lost in thought beneath the impassive gaze of Christ on the cross, the army commander was letting a mug of tea grow cold.

"The Soviet Union is inviting us to sit down at the negotiating table again," Airo told him. "I have the terms of the new proposed treaty with me."

Stalin had lost some of his arrogant attitude. Having been convinced he could bring Finland to its knees in a fortnight from the month of December, it was now February and he was facing the bitter reality of a much less triumphant outcome. His troops had still not advanced more than ten kilometres into the territory he had set his sights on, and the weather was against him.

In a few weeks, the climate would change. One after the other the Finnish lakes were going to thaw. In a country with almost 180,000 of them, the Russians would no longer be able to cross the water, but would have to fight their way round every one. At the same time, the snow would be melting, turning the earth into mud.

But what the Soviet dictator feared above all was not what would happen in Finland.

Stalin was beginning to look ridiculous in the eyes of the person he was afraid might want to invade Russia. Every additional day presented Hitler with the image of a country less powerful than it claimed to be, stoking his own ambition like a fire. And if Stalin added to his fears by reading the latest telegrams from his spies in Paris and London, informing him that France and Great Britain were considering intervening militarily in Finland, what he had at first thought would be a lightning conflict could turn into a quagmire.

Seeking to play the ogre and devour his tiny neighbour, he had only succeeded in drawing attention to himself. This war had been going on too long, and it had to be concluded, but without losing face.

And so Mannerheim and Stalin were talking to one another without speaking. From a distance, so as not to get their hands dirty. To communicate, Russia contacted a Swedish diplomat, who in turn got in touch with the Finnish ambassador in France, who passed the message on to his foreign minister in Finland, who relayed the information to Aksel Airo.

"New terms for a peace treaty, you say?" the field marshal repeated. "Are they really new?"

"Absolutely not. They're identical to the ones they proposed before the war, and identical to what they proposed in January. Stalin is demanding use of the port of Hanko for 30 years …"

"Obviously. The port that controls the entrance to the Gulf of Finland, and the opening to the West. That is unacceptable."

"He also wants Petsamo and the port of Liinakhamari …"

"To gain access to the Arctic Ocean and the nickel mines. That is not acceptable either."

"Then he wants to establish military bases in—"

"I'm well aware of what he wants," Mannerheim interrupted angrily, knocking over his mug of cold tea. "I haven't sent all the able-bodied men of Finland to the front, and I haven't lost more than 15,000 soldiers already, just to accept today what I rejected yesterday."

The negotiations to find a diplomatic way to end the Winter War were like having two mules confronting each other: neither would back down.

"President Kallio agrees with you," Airo said. "But he's not living under the Russian bombardment. Their army has launched 250,000 shells on our frontlines in a single day. That's more than we have had for the entire war. As for Kollaa, that's a real mystery. I cannot understand how so few soldiers are managing to hold off six complete divisions. And you know very well that if your line or Kollaa falls, then all of Finland opens up to Stalin. So I simply wonder how much longer we can resist?"

A good part of Europe was asking itself the same question, each one of them putting their own self-interest first.

"Stockholm and Berlin are calling on us to accept Stalin's terms. Paris and London are asking us to wait, and promising to send soldiers."

"I know that, Aksel. Daladier is talking of 40,000. Chamberlain almost 100,000. But when will those troops arrive? For now, all they're doing in France is splashing me on the front pages of their newspapers. Promises, promises! I cannot load my guns with promises! The minutes that tick by while I wait for their soldiers are not made up of seconds, but of our dead."

"Am I to understand you wish to negotiate with Stalin?"

"Certainly not. Contact Tanner.[24] I want to talk to Daladier. I need to know if France is with us. If it is, Great Britain will follow. This war is not yet lost!"

59

South of France, February 1940,
fifth-year primary class at Saint Joseph's School

At least the other pupils' poems rhymed. Their poems were not full of spelling mistakes either. And yet he had put his heart into his, and spent most of the previous evening on it, even if the result did not altogether show that. With his crumpled sheet of paper covered in clumsy handwriting laid flat on his desk, the nine-year-old schoolboy dreaded hearing his name called out, having to cross the classroom, stand up on the platform and recite his work. From the invention of schools to the present day, generations of clammy hands preceded him, and more generations would follow.

"Jean Chaignon," the teacher called out. "Come to the front."

Everywhere in France, it had been considered important for classes to talk about Finland, of the sublime combat of those who were supposed to capitulate within a few days and yet were still resisting. If the Finnish David could hold out against the Red Goliath, then there was hope for every country. And if compassion could be made a part of a composition exercise, so much the better.

His accent full of sunlight, the boy read his text with a touching awkwardness.

Dear Finlanders. I'm not rich at orll, but I take five francs from my piggie bank for you. My papa also will go to war to defand us from the Germains. I finish my litul letter shoutin: Long life Finland!

In a little more than two months, Germany was to launch the battle of France by invading the Netherlands, Luxembourg and Belgium. A few weeks later, Nazi boots were clicking their heels on the streets of Paris. The schoolteacher knew nothing of this, but if stories for children are meant to give them the means to confront the misfortunes of life – divorce and being abandoned, fear and hunger, even the loss of a loved one – then there was nothing so terrible about talking a little of war, even in distant Finland. "It doesn't rhyme, and his command of French is poor," the teacher thought, "so he doesn't deserve top marks." But the boy had given practically all his savings, and although his text did not have much literary merit, it showed that his heart was in the right place.

From his desk, the teacher picked up a little piece of cardboard with "Good effort" on it and handed it to the blushing pupil.

*

Paris, February 1940, Quartier Saint-Germain

The wrestling match had been advertised throughout the French capital on hundreds of posters and on the radio. Angiolino Giuseppe Pasquale Ventura, known as the "Italian Rocket" (Lino Ventura to his friends), a big-hearted giant with an iron fist in a velvet glove, had accepted this charity match for the "tiny" nation at war with Russia. He had not hesitated long, because, like everyone in Europe, he had been impressed by Finland's courage.

The Second World War had been declared more than six months earlier, but by February 1940 neither France nor Great Britain had been affected. There was a war in progress, but it was invisible. There was no lack of leisurely customers on the terraces of Parisian cafés, talking about Finland as though, lacking a conflict in their own land, they had to find another one to discuss.

Théodule Blanchard circled the paragraph in *Paris-Soir* that had a photograph of Lino, face covered in a black-and-white mask, fists at the ready, pectorals flexed. There had been a series of rain showers that day, and Théodule and his friend had used this as an excuse not to leave the café all afternoon.

"We mustn't miss this!" Théodule exclaimed. "And besides, it's in a good cause!"

"Finland? And to think that a few weeks ago nobody even knew where to find it on a map."

"And now it's all people talk about! Wait …"

Blanchard turned the pages of his newspaper, looking for the article that had caught his eye, and which summed up the worldwide interest in this minuscule conflict.

"Here it is," he said, pushing his glasses up his nose. "In England they're having an auction of works of art with all the profits going to the Finnish Army. In Belgium, they're marching with banners saying 'Down with the aggressor' and 'Honour to the Finnish soldiers'. The Pope is raising his voice from the Vatican. And in Geneva, the League of Nations has condemned this unjust aggression. Sweden has sent planes, guns and ambulances, and on its national radio organised a collection that has reached a million marks. Even the great Greta Garbo has given five thousand dollars from her own pocket. The newspaper says that as we speak on Broadway somebody called Robert E. Sherwood is putting on a play about the Winter War."[25]

"What about us? Does it mention France?"

"Of course. Did you think France would remain a simple spectator of history? Edith Piaf has sung at a charity concert in support of the Finnish cause, and we have also formed an aid committee. It says here that 72,600 francs has been collected, as well as pairs of old skis. And the French being French, that is seeing themselves as the centre of the world, some have even sent their ration coupons!"

"The Finns are going to have a long walk if they have to come to Paris to get their loaf of bread and kilo of sugar! But some money and pairs of old skis is a bit lukewarm as a commitment, don't you think?"

"A bit lukewarm?" Blanchard protested loudly, as if the

comment had been directed at him personally. Other customers in the café turned to look at him.

By now he was standing up in his elegant suit and dropping some coins onto the table for a fresh round of drinks. He glanced at the barman to reassure him he would lower his voice.

"Their army commander is on the cover of *Paris Match*," he said, sitting down again. "Someone by the name of Mannerheim: his photograph fills the page! And Léon Blum is talking of the 'Soviet crime' ... Lukewarm, you say? You'll see tonight if Lino is lukewarm."

*

Paris, Palais des Sports

Seated in the front row of the smoke-filled hall, Théodule and his chum had completely forgotten about Finland. The spotlights trained on the ring made the skin glisten on the two giants who were playing their parts, half-serious and half-show, as they followed a careful choreography. The "Italian Rocket" sent his adversary flying under and over the ropes. Each time, the men applauded and the women stamped their high heels.

"It's a headlock, followed by a body press," the radio commentator bellowed.

Lino lifted his opponent, a burly man from Montmartre who said he was a Turk to add a touch of exoticism even though he had never left Paris. His body was so oily he slipped out of Lino's grasp, but, in a swift move, the Italian got behind him, forced him to his knees, and put him in a half nelson. Groggy, pretending he could not breathe, the Turk slapped the canvas, but there was no way he was going to be allowed to throw in the towel so easily.

"Two chops to the throat from the wonderful Lino! What a sight! Now he's got him by the legs ... Yes, go for it!"

Lino grasped his willing opponent firmly by the heels, spun him round once, twice, then sent him crashing in a heap at the foot of the referee, who signalled the end of the round. Panting for breath, the two giants regained their stools.

"They're the ones we should send to Finland!" Blanchard exclaimed in the interval between rounds. "They're worth at least ten soldiers!"

"So you think we're going to send soldiers?"

"I can't see Daladier, and still less France, abandoning a democracy attacked so unjustly. Of course we're going to help them."

"You, for example, you've done your national service, haven't you?"

The enthusiasm and excitement immediately drained from Blanchard's face, replaced by an apologetic expression.

"You know me, and you know I'm furious I couldn't enrol, but this pain in my hip ... Last summer ... Well ... it's all very tragic."

And since at these fervent sporting events conversations never remain private, an obviously well-informed young man leaned forward from the row behind.

"Joining in the conflict now would be suicidally irresponsible. I don't think Finland has yet had to face the worst of what Russia can throw at them. Don't you read Kessel's articles? It appears Stalin is preparing an attack that could bring this famous Winter War to a swift conclusion."

This emotive news deserved further discussion, but slipped out of everyone's mind when the bell rang and the two athletes stood up again, ready to renew their combat.

In the Palais des Sports as elsewhere, the Winter War was at the heart of many discussions and led to a great number of passionate speeches. But apart from widespread and sincere sympathy, fine words, poems, a few chops to the throat and pairs of old skis, on the eve of an unprecedented Russian strike, Finland was still fighting alone, isolated and abandoned.

60

Gulf of Finland

Nobody had seen it coming, because nobody ever thought the Russians would dare attempt it. The Red Army had been rethought, reorganised and galvanised. Timoshenko, the mastermind behind this transformation, believed he could do anything.

With January past and February well under way, the war of attrition came to an end. Man-to-man fighting resumed on the Mannerheim Line and on the Kollaa front. But alongside this, and in the greatest secrecy, an astonishing operation had been envisaged: to invade Finland across its frozen gulf. On the new skis they had only just learned to use, the Red Army soldiers intended to cross the Gulf, take Viipuri – one of the biggest cities in Finland – and if fortune smiled on them, go on to storm the Mannerheim Line from the rear. After that, nothing would be able to arrest their advance or delay their victory.

However, a volcanic eruption would have been quieter than the movement of tens of thousands of men and horses, thousands of cannon, and hundreds of tanks. Before the first Russian so much as placed his skis on the frozen gulf, the Finns were already waiting on the far side, still not quite able to believe what they were seeing.

From one frozen bank to the other, 120 kilometres separated the two armies.

A new division had been formed from men taken out of the Mannerheim Line. They were deployed along the coast to defend the Gulf and its islands, scattered like confetti across the ice.

For several weeks, Viktor Koskinen had been attached to a gunner and had learned the rudiments of his trade. When the gunner was hit at the base of his spine and left paralysed, he had begged his companion to finish him off. Viktor had not hesitated. He had then taken his warm boots and his position before being chosen to go and participate in a new kind of conflict, only a few kilometres from where he was in the Gulf of Finland, and where the artillery would play a major role.

*

Some 90 days earlier, at the beginning of the war, when the marshes and lakes had first frozen over, a large number of Russian soldiers had overestimated the thickness of the ice, and it had given way beneath them. It was already −30°C, and if they were soaked from head to toe, they could not be warmed up again. They solidified after a few steps, or even in mid-air, frozen in mid-stride, with one foot forward and the other back, or with a hand outstretched, begging for help.

Since then, the orders were clear. Like a headless chicken, a wet soldier is the only one unaware that his life is over, and nothing can be done for him. His new friend Death had already put her hand on his shoulder and accompanied him for just a few steps more, while the other soldiers looked on disconsolately, almost apologising for abandoning him while he was still alive.

But winter, like the war, had progressed, and historically low temperatures had been recorded. With the thermometer showing −50°C, the Kremlin decided the Gulf could be crossed. And as with every order from Moscow, there was no questioning this mission.

In this white desert where the snowflakes whirling in the wind blotted out all contours, eyes stared blankly at the infinite horizon.

Everybody on the Finnish side knew of the plan, but they would have to see the Russians to believe it. Were they really going to undertake this folly? Was this perhaps a diversionary tactic, or did the Soviet high command really have so little regard for their soldiers' lives?

The thick layer of ice in the centre of the Gulf would have borne the weight of a fully loaded bomber, but, as any child could have foretold, the ice was thinner at the edges, and the first Soviet tank sank straight to the bottom. So did the enthusiasm of the soldiers who witnessed this terrible spectacle and heard the crew inside screaming for help.

Men were sent to look for more secure routes onto the ice, while Soviet engineers built wooden bridges so that the artillery and armoured vehicles could avoid the edges and land directly on a layer of ice thick enough to support them. After more than a hundred human losses, the remainder of the troops and their artillery could finally advance in close order. They advanced clinging to one another, falling one after the other, pushing forward blindly as there were no distinguishing features in the white cotton wool enveloping them.

On the first day of the assault the wind got up and gave them no respite until dusk. Huge sheets of white powder split up the units, and the soldiers – sometimes only a few metres from their colleagues – became completely lost. Even their shouts were snatched out of their mouths by the howling wind; many of them died firing at each other, convinced they were facing the enemy.

These same blizzards prevented them from seeing the many islets that were not defended like the larger islands but were just as dangerous because around them the icy surface was thinner. The blinded Russian tanks did not slow down as they approached these invisible shores, and only the infantry heard the crack echoing like a whiplash or metal cables about to snap deep in the water that announced their imminent demise. All at once the ice would part beneath them, the tanks plunging to the bottom as rapidly as a ship's anchor. As they toppled they created jagged cracks that zigzagged across the surface beneath the soldiers' skis, the horses' hooves, before the ice gave way completely and they were swallowed up. The thermal shock was so great that neither men nor horses could emit any sound, all of them dying in silence. A few managed to clamber out of the water; others clung on to the jagged edges before letting themselves go under.

The 120 kilometres became a whole continent to cross. Before they even reached the defended islands of Teikari and Tuppura, the Red Army had lost more than 2,000 men.

On the deserted island of Teikari with gently sloping beaches of cold sand and covered in a forest of pines as dense as a knitted jumper, neither Viktor nor his unit could as yet quite believe in an attack as absurd as it was reckless. It was only because they had been ordered to do so that they had set up their machine guns and artillery there.

Yet the Russians did arrive. Heralded by the rumble of engines. Then by their silhouettes, like a supernatural army of shadows, so unsubstantial that it seemed all bullets, all thrusts could pass straight through it.

And the most obvious Finnish command was finally given.

"At my signal … Aim at the ice!"

Viktor, who Pietari had thought too frail to go to war, Viktor, who everyone thought would be unable to survive a single day, was there, erect and determined, directing where to aim his cannon, loading it with shell after shell.

Everywhere, as shells and bullets exploded, the ice groaned as it broke up. As if sucked towards the seabed, the Red shadows vanished. Terrified horses reared and clambered over each other, bolted and injured their companions, whinnying painfully before going under as well, taking their riders with them. Out of compassion, the surviving soldiers shot men and animals before hastening on so as not to be separated from the others.

The Russians, whether forced men or patriots, blindly obeyed and advanced nevertheless. It was only thanks to the flashes from the Finnish guns lighting up the thick fogs that they knew where to aim.

The first night fell on the Gulf. The firing paused for a few hours in a truce imposed by cold and fatigue. Before dawn, the Soviet officers woke the living, left the frozen bodies where they lay, and at first light reached the island, only to discover that the Finns had already abandoned it to regroup on the next island and organise its defence.

On his way between the two, Viktor followed the horses pulling the cannon and mortars. In the vanguard without having been ordered to be there, he huddled close to his companions and concentrated on the metre in front of him, wiping the snow off his compass to make sure he was going in the right direction. Suddenly a shadow appeared before his eyes. He raised his fist calling for silence, and his bewildered officer repeated the gesture.

Like some huge bear trap, spikes and metal tips stuck up out of the ice in front of them. Viktor stepped forward warily, rifle at the ready, then advanced a little further, until he understood. He and the others walked on in respectful silence through this cemetery of Russian soldiers, caught the previous day in the freezing water and frozen before they could even sink. Their arms, rifle barrels, bayonets, skis and ski poles, even the top half of some bodies, bristled on the surface of the Gulf like weeds made of flesh, wood and metal. The heads of dead horses also emerged, manes like motionless black waves glistening with snow crystals, the ivory foam of their final struggles on the corners of their mouths.

Here and there under the surface of the ice they could make out the white faces of those who had gone down in the glacial blue water, then tried to resurface, only to be blocked by a transparent ceiling, mouths wide open in a last desperate attempt to breathe. Without compunction, the Finnish soldiers had to advance over them.

By midday Viktor and his unit finally reached the island of Tuppura, there to be greeted by a colonel who repeated the order he had been given.

"Mannerheim will not allow us to lose a single island in the Gulf. You've come from Teikari, now you have to go back there."

Back and forth for seven days, from islet to island, from fragile victories to terrible defeats, Russians and Finns killed one another with the same fury, with the same fear in their guts.

Six thousand, five hundred Russians lost their lives there.

Five thousand, two hundred Finns died with them.

Almost twelve thousand dead, until finally a few Soviet units reached the coast of Finland. They then had to make their way to the Mannerheim Line to support the rest of the Red Army in the hope of breaking through.

The climax was approaching. Without help from abroad, Finland was facing certain invasion and unavoidable surrender. Everything now rested on the shoulders of its exhausted soldiers. And the impossible was going to be demanded of the soldiers on the coast, on the Mannerheim Line, and on the Kollaa front.

To continue to resist.

61

End of February 1940, Kollaa front

That night, Simo dreamed of Toivo and his village, Rautjärvi.

"Did you know they're so scared of you they've given you a nickname?" Toivo had said to him, a piece of straw in his mouth, the summer sun burning his face as he lay on a field covered in a blond haze, a big red stain on his chest. "*Belaya Smert.* The White Death ... I've seen you crying over grazed knees, and defended you from your sisters' teasing, and now here you are, a legend."

Simo had stretched out his hand to press it on Toivo's wound and staunch the blood oozing out, but his friend had disappeared, swallowed up by the corn. When Simo woke, he could still hear Toivo's voice, almost warm inside his head. Then the bombardments took over, louder and louder, and the cold forced its way into every pore of his body.

"Come on! There's coffee and ginger biscuits," Onni told him. "Some new lads as well."

Since the battles had intensified, Simo only very rarely left on his own to hunt the enemy. The Soviet 8th Army was drawing closer, and their artillery often found their positions. They spent as much time in the trenches responding with mortars as they did sheltering in the wooden bunkers, praying they would still withstand the impact of the shells.

Crouching as usual, Simo and Onni crossed the camp to join Karlsson who was greeting the latest arrivals with coffee and biscuits. Unlike the Russian hydra, the Finnish troops could not be replaced *ad infinitum*. The wounded were no longer kept in the field hospitals, but given places in defence positions or returned to combat if they had recovered. There were not enough men available to be fussy, which explained why among the 20 or so new volunteers there was one with a limp, another with a heart murmur, a one-eyed man and a boy who was far from being an adult.

The officers no longer knew their soldiers, who were dispersed among different units; the rattle of machine guns in the distance and the thunder of the artillery all around them left them feeling disoriented.

"I am your designated commander," Karlsson addressed them after getting them to form up. "Look at me. Look at one another. Remember your neighbours' faces. The Russians are now also wearing white snowsuits, and our weapons look like theirs – because they are theirs, snatched from their arms in attack after attack. In blizzards, nothing looks more like a soldier than another soldier, so try not to kill one another."

They all obeyed his instructions, studying each other's faces so that they were no longer strangers but brothers-in-arms.

"Outside the trenches," Karlsson continued, "I don't want to see anyone standing upright. You crawl to get around. You stay flat to grab your gun, to reload, to take off your skis. Even to piss you stay flat."

By now in the motionless ranks jaws were clenching with cold, limbs stiffening with cramp. Their whole bodies were one big shudder, an unceasing wave of violent trembling.

"Embrace the pain, or you'll go mad! And don't touch any metal with your bare hands. Vehicles, weapons, shells – wear gloves, or strips of your skin will be torn off."

Karlsson ordered Onni and Pietari to take the new 6th Company recruits to the rear base, where their equipment, camouflage suits and rifles were waiting for them. Then he gestured to Simo to come up, and introduced him to the boy who was far from being an adult, who already had his gun.

"This is Yrjö," Karlsson told him. "He's come from the Viipuri Civic Guard. He hasn't completed his training, but he impressed on the shooting range. You're to take him under your wing, teach him what you know, and how to survive. You're to …"

But Simo was no longer listening. He wasn't looking at Yrjö, but at his uniform. At his chest. That almost invisible mended hole in the exact same place where Toivo had been mortally wounded. What were the chances?

"I saw you at the Civic Guard national shooting championship," the youngster said, recognising Simo, his words mangled by his chattering teeth. "You're even talked about on the radio. It's an honour to …"

A gust of wind carried off the rest of his sentence. Yrjö pulled up his collar, revealing on the back the small square of Finnish-blue cloth sewn there for someone else. Toivo's face became superimposed on that of Yrjö, and Simo's heart leaped.

*

Road to Loimola, Russian side

Attached to a crane by a massive steel chain, the enormous wrecking ball smashed the last farmhouse still standing in a doleful cracking of splintered wood and clouds of sawdust.

Since the outset of hostilities, the villages scattered along the road to Loimola had for the most part been destroyed by fire, but a few houses that had been spared, or what remained of the ruins of others, obstructed the view of the Russian gunners, and nothing now should stand between Stalin's troops and the Finnish defensive line. No villages or forests. Everything had to be destroyed.

The Stavka's envoy Fiodor Komarov had Shtern's ear, and as a result was appointed to lead this demolition operation, backed by his military officer, Captain Anikine.

With houses and farmhouses reduced to rubble, Komarov

turned towards the centre of the massacred village, contemptuously surveying the only building left standing.

"The church as well. Knock the church down."

The crane rumbled across. The metal ball slammed into the stone wall of the aisle and the stained-glass windows exploded in thousands of coloured stars. Inside, the wooden crucifix in the choir, as tall as the church, swayed, came off its supports, and toppled, splitting in two.

To Captain Anikine and his soldiers, all of them fervent Orthodox Christians, this was too much blasphemy. Many of them crossed themselves to ward off divine thunderbolts.

With the space cleared at last, Komarov had the cannon brought and lined up. Their muzzles were aimed at the vast forests that hid the Finns, the 30 kilometres of interconnected trenches that Russian patrols had still not been able to map properly, the Finnish Army's camp and, somewhere yet more hidden, their rear base.

"Fire. Keep on firing at that damned forest. I don't want a single branch left. And when it is wiped off the map, move on to the next one. I want to be able to see as far as the horizon, right inside their tents!"

The Red Army no longer seemed so much to want to win a war as to annihilate a country. Komarov was determined to play his part zealously.

The cannon fired almost a thousand shells in the same direction. When the fog of sawdust settled and the wind blew away the smell of gunpowder, all that was left was the fresh, spicy aroma of pine resin strangely floating among the troops.

A flare was sent up into the heavy clouds, lighting them like a beating heart. Then the order was given to launch the infantry in a wave of thousands in the direction of Kollaa.

Above them, a few hundred metres away, floated three giant helium balloons. Beneath them hung baskets, in which, glued to their field glasses, lookouts followed their troops, searching in the distance for the slightest trace of the Finnish phantoms.

*

Simo had accompanied Yrjö as far as the soldiers' tents. Because being a marksman meant remaining motionless for long periods, he had advised him to wear as many layers of clothing as possible. It took Yrjö some time to do this, sufficient to give the sniper the chance to abandon a pupil he had never asked to look after or be responsible for.

Yrjö found himself alone, swathed in clothes. In the distance the forest was lit up by deafening balls of fire, and only 200 metres from him the frontline trenches kept firing incessantly, feeding their machine guns with belt after belt of ammunition. All at once he was swept up by an unknown officer who made him part of a unit that was not his for the remainder of that day.

The 34th Regiment was protecting the Kollaa front; the 35th had been sent to engage the Russians inside the forests; and the 36th had split up into *Sissi* to launch attacks along the road.

Until nightfall Yrjö shot straight ahead of him, cutting down one after the other of what he preferred to think of as white silhouettes. His trench was spared when the adjacent one suffered a direct hit from a shell. For more than an hour he fired his sub-machine gun to cover the orderlies recovering the wounded from the bowels of the earth, and the ones on skis pulling the stretcher sleds behind them.

When finally he was relieved by the replacement company, Yrjö had no idea where he was, and had to ask his way back to the 6th Company camp like a little boy lost in a big city. Just a kid who for the first time had killed once, then ten times, and had finally given up counting.

There was no room close to the burning stove. The wind was whipping against the canvas of the tent. The layer of peat and moss covering the ground had recently been changed and the organic smell they gave off helped reduce the usual stench a little. Yrjö was about to go humbly in search of some human warmth on the wooden bunks, when Simo, who had abandoned the newcomer that morning, squeezed up against his neighbour to make room for him. Yrjö sat down without saying anything or uttering any reproach. Simo was a legend, the Magic Marksman, the White Death, and he would consider himself very fortunate to one day observe him in action.

"It seems Juutilainen is on his way back," Onni announced, heating up his pea soup on the embers: the soup always went cold as soon as they raised it to their mouths.

"Already?" Pietari said, surprised.

"Yeah. It appears he started several fights in the hospital and the doctors were so sick of him they're sending him back early."

The faces round the stove looked downcast at the news. In recent days, Karlsson had repeatedly assessed the risks of each of the missions he was undertaking. He worried about his men and positioned himself in the first line for every attack. When there was a risk of needless danger, he had had the courage to turn back. As a result, the men gave him their absolute loyalty, almost friendship. So when they heard the news of the legionnaire's return, some of them expressed their dismay and fear out loud. Others more surreptitiously even proffered insults. Before this could grow into open insubordination, Karlsson had to intervene.

"We'll eat well tonight, one of the Lottas has a soft spot for me. We'll drink as well: I've hidden a few bottles. We'll even sing, so loudly the Russians will think we've come to love war. Then tomorrow, under Lieutenant Juutilainen's orders, we'll continue the fight. But at the first lack of discipline, the bullet up your backside will come from my gun."

Even if they did not believe him, they took him seriously.

Despite the incongruously buoyant mood that evening, the

men did not last long before fatigue overcame them. Simo was left on his own beside Karlsson.

"We've already lost lots of men for Operation Talvela north of our position. In the south, the Mannerheim Line has a huge appetite for soldiers, so we are going to lose another regiment tomorrow to help fortify it. They will be facing seven times as many Russians. One Finn to seven Russians, can you imagine?"

Simo could. He stuffed another frozen log into the open stove.

"The Terror's return means we'll be on the frontline again, you know. And that means more of your sniper missions. I'm afraid he will ask the same of Yrjö. And the lad isn't ready."

Simo knew this too. Karlsson did not ask him anything more, but left to sleep in the officers' tent. On his way he snatched a bottle of *viina* from the grasp of a sleeping soldier.

In the chorus of snores, howling wind and endless bombardments, a voice was discreetly and fervently saying a prayer:

Eternal, merciful God, you who are a God of peace, love and unity, we pray to you, Father, and beg you through your Holy Spirit to bring together all that is scattered, to reunite and restore all that is divided …

"For the love of Him!" his neighbour protested. "I heard you reciting that throughout the three days it took us to get here. Don't you know anything else?"

"That one suits me," Yrjö whispered. "I mean, it's worked so far. But I'll continue in my head, if you prefer."

He slipped his hand under the neck of his jersey and pulled on the silver chain on which hung a gold crucifix and a sparrow-shaped amulet his sister had given him so that his soul would not get lost in his dreams. He shut his eyes tight with the same fervour, and returned to his now silent prayer.

"Yrjö," his neighbour said.

"Yes?"

"Actually, I don't mind if you continue quietly."

Like old people and those condemned to death, the soldiers wanted to draw closer to the Almighty in case they were soon to meet Him. Besides, Yrjö's voice made a good lullaby.

So that we may have one sole heart, one sole wish, one sole science, one sole spirit, one sole reason and, turned entirely towards Jesus Christ our Lord, we shall, Father, praise you with one sole mouth and give thanks to you, through our Lord Jesus Christ in the Holy Spirit, Amen.

"Amen," responded several anonymous voices in unison. It was a cold, restless night. When one of them fell asleep, another woke up screaming. They were killing endlessly, and when they returned to camp they had to count their missing friends. The unbearable and intolerable were becoming routine. Even so, once they closed their eyes the savage, atrocious images of that day, piled on top of those from earlier days, flashed time and again through their minds. The screams and dying breaths were branded on their souls, by now as moth-eaten as old wool. Would they ever sleep peacefully again?

Before dawn, Yrjö felt someone shaking his shoulder. Opening his eyes, the cold immediately struck him; he had to get used to the darkness before he finally saw Simo's silhouette, perched on the edge of one of the wide communal beds.

62

Going round obstacles was no longer an option. Day after day, section after section, the Russians had destroyed the 20 kilometres of forest separating them from the Kollaa front. Sitting on top of a rock that looked down over this sinister devastated landscape, Simo surveyed the scene, controlling his anger.

He jumped back down in two agile leaps, took out of his rucksack the map that showed where the Finnish mines had been laid, and drew a circle with a red pencil round what had once been a lush forest.

The Soviet 8th Army was abandoning the road to Loimola and adopting a different strategy. When Finland was as bare as the *tunturi* of Lapland,[26] there would no longer be anywhere left to hide. That was how the Russians seemed to want to win this war, with all the subtlety of a steamroller.

Yrjö's training could wait: the rear base had to be alerted, and so the two men turned back to find the River Kollaa and the frontline along it. But after only a few minutes on their skis Simo saw a cloud of carrion crows flying in concentric circles high in the sky. These birds usually fed on dead animals, but since the theatre of a merciless, shatteringly noisy war had invaded their territory, all the game had vanished. So what were these dozens of black silhouettes circling round? His curiosity piqued, Simo decided to go closer.

All around them artillery thumped and machine guns rattled. Either in vicious combat or simply to unfreeze the weapons, both sides fired them without stopping, so that the temperature of −50°C did not completely jam them. They had even kept big bonfires alight day and night and stacked rifles, mortars and cannon round them to keep them at a temperature only slightly below zero.

The cold that froze engines and weapons also dulled the smells, otherwise Simo and Yrjö would have long since realised what was in front of them and above which the crows were dancing.

A mass grave of at least 500 dead created a mound ten metres high that was only half-buried. Ten metres of frozen flesh covered in black parasites, torn to pieces by ravenous beaks and claws. The Kremlin repeated endlessly that the Winter War was not killing the children of the Motherland, and so these bodies that the propaganda insisted did not exist had to be abandoned. The pair took off their skis to walk round the pile. The sight of this hideous 500-faced monster, some of the bodies frozen in pain, others with a strange look of surprise, made Yrjö want to pray again. Suddenly Simo's hand was clamped on his mouth.

Fifteen metres away, a silent group of 20 Red soldiers was struggling to pull sleds piled high with fresh bodies.

Simo threw his rucksack, skis and rifle to the ground. The soft snow swallowed them up. With one knee on the ground, he lowered the baggy hood on his snowsuit in front of his face. Yrjö copied his every move; white on white and perfectly motionless, they disappeared.

The Russians passed right in front of them. They hauled the bodies off the sleds and, exhausted by the effort and unable to throw them on top of the mound, left them where they lay. A packet of cigarettes passed from hand to hand, and as they exhaled, the smell of brown tobacco reached the two invisible Finnish soldiers concealed less than two metres from them. Yrjö was trembling with fear and cold. They had to breathe as faintly as possible, allowing only a thin stream of air to leave their mouths to prevent creating a telltale cloud of vapour forming around them. Simo felt gently under the snow for the stock of his rifle, ready for any eventuality.

Caught up in their work as gravediggers, and suffering from the cold and fatigue, the Russians only looked straight ahead of them like dray horses. Dragging their now empty sled behind them, they passed by Simo and his apprentice once again without noticing them in this petrified ivory landscape.

Coming out of near apnoea, the two Finns could finally take a deep breath. They searched in the snow for their weapons, skis and rucksacks, then stood up – only for a gunshot to ring out. Simo turned to Yrjö, convinced he must have been hit, but all he saw was a white-faced youngster with a small puff of smoke emerging from the muzzle of his gun. Yrjö's hands were so numb he had not felt the pressure he had put on the trigger. And if that involuntary shot had been a friendly one, the following ones were definitely Russian.

Simo grabbed Yrjö by the collar and they began to run as fast as possible, hampered by the skis they were carrying, rifles slung over one shoulder and their packs over the other. Bullets whistled past them as they struggled through the snow.

The sniper spotted a mound of snow and they threw themselves behind it: definitely the worst hiding place imaginable, offering no protection at all. Russians were coming towards them, and if they were the gravediggers, that meant there were 20 of them.

The two Finns were caught in a trap. Bullets ricocheted off the flat granite boulders, demolishing what was left of the trees torn apart by Komarov's shells, piercing their useless shield of snow. The Russians did not aim carefully but kept up a steady stream of bullets. It was only a matter of seconds before Simo and Yrjö were shot or, worse still, captured. Simo thought of his farm, of Toivo, and was astonished not to see his protective fox. He had been convinced it would come to him in the last moments of his life, to envelop him in its warm fur and musky smell. Another bullet whizzed so close he even thought he could feel the wind it displaced as it sped through the air. There were 20 of them. In a heroic last stand Simo could kill five in as many seconds before needing to reload, but the remainder of the Red unit would surely finish them off.

Ready to meet the swan of the land of the dead, Simo closed his eyes, grasped his weapon, and prepared to inflict his last feat of courage on the enemy. But he did not even have time to stand up.

"I am Simo Häyhä!" yelled Yrjö defiantly, even though he was quaking with fear, his back against the mound of snow. "The White Death! *Belaya Smert*! I have a bullet for each of your filthy faces! Do you want to croak here or see the sun tomorrow?"

The firing stopped at once.

To make himself understood, Yrjö had mixed a few words of Russian into his Finnish and that, it seemed, had done the trick.

On their side, the Russians were talking this over. Ordinary soldiers had been chosen for this burial duty, so they were weighing up the situation without any officer.

"*Belaya Smert*? Do you know what the reward is? Whoever brings back his head to Komarov can go home," one of them said.

"Yes, but all those who've tried have a hole in their uniforms. It seems he is immortal."

"All the same, there's 20 of us, and only two of them ..."

"So what shall we do?"

Simo let a minute go by and, when he did not hear any more noise, cautiously raised his head above the mound. Not a single Russian left. Taken aback by Yrjö's presence of mind, his audacity and nerve, to which he owed his life, Simo was surprised to find himself laughing out loud.

"Yeah," his smiling pupil said, "I almost got you killed, but I reckon that I also saved you just by shouting your name at them."

*

Simo had changed his mind. On the way back, in a part of the forest a few kilometres from their camp, he laid down his rucksack behind a fallen branch left clinging to the trunk only by its bark.

When Simo had seen the way the forests had been devastated, he had decided to leave the lesson for his pupil until after he had reported back to the rear base. But their unexpected meeting with the Russians had confirmed, if need be, that "later" was at best an uncertain notion in their current situation. As in every conflict, throughout this Winter War there was nothing more hypothetical than "later".

Simo took out his rifle and propped it on the tree trunk. Yrjö repeated his movements, as if in a mirror. Simo thought about what he should tell him. As this might be his only chance, he needed to explain everything, to transmit years of techniques and knowledge. He tapped the stock of his rifle.

"This is an M28/30, birch-wood stock, serial number 60974. One day you'll remember that as easily as your birth date. It's 1.19 metres long, barrel length 68.5 centimetres. It weighs 4.3 kilos altogether when empty. It fires D166 13-gram rounds at a speed of 705 metres a second. They are lethal at a distance of up to two kilometres. My rifle is the same as yours, but each one is different, even if it is the identical model. Never change the rifle you know and which suits you, unless it's damaged."

Every word imprinted itself on Yrjö's memory like a sacred text.

"Before you set out you need to pick up the latest maps. They will only help you identify the most recent positions of our mines: if you need a map to tell you where you are, then you're already lost. When you leave your tent, take a handful of ashes from the stove and rub them on the oiled gun barrel. That way you avoid any glint from the sun that could give away your position. Put some sugar and bread in your pocket. Don't forget to give a hug to the ones you love. Your return is not guaranteed."

Simo smartly ejected the magazine from his rifle and showed it to Yrjö.

"Your magazine holds five rounds. Always take several with

you. Keep them in your pocket. Frozen rounds are heavier, and lose one metre per second. Absolutely everything can change their trajectory. The bullet travels in an arc – just like an arrow. If you are firing with the wind, it will climb; against the wind it will drop, and the same with rain or humidity. Then you have to find a good firing position."

Simo stretched out on the ground. Without taking aim, he pressed the stock into the hollow of his shoulder.

"First of all, look around you. Nobody walks so slowly they leave no trace. The ground, branches, leaves and above all the snow will tell you what you need to know. How many enemy soldiers have passed by, if they came to a halt, if they were pulling cannon or heavy machine guns. Look calmly, with the least possible effort, because once you are in position sweat will freeze your whole body. Do not shoot from a house or building – a single shell fired by the Reds would leave you among the rubble. Do not fire from high up in a tree – if they discover your position, you'll never have time to get down. Try to have the sun at your back so that your adversary is blinded by it. Finally, choose a spot with a clear way out in case you have to retreat. And if you do have to get away, don't forget to throw a few 'sparklers' behind you so they regret ever having declared war on us."

As he said this, Simo turned on his side and showed Yrjö the three grenades hooked to his belt. These were what he called "sparklers".

"Now you have to set up your shot. First, never put your finger on the trigger, but on the guard. That will avoid any accidental shot and mean you won't have to shout my name again to save your life. You will be motionless for long periods, and only your willpower can help you control your shivering, fatigue and fear. So you need to know your strengths and your limits. Don't rely on the first of these, but listen to the second. Never use a rifle scope, because again the sun could catch the lens and reveal your position. A lot of Russians could have confirmed that, if I hadn't come across them. Put a handful of snow in your mouth to prevent vapour, and if your rifle is on the ground, pat the snow in front of you solid so it doesn't fly up from the rush of air from the muzzle. Concentrate on what is in front of you, don't worry about the sky. Even if shells cause three-quarters of the casualties, there's no knowing where they will land; there's nothing you can do about it."

Then Simo lined up with his rifle as if they were one, closed his eye and aimed in the distance.

"When the enemy is in the centre of your vision, you have to choose. Find the best target, not the easiest one. If there are several, make a list. Their marksmen first and foremost. The one manning the machine gun next, then the men with the artillery or mortar. The officers fourth. The others can die last if they haven't already run away. They're not really important, because they are only ordinary soldiers and most of them never asked to be there. Calculate the distance carefully. If it's a moving target, fire 50 centimetres in front. If they are running, add a metre. Don't aim at the head, that's showing off and is no more effective than any-where in the upper body. Gently squeeze the trigger: let yourself be almost surprised by the shot. If you score a hit, repeat. If you miss, change position. Two emotions can spoil your shot: the fear of missing, and, since we are not assassins ... the fear of hitting your target. Unfortunately, after a few days you won't feel so guilty. That's it, now you know just about all there is to know. The rest is practice, and you're bound to get plenty of that."

Because they were close to camp and it seemed like a deserted spot, because Yrjö wanted to show the Magic Marksman that he too was talented, and finally because a lost crow had followed them and settled on a broken branch 50 metres from them, Yrjö killed it with a single shot.

"Are you going to eat it?" Simo said.

All his disciple's pride evaporated.

"I only kill because it is right to defend my country," Simo scolded him, "and because the Russians would do the same if they had the chance. Apart from that, I only kill what I eat. So go and fetch that crow. That's your dinner tonight."

*

Simo and Yrjö arrived as night fell and joined some of the 6th Company soldiers. They were doing their best to get some rest, even if it was only to close their eyes, because war never slept, and shells thumped all around them, a perpetual shuddering that entered through their feet and resonated up to their brains. It was endless torture.

Seven men from the company died that day, which could seem not a lot. But that was just one company, and six companies were needed to make up a battalion, three battalions to make a regiment, three regiments to a division. And just one division, the 12th, to defend Kollaa. Confronting them, the Russians in the 8th Army had six divisions, three of which had been renewed in men and materiel.

Throughout this new night and its cortège of nightmares, the soldiers, without daring to confess it, were waiting for Yrjö's soft voice and his prayer. But the day had changed things, had changed Yrjö, even though his voice was still soft as he said his new prayer.

"Lord," he began, "give me the strength to aim truly. Accompany the arc of my bullets so that they strike the demons invading our country. Whatever my fear and however cold it is, I will never forget the words of Simo, the most valiant of your sons. Never change the rifle you know and which suits you, unless it is damaged. Put ashes on your gun barrel, bread and sugar in your pocket. Hug those you love, your return is not guaranteed ..."

Not one of Simo's instructions was left out. Each one led to the next. And so the sniper's prayer was born.

63

It seemed that every day would be the last, the day Finland surrendered. Each evening on Teittinen's desk, hundreds of snapped dog tags from fresh deaths at the front piled up.

And yet Finnish nature had done all it could. The forests had been protective allies, their trees solid walls. The country was adorned with lakes like so many blue diamonds. But winter had covered them with an unbreakable layer of ice that could even bear the weight of tanks. As for the forests on the Kollaa frontline, all that was left were uprooted trunks and ravaged earth, scarred by almost a hundred deadly days of fighting.

And yet Finnish nature had done all it could ... It subjected the enemy to deadly temperatures and constant blizzards. But now the Russians were properly clothed, had been provided with skis and better food, which meant that most of them could bear the Arctic conditions. Of course, every day Shtern lost dozens of men to the freezing cold, but this was a kind of natural selection. The strong survived, the weak perished, and it was enough ruthlessly to replace them, because there was what seemed like an endless supply waiting patiently at the frontier.

And yet the Finnish soldiers had done what they could ...

None had deserted or surrendered. Their *sisu* was like a fire in the belly, helping them resist tenaciously even though they knew victory was impossible, obstinately clinging to their rifles and cannon, standing tall to face the enemy. But whereas in December they had been fighting shoulder to shoulder, now they had to stand a good ten metres apart to cover an area, carry out a patrol, or defend a position. This morning, a Lotta preparing food had told Onni that she was now cooking for two times fewer men as at the outset of the war.

The Russians were there day and night. Skirmishes took place five kilometres in front of the defensive line or hand-to-hand in the trenches. Twice a day the quartermaster unit shovelled out these endless pits filled with a mixture of earth soaked with blood, brown snow and fragments of dead bodies.

For the first time the Russian shells reached the Finnish companies' camps, although not the base headquarters. A few tents had been spared, but what use were they? The incessant waves of Soviet troops made any rest impossible, and the rolling fire of shells was so deafening nobody spoke any more. Kill or be killed – every second, the same, unique option was repeated. Everyone's uniform was stained with blood, whether Russian or Finnish. The soldiers spoke of Hell unapologetically, because even the chaplain wondered what the Devil could come up with which was worse than the Winter War.

And yet, right in the centre of the storm, one man was happy. Just before taking command of two *Sissi* and heading out for battle, the newly recovered Juutilainen bent down to Karlsson and delivered his thought for the day, just like someone having a fireside chat.

"I've spent my life defying death. Strange sort of an existence, isn't it?"

*

The 6th Company did not have to ski far before they met the first enemy troops: they were everywhere.

Karlsson had raised his hand to demand silence. Only a few metres away they had to distinguish between the warlike cries of units engaged in combat and the more piercing cries of pain.

The important thing was to discover who was making them, and so they crawled towards the sound to find out.

The Terror's 60 men were now facing nine Russian soldiers caught in a long roll of barbed wire concealed under the snow. Every attempt to free themselves had only driven the steel spikes further into their flesh.

The Russians gazed at them like trapped animals, begging for their lives.

"If we take them prisoner, we could get them to talk," Karlsson suggested.

One of the Russians, face streaked with metal, began to plead with them. They had no need to understand Russian to comprehend what he was saying. Paying no attention, Juutilainen took out his pistol and shot them one after the other, taking his time so that the last man could see his death coming.

"What did you want to learn? That we're at war with them, and that they've never been so close? Oh, I know your soft heart has made you loved by my men. But it's not the heart that wins wars."

He ordered Pietari, Simo and Yrjö to search the bodies before they froze while the remainder of the company formed a protective circle round them. Suddenly a fluty voice could be heard further off ...

"Don't shoot! Don't shoot!"

Pulkki the messenger boy, a green lantern held high above his head in the midst of the blizzard, was heading in their direction.

"Still not dead then?" the Terror greeted him in his usual fashion. "Almost a hundred days unarmed, and you survive better than a soldier."

Pulkki did not respond. No time. He pointed at a place on the map he had just unfolded on a fallen tree trunk.

"There," he panted. "The 4th Company is coming under fire from a heavy machine gun. They're surrounded. They've already lost a third of their men. I was going along the line looking for reinforcements."

"You've found them, my boy," Juutilainen said with a smile.

*

Further down, lying flat in a 20-metre long trench, what remained of the 4th Company was facing a steady barrage from close to a hundred sub-machine guns, as well as an impressive heavy machine gun that could fire as many rounds as could 30 men, with rounds five times larger. Its gunner was hidden behind two protective metal sheets. Only the top of his head was showing.

That was enough for Simo to slice through it with a single bullet.

While another Russian was plucking up the courage to replace him, the 6th Company had time to join the 4th in their trench.

"Have you dug your own grave?" Pietari scoffed. "Did you want to save the Russians time?"

The air was saturated with lead. The Finns were firing blindly, not even daring to raise their heads. Only the barrels of their guns poked out. Juutilainen recklessly took a look over the top. A 70-metre-wide strip of flat granite boulders separated them from the Russians. In the front was their heavy machine gun, mounted on a metal sled. Behind it, the men with sub-machine guns were hidden behind a rocky outcrop. The legionnaire ducked down and spoke to Simo.

"Maxim PM1910 at 70 metres! Seventy metres: can you cover me?"

Simo nodded.

Juutilainen turned defiantly towards Karlsson.

"I'll show you how to win your men's respect."

Checking that his sub-machine gun had plenty of ammunition, he got them to hook as many as possible of what Simo called "sparklers" round his waist. Loaded down with grenades, the Terror took three deep breaths, then gave the signal to his marksman.

Standing up, Simo just reached the top of the trench. The machine gun had come back to life and was spraying the Finnish position incessantly. To cover his officer at this distance would demand quite a lot of skill, and a lot more luck.

Two soldiers lifted Juutilainen and almost threw him over the top of the trench. Before he could even begin to run across the granite, Simo had stood erect and unerringly shot off the top half of the new machine gunner's brain. At 70 metres, he could have aimed at his eye and pierced the pupil.

The legionnaire sprinted, and Simo shot three more Russians before they could open fire. Some of the enemy retreated behind cover, while ten of them fired at the Terror. He had already covered 20 metres and was emptying all the rounds in his magazine at them. He still had more than twice as far to go to survive. Simo downed four more Russians with as many shots, but saw five, then six, then seven drop to the ground. When a new machine gunner stepped up to the gun, he also fell backwards from the impact of a bullet. Behind Simo, Yrjö was standing tall, rifle still smoking.

Thirty metres from his goal, and with his weapon empty, Juutilainen seized the grenades two by two, tore the pins out with his teeth and threw them in front of him, creating a tremendous wall of explosions.

Another new man was at the machine gun. Its burst of fire seemed to be pursuing Juutilainen, smacking into the granite and raising plumes of snow just behind his heels, getting closer and closer. Moments before the bullets could hit the legionnaire, Simo downed the Russian. Disorganised and terrified by the legionnaire's suicidal manoeuvre, the other Russians now cowered flat on the ground, trusting to the destructive power of the Maxim PM1910.

The Russian officer chose a new machine gunner. When he

refused point-blank to sacrifice himself, he was executed with a bullet to the head. Having no choice, the next one crawled towards the beast, but he never made it, aimed at and struck by the White Death and his disciple. When the Russian officer searched for someone else to face certain death, he was the one who took a bullet in the throat from one of his own soldiers. He collapsed, bloody hands clutching his neck, unable to believe this treachery. At which moment, a wild-eyed madman appeared, on his face an icy smile that showed all his teeth.

Juutilainen kicked aside the dead body slumped behind the machine gun. He turned the sled 90 degrees and began to pull the trigger. Like a scythe cutting corn, he chopped down almost 30 Red soldiers before running out of ammunition. Some of the survivors dropped to their knees, hoping the Finns would take them prisoner; the others ran as if they had met Death in person, an accurate enough description of the legionnaire.

This manoeuvre had created so much noise that none of them heard the engine of a T26 tank that reached the edge of the Finnish trench. At the top of a slight slope, its tracks rose in the air before crashing down in a cloud of snow, its gun barrel pointing directly at the men from the two companies crouching in the depths of the trench. The tank's machine gun sprayed the trench, and those who had not scrambled out in time were killed without suffering by the hail of bullets.

Pietari and Onni, who since the start of the conflict had disabled more than ten T26s, silently agreed on what they should do. They sprang out of the trench, Onni with a Molotov cocktail in his hand and a log in Pietari's. They raced towards the monster. The petrol bomb struck the tank's weak spot close to its air vents, but for the first time the flames were not sucked in, continuing to burn on the body of the tank without penetrating the cockpit. Pietari got ready to jam his log into the tank tracks to immobilise it, giving Onni time to light a new cocktail. But as he raised the log, Pietari realised that the T26's tracks had been armour-plated to prevent them being dislodged or immobilised.

On Stalin's orders, Timoshenko had rethought the Soviet Army. He had also improved and reinforced its tanks. The T26 was ablaze, but still seemed invincible. Onni and Pietari were so stupefied their attention wavered. The barrel of the tank had swivelled, so that its single eye was looking straight at them. But here too something had changed. The gun barrel was different: its diameter was so tiny it could never fire even the smallest shell. Then there was the smell of fuel coming from it ... Onni understood in time, and flung himself to one side, just managing to avoid the thick tongue of flame spurting from the barrel. The heavy, sticky flame engulfed Pietari, who became a screaming human torch. He twisted round on himself before falling to his knees with a guttural croak. A bullet to the heart put an end to his unbearable suffering. Simo had fired without even aiming. He lowered his rifle; the world around him turned hazy.

He barely saw Karlsson throw two grenades onto the roof of the T26, then run as fast as he could to find cover. One detonated under the turret and the force of the blast almost completely detached it from the hull. The other slid off, but before hitting the ground it exploded on the tank's left side.

He barely saw the mutilated tank, now marred by a deep scar on one side that obliterated the centre of the Red Soviet star painted there, as it turned round and disappeared over the far side of the slope.

He barely saw Onni covering Pietari Koskinen with snow to extinguish the flames, his skin melted charcoal, his snowsuit charred.

*

Five hundred kilometres away, Mannerheim was hesitating less and less over accepting Stalin's terms.

Four hundred and fifty kilometres away, Viktor Koskinen was writing another letter to his brother.

Seventy metres away, Juutilainen finished executing the Russian survivors, heedless of their pleas.

And a few centimetres from Pietari, Simo crumpled to the ground. He took his friend's burnt hand and brought it to his lips for a last kiss.

"Let a bullet go through me now. Let there be an end to all this," he prayed silently.

64

Main headquarters, Mikkeli, Finland,
February 28, 1940, fifteen days before the end of the war

On the field marshal's desk lay the almost insulting peace terms sent by Molotov. Signed by Stalin and received that day, not a comma had been changed, not a kilometre of territory that the Russians were demanding. This time, however, Mannerheim was contemplating them with a certain fatalism.

"Do we have any choice?" Aksel Airo said. "Viipuri and Kollaa will fall any day now, we can be sure of that. And the French and British troops have still not arrived, and perhaps have not yet even been despatched."

Mannerheim closed his eyes. A succession of images streamed behind them: the deadly battles on all the fronts; men dying; villages in flames; cities sinking beneath waves of fire.

"Tell Tanner to contact the Swedish ambassador. Tell him we look favourably on the peace treaty Russia is proposing. He'll know how to get that information to them."

*

February 29, 1940, fourteen days before the end of the war

It was not simply a question of bringing the war to an end, but to get out of it thanks to a hypocritical peace treaty that over the years would have the same consequences. The doors of the country would open to Russia, which would only have to absorb Finland region by region into the all-powerful Soviet Motherland.

To both the Finnish government and military headquarters,

the idea of seeing their country lose its only recently won independence was so painful, so viscerally unacceptable, that the least sign of support, the least hope of an Allied collaboration, could still make them hesitate over accepting Stalin's peace treaty.

And the sign arrived.

The door to Mannerheim's office was flung open by a visibly excited Aksel Airo.

"We've had news from France!"

*

Hôtel Matignon, Paris

Since the negotiations between Finland and Russia travelled between the ambassadors and foreign ministers of several countries, they were far from secret. And Édouard Daladier, the French prime minister, got wind of them almost as soon as they took place.

The Finnish ambassador was sitting in front of a ridiculously large desk that made Daladier seem tiny by comparison. Notably apprehensive, the French prime minister had two of everything in front of him. Two telephones. Two fountain pens. Two notebooks. Two blotters. And two gigantic chandeliers framing a mirror so tall it reached the ceiling and made the room appear even larger, so that Holma, the Finnish ambassador, hurriedly summoned to the Hôtel Matignon, did not at first notice the discreet man standing at the far end.

"What shall I tell them?" Holma said, his hand on one of the two telephones.

"Above all, not to accept!" Daladier said. "Tell your prime minister we are ready to send many soldiers."

"I'd like to be precise. How many shall I tell him?"

Daladier thought for a moment, as if calculating the price of something whose value he was not sure of.

"Tell him 20,000 troops. No, say thirty. Thirty thousand soldiers.

Perhaps even as many as 40,000! And that's without support from the British, which will soon come."

"Twenty and forty are hardly the same," Holma said, deeply anxious. "But above all, how are they to reach the frontlines? You'll be up against Sweden, which always plays its card as a neutral country to refuse to let Allied troops pass through."

"Ah yes, of course, Sweden's ambiguous neutrality," Daladier sighed. "They send a handful of men to Lapland to support the Finns, they supply them with weapons, but at the same time they sell all the iron from their mines to the Third Reich. Let's see if your minister is ready to listen to me."

"You could also speak to him directly, sir. I think he would be reassured to hear from you in person."

"No, politics is not that simple. Everything is prepared by intermediaries. Only signatures are added by the interested parties."

A career diplomat, Holma knew exactly why intermediaries were needed. If by any chance everything went awry, they would be the ones accused of having misunderstood things or misinterpreted them. And there was indeed a lot of room for debate between 20,000 and 40,000 soldiers.

Holma picked up the telephone and, with the others looking on, repeated what the French were promising. Daladier and the Finnish prime minister did not say a word to each other. The ambassador hung up, a smile on his lips.

"You have been listened to. Our reply will follow. But a clearer idea about the number of soldiers would be greatly appreciated. Time costs us lives, and we are cruelly short of them."

"Reassure him and tell him that I foresee we will do all we can."

Once Holma had left, Daladier turned to his discreet collaborator, who had so far remained silent despite his position as the foreign minister's private secretary. When he was fulfilling that role, he was Alexis Léger, but when he was a poet he was known under the pseudonym Saint-John Perse.

"I was against letting you sign the Munich agreement," Léger began guardedly, "but you did not listen. By allowing Hitler to dismember Czechoslovakia and annex Bohemia, Moravia and Silesia, all we have done is demonstrate our weakness. Now, if we go to Finland's aid all we will do is weaken our army at the moment when German troops are on our doorstep."

Daladier protested mildly.

"But to get to Finland, my dear friend, we will have to pass through Sweden. Who could then stop us seizing their iron mines and cutting off Hitler's supplies?"

"And what if Hitler sends his troops to meet you? That iron is his army's lifeblood, and I cannot imagine him simply handing it over to us."

"So then we'll meet him up there, and send more soldiers. Going to war in Scandinavia rather than on our own territory is after all more ..."

Daladier searched for the right word.

"Comfortable?" Léger suggested.

"If you wish. In any case, you are now to contact the French and British ambassadors in Helsinki. Have them go this evening to meet the Finnish foreign minister to confirm what we are promising."

"So in the end, how many French soldiers would stay in Sweden, and how many would continue on to Finland?" Léger persisted.

"Let's say around half of the 40,000."

"Or half of the 20,000 ... I get the impression that you're not entirely convinced. You promised their ambassador we would do 'all we can'. I'm afraid he'll tell them 40,000."

"That's what intermediaries are for, my dear Alexis. Let him announce what he thinks he understood. Just so long as Finland does not sign any agreement with Stalin ... Is there anything else you are worried about?"

This was his way of dismissing Léger. And if the poet was

aware of the nuances, the politician in him also knew how to read between the lines.

As the padded double doors closed behind him, his adviser in the waiting room came up to hear his news. Léger hid nothing from him, not even his doubts.

"This telephone call is going to relaunch the war in a country that was about to sign for peace. A peace that is what it is, but a peace all the same."

"So Daladier insists we send our soldiers there?"

"The secret ultimate goal of French policy is exclusively aimed at gaining control of Swedish iron ore.[27] I really hope our troops will go no further."

"How many does he want to send?" his adviser enquired.

"He himself does not really know. He has made a promise to a country that is going under without being certain that he can keep it."

In concluding, the politician Léger gave way to the poet.

"Shadowy strategies are at work, and I fear Finland is nothing more than the plaything."

*

March 2, 1940, eleven days before the end of the war

That day, following the French undertaking, the Finnish government decided to continue fighting. Stalin's terms were sent back to him, as an affront: to die rather than surrender.

Finland believed in Daladier's words out of necessity.

Russia believed them as well, but for different reasons.

Reassured by his spies with flapping ears, Stalin had concluded that Franco-British aid to Finland was imminent. In fact, his paranoia had decided this for him, and his spies had simply followed his wishes after a conversation with Molotov that in a theatrical farce might have sounded something like this:

MOLOTOV: "Stalin is afraid of an intervention by the French and British."

SPY: "And they are afraid of Hitler. According to my sources, Finland isn't the goal, merely the pretext. They will probably stop at the iron ore fields in Sweden."

MOLOTOV: "I understand, but he fears an intervention by the French and British. Do you want to tell him he's wrong? That his judgment is not sound?"

SPY: "I assure you, I don't want you to do anything of the sort. But now that I think of it, I believe I did hear strong rumours to that effect."

Reigning by terror, the Little Father of the Peoples was told only what he wanted to hear, and the truth could go hang.

Stalin was also afraid of the thaw in Finland, and so everything conspired to persuade him to fling the rest of his troops into this ludicrous conflict that, with all the men and weapons at his disposal, he should have long since won, but which he was now unable to disentangle himself from.

*

The next few days would be the worst, even though on the Kollaa frontline and the Mannerheim Line they seemed to have already faced the worst for weeks.

And neither French nor British boots ever did land on Finnish soil.

65

Kollaa front, March 3, 1940, ten days before the end of the war

Teittinen's command tent was one of the few still standing, but inside the news was as grim as the weather outside. The colonel's face was drawn with fatigue, his eyes bloodshot from exhaustion; opposite him as usual was Juutilainen, stinking of alcohol. Karlsson entered the tent, accompanied by the young man he had been sent to find. The legionnaire had met him already.

"Do you remember our friend here?" Teittinen asked the Terror. Juutilainen looked him up and down.

"Yes. It was you, wasn't it, who diverted a radio cable so you could listen in to the Russians? Antero. You are the soldier Antero."

The others were amazed at the Terror's powers of recall, when they thought he must always be too inebriated to recognise his own reflection in a mirror.

"I only remember the names of brave men, of the women I've laid on their backs, and the soldiers who annoy me," an amused Juutilainen said, to justify himself. "And if you're here, that's because you've done it again."

"Only for a few hours, before the Russians could discover it. The risk is that the Ivans find out and start feeding us false information."

"Tell him what you heard," Teittinen said, going over to stand in front of a much bigger map than normal, one that extended beyond the limits of the current frontlines.

Antero walked over to the map. The others followed him, soldiers and officers shoulder to shoulder, their faces lit by an oil lamp.

"It's here, look. Twenty kilometres south, at Ullisma. Commercial forests. I heard the *Ryssät* talking about widening the paths so that their tanks and cannon could get through. Five engineering units are already at work. They will shortly be joined by two infantry divisions and an artillery battalion."

This was the new information. The analysis began at once.

"They have already understood that destroying the forests is easier than going round them," Teittinen reminded his audience. "But it will take them half a year to flatten them."

"So now they have found a less dense forest," Karlsson said. "A commercial forest just below our positions, with paths that criss-cross it which they can use."

"Yeah," Juutilainen fumed. "They only have to widen them and their heaviest weapons will be able to get through. Cannon and tanks. Part of the 8th Army could outflank us to the south while the rest continue to bombard us from the east on the Kollaa front. A pincer movement, in other words."

Teittinen challenged him.

"The information could be a diversionary tactic. Or we could have misunderstood it. What do you think?"

"What surprises me most is that there are no battalion commanders round this table. All I command is a single company."

"Yes, but it's the 6th Company. And I've sent you on so many missions over the past three months and more you must think I want to get rid of you. But I have to decide if their manoeuvre makes sense, and I can't think of anyone better placed than you to answer that."

Juutilainen slid his hand across the map from the Kollaa front to the Ullisma forests, as if feeling the contours beneath his fingertips.

"More than 20 kilometres of skiing and marching," Teittinen said, "at temperatures of between –30°C and –50°C. And you'll have to travel at night."

"And it's too far to lay a radio wire from here to Ullisma," Antero said.

"So you'll be effectively on your own, cut off from the rear base," Teittinen told them.

The legionnaire and Karlsson exchanged a knowing look.

"We have to go and see what they're up to down there. It's unacceptable for us to run the risk of being surprised from the rear."

"That's true," Teittinen agreed. "But I can't spare you many men. Three battalions, no more."

"We know that."

"Nor can I strip Kollaa of its artillery units. If it's a real threat, your chances of getting back are slim."

"Has it ever been any different?" Juutilainen said.

*

Rear base of the Soviet 8th Army, headquarters

The Red Army was forever being reinforced and rebuilt. As far as possible it preferred to draw new soldiers from neighbouring countries protected or dominated by Russia and send them to the fronts rather than from its own offspring. But as the ranks were made up of so many different peoples, the troops became increasingly complicated to command, speaking as they did Armenian, Azeri, Byelorussian, Georgian, Kazakh, Kirghiz, Romanian, Tadjik, Turkish, Ukrainian, Uzbek, Chinese, Mongolian, Japanese and even the Samoyed languages of the semi-nomads from Siberia. Sometimes an order had to be translated ten or fifteen times before all the troops understood.

On the other hand, the "true" Soviet soldiers were no easier to command. Komarov therefore told himself that if he armed them for the apocalypse, they would be much less inclined to disobey. He had friends in the air force, and these friends had filled an entire wagon in the supply train for him.

The unlabelled wooden crates arrived early one morning. One of them had been opened and was the centre of attention even though at first glance it contained only more munitions.

Komarov the *politruk* stood behind Grigori Shtern, the commander of the 8th Army, as they watched the soldier loading his rifle magazine from the crate. Around them, other battalion commanders were observing the demonstration.

The soldier pushed the rifle bolt forward to load the round, glanced at a spruce ten metres in front of him and aimed at the centre of its trunk, so broad that the tracks of a tank would not have flattened it. Then he fired. Almost simultaneously, the observers heard the report (normal), heard the sound of the impact (deafening), and above all saw the result on the tree (stupefying).

The bullet had not gone straight through it, but had ripped it apart, its fibres torn off and smoking. Then the top of the spruce collapsed like a factory chimney demolished from below.

"Explosive ammunition," Tomarov almost crowed. "We're not going to use them for our sub-machine guns because there won't be enough for everyone, but we do have sufficient to equip our marksmen."

The soldier reloaded and chose a fresh target. An ancient Siberian pine with a trunk twice as thick as the spruce. It was some 30 metres high, and stood out above the forest canopy, its top bent by the weight of its snow-laden branches like an old wise man looking down on the world below.

After the blast and the cloud of wood chips, all that was left was a huge hole in the middle of the pine trunk. The soldier passed his arm through it. Seeing all the astounded faces, Komarov, as proudly as if he had designed them himself, explained how these munitions worked.

"It has an explosive charge that fires the bullet, and inside it the equivalent of a miniature grenade that explodes at the first contact. You can bring aircraft down from the sky with it! Just imagine the effect on Finnish soldiers. We'll be able to pluck off their heads just like plucking a flower petal."

In order to say it once and then forget it, Shtern wanted to hear confirmation of something.

"Are these the munitions that were banned for soldiers by the 1868 Saint Petersburg Declaration?"

"What Russia offers, it can take back," Komarov defended himself. "And what it decides, it can rescind. Who is going to come here to examine the evidence?"

66

Kollaa frontline, March 4, 1940 (–30°C),
nine days before the end of the war

So the Russian tanks were better equipped? Well then, the Finns would hit them harder ... Karlsson, Simo and Onni had spent part of the evening fashioning satchel-grenades: a 30-centimetre-long piece of wood; four sticks of TNT round it, amounting to five kilos of explosives; four metal plates covering them; and everything held in place by string. But the desperate lack of munitions meant that they could only make two of them.

Yrjö had wanted to come with them to the forests of Ullisma. Simo had been against it, but he was neither his father nor his officer. Before midnight they left the camp at Kollaa that was still being shelled non-stop, leaving behind them a frontline that could be breached at any moment.

*

March 5, 1940, 04.30 hours (–40°C),
eight days before the end of the war

For many, this march had been the most exhausting of all. They had to make sure they did not get lost in the night, and to sweat as little as possible or risk freezing on the spot at the first break they took. The often thigh-high snow exhausted the leading man, so they had to keep changing the order from front to back and check that the men were still following. Sometimes when the others turned round and saw two or three soldiers were missing, swallowed up by the forest as payment for all they had made it suffer, they merely crossed themselves hastily.

The three Finnish battalions eventually came to a halt two kilometres short of Ullisma. At 15.00 the soldiers completed their bivouac of tents half-submerged in the ground, surrounded by shallow trenches. Since making fires was forbidden, the 2,000 soldiers huddled together like birds on a branch, shivering, teeth chattering, their muscles seized up with cold.

An hour later a patrol of scouts returned, and the officers were able to assess the forces in play.

"There are more than 12,000 Ivans facing us," the scout reporting to them said.

Two thousand Finns facing six times that number of Russians. In view of their blatant inferiority in numbers, no army would have chosen anything other than defence. The Finns therefore opted to attack.

"Distribute bread, sugar, jam and *viina*," Teittinen ordered. "We'll move out before sunrise."

*

March 6, 1940, Ullisma forests, 04.00 (–50 °C),
seven days before the end of the war

Simo, Onni and Yrjö had spent the night keeping watch on one another to prevent any of them falling fast asleep. Some brothers-in-arms had not been so lucky: they were discovered, eyes as white as porcelain marbles, faces contorted in death throes. Even their rifles had frozen.

Yrjö copied Simo and stuffed his M28/30 between his snow-suit and body to keep it warm. Then he slipped a magazine into each pocket and, after rubbing it a little, another one into his underpants.

The battalions divided into a three-pronged attack; their companies also split up to encircle as best they could such a formidable adversary with so few men. The commercial forest was made up of 48 squares like a chequerboard, separated by paths named after streets in Helsinki: Simonkatu, Unioninkatu, Sirkuskatu and even Hallituskatu ...[28]

The 6th Company bade farewell to the 4th and 5th companies. The soldiers took time to hug one another and exchange a few words. Then, with Simo and Juutilainen in the lead, they headed for the position chosen the previous evening. The sun was still asleep, the moon was high in the sky, and its reflection on the snow brightened the night. It would soon be 05.00, and to ensure almost total silence orders were passed in a whisper, repeated every third man from officer to soldier until they reached the men pulling the ammunition sleds and the still-empty stretcher sleds at the rear of the column. Barely a month earlier these would have been pulled by soldiers, but by now the Finnish Army was bled almost dry, so that during these final days of the war, men, women, soldiers and Lottas all played their part in the defence of their country. A Russian pistol stuck in her belt, Leena dragged her stretcher sled along without a murmur of complaint.

Shortly before reaching their chosen position, Juutilainen gestured for absolute silence. There were 50 of them, and at the meeting of two paths in the forest a unit of 200 Russians appeared, surrounded by the amber halo of their lanterns. Behind them came the sound of an engine, like a growling animal. Through his field glasses, Onni saw a tank damaged on one side, a lengthy scar along its red star, the machine gun and turret that Karlsson had almost torn off newly repaired. When they saw it, the 6th Company threw themselves down and merged with the snow.

The flame-throwing tank focused all of the Finns' anger. It had become Russia itself, representing everything about this unjust war, these 97 days of carnage. Essentially, it was a desire for revenge that tore at the soldiers' guts.

Rising to his knees, the legionnaire ordered his men to prepare.

Just as consumed with anger as the others, Simo had, however, taken the time to glance up at the sky. The moon was still shining so brightly that it would reveal their every movement. Before the order to advance could be given, he grasped Karlsson by the shoulder and pointed to a heavy black cloud that was almost on top of them. Karlsson understood at once, and in his turn managed to stop the Terror giving the command.

The cloud advanced unbearably slowly. So did the Russians. They would soon be so close the effect of surprise would be lost. Then, as Simo had foreseen, the cloud passed in front of the moon, masking it. The whole planet seemed to be snuffed out.

Soon only flashes from gun muzzles lit the darkness. As the Finnish machine guns crackled, the trapped Russians fell one after another. They responded blindly, firing wherever they heard a noise, wounding a Finn, killing one of their own, or running away to hide. By the time the cloud had drifted past the moon, all that was left of them was one lost tank and a few men defending it.

Karlsson took out one of the satchel grenades; Onni did the same. With Simo covering them, they skied towards their quarry. The tank spat a thick tongue of flame that flew narrowly over their heads. Reaching the side of the tank, Karlsson managed to toss his explosives under its tracks. A second's suspense. The mechanism, the fuse: anything could still fail. Then came a magnificent explosion. The blast flipped the tank over with a metallic crash, before it settled on its side like a wounded animal. Onni threw the second satchel grenade: it blew open one side of the vehicle, revealing the crew imprisoned in the cockpit, stunned, ears bleeding, eyes scorched. One of them crawled out of the turret. Simo shot him.

Onni approached the tank as if the war had come to a standstill, oblivious to the whizzing bullets and the fury of the battle of Ullisma raging all around him. Snapping the top off a Molotov cocktail, he poured the ethanol straight into the tank's wound, then lit the storm match and dropped it into the gap. The interior caught alight in a blast of heat. The two crew members screamed and when they tried to recover their breath, fire filled their lungs. Simo looked on. The Finnish soldiers were not monsters or assassins. And yet they looked on coldly at this revenge which would never be sufficient to satisfy them.

*

The Russians had abandoned all thought of retaliating precisely. Their artillery fired indiscriminately into the midst of the combatants. A smell of cordite and blood hung over the chaos; the gurgling cries of the dying haunted the battleground; the blasts from rifles and cannon pierced eardrums. The shelling forced the Finnish companies to split up, leaving only small groups of isolated soldiers.

In the forest, after a skirmish, the Sirkuskatu path defended by the Russians fell into Finnish hands. Unioninkatu, held by the Finns, became Russian after an assault. In each of the 48 squares the same merry-go-round was taking place. A hundred metres won. A hundred metres lost. But Ullisma had to be held to protect Kollaa, and the Finns would not stop until they ran out of bullets, or one pierced their hearts.

Juutilainen's men were at the throats of a Russian battalion they had encircled grenade by grenade, Molotov after Molotov. They had reached the edge of the forest, where the last pines gave way to a plain dotted with frozen marshes bordered by stiff, icy reeds. The enemy soldiers split into small groups, forcing the legionnaire to do the same with his men, so that soon the 6th Company divided into small units to pursue them. Karlsson, Onni, Yrjö and Simo were one such group. As they emerged from the forest they were met by intense gunfire. Next to Simo a tree trunk exploded, torn in half. In front of him, a clump of frozen earth the size of a car was flung 20 metres into the air.

"*Perkele!*" Onni shouted. "What are they shooting at us with?"

That morning alone, more than 40,000 shells had already pitted the ground with as many deep craters. The four men flung themselves into one. Ensnared like this, the Russians would simply have to aim accurately to destroy them with a single mortar bomb. If any of them were to survive, the group would have to separate again. Karlsson grabbed Yrjö by the collar and told Simo and Onni to cover them as they leaped from crater to crater, ever closer to the Russians, by now only 20 metres away. Bursts of machine-gun fire tracked the pair as they ran. Karlsson had barely taken cover when he began to shout orders at Yrjö.

"We're close enough to hit them with grenades ..."

But Yrjö wasn't listening. He couldn't take his eyes off his officer.

"First we'll empty our machine guns on them so they have to keep their heads down ..."

Two red buds were spreading across Karlsson's white snowsuit like a blossoming flower.

"Then we throw all our sparklers ... And as soon as ..."

The cold and adrenaline numbed the pain. Karlsson had not yet realised he had been shot twice in the stomach.

"And as soon as ..." he said again. "As soon ..." he repeated, unable to get any further, as if out of breath. "As ..."

He looked down. Incredulous, he pressed both hands on the wounds, saw them covered with warm blood, and then collapsed on his back, gazing up at the sky with no pain or anger. This is how a soldier's life ends.

"So ... so it's today?" he said with his last breath.

Yrjö was paralysed. The air was filled with dust, floating bits of earth, ashes and dirty snow. The fiercest fighting reached him as a muffled murmur. Karlsson's blood froze as it flowed out, creating small scarlet stalactites that grew towards the ground as the drops fell. Yrjö stretched out his hand to tear off the officer's dog tag, then stared at it in the palm of his hand. Not even the Russian soldier who jumped down into the crater could rouse him from his torpor. Yrjö stared at him in wide-eyed astonishment. The Russian pulled his trigger twice – *click, click* – but nothing happened. Yrjö stood there peering at him, utterly unaware of how lucky he was. His adversary nervously tugged at his jammed rifle before throwing it away and pulling a pistol from his belt. By the time he raised his head to shoot, Yrjö's bayonet had already travelled through his body so far that the metal point stuck out of his back. He could feel the young Finn's breath on his face and neck.

Twenty metres away, Simo was loading, firing, killing. Emotionless, Simo loaded, fired, killed. Without once missing his target, Simo loaded, fired and killed with such cold fury and precision that Onni's sub-machine gun became the least of the Russians' worries. They were up against a Finnish sniper, and had to get rid of him. Their explosive bullets would never be put to better use.

Dispersed by an attack on one of the other squares on the Ullisma chequerboard, ten or so soldiers of the Finnish 4th Company had also been pushed to the edge of the forest. They backed into the same Russian unit that had already lost close to 40 soldiers, most of them at the hands of the one they called the White Death. Yrjö took the opportunity to climb out of the crater.

When Simo saw him running on his own, he realised they would never see Karlsson again. He and Onni covered the youngster as he sprinted the last few metres, emptying one magazine after another. Finally reunited, they threw their remaining ammunition to the ground to share it out. Perhaps they could hold out a few more minutes? There were about 30 Russians left out of the initial 70, and there were only three of them in the shell crater. But with what was left of the 4th Company, with the *sisu* that made them invincible, and in the knowledge that their cause was a just one, they knew they would find the courage to resist, and perhaps even the impertinence to be victorious.

In the time that Yrjö aimed and hit once, Simo did so three times. And when the two marksmen had to reload their magazines, Onni fired a continuous stream of bullets to protect them.

Opposite them, the Russians got to their feet and fired, holding their sub-machine guns with two hands at hip level, spraying the Finnish position. This left a small window of opportunity for their own marksmen, in a tactic similar to the one employed by those resisting them. One of the Red snipers moved away from the exchange of fire and crawled to a spot that would allow him a few seconds to take aim. When Onni and his machine gun were in his sights, he pulled the trigger. But just at that moment Onni ducked, and the two Finnish snipers stood up.

The Russian explosive bullet sped through the air.

It passed through Simo's cheek and exploded against his lower jaw, setting off the second charge. This blew up in his open mouth, tearing off his other cheek, part of his upper jaw, and a number of teeth. He turned calmly towards Yrjö, eyes open wide as if he could not believe he had been wounded. His face torn apart, the gaping hole from nose to neck left the pink inside of his throat visible. His jaw hung down, flapping to and fro, smoke pouring out of his mouth, snowsuit stained with his own blood … Simo collapsed, unconscious.

The Russian sniper never knew who he had shot on this day, March 6, 1940, seven days before the end of the Winter War. And nobody bothered to remember him, or glorify the name of the person who, for the first and only time, had hit Simo Häyhä.

*

Ullisma grew calmer as night approached and yet another snowstorm blew in. The Finnish and Russian forces withdrew to spend the night in their bivouacs two kilometres from the commercial forest.

Leena had lived up to the legend of Lotta Svärd. With no

thought for her own life, she had spent more than eleven hours going back and forth, hauling her stretcher sled loaded with the wounded from inside the forest to the field post, where they were examined and either attended to or evacuated. Further off, in endless rows, waited the dead.

Now Leena was sitting on a rock, her eyes fixed on the icy forest. She watched anxiously as the remaining units, or what was left of them, straggled back, still hoping to see her friends. Juutilainen came to join her. More at ease with the dead than with the living, he could only blurt out clumsily:

"They're not coming back."

"What do you know?" Leena protested. "And if that's all you have to say to me, go off and snarl at your men, I don't need you. Are you planning on leaving Simo Häyhä out there? And Karlsson? And Onni? Do you really think that's what they deserve? Simo never left anybody behind. Ask your soldiers."

Juutilainen looked down at the ground then stood up and left her there on her rock. He was as contrite as if he had been reprimanded by a general or by Mannerheim in person.

Ten minutes later, a pair of strapping youths armed with a sub-machine gun and a rifle appeared, each of them pulling a sled. They were Eino the infantryman and Rasimus the sniper, both from the 5th Company. Another Simo, another Toivo, another Karlsson, another Hugo, another Pietari, and their story, that of their hundred days of war, could have filled a book.

"Leena?" Rasimus said. "Juutilainen sent us."

67

Covered with lichen and branches in their shell crater, Onni and Yrjö spooned one another as they struggled to resist the cold and the dreaded temptation to fall asleep. Simo's shattered body, his face swathed in a bandage so that they did not have to look at it, lay alongside them. They had to get through the night in this tomb where the Russians had cornered them, abandoning them there when night fell and a fresh blizzard arose. They had to survive, force their hearts to continue to beat, stay awake, talk.

"I was going to get married," Onni said. "Look, here's my ring."

His trembling hands were blue with cold. On his ring finger the gold looked as if it were molten, almost magical.

"We're not dead yet, are we?" Yrjö said. "Besides, I've never been invited to a wedding!"

"I'm going to need friends around me, and I've lost a lot of them. So you'll even be on my table."

A second later, Onni drifted off, then almost immediately woke up with a start, his stomach churning as if he had saved himself from a fall at the very last second. To fall asleep would be fatal. He was frightened not of dying, but of being abandoned. Him and his friends.

"My name is Onni," he said, shivering. "I live in the village of Rautjärvi. You'll have to find Simo and Pietari's families and tell them what good soldiers they have been. You need to find my wife as well. And tell her that—"

"Be quiet!" Yrjö cut him off.

"No ... you must listen to me! Rautjärvi, will you remember that?"

"Be quiet," Yrjö said again. "I can hear someone."

Through the snowstorm a stifled but clear voice seemed to be calling their names. "Simo?" "Onni?" "Karlsson?" "Yrjö?" Was this the siren's voice welcoming them to Tuonela, the land of the dead?

Onni lifted the covering of branches and in the distance spotted a lamp with a green filter. Searching in his rucksack, he pulled out his own lamp and answered.

*

Struggling against the gusts of wind and snow, Rasimus and Eino recovered Karlsson's body from a crater further off and loaded it onto one of the stretcher sleds. With gentle gestures and heavy hearts, Onni and Leena did the same for Simo. Then, next to the two bodies, the four soldiers and Leena huddled together beneath the branches, wrapped themselves in the blankets Rasimus had brought, and waited for the storm to pass.

"How did you …?" Onni began.

"The 4th Company," Eino the infantryman said, his voice quavering. "They told us they fought beside you in the late afternoon. They thought you were dead. We thought you were all dead."

In less than an hour the storm eased, but it would only take a few minutes for it to start up again, so the team wasted no time. Rasimus the sniper stared down at the legend Simo, stretched out motionless on the sled. The invincible White Death whose demise would sap the morale of the entire Finnish Army. Respectfully crossing himself, he gave the order to head for the bivouac near Ullisma, four kilometres away.

*

When they arrived at the camp, even though it was late at night the survivors from the battle had formed a guard of honour that was so ragged, so wounded, so exhausted, it was magnificent. Juutilainen was at its head.

Rasimus was pulling Karlsson's sled. Leena the one carrying Simo.

Behind the half-buried tents stood the rows of dead bodies that had to be taken back to the Kollaa frontline, and from there to the thresholds of their homes. Each was in a wooden coffin with half of the dog tag nailed to the top, a coffin made from the forests of Finland where they had lost their lives. Karlsson and Simo were laid to rest with the others, and because of the biting cold, only a rapid prayer was said for them. The sun was already on the horizon, ready to shine on a fresh day of battle. After the last "Amen" they had to return to war. Leena and Onni were left together, then Juutilainen called Onni, and Leena was all alone.

And yet, in this heap of dead bodies, one heart was still beating ... so feebly each beat might be the last.

The fur brushed against his skin in a silky caress. Soon it enfolded him as if it was coiling round his chest. The sharp musky animal smell called to him from far away, from the shores of Tuonela. The huge fox's rasping tongue began to clean him, cleansing his soul and his wounds. Then the fox opened its mouth right above the bandage-swathed face and blew gently on the life that had not yet altogether abandoned him, on the remaining embers of a dying fire. They began to glow in Simo's body.

Nobody in the camp would have seen these invisible movements, but Leena had gone on praying, and when she saw a boot stir amidst the bodies, her heart gave a leap.

She flung herself towards him, tugged at his legs, and then hastily unwound the bandage. As the last few inches came off, the soldier's terrified eyes appeared, crying out in pain ... only to close once more as he lost consciousness.

"He's alive! Simo is alive!"

Rasimus came running, followed by a sceptical Juutilainen. They were soon joined by Onni, Yrjö and many more. Seeing his chest rise, however weakly, they all had the same thought.

"Immortal. Simo Häyhä is immortal."

Leena returned carrying blankets and wrapped them round Simo to warm him. She insisted he had to be evacuated and that they needed a sled and some morphine.

"Do as she tells you, *perkele!*" Juutilainen barked.

*

Of course, the battle of Ullisma did not stop with Simo's terrible mutilation. The legionnaire had to give priority to the fighting rather than his sniper's evacuation, and so Leena and Onni left the camp at daybreak, each of them hauling a rope on the sled.

Twenty long kilometres lay in front of them from the forests of Ullisma to the Kollaa front, where they hoped an ambulance would be available to take them to the base hospital.

In spite of the morphine, the pain kept Simo in a drugged, drowsy state, with on the one hand a pleasant desire to let himself slip away, and on the other a visceral wish to fight on. Stretched out on his stomach so that his jaws would be supported by the bottom of the sled, with his one good eye Simo watched the snow glide past, just as the landscape does on a train journey. As they progressed, he had moments of awareness followed by lapses of consciousness. When she heard Simo's groans intensify, Leena insisted to Onni they stop and give him another morphine injection.

She removed her skis and knelt by the wounded soldier. She was horrified when she raised her hands to his mouth and saw his face was blue, convulsing, desperate for oxygen that could not find a way through. They had dragged him over rough terrain, crossing frozen marshes and ravaged forests, and the gaping hole in Simo's throat had become blocked by leaves, pine needles, earth and snow, as if he had vomited them.

Leena removed her gloves and without a second thought plunged her fingers into Simo's gaping mouth, as far down as the trachea. She pulled out handfuls that were choking him. A noisy, unexpected intake of breath told her Simo was breathing again.

"That's the second time you've saved him," Onni told her.

*

Before long they came to the forward defensive positions, still some way before Kollaa. Suddenly in front of them they saw a unit of 30 or so silent men. Russians? Finns? Onni swivelled his machine gun in front of him, ready to fight one last time if need be. Leena pulled the pistol from her belt, keeping the barrel lowered, hesitant about shooting.

"*Oh Emma!*" she began to sing instead. "*Do you remember that night when the moon was full and we left the ball?*"

A moment's silence. The Russians did not know the song: "Emma" meant nothing to them. Not their style. Not their language. And the words of this waltz that all the radios in Finland played over and over on the eve of the conflict was tantamount to waving the blue-and-white Finnish flag.

"*You gave me your heart, vowed to love me and promised to be mine …*" came the response.

They fell into each other's arms, and when the unit they had come across learned the identity of the wounded man on the sled, they made it a point of honour to escort them until the Kollaa camp came in sight. Then they went back to their war, galvanised by the tenacity of this simple farmer who had become such a redoubtable soldier.

Arriving an hour later, only a few metres from the defensive line and the first trenches, Onni collapsed exhausted, incapable of taking another step. Leena also fell to her knees in the snow. She summoned what strength she had left to raise her lantern in the ivory fog.

War memoirs of Doctor Aarne K.E., main base hospital at Kollaa

That evening there were even more casualties than usual, which we blamed on the non-stop artillery bombardments. We examined the wounded with an X-ray machine, which was also used for fractures. Before the operations we gave blood or plasma transfusions and administered any necessary medication. The operating table was lit and warmed by Petromax lamps. This was the daily routine in the field hospital, or rather the nightly routine, which lasted until morning.

I can recall one patient in particular who pulled through thanks to a stroke of luck. I had just completed a difficult operation and realised my tobacco tin was empty. I stepped over the patients laid out on the ground to go and look for some more in our store. To my mind, tobacco was the best way to relax after hard work; in between operations we all smoked and drank coffee. Returning from my expedition, I noticed a patient on a stretcher who an hour earlier had been classified as being in a stable condition. His face had suddenly turned blue, and I told myself his respiratory tracts must be blocked. The temporary bandages that had been applied were a shapeless bloody mass covering the bottom half of his face. He was conscious, but the bandages prevented him from talking or expressing himself. The situation could rapidly deteriorate, so I had him transferred to the operating table at once. I quickly realised that time was of the essence. His jaw was shattered and a mixture of bone fragments, bits of flesh and clotted blood were blocking his throat and preventing him breathing.

Had the transfer from the cold into the warmth provoked this by softening the flesh of his face, or was it a result of being transported? I didn't have the time to reflect on this. I didn't even have time to apply an anaesthetic, but by now the patient was unconscious and so it was not necessary. I solved the problem by performing a tracheotomy and giving him artificial respiration. The patient started to breathe again thanks to a metal tube protruding from his throat, and he stabilised sufficiently for me to consider operating on his jaw. I extracted the splinters of bone and flesh stuck in his throat and sewed up the still intact areas of flesh. With the help of a dentist we had at the hospital we managed to reconstitute his lower jaw by readjusting the two halves. Finally his entire jaw was held in place thanks to metal wires and plaster, so that little by little he could breathe naturally again. At that moment I realised that the patient was the senior corporal Simo Häyhä, who had become famous as a marksman.

68

In the former school now transformed into a hospital, exhausted from unrelenting days of surgical operations, Aarne gave himself permission to smoke his cigarette without leaving the building. Finally on his own in the calm of what had once been a primary classroom, he contemplated the bloodstained upturned door that served as an operating table. On its underside it still bore a map of Finland and its frontiers – frontiers that almost 400,000 men had defended from the first day, and that 300,000 were still defending. The floor was covered with blood-soaked compresses, reminders of the operation that had saved Simo's life, and the image of a battered nation.

Elsewhere in the hospital morphine spread through veins and calmed cries of pain.

The door to the building opened and a male nurse appeared. A medical bus was arriving, full of "our lads" hovering between life and death. Then the nurse referred to Simo, who everyone was talking about.

"It seems they hit him with an explosive bullet ..."

Aarne finally comprehended how such unusual injuries had been caused. Until now he had attributed them to a point-blank machine-gun burst to the face, or the blast from a mine or grenade.

"But if it was explosive ammunition," the nurse asked, "why didn't his head simply explode?"

Aarne thought this over for a moment. A few notions of anatomy could explain this miracle.

"The bullet passes through the cheek," the surgeon began. "It explodes when it comes in contact with the jaw, but as his mouth is open, the blast has an exit and escapes. If his mouth had been shut, his head would have been blown off."

So that day Simo Häyhä ought to have died five times, and five times he was saved.

By his open mouth, which left a way out for the blast.

By Leena, who saw him stirring among the dead bodies.

By Leena a second time, who prevented him from suffocating as he was being evacuated.

By the surgeon who discovered him among the stable patients, strangled by his torn-off flesh, his teeth and his shattered bones.

By the surgeon once again, thanks to an interminable operation of wartime improvisation. An operation that had to be carried out again in better conditions with better equipment, free from the fear that at any moment the hospital could be destroyed by a Russian attack.

*

As Aarne walked through the building to the school yard where a full medical bus was already drawing up to deliver a new crop of wounded, he spotted Onni and Leena. They both had a mug of hot chocolate in their hands and blankets round their shoulders. The soldier was asleep on Leena's shoulder.

A nurse came up to him to ask how the operation had gone. Smiling, she went over to Leena, whom she already knew.

"Simo is alive," she told her.

Leena took Greta by the hand and hugged her. Then she closed her eyes with relief.

"You are Lotta Svärd," Greta whispered in her ear.

Leena had honoured the legend, and now she had become part of it.

69

March 8, 1940, five days before the end of the war

Scandinavia had remained neutral. Europe had stayed out of the war, worried about taking on too much as Hitler drew ever closer. And neither the French Daladier nor the British Chamberlain had kept their promises – promises that had plunged Finland into two more weeks of conflict that were as pointless as they were bloody.

On March 8, two days after Simo had been so badly wounded, Mannerheim received alarming news from all the fronts. The Russian victory was a matter of days, if not hours, away, and rather than the territories Stalin was demanding, the whole of Finland was at risk of becoming Soviet.

The commander-in-chief of the Finnish forces confessed to Airo how hopeless the situation was. They had quickly to reach a peace agreement before Stalin realised it would only need one more push to enable his army to invade the entire country.

"We're wounded, but they have to think we're invulnerable. We're on our knees, but they have to think we're invincible. No-one must know how close we are to surrender."

And so on March 9 the Rolls Royce Silver Ghost roared its way from military headquarters in Mikkeli to the seat of government in Helsinki, where Mannerheim urged President Kallio to restart the negotiations and establish an armistice at all costs.

Finally on March 12, 1940, facing Molotov and Stalin himself, the Finnish prime minister Risto Ryti signed the Moscow peace treaty on more punishing terms than ever. This time it was impossible to reject them.

Ten per cent. of territory was amputated from Finland, as well as 20 per cent. of its industries, four islands and the military base at Hanko. Viipuri, so dearly defended during the Gulf of Finland war, was annexed and given the Russian name of Vyborg. When the borders were redrawn, close to half a million Finns had to go into exile, abandoning their houses and farms to the Soviets.

And yet, although it seemed that Russia had won the war and Finland had surrendered, the reality was the very opposite. An ogre nation with 171 million inhabitants had failed to overpower a peaceful country of only 3.5 million, or to advance any further than fifteen kilometres into the coveted territories. A defeat that was not one became a shameful victory for Stalin. A bad winner, he sent that same day an official order and a secret one. The Finnish prime minister was aware only of the official order. As agreed in the treaty, it instructed the Red Army to cease hostilities on March 13, and called for the restoration of friendly relations between the two countries.

At the same time, the secret order was sent to every frontline commander. An order steeped in rancour and malice, one clearly reflecting all the inhumanity and cruelty of the person who had devised it.

On paper, the Winter War was over. But the blood had not ceased to flow.

70

March 12, 1940, last day of the war

The sealed instructions left the Kremlin, one for each of the fronts. The adjutants tore them open for their generals and colonels and read the contents. Often those same perplexed generals and colonels asked them to repeat the secret order they contained.

"Peace has been signed with Finland," the young soldier read out a second time to Grigori Shtern. "It will come into force tomorrow, March 13, at 11.00 hours. There is one more day of war left, and our divisions are ordered to return with no unused munitions."

This meant they should kill as many Finns as possible, as quickly as possible, before they became good neighbours once more. Shtern, the commander of the 8th Army, was unfortunate enough to disapprove out loud of Stalin's secret order. Komarov, his political commissar, did not forget to mention this in his report.

However critical he might be, Shtern had no choice but to obey. An hour later a cohort of Russian officers, crammed shoulder to shoulder in his tent, listened to him with astonishment.

"Our logistic supplies are ceasing from today," he announced. "We still have more than a week's worth of munitions, but we will not be returning to Russia with any of them. In a final salvo, we are going to use what we would normally use in seven days."

Some of the career officers looked at one with embarrassment. They were not at all proud of the way this war was ending, shamefully and with the opposite of any military glory. They had fought poorly from the first day, and swore quickly to forget this last one.

Yet again, this widespread reluctance did not escape the notice of the *politruk*, who dutifully retained the names of the objectors in his mind. He was so irritated that he interrupted and translated the order into precise instructions.

"Not a single round! Not a single shell! Prepare all the cannon, all the mortars, all the rifles, all the machine guns. Before peace is declared, fire constantly, without pausing, without resting."

*

Mannerheim Line, March 12, 1940, last day of the war

All the munitions the Finns had left could fit into their pockets. Viktor Koskinen counted his rounds, and they did not amount to 50. His companions in the trench were no better equipped. But news of an armistice had arrived, and with it the promise of the end of this hell.

The war would end the next day at precisely 11.00, and what Russian would be mad enough to die today?

Viktor thought of his brother and how impatient he was to see him and his family again. Of his father's pride, a pride he had had to win at the risk of his life. Of the stories he would tell them, and the ones he would keep to himself that would haunt his nights. Of the sweetness of a Finnish summer, the lilacs on the edge of the lake just by his farm that seemed to be adorning it with a sapphire necklace. He could have spent the day strolling among them, but a shout from his officer tore him out of his reverie. Before the man could dive into the trench for protection, the blast from an explosion sent his torn-off limbs a hundred metres away.

At the same moment the sky darkened with a storm of shells like a murmuration of starlings, rising high in the air before plunging onto the Mannerheim Line. The ground disintegrated as everything was thrown into the air. In broad daylight, a night made up of burning debris enveloped the 132 kilometres of the

Mannerheim Line. Above the soldiers all was darkness; in front of them, waves of fire and an extraordinary hurricane of molten metal.

The S.B.2 Russian bombers dropped all their bombs. Inadequately armed, the few Finnish fighters pursued them through the sky, the wings with the Soviet red star almost brushing against the ones with blue swastikas.

The soldiers on the Mannerheim Line had run out of ammunition. Viktor and the others spent the night praying in the trenches, visited by the military chaplains, all of them terrified they would be the last to die. They stuck closely to the youngster, jostling to get near him, Viktor Koskinen, nicknamed the Lucky One, hoping he still had some of it to share.

One last shell. One last burst from a machine gun. The night was over. So was most of the morning.

At 11.00, silence returned. Absolute silence, something none of them had heard for exactly 105 days. And yet for hours now and years afterwards, the tumult and fury of the Winter War would continue to reverberate inside them.

The veil of dust fell from the sky like a heavy blanket. As the sky cleared, it revealed a desolate battlefield carpeted with shredded uniforms.

It is said that some of the Russian soldiers who were closest to the frontline exchanged cigarettes with the Finns. Some even shook hands – but Viktor did not witness this.

Covered in earth and blood, freezing from the snow, he clambered out of the trench, dropped his rifle at his feet, and swore he would never pick it up again. Neither that one, nor any other. His father would understand, or not; either way he would not care less.

*

Kollaa front, last hour of the Winter War

There has to be a first death; you have to see it with your own eyes to truly believe in war. And there has to be a final death to bring the war to an end.

At Kollaa, Yrjö was the one.

A few minutes before eleven, he had come face to face with a Russian infantryman. Both of them had fired and both were mortally wounded.

Soon afterwards came shouts of joy at the return of silence. From both sides of the frontline. Light streamed over Yrjö's closed eyes, over his prostrate body and its stilled heart. All around him, the last day of war had littered the ground with bodies in their thousands, staining the snow red. Amongst the other corpses, he was no-one. No more precious, no more important. In death, only their uniforms set them apart. They were enemies, now they lay side by side. Here, hands touched; elsewhere, lifeless faces confronted each other. They had spent the whole winter killing one another.

The dead from previous weeks were half-hidden in the earth. Only vestiges remained: their still visible helmets, occasionally parts of their backs. Their arms were like aerial roots, as if growing out of the ground itself, ready to rise, get to their feet and haunt all those who had decided on this war, entirely forgotten by the world almost a century later.

Their blood would saturate the ground, their flesh would nourish the trees, mingle with the sap. They would be in every new leaf, every new bud.

There were more than a million of them, and when, tomorrow and beyond tomorrow, the wind blew through the branches of the forests of Finland, it would also carry their voices.

*

As Stalin had dictated, the Red 8th Army had killed as many as possible, dishonourably and crudely, until at 11.00 precisely here and throughout Finland the Winter War came to an end.

Komarov smiled at finally being victorious, already imagining his triumphant return to the Motherland. With the spring thaw, the stench of carcasses and putrefaction would rise from the forests and he could leave all that behind him as a souvenir for the Finnish people.

"Of course," he admitted to Shtern, "the story will have to be rewritten, to lend it a heroic tone. But first give it time to be forgotten, then, one day, you'll see, it will be celebrated at its true worth."

For his part, Shtern did not see that as any consolation.

"All we've done is take enough territory from them to bury our dead in," he said sadly.

71

Kinkoma Hospital, Jyväskylä, central Finland

In the staff room where doctors and nurses bumped into one another the smell of coffee mingled with that of alcohol and ether. The radio quietly transmitted Mannerheim's clear voice. It drifted along the corridors and even into the hospital rooms, as if the field marshal was visiting each of them in turn, even though he was speaking one last time to his soldiers:

"You did not hate them, you wished them no harm. We waited for help that never came ..."

Simo's hand twitched; his fingers grasping part of the white sheet. It might be supposed that he was brought round by the squeak of pens signing the iniquitous peace treaty or by the din from the last abject, wretched bombardment Stalin had ordered, because after eight days in a coma, he woke up on exactly March 13, 1940, the very last day of the Winter War. When he opened his eyes, the first thing he saw was Onni, asleep on a chair at his bedside.

"He's been watching over you ever since your transfer," a low voice said next to him.

The last time he had seen Leena, he had thought it was in a dream. She was walking in front of him, straining all her muscles to pull a stretcher sled through a snowstorm, turning round regularly to keep an eye on him, her Lotta's uniform smeared with earth and the blood of his brothers-in-arms.

Now she was wearing a long, clean dress that reached down to big fur-lined shoes. Her hair was tidy, and she smelled good.

"Don't try to speak, you won't be able to," she told him. "You have to be patient."

She stretched out a hand to the bedside table on which lay a notebook with clipped sheets of paper and a pencil. She picked these up and laid them on the bed for him. Simo scrawled a few words on the paper and passed it to her.

"No, we haven't returned home. The situation is still complicated. The borders have been redrawn and lots of us have lost our farms and houses."

Simo picked up the pencil again.

"Rautjärvi?" she read. "I'm so sorry, but our village was cut in two, and your farm at Kiiskinen is on the Russian side now."

A grimace of pain spread slowly over Simo's face, and Leena realised more morphine would soon be needed. As she was getting up to look for a doctor, Onni woke up.

"Simo! My friend!" he stammered, still bleary-eyed. He flung himself willy-nilly into his arms, lying almost horizontally on the hospital bed. He wept warm tears from joy that they were both alive in spite of everything.

Simo picked up the pencil again.

"Juutilainen?" Onni read. "He survived, of course, that's what he does best."

Could it be that one is inoculated against love and death from wanting them too much? The legionnaire had fought right up to the last moment and his last bullets. Now he was looking for a new job, provided it allowed him to wear a uniform and shout at soldiers.

Simo picked up the pencil again.

"No, I'm sorry, your rifle stayed down there. Maybe one day when we're old we'll go back. To remember, if we ever forget. But an officer came yesterday to return your rifle of honour. I know you don't think much of it, but one day it will be in a museum, I promise you."

Simo picked up the pencil again.

"Yes, Kollaa held out. Right to the end, even though we lost half our men. The Mannerheim Line as well. I've no idea how we did it."

More questions tumbled through Simo's still hazy mind: now the image of a young soldier flashed in front of his eyes. Through the bandages covering his head, only Simo's eyes were visible, and now they appeared concerned. He wrote hastily.

"Yrjö?" Onni read. "Don't think about that any more, you need to rest. And above all stay discreet. I'm not sure it's a good idea for the *Ryssät* to learn you are the White Death and have survived. Their spies are everywhere again."

Their hands still covered in the warm blood of Finland, the Russians had once more become their neighbours and allies. When he woke up on March 13, 1940, Simo found he had lost his entire life.

His face. His farm and his hamlet, now Russian.

Toivo, his dearest friend. The Winter War ...

And he had even lost the right to speak about any of it.

First Epilogue

There was no celebration of the Winter War when Komarov got back to Russia. All the military archives were transferred to the Kremlin and kept under lock and key so that they would be forgotten by Russian history. Komarov with them.

In Soviet school textbooks, nothing in particular happened between November 30, 1939 and March 13, 1940.

However, close to 400,000 men in the Red Army were wounded, or killed, or went missing, although the official figure was 350. The rest were to be forgotten. The rest brought shame. The Finnish Army lamented the loss of almost 70,000 men. It also took 6,000 Russian prisoners, who were repatriated the day after the armistice. But they could not tell their Winter War either. Four hundred were executed as soon as they returned, and 4,000 were sent to the gulag, their memories gagged in the depths of cells.

Grigori Mikhailovich Shtern became the object of rumours accusing him of being a German spy. Imprisoned and tortured, at first he defended himself, but after one eye was gouged out, he confessed to what they wanted to hear. Shot by firing squad on the orders of Lavrentiy Beria, the head of the N.K.V.D. (People's Commissariat of Internal Affairs) and therefore Komarov's boss, his name was only re-established fourteen years later on the grounds of what the chief prosecutor termed "a lack of proof".

*

Finland was badly wounded, both victim and victor. But this war, seen as a necessary common sacrifice, helped to create an unshakeable national identity.

Later on, Carl Gustaf Mannerheim became President of the Republic of Finland. He remained haunted all his days by the number of soldiers he could have saved if he had accepted the Russian terms at the outset of negotiations.

Aarne Juutilainen signed up for war after war, but was unable to be killed in any of them despite his best efforts. He ended up alone and alcoholic, and for the first time in his life retreated: to a care home.

In 1946, when France was rebuilding after the Second World War, it had no scruples about asking Finland for the reimbursement of 400 million francs for the rifles, cannon and heavy machine guns it had sent, most of which had not arrived until long after the end of the Winter War.

*

Russia's hard-won victory attracted the attention of Adolf Hitler, in the same way that a wounded animal entices a predator. The German Army's original plan was to stabilise the western front and only then attack Russia. But, seeing the Soviet Army's dire performance against Finland, the plans were changed and almost four million troops were hurled against the weakened Soviet Union in the largest invasion in military history, in what was called Operation Barbarossa ...

Without Simo's courage, without the *sisu*, that soul of ice and fire, nobody can imagine what Europe or the world would be like today, nor what forces would hold power. Nobody in our day really knows how much we owe to the Finnish soldiers of the Winter War.

Second Epilogue

Finland, 1976, Valkjärvi farm

Time had gone by, and for years now Simo no longer had to conceal his identity as *Belaya Smert*. He was a legend in his country,
invited to commemorations and inaugurations in military acade-
mies and Civic Guard garrisons as the hero he had been and the
myth he had become.

He attended these events politely and unpretentiously, often
surprised at all the attention, considering himself no braver than
the soldiers he fought alongside.

After he was wounded, he was operated on another 26 times
in fourteen months: an operation every fortnight for more than
a year. If for Simo the Winter War had lasted 98 days, it took
him four times as long to recover from it, physically at least.

To compensate for the lands he had lost to Russia, the Finnish
government offered him a farm and a portion of forest. This
morning, thick snowflakes were falling on them, softly blanketing
the yellow VW Beetle parked outside his door.

Simo had never married or had children. The company of his
horse and his dog Kille seemed all he needed. He did, however,
know how to receive visitors when necessary. He had made black
tea and been to the bakery, because although he preferred to talk
about the war only with his brothers-in-arms he had ended up
giving in to the persistence of a young woman journalist who
was already knocking on his door …

She took off her coat, unwound her scarf, and put her big
hold-all on the floor. Then she sat in the comfortable armchair he

was offering and switched on the Dictaphone on the low table between them. Simo drank some of his tea and tried to warn his guest in his wounded voice that his shattered jaws sometimes made it hard to understand what he was saying. She reassured him, then sank her teeth into one of the *joulutorttu*,[29] covering her upper lip in white icing sugar.

She had insisted on meeting him; he had admired her spirit, and as he watched her wiping her mouth on her pullover sleeve, he was briefly reminded of Leena.

"The Finnish Army continues to follow your advice, and your name is mentioned with respect in armies all over the world," the journalist began, still munching on the cake.

"I did what was asked of me, as well as I could. There would be no Finland if all the other soldiers hadn't done the same," Simo said humbly.

"Your gun is exhibited in the Heritage Room of the Karelia Light Infantry. With it you killed 542 Russian soldiers, and a similar number with your sub-machine gun. That makes you the best sniper in the world."

In fact it was his rifle of honour displayed in the glass case in the Heritage Room, but Simo did not correct her. Far away in the forests of Ullisma, his own rifle was growing rusty and old like him.

"I fired and reloaded as often as there were enemy soldiers in front of me," he said. "But war is not a pleasant experience."

"And what did you feel when you killed for the first time?"

"The recoil of my rifle," he said somewhat tartly, because he refused to revisit memories of Kollaa.

The interview lasted until the yellow Beetle had turned white. At the end of the morning, Simo politely accompanied the journalist to the door, aware he had not been as forthcoming as she had hoped.

She found her car, but just as she was opening the door the

sound of an engine came from behind the first pines bordering the farm. Then another. She barely had time to step aside to let past in a flurry of snow the two gleaming black saloons accompanying what must be an official vehicle.

First three men in black got out and looked briefly all round them. One of them opened the boot and took out a rifle case, while the second one opened the rear door. When she recognised the man stepping out, the journalist searched hurriedly in her bag to find her camera and take the perfect photograph to accompany her article. But before she could even focus, the third suit came striding over to inform her that visits from the president, however routine they might be, were still private. These moments concerned only two old acquaintances.

As the wind blew away the clouds to allow the sun's rays through, Urho Kekkonen asked to be left on his own. Just like any ordinary visitor, the President of the Republic of Finland, rifle slung over his shoulder, walked across the yard, climbed the three wooden steps, and knocked on the door of the Häyhä farm.

"Are you ready, my dear friend?" the head of state asked when Simo opened the door.

Simo whistled to his dog, put on his coat and took his rifle down from the hook on the wall.

"We'll see what the forest has to offer us," he said. "And see if we should take it."

FINIS

"What I remember most about that war was our army's incompetence. It could not even manage to deal with a handful of Finns. They were the ones who taught us how to wage war."

*Georgi Prusakov, doctor with the
100th Battalion of volunteer Russian skiers*

*

"The Finnish people have demonstrated that an undivided nation, however small, can show an unprecedented ability to fight. The Finnish people have won the right to live independently as part of the family of free nations."

Carl Gustaf Mannerheim

Photographs of Simo Häyhä, Toivo Varis,
Carl Gustaf Mannerheim, Aksel Airi

Photographs of Wilhelm Teittinen, Aarne Juutilainen,
Vilho Nenonen, Grigori Shtern

Bibliography

La Guerre finno-soviétique (The Finnish-Soviet War), Louis Clerc, Economica, Paris, 2015.

Tulimyrsky Kollaalla (Fire Storm at Kollaa), Hannu Narsakka, Painopalvelut Yliveto, Jyväskylä, 2017.

Unknown Soldiers, Väinö Linna, trs. Liesl Yamaguchi, Penguin, London, 2015.

The Face of War, Martha Gellhorn, 1959, updated 1993, Granta, London, 2016.

Histoire politique de la Finlande xix e–xx e siècle (A Political History of Finland), Seppo Hentilä, Osmo Jussila et Jukka Nevakivi, Fayard, Paris, 1999.

Official Report of the surgeon Aarne K.E., who operated on Simo Häyhä, Kansa Taisteli, Bonnier, Paris (I could only find an old copy giving a reference to this publisher, but I do not know if the text was really published).

Sisu: the Finnish Art of Courage, Joanna Nylund, Gaia, 2018.

Stalin and the Inevitable War, 1936–1941, Silvio Pons, Routledge (The Cummings Center series), Abingdon, 2002.

The Winter War: The Russo-Finnish War of 1939–40, William R. Trotter, Aurum, London, 2013.

Parlamentin Palkehilta Kollaan Kaltahille (From the steps of parliament to the shores of Kollaa), Antti J. Rantamaa, Werner Söderström OY, Helsinki, 1942.

Interviews with Aarne Juutilainen by Jyrki Mäkelä.

Secrets et leçons de la guerre d'Hiver (Secrets and Lessons of the Winter War), Izdatelstvo Poligon.

Simo Häyhä: Tarkka-ampuja (Simo Häyhä, marksman), Veli Salin, Revontuli, Tampere, 2012.

Kunniamme Päivät, Suomen Sota 1939–40 (Days of Honour, Finnish War 1939–40), Maan Turva, Werner Söderström OY, Helsinki, 1940.

Onnen maa: Suomi elokuussa 1939 (The Land of Happiness: Finland in August 1939), Denise Bellon (photographer), Finn Lectura, Helsinki, 2004.

Suomi Sodassa (Finland at War), Valitut Palat (*Reader's Digest*), Helsinki, 1983.

Finland from East to West, documentary film directed by Olivier Horn, Arte, 2017.

Kaputt, Curzio Malaparte (1944), New York Review Books, New York, 2007.

White Death: Simo Häyhä, The World's Best Sniper, Petri Sarjanen, Suuri Suomalainen Kirjakerho, Helsinki, 2015.

The White Sniper: Simo Häyhä, Tapio Saarelainen, Casemate, 2016.

Notes

1   *Perkele*: Damn, Shit or Bother.

2   *Ryssä* (pl. *Ryssät*): slang term for "Russian", like "Russki" in English.

3   *On koira haudettuna*: equivalent to "There's something fishy here".

4   In those days the sauna took the place of a bathroom, and every family had one. The sauna was some way away from the house, and the phrase "take someone behind the sauna" means to quietly get rid of someone.

5   Lapatossu: a comic character played by Aku Korhonen.

6   "Emma's Waltz". Words by V. Sükaniemi. Sung in 1939 by Ture Ara.

7   Artificial bramble: the term then used for barbed wire.

8   *Sissi*: light infantry platoon. There were four platoons in each company.

9   Oblast: an administrative region in the U.S.S.R.

10   *Khorosho*: O.K.

11   *Viina*: colourless Finnish alcohol, similar to vodka. About 40 per cent. proof.

12   *Mummo*: granny, grandmother.

13   *Politruk*: political commissar.

14   *Puukko*: traditional Finnish knife with a short, one-sided blade and hilt made of birch wood or reindeer horn.

15   *Talvisotakäsikirja*: manual of winter warfare.

16   *Motti* in Finnish means "a stockade of wood" and means to encircle enemy forces. When they surrounded the Russian forces for the first time, the Finns gave the tactic the code name "*Motti*", and it stuck.

17   *Kettu*: fox.

18   *Yle Radio Suomi*: Finnish national radio.

19   *Selvä, selvä*: O.K., O.K. ...

20   *Tarkkailija*: spotter or observer.

21   *Hyöky*: tsunami.

22   *Kaamos*: when the sun no longer appears, either due to the weather or to a polar night.

23   *Taika-ampuja*: the Magic Marksman.

24   Tanner: the Finnish foreign minister.

25   *There Shall Be No Night*. Première at New York's Alvin Theatre on April 29, 1940.

26   *Tunturi*: a bare hill rising above the tundra.

27   Extract from the dossier "Ski" in the historical archives of the French Naval Defence.

28   *Simonkatu*: Simon Street; *Unioninkatu*: Union Street; *Sirkuskatu*: Circus Street; *Hallituskatu*: Government Street.

29   *Joulutorttu*: a star-shaped cake, a Finnish speciality.

Acknowledgements